Corrupted Coil

A Young Adult Epic Fantasy Adventure

Theo Mann

The Invisible Publishing Company

Corrupted Coil Series

Book 1: Corrupted Coil

Book 2: Staff of Life

Book 3: Dark Poison

Book 4: Broken Cradle

Book 5: The White Spire

Contents

Chapter 1   1

Chapter 2   9

Chapter 3   15

Chapter 4   21

Chapter 5   27

Chapter 6   33

Chapter 7   39

Chapter 8   47

Chapter 9   53

Chapter 10   63

Chapter 11   71

Chapter 12   79

Chapter 13   87

Chapter 14   97

Chapter 15   103

Chapter 16   107

Chapter 17   113

Chapter 18   121

Chapter 19   127

Chapter 20   135

Chapter 21   141

Chapter 22	149
Chapter 23	155
Chapter 24	161
Chapter 25	171
Chapter 26	177
Chapter 27	183
Chapter 28	189
Chapter 29	195
Chapter 30	201
Chapter 31	207
Chapter 32	213
Chapter 33	217
Chapter 34	223
Chapter 35	233
Chapter 36	239
Chapter 37	245
Chapter 38	251
Chapter 39	257
Chapter 40	265
Chapter 41	273
Chapter 42	279
Chapter 43	285
Chapter 44	295
Chapter 45	305
Chapter 46	313
Chapter 47	319
Chapter 48	325
Chapter 49	333

Chapter 50   341

Chapter 51   347

Chapter 52   355

Chapter 53   363

Chapter 54   369

Chapter 55   375

Keep Reading   379

Sign Up Once--Get all Theo Mann's free books including brand new   381
releases

About Theo Mann   383

Also by Theo Mann (so far)   385

Chapter 1

"Darklings attacking!" Yann Dilnao yelled up the line of Watchmen posted on his right.

The men of the Black Watch stood twenty feet apart along the magical barricade protecting the town of Middleborough from the chaos of wild magic outside.

The barricade formed a huge transparent dome over the messy collection of low, roughly thatched houses cramped inside the town.

The magic surface protected Middleborough from hurricane winds of red, black, and burnt-orange currents moving out in the Coil.

That protection wouldn't last, though. Magical vapors sent waves of sparks shimmering across the dome and around the town's perimeter wall. Those sparks gave the only evidence that the dome was still there protecting the town from destruction.

Yann tightened his grip on his war glaive and braced himself for the incoming attack. Monstrous shapes erupted from Dark Layers beyond the barricade.

Gargantuan slithering creatures poured from shadows between the Dark Layers. The Darklings undulated in the shifting undertow of magic and potential to surround the town.

Then turned their hideous fanged mouths and tentacles on Middleborough.

Men's voices yelled up and down the barricade on Yann's right. "Stand fast!" his father bellowed. "Hold the line!"

"They're coming in fast!" Rien Dugas called back.

He said a few other things Yann didn't catch over the noise. The barricade muffled the wind rumbling and booming outside. The Darklings added their thunderous roars to the pounding din echoing across the shadowy landscape out there.

These Darklings were nothing like the creatures the Black Watch had faced in the past. These were ten times bigger, much faster, and a thousand times more hideous.

Spikes and razor edges lined their whipping tentacles. Their jaws cracked to reveal bristling fangs dripping with poison. Magic flashed and crackled on the Darklings' skin to light up the shadows beyond the barricade.

The Dark Layers rippled through the night disgorging hundreds of Darklings. They ranged down the barricade to encircle the town. The Darklings would overrun the Black Watch, break through the barricade, and that would be the end of Middleborough.

The town had lost contact with any other isolated Islands of stability in this remote corner of the Coil.

Middleborough had been living on borrowed time for months. The Black Watch couldn't hold the Coil's shifting magical forces at bay for much longer.

Then the Coil would swallow Middleborough along with every other Island in this sea of chaos.

Was tonight the night? Was this battle the moment when the forces of mayhem and destruction annihilated Middleborough and everyone inside it? It was only a matter of time.

The Black Watch alone stood between the town and certain doom. Yann faced down the thickest knot of Darklings coming straight for him.

He planted his legs wide and brandished his glaive to take the full brunt of the assault. His father, Yvan Dilnao, Commander of the Middleborough Watch, had posted Yann at the farthest end of their line.

Yann was the youngest Watchmen in Middleborough. Yvan usually put Yann here to keep him out of the thickest fighting. Tonight, that strategy turned out to be a huge mistake.

The Darklings came thickest from Yann's left. No other Watchmen guarded the wall down there. Yann faced the full Darkling assault by himself.

The nearest Watchman to him was twenty feet away with the others spaced farther down the wall to his right. They couldn't leave their posts to help him—not without leaving the rest of the barricade unguarded.

Yann spent his life training to be a Watchman, but nothing prepared him for this. This was it. He wouldn't be able to stop the Darklings from overrunning Middleborough. At least he would die in battle. He wouldn't have to live with his failure.

He took a step back from the barricade as the Darklings advanced. They loomed out of the shadows and towered over Middleborough.

The barricade and everything underneath it looked so small and frail compared to these creatures. His glaive wouldn't make a dent in even one of those things, much less dozens of them.

Screams and running feet echoed out of the town behind him. The townsfolk ran for cover, but nowhere in town would be safe once the Darklings got inside. They would leave no one alive.

Sparks and explosions erupted from the Darklings' skin, but for some reason, they didn't come any closer.

They could flatten the barricade in seconds, but they stood off. More flashes gave Yann a clear view of their vast, grotesque bodies.....and then he saw it.

The forks of light and flame cascading down the Darklings' bodies gave him a glimpse of silhouetted figures moving around out in the Coil. They were tiny compared to the Darklings, but he saw at one glance that they were all human.

"Hey!" he yelled up the line. "There are people out there! Someone's out there fighting the Darklings!"

"Stand fast, boy!" Rien hollered back.

Yann stared at the strangers dashing back and forth in the gloom. Their clothes billowed and slashed in the storm.....and then more bursts of light showed him exactly what was going on out there.

Light flared down on the ground as a tall figure stabbed something into one of the Darklings. A magical discharge exploded across the Darkling's skin and the creature thundered in rage and pain. The monster rounded on the tiny stranger who dared to attack it.

The Darkling reared and arched its yawning mouth downward. The creature prepared to snatch the stranger when another outline zoomed out of the Coil.

This one was smaller with long dark hair whipping from the head. The lithe body had the curves of a female, but she looked much younger than the first figure.

She darted between the wizard and the Darkling, planted herself there, and thrust out a short staff gripped in both hands. The shaft struck the Darkling broadside and a devastating blast of magical lightning ricocheted back at the monster.

The thing arched even higher, but it didn't attack. It roared so loudly that the sound shook the barricade. Then the monster detonated with an almighty boom. It shattered into a million black shards that evaporated into the wind.

"Hey!!" Yann bellowed down the line again. "There are people out there fighting the Darklings! Father—come down here now!"

Yann didn't dare to turn away. He stared unblinking at the strangers battling for their lives against a mounting horde of Darklings. More of the fiends disgorged from the Dark Layers all over the place, but the strangers held their ground.

Running feet approached Yann's post from his right. His father, Rien, and Omer Veco rushed to Yann's position. None of them said a word as the strangers backed closer to the barricade.

The girl stood shoulder to shoulder with the tall wizard. Four more wizards gathered from out of the dark. Each one fought the Darklings back as best they could, but none of them could defeat the monsters the way the girl could.

The battle ranged farther to the left. The Darklings shifted their attack to flank the strangers. The more firmly the strangers entrenched themselves to defend their line, the farther left the Darklings migrated.

"What the hell?" Rien growled under his breath.

"They're adjusting their strategy," Yann pointed out. "They're anticipating us."

"Us!" Rien snorted. "Those people aren't us. They're Coil rats. They don't belong here."

Yann almost made the mistake of pointing out that these strangers were the only thing stopping the Darklings from taking Middleborough, but he stopped himself from saying that.

Four Darklings slithered sideways and came at the strangers from an angle. The wizard on the far end swiveled to confront the monsters. This wizard looked like a woman, but Yann couldn't be certain from this distance.

The lone defender raised two star-shaped weapons, one in each hand. Sparks and flashes burst from the points. They shot through the darkness and hit two Darklings, but she couldn't fight them all.

One Darkling shrank back and the other three struck without mercy. They pounced on her, devoured her, and then charged behind the other strangers trying to save themselves from even more monsters.

The girl held her position for a second while the Darklings encircled the strangers and made a dash for the barricade. "Incoming!" Yann roared.

Watchmen charged him from all over. They left their posts to surround him, but the girl got there first.

She sprang between the Darklings and the barricade. She landed less than ten feet from Yann, but he still didn't get a good look at her face. Her hair lashed wildly in the storm and her sudden movements kept casting her features in shadow.

She landed in a crouch facing outward against five Darklings. Every muscle tensed and she burst into a wild rotating maneuver spinning her staff in all directions.

Magical blasts fired from both ends. She jabbed it at the Darklings, spun it back and forth, and ejected dozens of torrents and explosions. Yann couldn't keep up with them all.

Three more Darklings evaporated under her assault before the tall wizard and their other companions retreated to the girl's side. Five strangers formed ranks in front of the barricade to defend the town from invasion.

None of the strangers could destroy the Darklings the way the girl could. She blasted away as many as she could, but the Darklings adjusted their tactics once again.

They split and closed around the strangers from both sides. The Darklings left the girl isolated in the center and moved in on the outer edges of the strangers' line.

Two Darklings pounced on a shorter man on the left. They devoured him and charged the barricade while the rest of the strangers were busy fighting more monsters.

Yann had a split second to see the Darklings coming before they crashed full force into the barricade. Nothing could stand against them. The barricade shuddered under the impact and magical discharges boomed down the Darklings' misshapen bodies.

The next instant, the barricade exploded in a deafening crash. Darklings flooded the town along with the pounding tempest of the Coil's wild magic.

Yann forced himself to stand his ground as a huge monster rushed him. Its tentacles whistled and hissed around his head. Its gaping mouth rose many times higher than the wall.

A tentacle slashed at him and he struck out with his glaive. He lopped it off and parried five more coming from his right. They cracked back to strike him. How much longer could he hold out before this fiend devoured him, too?

He chopped off three more tentacles and the creature roared. It reared its boneless body and he saw it about to consume him the way the Darklings consumed the wizards outside.

Only ordinary human men joined the Black Watch. None of the Watchmen had magical power. No way could a junior Watchman defend himself against one of these things.

He couldn't do anything to stop that mouth coming for him. Each fang embedded in the creature's jaws dwarfed him by a mile.

He had one chance to get away from it. He counted down the seconds before the mouth swallowed him and then he sprang out of the way. He made it as far as the creature's side and slashed his glaive across the edge of the creature's mouth.

He caught his blade edge on the outer lip and ripped up the monster's side. Black blood poured from the wound and saturated Yann's clothes and hair. It got in his eyes and nose, but he was already too out of his mind with battle rage.

He stabbed his glaive into the creature's side and a vicious crack of magic ricocheted up the shaft into his hands. It locked his fingers to the shaft so he couldn't let go.

The creature recoiled from his assault and rolled away from him taking his weapon with it. He held on against his best efforts to let go and the creature's movements carried him skyward along with it.

It whipped him upward until he flopped right on top of it. He looked down at Middleborough descending into chaos.

Watchmen, strangers, and townsfolk fought side by side to drive the Darklings out of town. Yann couldn't tell from here if the townsfolk were winning or not.

He scrambled onto the monster's back and pure blood rage wiped out every other thought. He flung his leg over the creature's body. Magical explosions hammered him all over, but he didn't care.

He ripped his glaive out of the monster's skin and stabbed again and again. Every strike sent another discharge of lightning through the shaft into Yann's arms, but they only enraged him and made him stab harder.

He roared in fury hacking the creature to pieces. Blood spurted from countless wounds, but at that moment, one of the creature's many tentacles coiled around and smacked him across the back of the head.

He fell on top of his weapon and fought to stay conscious under a hail of blows coming from all directions. He lay bowed and beaten under the assault......and blinked down at the battle on the ground.

His father and the other Watchmen battled Darklings side by side with wizards, but Yann barely saw them. He stared as the girl zoomed out of nowhere and attacked the Darkling from the side.

She stabbed her staff into the other side of the creature's mouth. It howled in agony and she unleashed a hellish barrage of blows, stabs, and explosions on the thing.

It contorted trying to escape. The creature rolled the other way and pitched Yann sideways. He grasped his glaive trying to keep himself from getting crushed.

The girl struck without mercy, jumped in front of the Darkling, seized her staff with both hands, and thrust it longways at the creature. She released a withering blast and the Darkling dissolved underneath Yann's sprawled body.

He slammed down hard on the ground blinking stars out of his eyes.

Chapter 2

Yann scrambled to turn himself over and searched everywhere for another Darkling coming in to kill him. He took a second before his mind cleared enough to see the assembled Watchmen and townsfolk driving the Darklings back into the Coil.

Five wizards from Middleborough joined together to reestablish the barricade. The Darklings slithered away and vanished into the Dark Layers.

Yann's father went over to the wizards and exchanged a few words with them before he went down the line checking the Watchmen.

Yann sank onto the ground gasping for breath. His whole body hurt and his head pounded. He didn't trust himself to stand up.

He shut his eyes and commanded his heart to keep still. He didn't want to face the Darklings like that again, but he would have to eventually.

They'd only been getting stronger and attacking Middleborough in greater numbers these last few years. They would always come back until they swallowed the town.

Some hint of movement nearby made him stiffen and his eyes snapped open. He froze when he saw the girl standing over him. Her dark eyes measured his battered body and the gore and ooze covering him all over. He could just imagine what he looked like.

She wore a black cloak over a random collection of patched clothing belted around her waist. Lengths of battered rope tied strips of cloth around her shoes and calves.

At this close range, he also saw that she carried a tattered leather bag over her shoulder. The strap crossed her chest under her cloak so the bag hung on her hip.

She leaned on her staff and skewered Yann with dark, unfeeling eyes. She jutted her chin at him. "You did well.....for an imp."

He relaxed back on the ground, but he didn't dare to take his eyes off her. Something about her made him want to guard himself against her. "I'm not an imp," he growled. "I'm a Watchman."

"Watchmen are imps. You have no magic."

"So what?" He scanned the town to distract himself from her intense stare.

The wizards who came out to help defend Middleborough and reestablish the barricade headed back into their houses.

Yann's father, Yvan, went from Watchman to Watchman giving orders and assigning them to new posts even though the Darklings weren't here anymore.

Yann heaved himself onto his elbow to push himself up. He would have liked to stand up and face his father on his feet. The pain in his ribs stopped him from going anywhere.

Before he could move, the girl shot out her staff, jammed the tip into his sternum, and forced him down onto his back. He tried to resist, but his strength failed him.

She pinned him and a surge of magic rushed into him from the end of her weapon. Her magic flooded his body and knit his bones back together.

The pain subsided and he wilted, groaning. "Thank you!"

"Keep still," she snapped. "You're no good to anyone the way you are."

He would have liked to argue back, but he couldn't do anything against a magic-user as strong as she was.

She was right. He was an imp. He had no magic. He wasn't good for much besides losing his life defending an unknown town like Middleborough.

"Where did you learn to fight like that?" the girl asked. "You handled your glaive very well."

He shut his eyes so he wouldn't see her staring at him. "I only know what I learned on the Watch. I'm not very good."

"You nearly killed that Darkling. I've never seen an imp come so close to killing one of them. Not even Wesh can do that and his magic is stronger than mine."

He dared to open his eyes, but she wasn't looking at him anymore. She surveyed the town with a critical gaze.

She was more beautiful than he first realized, but she had a hard, unforgiving air that told him to watch his step around her.

Her dark hair and eyes gave her a haunted look and she never slackened her grip on her staff. Heaven only knew what she could do with that thing.

The tall wizard that Yann had seen fighting outside came over to the girl. He wore a knee-length grey tunic with a large, decorative gold cross embroidered on the chest.

He wore his shoulder-length grey hair combed straight back from his face. A curved handlebar mustache covered his upper lip and surrounded his mouth to point down to the ground.

"Are you hurt, Eliska?" he asked the girl. "We lost Ines."

"And Ramon," she added. "I wonder how many wizards this town has."

"I think I saw ten just now." The wizard squinted toward the houses, taverns, and buildings lining Middleborough's main street. Light flooded the night from dozens of windows.

The light left the slumped houses in darkness. Barely enough light made it to the wall for the Watchmen to see.

The tall wizard had scraggly grey hair and an unkempt beard, but his ice-blue eyes flashed with hidden fire.

Another wizard in a matching grey tunic came over to join them. Yann didn't see any other newcomers inside the barricade. These three must be the only survivors.

This wizard was a younger man with a burly build. He carried no weapons at all, but magic kept fizzing and sparking from his fingers when he glared around the town.

"You have a bad burn on your shoulder, Mael," the girl told him. "Let Wesh heal it for you."

The tall old wizard moved over to Mael's shoulder. Wesh raised his hand to Mael's wound, but Mael rounded on him snarling and smacked Wesh's hand away.

"Don't touch me!" Mael snapped.

Wesh raised both hands in surrender. "All right, all right. I wasn't going to hurt you."

Mael gritted his teeth and grimaced. "Later. It hurts too much."

Wesh happened to notice Yann lying there. "Is the boy hurt?"

"He was," Eliska replied. "I healed him. He just needs to rest. He's exhausted."

"You did very well, boy," Wesh told him. "I have never seen an imp come as close to killing one of the Darklings."

Eliska sneered down at Yann. "I already told him that, but he didn't believe me. Maybe he'll listen to you."

Yann didn't like them talking about him like a specimen under a magnifying glass, but Wesh took a step closer and extended his hand. "Come. You're strong enough to stand up now."

Yann held out his hand to accept the wizard's help, but at that moment, another glaive flashed between them. The shaft knocked Wesh's hand down and the Watch Commander stepped between them. "Do not touch my son!" Yvan snapped.

Wesh spun around fast. Mael and Eliska both moved closer to Wesh to defend him.

"We were trying to help the boy," Wesh explained. "Eliska healed his injuries. He's fine now, thanks to her."

"You're all under arrest for breaching our barricade," Yvan announced and five more Watchmen moved in to back him up.

"We defended your town, you idiot imp Watchman!" Mael snarled. "You would all be dead now if not for us. You saw that yourselves. You watched our people die while you remained safely behind the barricade and let us fight the Darklings for you."

Mael's broad shoulders stiffened even more. The magic flashing from his fingertips built to a steady crackle.

Wesh laid a hand on Mael's arm to stop him, and this time, Mael didn't lash out.

"We came here to defend your town," Wesh told Yvan. "We did everything we could to stop the Darklings from breaching your barricade, but there were too many of them. You saw that for yourself. You have no reason to arrest us."

Yvan raised his eyebrows. He barely came up to the wizards' chin, but Yvan didn't back off. "You came here on purpose, did you? So you knew about this attack? How am I to know you didn't plan this? Maybe you used the incursion to get inside the barricade when you couldn't manage it on your own."

"Listen to me, Commander......" Wesh began.

"This is stupid," Eliska muttered. "We never should have helped them. We should have let them die. The world would be a better place without them."

Yann couldn't listen to this. He clambered to his feet and hustled over to his father. "He's right, Father. They held the Darklings off three times before they breached the barricade. At least four of their party lost their lives out there. I saw it all from my post before you got there."

Yvan completely ignored him. "We have laws in this town. I have no choice but to arrest you while I investigate the matter. If I find out you didn't trespass, I'll release you. Until then, please come with me."

He waved toward a nearby building. It was just another house that had been converted into the Black Watch's headquarters.

The Watchmen lived upstairs. The basement served as the Middleborough jail on those rare occasions when the Watch had to arrest someone.

"You're making a mistake, Commander," Wesh insisted. "We can help you defend your town. The Darklings will come back for you. We're the only people who can help you defeat them."

"No one can defeat them," Eliska growled under her breath.

"*You* can," Yann countered. "How did you do it? How did you destroy them like that?"

"That's neither here nor there," Yvan interrupted. "Come with me, please. Don't make us use force."

Three more Watchmen appeared behind Rien and Omer. All the others came armed.

They confronted the three strangers in such a menacing stance that the standoff threatened to explode into another battle.

It wouldn't be a battle, though. These three wizards could flatten the Watch in seconds, but they didn't.

Wesh elbowed Mael. "Go with them and cooperate with their investigation. It's the only way to make them listen."

"To hell with that," Eliska snapped. "I am not going to jail because some imp is too stupid to listen to reason."

"Watch your mouth, girl!" Rien fired back. "You'll go where we tell you to go and you'll like it."

Wesh turned to Eliska. "Go with them. Please. They'll hear what we have to say and then they'll release us."

"*I'll* release us," she snarled. "There isn't a man in this town who can hold me against my will."

"We'll see about that," Rien replied.

"Don't resist," Wesh told the girl. "Cooperate with them—for now. If things turn against us, I'll let you know."

She snorted, but she didn't say anything. Yvan waved toward the house again. Neither Mael nor Eliska moved until Wesh physically shoved them forward.

The Watchmen guarded the party on their way to the house. Eliska and Mael kept glaring at the Watchmen as menacingly as the Watchmen glared at them, but Wesh's influence prevented the confrontation from disintegrating into another fight.

Yvan stopped outside the house and pulled up the storm doors leading into the basement. The Watchmen gathered in a semi-circle to surround the strangers. Eliska turned backward and brandished her staff at them to hold them off.

Yvan went downstairs first followed by Wesh and then Mael. Eliska went last. She never turned her back on the Watchmen.

Yann stood off to one side and watched the strangers out of sight. He didn't threaten them and he didn't help to guard them.

He didn't understand why his father would put these people under arrest at all, but Yann wasn't Watch Commander.

Yvan was solely responsible for the safety of everyone in Middleborough. He ran the Watch his own way. Yann was his most junior subordinate and not in any position to question his Commander's decisions.

Yann could well imagine the scene going on downstairs. Eliska alone could blow this house to smithereens. She could probably level the whole town if she wanted to. Locking her up would be the worst idea ever.

Yann didn't say that out loud—not yet. He waited until his father came out alone, closed the storm doors, and faced the other Watchmen.

Yvan gave them their orders and the Watch dispersed before he came over to Yann.

"Are you hurt, son?" Yvan asked.

"Not anymore. That girl healed me."

"You did very well in the battle. I'm proud of you."

Yann glanced toward the house and lowered his voice so no one else would hear him. "Was it really necessary to arrest them? That girl destroyed four Darklings. We should be trying to recruit her, but she'll never help us now. She hates you for doing this to her."

"We can't recruit her, son. She's a magic-user. We're imps."

"You know what I mean. This town is on its last legs. We need all the help we can get."

Yvan shook his head. "If we don't keep the laws, we won't have a town worth saving. You're too young to understand this, but you will in time."

"I'm not too young to recognize an ally when I see her. All three of them risked their lives and lost their comrades defending us. How could you turn them against us like this?"

Yvan turned away with another shake of his head. "Go change your clothes and clean yourself up. Then you can go back on watch at the same post. You did well to raise the alarm when you did. Keep your eyes open for any Darklings coming back."

He walked off and left Yann standing there fuming. What was the point of keeping his eyes open when the Watch lacked the firepower to fight the Darklings at all?

Did his father really plan to keep the only three wizards capable of fighting the Darklings locked up in a basement while the Watch went down trying to hold this town? Yann couldn't think of a more ill-conceived plan.

Chapter 3

Eliska shifted her weight on a cold stone bench in her bare, bleak cell. She couldn't get comfortable.

She'd gotten herself into a lot of dangerous situations, but she'd never been in jail before. She always managed to avoid this until now.

She cursed that idiot Watch Commander for his short-sightedness. Not even him being a powerless imp could excuse him treating her party like this.

Eliska and her fellow travelers had been the only thing to stop the Darklings from destroying this flea-bitten town. He knew that and he arrested them anyway.

She hated him for that, but at least he couldn't hold her here. If the Darklings attacked again, she would break out of this house and abandon the town to its fate. That was the least they deserved after this insult.

The Watch Commander took her staff, but he couldn't take her magic. It worked better when she channeled it through some object, but she could use her magic perfectly well with her bare hands if it came to that.

She could have killed him. She could have killed the entire Watch.

She wanted to, but that boy stopped her. He stood up for her.

She couldn't remember anyone ever doing that for her before. He stood up for her to his own father. That counted for something.

Would she have the guts to abandon *him* to certain death? She would be if she left him in this town.

He was an imp. He fought well against the Darkling, but he wouldn't survive another battle—not without her there to save him.

She pushed those thoughts out of her mind. She couldn't start caring about some imp boy in some no-name town in a forgotten corner of the Coil. He was nothing. He certainly wasn't important enough for her to risk her life to save him.

She tried one more time to find a comfortable sitting position when the storm doors crashed open above her head. Sunlight streamed into the basement and she braced herself for another confrontation with the Watch Commander.

She stiffened when the boy climbed down the stairs into the basement. He wasn't as tall or imposing as his fellow Watchmen. He couldn't be more than seventeen, but he had a sturdy, solid air about him. He didn't move fast—not now.

He moved plenty fast during the battle. She wouldn't have expected an imp to be so quick and ferocious.

He had cleaned himself up and changed into clean clothes. His dark hair was still wet and it hung over his eyes. They sparkled with a dark light when he studied her through the bars of her cell.

He wore the same black uniform as the rest of the Watch with a small gold insignia embroidered on the upper left shoulder. Other than the insignia, the uniform was solid black pants, shirt, and jacket.

A single gold pip marked the corner of his plain, banded collar buttoned tight around his neck. The Watch Commander wore an oak leaf on his collar. The other Watchmen wore more than one pip depending on their rank, but this boy only had one.

He held up a plate covered with a cloth. "I'm Yann. I brought you something to eat."

"Leave me alone," she snapped. "If you aren't here to let me out, you're useless to me."

"I can't let you out. Only my father can do that."

"Then go away. I helped you and this is how you repay me."

"I tried to stop him from putting you in here. You heard me."

"Do you always do what he tells you? Did he tell you to come down here and interrogate me? He's a coward if he didn't come himself."

"He didn't want me to come. He wanted to send Rainier to bring you this, but I asked him to let me bring it. I wanted to talk to you."

"I don't want to talk to you. Get out. You're his dog if you do what he says."

"He's my Watch Commander. I'm under his orders whether he's my father or not."

"Then go lick his boots. Maybe he can save you from the Darklings. I sure won't."

He didn't leave. The way he looked at her was really starting to piss her off.

He squatted down outside the bars and slid the plate across the floor into the cell. He pushed it as far inside as he could reach, but she didn't move. She refused even to look at it even though she was hungry.

She hadn't eaten in four days, but she wouldn't show him that. This food was another trick just like so many others.

These imps wanted to manipulate her and then pull the rug out from under her. She'd seen it a thousand times before.

He stepped away and leaned against the opposite wall—far enough away that she wouldn't see him as a threat—as if he could possibly threaten her.

He put his hands behind his back and rested his weight on one foot. "I've never seen anyone who can defeat the Darklings the way you can," he remarked again. "I was wondering if I could convince you to help us."

"I will never help you again—ever," she spat back. "I hope you die out there. That's the least you deserve. Your father deserves to watch you die in battle against the Darklings."

He didn't react to her insults. He just kept studying her. "Who are you? Where do you come from?"

"Why should I tell you—so you can run home and tell your father all about me? I hate you."

"He didn't want me to talk to you about any of that. He thinks you're dangerous."

She burst out laughing. "I'm dangerous to him. Go home and tell him I'll kill him the first chance I get."

"You could kill him now. You could destroy this whole house with the whole Watch inside it. You could kill everyone in town and be on your way into the Coil where you belong."

She looked away. She didn't like where this conversation was going.

"Where did you come from, Eliska?" he asked in a much softer tone. "How did you wind up out in the Coil?"

"How the hell should I know?" she grumbled. "I've been out there as long as I can remember."

"Don't you have any family?"

"Of course not. Do you think I would be wandering around in the Coil if I had any family? I'm an orphan. Is that what you want to hear? Be grateful you have a father who wants to get you killed. It's better than nothing."

"You must have incredible magic if you've survived out there for that long. Where did you learn it?"

"I didn't learn anything. I picked up a few things here and there. That's all." Her resolve crumbled and she bent over to pick up the plate. She might as well eat if he was going to stand there shooting questions at her all day. "No one ever sticks around for long. I travel with someone for a day or two and then they either die or disappear or I disappear. It never lasts."

"So you don't know how you developed the ability to defeat the Darklings?"

"I have to keep myself alive somehow. What difference does it make how I do it?"

She took the cloth off the plate and started eating. He'd brought a hunk of bread, a piece of cheese, and a shaved pile of juicy roasted meat.

Yann didn't interrupt for a minute. She tore off a hunk of the bread and then started stuffing the meat into her mouth. It tasted mind-blowingly delicious.

"Your friend Wesh said your group came here on purpose to stop the Darkling incursion," Yann finally went on.

"Wesh isn't my friend," she mumbled around a mouthful of cheese. "I don't even know the guy."

"You acted like you knew him outside. You and Wesh and Mael stood together and talked after the battle."

She shrugged. Telling him this wouldn't make any difference in the end, especially if he didn't plan to tell his father what she said.

"I just bumped into them yesterday. I've never seen them before in my life. They were on their way here. Wesh said I might be able to get work here so I came with them. Then we got caught in the battle. That's all I know."

Yann frowned at her. "My father thinks Wesh and the other wizards who were with you might have brought those Darklings here for some reason."

She snorted. "Your father isn't the sharpest, is he? The Darklings came out of the Layers. You were standing right there. You saw."

He cocked his head the other way. "How do you know I was standing there?"

"Because I saw you, punk! Do you think I'm blind? I saw you through the barricade. You were on watch when the Darklings overran us. They rushed the barricade and we moved between you to defend the town."

He didn't answer. He kept frowning down at the floor thinking something over.

"Your father doesn't think much of you if he doesn't take the report of his own Watchman," she went on between mouthfuls. "He said he'd investigate our claim, but he hasn't done that if he didn't even ask you what you saw."

"I already told him what I saw."

"Then he's a fool who doesn't deserve his post. Someone else should be Watch Commander—you, maybe."

Yann laughed and pushed himself off the wall. His eyes twinkled and his face lit up when he laughed like that. "I'm too young to be Watch Commander. The other Watchmen wouldn't take me. They wouldn't listen to me any more than he does."

"He's going to get you killed. A Watch Commander is supposed to defend humankind, not put people in danger for no reason."

He met her gaze, but he didn't stop smiling. He looked like a completely different person. His whole countenance glowed in an unsettling way.

She found it impossible to hate him when he looked at her like that—like he might actually like her as much as she was starting to like him.

"I'll tell him what you said," he finished.

"You said you already did. What will telling him again do?"

"I don't mean about the Darklings coming out of the Layers. I mean I'll tell him what you said about only joining up with those wizards yesterday and about getting caught in the battle when you had no idea where they were going. Even if Wesh and Mael knew the Darklings planned to attack the town, it means you didn't. My father will release you."

"You hope he does, you mean. You can't guarantee he will."

Yann shrugged. "You're right, but I'll still tell him. He'll let you out and then you can leave us all to our deaths if you want to."

He waited for her reaction, but when she didn't give it, he walked away, climbed the stairs, shut the storm doors, and his footsteps got farther away in the street outside.

She turned back to her plate. Half the food still lay there waiting for her to eat it. He didn't take it away from her for being rude and hateful to him.

Maybe he wasn't as bad as all that, but she couldn't say the same about the Watch Commander or his other Watchmen. None of them stuck up for her or tried to change the Watch Commander's mind about her. She didn't owe them anything.

She suffered a pang of guilt about Yann, though. He was right. The instant the Watch Commander let her out of this cell, she would leave Middleborough and go her own way.

She'd survived in the Coil long enough on her own. She never stuck around anywhere for long.

She didn't mind leaving all of these other people to die, but she couldn't feel the same way about Yann. No one had been this kind to her in a long, long time.

In fact, she couldn't remember anyone being this kind to her. Would she really leave him to die, too?

He would stay. He wouldn't leave Middleborough even if she offered to take him with her—which she wouldn't.

He was a member of the Black Watch. They didn't run.

He would stay and fight and then he would die just like all the others. Members of the Black Watch only died one way. They died on the wall.

If she wanted to help Yann, she would have to stay, too, but she would never do that.

She would never die on the wall defending a flea-bag town like Middleborough.

She'd spent too many years and too much blood keeping herself alive to throw it all away for nothing.

Chapter 4

Yann strode back to the house, went inside, and found his father and Rainier Terriau in the Watch Commander's office. Yvan looked up when his son walked in. "Did she say anything—anything she didn't say last night?"

"She says she doesn't know the other two wizards she came in with. She says she just met them yesterday and they traveled together before they got caught in the battle. I believe her."

"You'd believe anything she told you," Rainier countered. "You're soft on her."

Yann bit his tongue. "You'll find out she's telling the truth. She's a wanderer. She has no family. She doesn't know those men. She wouldn't travel with them if she did. She prefers to travel alone."

"We have more important business to attend to right now," Yvan interrupted. "You come with us, son. We're going to interrogate the wizards."

Yann hung back and let his father and Rainier leave first. Rien joined them on the way out of the building. The men went down into the basement on the other side of the house.

They found Wesh and Mael locked in two adjoining cells. A stone wall separated them from Eliska's side of the jail.

Wesh sat up on his bench and squared his shoulders when the Watchmen entered.

Mael lay stretched out on his bench. He didn't even bother to raise his head when the Watchmen lined up outside his cell.

"What can I do for you, Commander?" Wesh asked.

"What can you tell us about that girl you came in with last night?" Yvan asked.

"I can't tell you anything except her name and that she has incredible magic. I've never seen anything like it before. She can destroy Darklings....but you saw that yourself. She might be one in a million. She says she's been alone in the Coil for as long as she can remember. She must have unbelievable magic to survive alone for that long."

"How do you know she was telling the truth about being alone in the Coil?"

Wesh made a face. "You've been behind the wall for too long, Commander. A girl her age doesn't become so hard and unfeeling and wary of people without going alone in the most dangerous environments. She traveled with us for maybe ten hours. In that time, I saw enough to convince me that she'd been in the Coil for a long, long time. There is nothing out there she can't handle and she prefers to handle it alone. She shuns people and I don't blame her. Anyone less powerful than herself would be a liability to her and likely to get her killed."

"Why did she stay with you, then? Why did she travel in your company?"

Wesh shrugged. "We told her we were coming to this town. She thought she might get work here or maybe supplies. She didn't say outright that she had nothing else to do and nowhere else to go, but she implied it with her careless attitude."

"Why did *you* come to Middleborough? You suggested last night that you came here on purpose."

"I told you already. The Darklings were sent here to raze this town."

"Sent by whom? The Darklings are unruly and attack without any direction at all."

Wesh raised one bony index finger. "Ah, yes! That's what we all think, isn't it? You saw for yourselves that they didn't do that last night. They attacked with a definite purpose. They coordinated their attack to get behind us so they could breach your barricade. Someone was directing them."

"Who would do something like that? Who *could* do something like that?" Yvan's eyes popped wide open. "Did the girl do it? Would she have enough power to do it?"

Wesh smacked his lips. "Use your head, Commander. If she wanted to coordinate the Darklings to wipe out your town, she wouldn't have risked her neck to defend you. She could have just stood off to the side and let them kill you all and then taken what she wanted."

"Wanted!" Yvan exclaimed. "Wanted what?"

"That's what I'm telling you. The Darklings came here for something. The Voyant Mendicat wants....."

"The what?" Rainier cut in.

"The Voyant Mendicat," Wesh repeated. "He's a sorcerer who lives in the White Spire. He's said to hold the power to direct the Coil where he wants it to go. They say he can cause it to ripple in one direction or another. He can use the Coil to erase towns and dimensions and even entire lands in one place while he creates Islands somewhere else that give rise to new civilizations."

"Do you believe that's true?" Yann blurted out before he thought to stop himself. "How could anyone hold that much power?"

Wesh shrugged again. "I don't know if it's true or not."

"How do you know the Voyant Mendicat sent the Darklings to attack us?" Yvan asked.

"My brothers in the Guardian Templars foresaw it in their scrying visions. They sent me, Mael, Ramon, and Ines to warn you and to defend you if we could, but we left the Temple more than two years ago. We've been traveling through the Coil ever since, but it keeps changing and shifting on us. Maybe the Voyant keeps moving it around to slow us down."

Yvan glanced over at Rainier. "Two years. That's when the Darkling attacks started to escalate."

"The Voyant thinks there is a certain element in this town that he wants," Wesh went on. "He sent the Darklings here to get it for him. He won't stop until he reclaims it."

"What is this element?" Rainier asked.

"I don't know that," Wesh replied. "I don't think anyone knows....except the Voyant himself."

"How are we supposed to stop him from taking it, then?" Rien asked. "We can't even stop the Darklings from invading this town."

"We'll do what we can to help you," Wesh replied, "but as you can see, it's just Mael and me now. Two of us won't be able to do anything."

"What about the girl?" Rainier asked. "She can defeat the Darklings."

"She won't help us," Yann interjected. "She's furious that you locked her up. As soon as you let her out, she'll leave."

"She wouldn't be able to help you anyway," Mael muttered from his bench. "She might have power, but she's only one person. She couldn't defeat them last night and the Voyant will send a bigger attack next time. She won't be able to defeat them and we'll all die. She's smart to leave and save her own life."

"How can you speak so highly of a useless Coil rat?" Rien growled. "She's as good as a Darkling herself if she walks away and leaves a whole town to die."

"She's no Darkling," Wesh replied. "I don't know what she is, but she doesn't belong to the Dark. She fears the Dark as much as we do."

"You say that," Rien countered. "She's nothing but a...."

Yvan stopped him by laying a hand on Rien's arm. "She's blameless. She had nothing to do with this. Maybe she's right to hate me for locking her up instead of listening to her."

He walked forward, pulled out his keys, and unlocked Wesh's cell. "You're free to go, old man. I would appreciate it if you helped us against the Darklings, but I would appreciate it even more if you could convince that girl to help us, too."

"Eliska," Yann interjected. "Her name is Eliska."

"Right." Yvan went over to Mael's cell and unlocked that, too. "I'm grateful for your help, both the help that you've already given me and any help you give me in the future, though I don't know what good it will do any of us."

"Go tell her," Wesh replied. "If you can't convince her, I'll come with you and try myself, but I don't think she'll listen to any of us. She'll say she's better off alone and I'm afraid she's right."

Yann agreed with him, but he didn't say so. Eliska would be more than happy to tell the Watch Commander to his face.

Yvan climbed the stairs and paused in the street outside the storm doors. "Rainier, you take Rien back to my office and wait for me there." Yvan gave Yann a sharp look. "You come with me, son. She listens to you."

Yann didn't ask why his father thought that. Eliska wouldn't listen to Yann any more than she would listen to any other Watchman, but he didn't argue.

Yvan pinched his lips together the way he always did when he had to do something unpleasant. He marched around the building and pulled open the other storm doors.

He climbed down and stopped outside Eliska's cell. She sat with one knee drawn up and her other leg stretched out on her bench. She glanced at Yvan and then her dark eyes sliced sideways to Yann.

"I am Yvan Dilnao, Eliska," he began. "I am Commander of the Middleborough Black Watch."

"Do you think I give a damn who you are?" she fired back. "You're nothing to me."

He held up his keys. "I'm the person who can release you from this cell."

"You can't hold me here. You don't have any power over me."

"Your friend Wesh tells me that you only met him and Mael yesterday," Yvan told her.

She allowed her eyebrows to lift slightly. "Wesh told you that? Not....*him?*" She glanced over at Yann again.

"I realize now that you didn't bring the Darklings here," Yvan went on.

She snorted in his face. "What did you do with my staff?"

"It's in my office. I'm here to release you."

"Really?" She glanced around her cell. "And yet I'm still in here."

"I came to ask you to help us defend this town against the Darklings. Prove to me that I'm not making a mistake by releasing you."

"If you're releasing me, then you already made a mistake by locking me up when you had enough information to know I never did anything wrong.....unless I was the one who made a mistake by helping you the first time. You punished me for helping you. I would be stupid to do it again."

Yvan sighed heavily. "You don't make it easy to help you, girl."

"You can't help me. I can help myself just fine. Just let me out of here and leave me alone." She turned her head away and pretended to look at the wall.

Yann's heart went out to her. He agreed with everything she said.

Why should she help the Black Watch? The Commander made a serious mistake by locking her up like this. He had no reason at all to do that. Now he would pay the price for it.

Yvan unlocked the cell. The door creaked open and he propped it aside. "There you go. You can leave now."

She refused to look at him. "Where's my staff?"

He compressed his lips even tighter and scowled at her, but Yann felt no sympathy for his father. The Watch Commander asked for this.

Yvan nodded at Yann and Yann bolted out of the basement. He ran back to his father's office.

Rien and Rainier both glanced up when Yann looked around for Elisa's staff, snatched it from the corner, and dashed back outside.

He slowed down when he spotted his father and Eliska standing outside the building talking to Wesh and Mael. Yann could just imagine how much success Wesh and Mael were having convincing Eliska to stay.

Her eyes lit up when she saw Yann coming back, but she didn't look at the staff. She was looking at him. Could she soften that much just because of him?

His spirits lifted and he held out the staff to her when, at that moment, another bone-crushing blow struck him across the back of the head. He felt himself going down and a sickening wave of cold nausea swept over him.

He stretched out his hand to Eliska, but she leapt away from him instead of coming toward him. He tried to call out to her to take her staff. She would need that when she left Middleborough and returned to wandering the Coil.

She spun away from him and her hair whipped out from her head. Yann's blood crashed in his ears and he collapsed onto his knees.

He tried to call out to anyone, but he couldn't move. All his limbs turned to water and he felt himself falling over.

He toppled onto his shoulder and stared in blank horror at a dozen absolutely massive Darklings surrounding Middleborough.

He had never seen Darklings this big before. Each one dwarfed the town by many times. They faced inward with their gargantuan fanged mouths gaping to swallow the town.

Howling winds blasted into town....except there was no town anymore. The barricade evaporated and the buildings and houses around the town's perimeter dissolved in the hazy cloud of chaos.

Shingles, windows, siding boards, water troughs, furniture, and bodies twirled in the wind, cartwheeled past the Watch standing in the middle of the street, and vanished into the whirling darkness.

Dark Layers rotated through town disintegrating everything in their path. The Darklings remained in position facing inward at the points of the compass.

They didn't dive in to attack. They didn't have to. Middleborough was finished. The Coil wiped it out of existence along with everyone in it.

Chapter 5

Eliska sprang backward and straddled Yann's fallen body. She couldn't let him get pulled away in this mayhem.

"Stand fast!" she roared into the howling wind. "Stay where you are and stay connected!"

"We need weapons!" Yvan yelled over the noise.

"You'll never survive if you leave now! Stay where you are!" She backed another step until she stood right over Yann. "Give me my staff!"

None of the Watchmen turned around even to look for it. Yann dragged himself off the ground to pick up her staff. He tried to pass it to her, but he couldn't rise. She didn't dare to turn around.

She extended her hand behind her groping for it when a Darkling tentacle whipped through town. It unwound between a few of the remaining houses and cracked straight for the party.

The tentacle snapped in Eliska's face and she struck out with her bare hand. She slapped the tentacle away and it snaked out of sight into the darkness. She didn't dare to put her hands down again as more tentacles hissed all around her.

They struck random people running through the street. The tentacles snatched livestock and yanked them away into the storm. Scraps, splinters, and razor-sharp debris peppered Eliska's skin and she heard screaming in the background.

Someone grabbed her ankle. She dared to glance down just long enough to see the cuff of Yann's sleeve surrounding the hand holding onto her leg. She didn't move nor did she try to shake him off. She wanted to make sure he stayed near her.

He crawled over to her and held onto her leg while he hauled himself to his feet. He planted himself between her and another Watchman on his other side.

He wobbled on unsteady legs, but at least he was upright—not that it would do any good. "Why don't they attack?" he yelled into her ear.

"I don't know!" she called back. "They don't have to, I guess."

"What do they want?"

She could only shake her head. She didn't want to take her attention off the Darklings in case they attacked again.

He turned aside, bent over, and picked up her staff, but when he straightened up to hand it to her, the Darkling right in front of them lunged for the party.

"Stand fast!" Yvan yelled again, but it was too late. That one Darkling reared high into the air and dove down on top of the town. Its enormous mouth widened to a colossal size and it crashed down on top of what was left of Middleborough.

The Darkling swallowed the town and an unbelievable force struck Eliska all over.

The black void enveloped her and she felt herself pinwheeling through space. Bodies and random stuff pounded her from all sides and she slammed down hard on some solid surface.

People landed on top of her grunting in pain and she groaned when they crushed her under their weight.

She scrambled to get out from under them trying to orient herself in the darkness. Her hand brushed her staff, but when she tried to pick it up, someone yanked it away from her. "No!" Yann yelled.

"It's me!" she called into the darkness. "It's Eliska!"

"Eliska......" His hands patted her all over, but she couldn't find her staff again. "Where are we?"

"We're in the Coil. Get up—quick!" She picked him up and pawed up to his face. "Is your head okay?"

"I'm fine. Where is everyone?"

She strained her eyes to see in the dark before the howling wind and tornado of debris hit them without warning.

It started as darkness and widened to include the murky whirling Layers, clouds, and mayhem of Middleborough....except that the group wasn't in Middleborough anymore.

Wesh, Mael, Yvan, a handful of Watchmen, and a few other townspeople got to their feet in the same positions where they started when the Darklings attacked.

None of the houses were there anymore. The Darklings were gone, too. Chaos and shadow surrounded the party.

Eliska pulled Yann into position between herself and Wesh, but she could already see that it was no good.

She didn't see her staff anymore. She just had to wait and pray the Coil spat the party out in some relatively safe place.

"Where are we?!" Wesh hollered.

"It looks like...." Eliska squinted into the shadows. "I think we're in Serenity Valley."

"Serenity Valley!" one of the Watchmen roared. "You call this serene?! It isn't a valley, either!"

Eliska remained tense and watchful as the Layers built to a punishing wind.

The townspeople tightened together into a knot facing outward from the center. Sections of darkness gathered into shapes out in the Layers.

"Here it comes!" Eliska yelled over her shoulder.

Yann bumped into her from the side. They both backed up a little more until he stood touching her on that side, but she didn't want him anywhere else. She didn't want him to get lost.

He started to say, "What is it.....?" and then he saw it, too.

The shadows collected in certain places with orange, red, and dark purple vapors slashing and crackling all around them.

Those shadows started to take shape and expand into Darklings, but at that moment, the ground under Eliska's feet caved in. The earth quaked and split apart.

The whole party tumbled into the fissure. Yells echoed out of the darkness and Eliska yelled out, too. She tried to grab out for....anything.....

She cartwheeled through multiple Layers, crashed into things, ricocheted off a few Watchmen, and slammed down hard on a shelf of solid rock.

Her face bounced on the stone hard enough to stun her. She shook the stars out of her eyes and tasted blood in her mouth before she dragged her head up to look around.

Her hair hung over her eyes, but at least she landed on something solid. Wesh, Yann, and the Watchmen writhed and groaned on the same rock shelf near her.

Mael lay right in front of her staring at nothing with his eyes open. He was dead. She didn't see any of the other townspeople who'd gotten out of Middleborough alive.

Eliska pushed herself up on all fours and crawled over to Yann. "Are you okay?" she choked.

He groaned, hugged his arm over his stomach, and howled through gritted teeth while he grimaced in agony. "NO!!" he gasped.

She extended her hand to touch him and heal him, but right then, a deep rumble shook the rock shelf underneath her.

She glanced around searching for the source of the noise. The shelf extended a dozen yards in every direction from where the Watchmen lay.

Then the rock cliffs plummeted away to nothing with Layers and Darkness on all sides.

The Layers swirled in a torrent of chaotic madness all around the shelf. The Layers whipped against each other and the colors slashed and pelted back and forth, but those howling winds didn't come onto the shelf itself.

"Where are we?" Yvan asked.

"We're in an Island." Eliska turned back to Yann and flattened her hand on his chest.

She felt right away that he had life-threatening injuries to his internal organs. He would die if she didn't heal him now.

Wesh went through the Watchmen attending to their injuries while he searched the surroundings, too.

"We can't stay here," Eliska panted. "We have to move."

"How can we when there's nowhere to go?" Yvan asked.

She made a face at him and then concentrated on sending a rush of magic into Yann's chest. "You don't know much about the Coil, do you? It will change soon. This part of the Coil is too unstable."

"The Islands are supposed to be stable," Yvan pointed out. "If we're in an Island....."

The same deep rumble vibrated the rock beneath the party and cut him off. Everyone stopped what they were doing.

Eliska looked around again, but she didn't stop sending her magic into Yann's body. She had to work fast, but his injuries took too long to heal.

The rumble kept getting louder until it built to a thunderous boom. No one could ignore it anymore.

Yann's eyes snapped to Eliska's face. He stared up at her in desperation, but she couldn't work any faster than this.

Tremors pounded the rock until the whole shelf jolted with deep, crushing blows. Without warning, sections of rock around the shelf's perimeter erupted upward into spikes.

They kept growing into hills and then cliffs and mountains. They grew outward as well as inward. They expanded to take up all the space on the shelf—the only space left for the party to stand.

Eliska lunged to her feet and grabbed Yann. "Everybody up! Get up! Come on! Run for it!"

She took off running, but she couldn't move fast while she dragged Yann with her. He staggered to his feet, stumbled, and kept going. He barely stayed upright, but at least he was still alive.

The rocky cliffs kept growing and growing and growing. They converged inward on the party.

The walls would crush everyone in the center if the group didn't keep running.

The shelf wasn't big enough for any of them to run anywhere. They would have run straight off the edge into the chaos Layers, but the landscape morphed and transformed too fast.

Eliska ran straight into another cliff rumbling, sprouting, and jutting out of the shelf in front of her. She didn't know what it would become or if it would crush her and the rest of the party any second now.

The Watchmen slowed down when they saw themselves running into a stone cliff. They dropped back, but Eliska sprinted forward.

She raised her hand to use her magic to blast the cliff apart, but Wesh got there first.

He fired a crackling bolt energy from his palm. It struck the cliff face, but the impact only made it expand faster.

Eliska raced to his side. She had to take one hand away from holding onto Yann.

Wesh glanced over at her, and when he saw her about to unload her magic on the cliff, he raised his hand a second time.

They both fired simultaneously this time. The cliff shuddered and boomed, but it still didn't collapse.

The Watchmen crowded around for protection from the upheaval. The surrounding cliffs rumbled, pounded, and crashed against each other as they all kept growing out of control.

They chewed up the shelf until no space remained. They would smash in on themselves and crush the party in the center.

"Again, Eliska!" Wesh bellowed over the noise.

She took both hands off Yann and plastered both hands against the cliff face in front of her. He buckled to his knees, but she could only help him one way.

"On three!" Wesh roared. "One.....two......three!"

Eliska summoned every scrap of magic she possessed and channeled it into the rock.

The cliff evaporated in a curtain of falling rock, rubble, and gravel falling right on top of the party standing underneath it.

The Watchmen yelled out. A brick-sized stone smashed Eliska in the head. She screamed in pain and raised her arms above her for protection.

Her magic formed a barrier over her and the others, but only for a second before the walls smashed together and the whole shelf dissolved in a deafening explosion.

What had been a rock shelf disintegrated into the Layers. Rock, dust, and boulders wheeled off into the surrounding chaos.

Eliska lost sight of everyone and everything in the Dark until she hit another solid surface.

This one wasn't stone. It gave a little under her weight, but only a little. She smelled dirt and pine trees, rolled down a slope, and landed in a puddle of freezing cold water.

Chapter 6

Yann's eyes fluttered open. He found himself lying on his back staring at the sky through the tops of some kind of trees.

He pried himself off the ground and looked around. His whole body ached, but at least he could move his limbs without pain.

He woke up in a clearing in some woods. A small stream ran through the grass nearby.

Eliska sat on a rock near him. All the other Watchmen who survived Middleborough were all in the process of waking up, sitting up, and looking around, too.

Wesh lay stretched out not far away with his eyes closed. "Is he.....?" Yann broke off. Maybe he shouldn't ask.

"He'll be all right," Eliska replied. "He got injured, but I healed him. He just needs to rest, but he'll wake up soon."

She eyed Yann for a second and then went back to working on a long tree branch stretched across her lap.

She passed a knife down its edges to shave off the extra twigs and bark, straighten it, and smooth it into another staff.

A fire crackled at her feet and she occasionally stopped working on the staff to add more dead sticks to the flames. She was the only person sitting up. She must have lit it.

She'd taken off her black cloak, propped some longer branches at angles near the fire, and spread her cloak on top of it. It must have gotten wet. Now she used the fire to dry it.

Yann found himself squirming under her direct stare. She only took her eyes off him to look at her work or to glance around at the other Watchmen.

None of them seemed to be injured—not seriously. Did she heal them, too? How many of them owed her their lives? They might not even realize that she saved them. They could have been unconscious at the time.

Yann definitely owed her his life. He knew he was going to die on that rock shelf, but she saved him then. Did he almost die this time, too?

Yvan distracted him by coughing. The Watch Commander got as far as his hands and knees and then fell back on his seat. Dirt and dead pine needles stuck in his hair and covered his uniform.

Yann crawled over to his father and touched the Watch Commander's shoulder. "Are you all right, Father?"

"I'm fine." Yvan coughed again, looked around, saw Eliska sitting there, and glanced up at Yann. "Are you all right, son? Did you get injured?"

"I did....." Yann didn't tell his father that Eliska saved him again. Yvan was too smart not to put the puzzle pieces together on his own. "I'm all right now."

Just then, Wesh jolted upright. He jerked out of a sound sleep, shot into a sitting position, and yelled out in surprise while his wild eyes darted around the forest.

"Stay calm, Wesh," Eliska murmured and raised her staff to sight down its length. "You got hurt, but you'll be okay. We're in another Island."

Wesh searched everywhere for a second before his shoulders slumped. He cast his gaze to the ground. "Mael is gone. I'm the last one."

"We have bigger problems than that," Eliska told him. "We're stranded in the Coil."

"Where are we?" Yvan asked. "What does it mean that we're on an Island?" Now it was his turn to look around. "There could be towns around here somewhere."

"Not here," Eliska told him. "This Island is too small. It will change soon."

"How can you tell?" Yann asked.

She held up the staff in her hands, rotated it to examine it from all sides, and then held it out so the end pointed at his face. "Do you see that? The growth rings are too far apart. This forest just grew out of the Coil a little while ago. We're still in the wild Layers."

"What does that mean?" Omer asked.

She didn't outright sneer at him, but she barely looked at him when she answered. "It means the Island can go as easily as it came. Islands are always popping up in the Coil. Sometimes they last a few minutes like that rock shelf we landed on. Sometimes they last a day or a week or a year. Then the Coil shifts again and the Island vanishes and reforms into something else somewhere else."

"So.....we have no way of knowing how long this Island will last?" Rien asked.

She let the staff fall down on her lap, turned around, and stared at him. "Don't you know anything about the Coil—anything at all? You don't even know what an Island is or how it works?"

"Of course I don't know anything about the Coil!" Rien fired back. "I've never been out of Middleborough in my life! Do you think I want to be some worthless lowlife Coil rat like you?"

"Rien!" Yvan snapped. "Stuff it."

Rien opened his mouth to say something equally insulting to Eliska, but he stopped himself in time, glanced at the Watch Commander once, clamped his mouth shut, and turned his head to look off in another direction.

Eliska scrutinized him for a second before she went back to shaving on her staff. "Don't worry. I'll go off alone and return to being the Coil rat that I am. You won't have to worry about me any longer.....but you might want to think about where you are and what you're doing here. Middleborough doesn't exist anymore. You're stranded in the Coil the same way I am....which means you're Coil rats just like me. I hope you're happy. Now you get to find out how I've been living for the last sixteen years. So good luck with that."

She stood up, gave her new staff one last critical inspection, twirled it through the air a few times, and then stabbed it into the soft soil at her feet.

She crossed to her cloak and squeezed it. It must not have been dry enough. She readjusted its position on its drying frame and went back to pick up her staff.

Yvan scrambled to his feet. "Thank you....Eliska....for everything you've done for us. I understand why you don't want to stay with us....."

"I doubt you understand very much of anything," she mumbled under her breath. "You and your dopey Watchmen will die out here. The sooner I get away from you, the better off I'll be."

"You would really go off and leave us alone to die—when none of us has any magic to defend ourselves?" Barsali Brun snorted. "You really are a Darkling."

"I'm not leaving you alone," Eliska told him. "Wesh is here. He'll help you. He came to Middleborough to save you. He'll do it if you even can be saved—which I doubt. You don't need me and...." She glanced at Rien. "You don't want me anyway. We're better off apart."

She took her staff and walked off into the trees. She must not have been planning to leave right away. She didn't take her cloak with her.

No one spoke until she passed out of earshot. "She's a wretch," Rien snarled.

"Did you have to insult her to her face?" Yvan fired back. "The very next one of you who calls her a Darkling or a Coil rat or any other insult will be out of the Watch. Is that clear? She saved our lives—more than once. We're alive right now because of her. All of you better start treating her with some respect. If you can't do that, then keep your mouths shut around her."

Yann didn't get involved. The other Watchmen didn't answer at all. Silence fell over the group.

Six Watchmen survived the destruction of Middleborough besides Yann and his father. The Watchmen had a mixture of reactions to Yvan's order about Eliska.

Neither Rien Dugas nor Barsali Brun would look at the Watch Commander. Rien kept fuming over there, grinding his teeth, and glaring at the surrounding trees on the opposite side of this clearing.

Omer Veco looked straight back at Yvan with clear, direct black eyes. Omer's sharp, angular features showed no surprise or offense at Yvan's order.

Then again, Omer never said anything insulting about Eliska, either to her face or behind her back.

Vidal Rom didn't treat the order like anything special, either. He squatted down next to the fire, used a stick to stir up the embers, added more wood, and spread his hands over the flames to warm his fingers.

"She's a resourceful young thing, isn't she?" he remarked. "She knows her way around the Coil."

"Of course she does," Wesh replied. "She understands its ways from long experience the same way you would be familiar with your own hometown. The Coil's many dangers are no surprise to her and she knows how to survive when things go wrong."

Neither Niyazi Trahan nor Niels Surette even seemed to hear Yvan's order. Both of them searched the surrounding forest for something that kept not being there.

"We should canvas the area," Niels suggested. "We might find a town....."

"She says this Island only sprang up recently," Omer pointed out. "It could be too new for any towns to develop."

"We still might find something," Niels pointed out. "We can't stay sitting here forever."

"If she's right about the Coil shifting soon and swallowing this Island, then we could wind up somewhere else anyway," Vidal added. "Canvasing the area would accomplish nothing."

Eliska came back just then. Everyone stopped talking the instant she stepped out of the trees.

She carried her staff in one hand and the headless body of some furry brown animal in the other.

She sat back down on the same rock by the fire, held up the animal by its back leg, and aimed her staff at the creature.

She fired a fork of magic at the carcass and the hide stripped off in one sudden rip.

The pelt fell to the ground at her feet while the bloody bare body still hung from her hand.

Yann burst out laughing at the sight. He realized as soon as it happened that he probably shouldn't have laughed. It wasn't the appropriate response to the situation.

His laughter slipped out before he could stop it. He stifled it immediately, but the sound startled everyone into spinning around and staring at him. Even Eliska stared at him.

He bit his lip and tried to shut his mouth, but he couldn't stop chucking at the way she skinned that animal. "Sorry," he mumbled. "It just looked funny."

She split in a matching grin. "It's easier than doing it with a knife, isn't it?"

Yann found himself grinning back at her. "Cleaner, too."

"Watch this. This is the best part." She picked up her staff again.

"Stop playing with it," Niels interjected.

She barely glanced at him before she turned back to her dead animal. She fired another steady beam of magic into its body, sliced it open, and all its entrails squelched out onto the grass next to the fire.

In seconds, she cleaned, gutted, and skinned the animal as expertly as any professional butcher could have.

"You're lucky," Yann told her. "Our butcher's apprentice trained for years to be able to do that."

"There are some advantages to being a worthless lowlife Coil rat." Eliska shifted off her rock, squatted down by the fire next to Niels, and laid her carcass on another rock while she constructed a spit to cook the meat.

The Watchmen fell silent watching her work. Did she plan to share any of this meat with them?

Yann's stomach tightened with hunger. His mouth started to water as the smell of roasting meat drifted through the clearing.

He didn't dare to ask her to share the food with him—not after the way Rien and Barsali insulted her. No one else asked, either. Yann really hoped the others were starting to realize the priceless resource they'd thrown away by kicking her in the teeth.

She helped them. She helped them a lot more than they deserved. She probably helped them more than they even realized.

Most or all of them could have gotten injured and nearly died when they fell through the Layers. She could have saved all their lives before they regained consciousness.

She could have been their greatest asset if they only treated her well. Now she would leave them to fend for themselves.

Yann glanced over his shoulder at the forest. It sounded peaceful. Birds chirped in the branches and insects clicked out of sight.

Sunshine streamed through the canopy. The smell of pine needles and fresh earth drifted on the soft breeze.

He couldn't remember ever seeing such a serene, inviting landscape, but it breathed with menace.

The Coil's swirling Layers of wild magic stormed just out of sight. Everything in front of Yann's eyes right now—this was nothing more than a veil of deception to stop him from seeing the danger lingering right behind those trees.

Chapter 7

W esh crossed the clearing to the edge of the stream. He stopped with his back to the group, moved his hands through the air in front of his face, and released a rain of sparks.

They formed a sheet of light shimmering with watery colors. Then they cleared to form a transparent surface.

A magical window opened to reveal another landscape beyond. It churned with Dark colors and then rose and fell in a constant shifting panorama of different environments.

The image started as a vast desert of dry, cracked flats with mountains in the distance. In a few seconds, a massive forest of towering pine trees erupted out of the flats and then a torrential thunderstorm hit the treetops.

Rain pelted the trees to smithereens, disintegrated the forest, and then crumbled the earth around the tree roots. The landscape exploded and everything collapsed into the Coil's confused Layers again.

"What do you see, old man?" Barsali asked.

"Eliska is right, of course," Wesh muttered without turning around. "This Island won't last more than a day or two."

"Is there anywhere we can go?" Yvan asked. "That gives us a day or two to find another safe haven—maybe one that will last longer."

"We should try to find a town," Niyazi suggested. "Any town will need the Watch."

"I'll try to find one," Wesh replied. "The Coil is becoming more unstable all the time. No town will be completely safe. The same thing that happened to Middleborough can happen anywhere."

"You said the Voyant Mendicat went after Middleborough to get whatever it is he wanted from there," Yvan pointed out. "If he destroyed Middleborough, he should already have whatever it is. He would have no reason to destroy the next town we go to."

"I wasn't referring to the Voyant," Wesh replied. "I was referring to the Coil itself. The Coil is becoming more unstable with every passing year. I've been alive a long time and I've never seen it this bad before. Towns can fall at any time. Landscapes shift and vanish along with any towns that happen to exist in those landscapes. All of that would be happening even if the Voyant didn't do anything."

"Didn't you say the Voyant controls the Coil?" Yann asked. "If he can do that, maybe he's the one causing all this instability."

"I said it was a rumor that he controls the Coil," Wesh replied. "We have no proof that he does."

"You're a member of the Guardian Templars," Omer interjected. "If the Guardian Templars don't know, then who does?"

"The Guardian Templars don't know everything," Wesh replied. "We spend our lives studying and trying to learn as much as possible, but we're only ordinary men at the end of the day."

"What do you know about the Voyant?" Yann asked.

"Only what I've already told you. He's a powerful magic-user. He might be the most powerful magic-user in the entire Coil. I can't imagine anyone more powerful than he is, but that doesn't mean he controls the Coil. I don't know if anyone can."

Yann automatically glanced at Eliska. She sat in silence listening to their conversation.

Did she have the power to control the Coil? She used her magic to protect the group, but she couldn't destroy that cliff without Wesh's help.

She must have been using her magic to get herself out of dangerous situations for a long time.

She might even have been using her magic to manipulate these landscapes to make them more beneficial to herself or at least less dangerous.

She caught him watching her and turned her attention back to the carcass on the spit. She turned it over to cook the other side and started carving off pieces of the already-cooked meat.

Everyone pretended not to notice when she put the first few pieces into her own mouth. None of the Watchmen said a word to ask her to share the food with them.

She showed no sign of noticing their behavior, either good or bad. She chewed in silence while she sliced off a few more pieces.

She handed the second portion to Neils who happened to be sitting closest to her. She actually smiled at Yann when she stretched her hand across the fire to pass him a wad of shavings.

"Thank you," he murmured.

"Did you really think I was going to eat all of this by myself right in front of you and leave you to go hungry?" She turned around to call over her shoulder. "Come get something to eat, Wesh. We might land in another rock Island with no life in it."

Wesh kept working on his magical window for a minute before he gave it up. He passed his hand in front of the window, wiped it out of the air, and crossed to the fire.

He sat down crosslegged on the ground on Eliska's other side between her and Yann. Wesh heaved a shaky sigh.

She dumped a handful of meat into his wrinkled palm.

"Thank you, my dear," he told her. "You're a truly generous soul to share this with us."

She licked the juice off her hand before she started cutting again. She stuffed another piece of meat into her mouth and talked with the food stuffed into her cheek while she served the other Watchmen.

"This one has a strange taste," she mumbled. "I've never tasted one like this before. There must be something in the local vegetation that gives it a different taste."

"What is it?" Yann asked. "What kind of animal is it?"

"I don't know what it's called. I call them squabbles."

"Squabbles!" Niyazi repeated. "That's an argument."

She shrugged. "That's just what I call them. I don't know their real name."

"It's a long-tailed gar," Wesh interjected.

"That makes no sense!" she countered. "They don't have a long tail."

"You would have been a genius if you only received some education," he replied. "There are four varieties of gar—the tailless gar, the mottled gar, the hyperlight gar, and the long-tailed gar. The long-tailed gar is called that because it has the longest tail of the four."

She shrugged that away, too. "I guess I learned something today, but I know more about what they taste like. I've eaten hundreds of these things and none of them tasted like this."

"You have me beat on that one, my dear," Wesh replied. "This is the first gar I've ever eaten."

Eliska turned the other way to survey the other Watchmen. She'd already given a portion of meat to Yvan, Omer, Neils, Niyazi, Vidal, and Barsali.

They all gathered around and thanked her as politely as possible when she served them. The gar kept getting smaller and smaller as she sawed the meat off the bones.

Rien sat off to one side with his head turned as far away as possible. He didn't watch the others eat. He didn't take part in the conversation. He made no move to come forward so he could accept her generosity.

She shot him a brutal look on the side and went straight back to what she was doing. She didn't insist that he come and get something the way she did with Wesh.

She took another piece of meat for herself and started passing out the last scraps to everyone else, starting with Neils in the same order she served them in the first round.

Yvan got to his feet, went over to Rien, and bumped his shoulder. "Come over and eat," Yvan snapped in that tone every Watchman understood instantly.

Rien had served under Yvan Dilnao for too many years not to understand that order as the command it was. The hair stood up on the back of Yann's neck when he heard his father's tone. Yann would never want his father talking to him like that.

Rien obeyed instantly, got up, and wedged himself into the circle between Omer and Vidal.

Rien mumbled, "Thank you," when Eliska gave him some of the food. She didn't respond.

"So where will we go if we don't scout the area?" Niyazi asked.

"I don't know," Yvan replied. "Maybe Wesh can help us with that."

"There's another Island three Layers down from this one," Eliska interrupted. "It has towns in it. You should go there."

Yvan's head snapped up to stare at her. "How do you know that?"

"It isn't hard." She wiped her hand on her pants, snapped her fingers, and made sparks fly from her fingertips.

She spread her palm and the sparks gathered there in a revolving miniature tornado. The tornado expanded into a six-inch representation of a coil and then widened.

The image zeroed in on a few different turns of the spiral. As it got bigger, more distinct Layers appeared with colors, shaded areas caught between the Layers, and tiny landscapes caught in the confusion.

The picture kept widening, but it never got any bigger. It stayed right there in the center of Eliska's palm.

She zoomed in on one particular Layer. The whole party looked in on a miniature picture of a forest.

"That's where we are," Eliska told everyone.

"That's amazing!" Barsali gasped.

The spiral turned a little farther and dropped down three Layers to another tiny landscape of hills, rolling farmland, towns, and roads crossing the countryside.

"It looks like a stable Island," Eliska remarked. "They don't have the Watch, though. It might not be very old as Islands go."

"You should come with us," Yvan told her. "You said you wanted to go to Middleborough to get work. You could do it there."

"No, I won't go there." She did something to the image and shrank it to show the Coil again.

The rotating spiral contracted to a ball-sized representation of multiple Layers all coiled on top of each other.

Layers in the upper sections collapsed on top of each other, exploded in arrays of light and sparks, compressed into Dark Layers, and swirled in different colors before they reformed.

"The Layers are too close to this Island," she pointed out. "It won't last."

"Why did you suggest that we go there, then?" Omer asked. "We could all die there if the same thing happened."

"It might not collapse for years." She closed her hand and the image vanished. "It might never collapse."

"Where will you go instead?" Yann asked.

"I'll stay out in the chaotic Layers. I know how to move around there. I'll find Islands like this one where I can stay a few days and then move on. It's safer than going to towns. I never go to towns unless I have to."

"Did you have to go to Middleborough?" Vidal asked.

Eliska stood up and squeezed her cloak again. It must have been dry enough. She took it off the rack, wrapped it around her shoulders, and tied it at the neck.

"I didn't have to go there and I don't have to go to that town. Staying away from people has kept me alive this long. I would be stupid to change my strategy now."

She walked away from the fire, walked down the bank to the stream, and squatted there to wash her hands and the blade of her knife.

She left the remains of the gar on the spit over the fire. At least half the meat still clung to the bones. She left enough for all the Watchmen to enjoy at least one more meal. She didn't try to take the gar with her.

No one said anything for a minute as the Watchmen took in this latest turn of events. She really planned to leave this food for them—for the same people who arrested her and insulted her to her face.

Yvan bumped his knuckles against Yann's elbow to get his attention and then jutted his chin at Eliska from behind.

Yann frowned. His father jerked his head toward her to tell Yann to go talk to her.

Yann didn't know what to say to her. He didn't want her to leave. He'd never met anyone like her. He understood enough of Wesh's comments to know that even Wesh had never met anyone like her.

Yann was starting to get a much clearer picture of what Wesh meant when he said she might be one in a million.

Yann also understood much better now why she didn't want to stay with the group. She developed a system for keeping herself alive in the Coil. That system didn't include other people.

She was right about one thing. She would be stupid to change anything about her methods, especially considering the dangers out here.

He had no earthly clue what to say to her. He did know he had to talk to her at least one more time before she walked out of his life forever.

He followed her down the bank, squatted next to her, and glanced over his shoulder to make sure the others were out of earshot.

"Can I ask you something?" he began.

She didn't look up from washing the grease off her knife blade. "If you want to."

"What's the earliest thing you remember? Do you remember where you were in the Coil when you first remember being out here by yourself?"

Her head shot up and she narrowed her eyes at him. "What do you want to know that for?"

"I'm just curious. You know so much more about the Coil than we do...."

She snorted in his face. "You don't know anything about the Coil. I bet none of you has been out in the Coil before, not just rat-face over there."

She didn't turn around to indicate who she meant. Rien didn't have a rat face, but Yann couldn't fault her for insulting him any way she chose to.

"So?" he asked. "What do you remember about where you were when you were that young?"

She bent over her knife and muttered under her breath. "I don't remember anything. Even if I did, the Coil changed too much back then. I wouldn't be able to find out where I came from if I tried."

"Are you sure? Maybe if you try, you could find out who you are and where you came from. You might have some family out there waiting for you."

"I already tried, okay?" she snapped. "Do you think I didn't spend years searching? Whatever Island I was born in doesn't exist anymore. The Coil changes too fast like Wesh says. That Island is long gone."

Yann looked away. Her words didn't betray any interest in the subject at all, but her tone sure did.

She tried to keep her voice dismissive and scornful of the whole topic, but a note of broken hopeless despair crept in despite her best efforts to hide it.

She distracted herself and him by pulling her bag forward, digging out a chipped piece of sharpening stone, dunking it in the stream, and rubbing her knife blade against the stone in a circular motion.

Yann couldn't look at her. He couldn't imagine a life worse than this—to wander alone in a landscape of destruction with no one.

It was worse than wandering with no one. All the forces at work in Eliska's life blocked her from connecting with anyone.

All those forces worked together to make it not only impossible for her to get close to anyone but actually benefitted her when she kept away from everyone. What a tragic waste.

She interrupted his thoughts. "What about you?" she asked. "The men of the Black Watch take a vow of celibacy and forsake all family. How did your father come to have you?"

"I don't know that. He never talks about it. I was born in the Watch and grew up in the Watch my whole life. The Watchmen are the only family I've ever had. It's all I've ever known."

"That's against the Black Watch oath, too," she pointed out. "Watchmen are supposed to volunteer of their own free will. The Black Watch isn't supposed to initiate anyone underage because they can't volunteer willingly with full knowledge of all the risks."

Yann shrugged that away. "I guess not, but it's the way it is for us. I wouldn't have it any other way."

"You don't know that because you've never known any other way."

He finally worked up the courage to turn around and look at her. Her dark eyes bored into him in ways he couldn't explain.

She studied him from inches away. He'd never spoken to her alone at this close range before. Her presence did something to him. He wasn't sure he liked it, but he could no longer deny the effect she had on him.

She looked away first. "You should go back to them. You wouldn't want any of my worthless wretchedness to rub off on you."

"Why would you say that?" he countered. "I'm trying to be nice to you. Why would you assume I think that way about you?"

"Don't be nice to me. Being nice to me gets people killed." She stuffed her stone back in her bag, slid her knife into her boot, stood up, and cast one last glance at Wesh and the Watchmen sitting around the fire. "You can make my excuses to everyone. See you later."

Chapter 8

Eliska braced herself to walk away from Yann. She did her best to keep her posture casual, but the longer their conversation went on, the more it hurt to walk away.

She shouldn't have gotten so attached to him. She kicked herself for that now. She couldn't even remember when or how it happened.

Some force she couldn't describe drew her to him. She didn't want to leave. She wanted to keep talking to him—about everything.

She had to leave, though, so she better bite the bullet and get it over with sooner rather than later.

Hanging around and dragging it out would only make it harder. She sensed that. She would keep talking to him. They would keep sharing details about their lives.

He would keep trying to be nice to her. She would keep doing things to help him and make his path easier.

All those things would only make the parting harder later—as if it wasn't hard enough already.

He got to his feet and faced her. He didn't say goodbye—not with words. His eyes said it.

She would probably never see him again. Wesh wouldn't be able to keep these helpless Watchmen alive in the Coil—not for very long.

Eliska didn't want to stick around long enough to watch Yann die. She wanted to be hundreds of miles away and preferably several Layers away when it happened.

Then she would be able to pretend that he wasn't dead when he was.

She tore herself away. She planned to cross the stream over the stepping stones, climb the opposite bank, and enter the trees over there. She wouldn't have to walk past the Watchmen or say goodbye to any of them or to Wesh.

Just then, for no reason she could figure out, the Watch Commander strode down the bank to where she and Yann stood talking.

The Watch Commander pulled up next to his son and squared his shoulders at Eliska. "I understand why you feel you have to leave, Eliska, but maybe there's another reason you might consider staying—and I don't mean so you can protect us. We all know you have the power to protect us and we would be so much better off with you with us than on our own. That isn't what I mean. There may be something we can give you—something you can't get by yourself—something that would make it worth it to you to stay with us and travel with us."

She tried not to raise her eyebrows too much. "Really? What would that be?"

"Companionship. You don't have to live alone anymore. You could have people in your life—people who want you around—people who care about you as much as you care about them. You've spent all these years alone. I'm sure you've met some truly terrible people in the Coil, but not everyone is like that. Things could be different if you found the right group."

"And you think you and your Watchmen are the right group for me?" She snorted at him. "I don't think your man up there agrees with you."

She did her best to block Yann out of her awareness when she said this.

The Watch Commander's words hit her hard, but not because of the Watchmen.

There was a right person here she could feel that way about. She could feel that way about Yann.

If any right person or people existed in the world, he was one of them. She felt that to the marrow of her bones, but she couldn't take him by himself. She would have to sign up for the whole group, including rat-faced Rien.

Yvan read her mind. "Rien is only one man and he has his own reasons to dislike those who live in the Coil. I've already spoken to him and Barsali about being rude to you. I give you my word they won't do it again. You don't have to leave. You don't have to live alone like this with your back against the world."

"Yes, I do," she snapped. "You don't know enough about the Coil. You wouldn't say this if you knew anything about it. Anyway, I'm already leaving, so it's too late. Goodbye and thank you for nothing, Watch Commander."

She turned to Yann, but the prospect of saying anything to him hurt too much.

The temptation to fall into deep, penetrating, heartfelt conversation with him became unbearable. She had to leave now or she wouldn't be able to leave at all.

She turned to face the stream and put out her foot to step on the first stepping stone.

At that moment, it started to rain, but this was no ordinary rain. Pelting shards of hail hurtled out of a clear blue sky. No hail could have come from there because the sky didn't have any clouds in it.

The landscape changed in a split second. A wall of wind, ice spikes, and flying splinters smashed in from the side to Eliska's right.

The tempest hit her hard enough to make her stagger. Yann and his father stumbled, too. The other Watchmen scrambled to get to their feet.

The hurricane wiped the blue out of the sky in an instant. The hail elongated until each piece stretched into an arrowhead.

Thousands of these projectiles hammered down from the sky, but Eliska still didn't see any clouds up there.

The wind erased the blue and stripped the sky aside to reveal the whirling shadowy colors of the Coil's most dangerous Layers.

The hail spikes stabbed downward at impossible speed. They fell from the highest atmosphere gathering speed as they came.

Omer roared in pain up on the bank. Wesh shrieked when three shards slashed down his face and left him bleeding.

Eliska heard the Watchmen yelling at each other as they crowded together. They raised their arms above their heads to protect themselves, only for dozens of the shards to stab into their arms.

Eliska fired her staff into the air and formed a dome of protection over herself.

She only realized a second too late that she was leaving Yann and his father defenseless outside it. She didn't usually have to think about protecting anyone but herself.

She sprang over to them. The hail spikes bounced off her dome, shattered, and each strike made a small crashing sound that built into a deafening, drumming din around her ears.

Wesh finally erected a similar dome over the other Watchmen. The rain put out the fire before the whole landscape descended into chaos—the same scene of chaos they had all just seen through Wesh's window.

The shards tore branches and needles off the trees. All those spikes acting together shredded the canopy and ripped the forest apart.

"Follow me!" Eliska bellowed to the two men nearest her. "Stay with me! Don't get too far away!"

They both understood and Eliska headed up the bank to rejoin the Watchmen. She wanted to combine her power with Wesh's to give the party the best chance of getting out of this alive.

Yvan grabbed his son and dragged Yann up the slope. Wesh had his hands full dealing with so many Watchmen. His dome was barely big enough to contain them all.

Rien, Barsali, Omer, Niyazi, Neils, and Vidal crowded body against body under the dome. They all held onto each other trying in every possible way to prevent any of them from accidentally sticking a body part outside.

Every man bled from multiple razor cuts to their heads, faces, arms, shoulders, and backs. Eliska didn't dare to check on Yann—not yet.

Wesh got stuck on the other side of the group. He didn't see Eliska coming toward him with the last two Watchmen sheltering under her dome.

When Wesh did see them, he tried to get the others to move closer so they could join up. Wesh and Eliska could combine their magic to create a bigger dome—big enough for all of them to fit under and maybe heal the Watchmen's injuries.

Wesh couldn't get all of them moving in the same direction at the same time—not without risking their lives.

That left Eliska, Yann, and Yvan to cross the last dozen yards to Wesh's dome.

Eliska cast one last glance behind her. The hail was rapidly hammering the forest into the ground.

As soon as the hail finished tearing the trees apart, all those millions of sharp projectiles would erode the ground under the group's feet. The Island would collapse and then.....

In that moment when she looked behind her, she spotted something in the Layers beyond where the treetops had been until just a few minutes ago.

The shadowy vapors between Layers separated. Dark shapes materialized from the background.

Some of those vapors whipped and snaked through the colored swirls. The shapes didn't disintegrate. They became more distinct.

Their movements became more deliberate....and then a torrent of Darkness poured down from the sky toward the devastation where the forest used to be.

The wave hit the ground with an earth-shaking boom and all that Darkness erupted upward to form monstrous, towering figures studded with spikes and tentacles. Ten massive Darklings shot upward fully formed around the two pathetic domes.

Eliska spun around and raised her staff to confront them, but the constant drum of the hail shards on the dome above her head changed her mind.

She wouldn't be able to fight the Darklings from under this dome. She wouldn't be able to protect Yann or Yvan in the middle of fighting those Darklings.

The minute she stepped outside—the minute she fired her very first assault against them—the dome would collapse.

Then the shards would kill both men right here. The shards would tear them apart so much quicker than the shards tore apart those trees.

She made a split-second decision, spun her staff around, and stabbed the end into the ground at her feet.

She discharged a massive jolt of magical power into the soil. The ground fractured from the impact. Fissures cracked and forked through the grass.

The landscape quaked and rocked. The Darklings bellowed in rage and took a dozen menacing steps closer to the party.

Eliska raised her staff above her head, summoned all her power, and slammed her staff down harder this time.

It worked. The ground completely caved in. It buckled in an avalanche of bedrock, soil, tree roots, torn grass, splintered tree trunks, and falling bodies.

All the Watchmen yelled in unison. Even Eliska yelled as the whole party tumbled through the breach into an open space under the ground.

They fell into another vapor Layer, but this time, an even more brutal wind struck from the left side.

It pummeled everyone with such force that they couldn't fall downward. The wind caught everyone, spun them through the Layer, and Eliska hit what felt like a curtain of water.

She broke through into a completely different Layer with bluish-purple and green vapors. They burned her skin when she fell through them.

The wind didn't blow here at all and the whole party instantly started falling again.

She lost track of how many Layers she passed through. Different kinds of magic operated in each one. In some, what looked like vapors slashed and cut a person's skin. Others didn't do anything and some actually felt pleasant and velvety soft.

She and the others barely entered each Layer before the shadows started to reform into Darklings. They lunged for the party and tried to attack.

Only the group's continuous falling and changing Layers saved them from each attack. The Layers changed rapidly from one to the next and the Darklings always reformed in each one.

Chapter 9

Eliska fell into a vast sea of sizzling energy sparks and, in the middle of that, another brutal torrent of magic slammed into her from the side. It swept her out of the sparks, through another hurricane wind, and she crashed full force into a vertical stone wall.

Gravity didn't pull her down to the ground, though. She stayed glued there to the side of the wall.

Her staff stuck to the wall next to her. At least she managed to hold onto it this time.

She tried to pull herself off and heard Wesh and the Watchmen groaning and cursing all around her.

She pried up her head...and realized she wasn't stuck to a wall at all. She lay sprawled on the ground in another Island of some stable landscape.

She peeled herself off the surface and pushed herself to her feet. She could stand all right, but her mind took a second to reorient to which direction was up.

The Watchmen started to sit up and stand up, too. They had the same problem and one of them lost his balance when he tried to get to his feet.

Eliska automatically picked him up. She didn't even know his name. She didn't know any of their names apart from Yann, Yvan, and Rien.

Everyone looked around. What she thought was a stone wall actually turned out to be a vast empty landscape of parched flats like the one she'd seen earlier. Not a single stick of vegetation grew anywhere.

The flats stretched all the way to the horizon with not a hill in sight. The Layers swirled and whipped beyond the edge of the land.

In that moment, Eliska got a split-second flash of an image in her mind. Towering Darklings loomed over the landscape.

Her vision gave her a clear view of herself, Wesh, and these Watchmen trapped in another ring of Darklings exactly the way they'd surrounded Middleborough.

Spikes and horns jutted from their faces. Whipping spiked tendrils lashed and cracked through the air trying to grab and tear the travelers apart.

"Now how do we get out of this?" one of the Watchmen grumbled.

"We gotta get out of here," Eliska murmured. "The Darklings are coming for us."

Yann looked up. "They are? How can you tell? They aren't here."

"Get up, all of you." Eliska heard her voice shaking. Her fingers tightened on her staff.

"Don't break us through again, Eliska," Wesh told her. "We can't fall like that again."

"Get up!" she snapped. "Come on! We have to get ready to move!"

"What's wrong?" a sandy-haired Watchman asked. "At least we're on the ground now."

Eliska opened her mouth to answer....and saw it. A piece of the dry flats crumbled near her foot. A tiny brown sprout poked its tip through the rough soil and started to grow.

"Run!" Eliska yelled and bolted forward. "Run for your lives!"

No one else moved. They looked around at each other trying to understand.

She didn't wait to see anything else. She didn't have to. That sprout kept growing....and growing....and growing....

It didn't stop growing—ever. It got longer and thicker. It sprouted side branches until it grew as tall as the Watchmen.

More sprouts erupted out of the ground all over the flats. The sprouts grew a few feet apart, and in a matter of seconds, they filled the whole landscape.

Thorns burst through their rough, woody brown stalks and spread to every branch. The vines twisted, bumped into other sprouts getting taller and thicker by the second, and knotted together to block anyone from going anywhere.

The Watchmen staggered away from the first sprout only to bump into others growing too close nearby. The tangled brambles grew higher than the Watchmen's heads. No one could see the top of the mass of vines.

Eliska made it a dozen yards away from the Watchmen before the landscape became completely impassable.

The brambles kept getting bigger....and they started to take shape. The branches compacted into Darklings with spiked thorns dotted all over their skin. Their vines whipped and cracked everywhere to slash and tear and kill.

Wesh whirled back and forth waving his hands and firing magical blasts at the vines to drive them away from the Watchmen.

They had to crowd in close to him for protection. Their presence stopped him from working as effectively as he might have, but they couldn't stay anywhere else.

Eliska could have blasted her way through and kept on running. She could have left the Watchmen behind and never looked back.

She didn't understand why she didn't. She fired her staff in front of her, carved a path through the thorn bushes, and then shot a second time behind her to clear the way for the Watchmen to catch up.

Yann reacted first, grabbed two men near him, and dragged them forward. "Come on!" he yelled. "Run!"

He took off in Eliska's direction pulling his closest companions with him. Eliska found herself slowing down to let them close the gap.

She had to fire continuous blasts of magic from her staff to slash the vines and brambles away from herself. She also had to constantly fire behind her to open the channel for the Watchmen to get through.

The others followed. Wesh waited until last. He bombarded the vines with dozens of pulses from his bare palms. The vines closed behind him as he caught up with the others.

Eliska started running again as soon as Yann and the others drew level with her. She bombarded the vines on both sides and in front, but they only grew faster.

They closed over her head. Her magic formed a tunnel through the thorns for the party to keep moving.

The shapes forming around the party became more distinct. The mass of brambles reared. Yawning mouths full of thorny fangs opened to devour the fugitives.

The Darklings roared in fury and dove down on top of the group. Eliska reacted without thinking and nailed the end of her staff into the ground with all her might.

The surface fractured immediately this time. The group plunged through, bounced off a dozen broken ledges underground and landed on another rock shelf.

This one turned out to be the same size as the last one, but with one distinct difference. The edges dropped away into a bottomless gorge between gargantuan mountains.

The peaks spiked into the clouds high above their heads. The shelf's sides plunged out of sight with no floor that Eliska could see.

The Watchmen slammed down on the hard surface. One of them fell too close to the edge. Rien and Yvan dove for the man and pulled him back just in time before he plummeted off to his death.

Everyone crowded to the center to keep away from the sides, but at least the Darklings didn't come here.

Eliska went through the group one man at a time healing all their injuries from the hail shards. She hardly looked at what she was doing. She kept casting glances behind her at the surroundings. "We're safe here for now."

"You call this safe?!" Rien snapped.

"We're safer here than we were in those brambles." She surveyed the landscape. "We aren't in the Layers anymore. The sky is blue. We must be in an Island."

"Obviously we're on an Island!" Rien countered. "We're on an Island in the air."

"She means we're on an Island of stability," Wesh interjected in a soothing undertone. "She means the landscape isn't changing—or not as quickly."

"But for how long?" Yvan asked. "We can't keep doing this."

"We should stay here for now," Eliska decided. "We're safe here and we've all just eaten a meal. We have no reason to leave until we absolutely have to."

The Watch Commander locked his eyes on her. "We're all in your debt, Eliska. I know you didn't want this. We're all beyond grateful for your help."

She looked away. She didn't want him thanking her. "I guess I'd be staying here even if you weren't here."

"What are we going to do?" a dark-haired Watchman asked. "We can't stay here forever."

"We won't have to," Eliska explained. "The Coil will shift eventually."

"Great," Rien snarled. "Just great."

"I didn't make it like this," she told him.

"The Darklings attacked us again," Wesh cut in. "They followed us through the Layers."

"What does that mean?" Yvan asked.

"It means they're still coming after us the same way they did in Middleborough."

"But you said they wanted something from Middleborough," Yann pointed out. "You said they attacked the town to get what they wanted."

"Obviously they didn't get it or they wouldn't be coming after us now," Wesh replied. "Whatever it is they want must be here—among us."

All the Watchmen whipped around to gape at him. Some gasped in horror. "That's impossible!" Yvan exclaimed. "We're imps! None of us have any magic."

"We don't know what it is they want," Wesh countered. "Whatever they want might be something non-magical—something one of you is carrying, perhaps."

The Watchmen looked at each other next. "None of us is carrying anything," Yann pointed out. "We all lost our weapons when Middleborough went down."

"Then perhaps the thing the Darklings want is one of you," Wesh suggested.

"Us! The Darklings can't want us!" Rien jabbed his finger at Eliska. "She's the one they want! She's the only one here with any magic besides you."

"But your Watch Commander told me the attacks on Middleborough started two years ago," Wesh reminded him. "Eliska wasn't in Middleborough then. The Watch Commander says the attacks had been escalating all that time and culminated in the attack that destroyed the town. Whatever the Darklings want must have been in Middleborough before she ever set foot in the town."

Another deadly silence fell over the group. Eliska flicked an invisible speck of lint off her pants. She didn't want to look at anyone.

She knew nothing about these people or their town or what some Voyant Mendicat might want from them.

This was yet another reason for her to put as much distance as possible between her and them.

She couldn't do that on top of this shelf. She could have destroyed the shelf and sent both herself and them into another Layer.

She could have used any of these Layers to separate herself from them. She could have sent them to one Layer while she traveled to another.

Falling through so many Layers and coming so close to the Darklings made her want to stay on this Island, at least for a little while.

One little haven of stability in a vast cosmos of chaos and danger—she had to take advantage of the lull while she had a chance. She might not get another opportunity to rest and regroup like this—not for a while, anyway.

Yvan scrutinized each of his men one after the other. "Are any of you carrying anything—anything at all?"

"We're all wearing our uniforms," Yann pointed out. "I don't have anything apart from that."

"I have this." The sandy-haired Watchman stuck his fingers down the collar of his jacket and pulled out a plain gold ring hanging by a chain. "I've worn it since I was a boy."

"What is it?" Wesh asked. "Where did you get it?"

"It's my mother's wedding band. She wore it for three years after my father died. She gave it to me the day she took it off." He looked down at the tiny gold circlet. His thick, muscular fingers made it look tiny and frail. "It reminds me of my family—my mother, my sisters, their husbands, and their children. They all lived in Middleborough. I joined the Watch to protect them...and now they're all gone."

"They might not be gone," Eliska told him. "They might have fallen into another Layer and survived. They could still be out there somewhere."

The man looked up at her. Tears brimmed in his deep brown eyes. "Truly? Do you really think so?"

His reaction made her throat constrict. She couldn't answer to tell him it was only a vague possibility—not a certainty.

Wesh broke the spell by interrupting. "What about the rest of you? Does any of you have anything on you—anything at all?"

"You just said the thing might not be a thing," Yann pointed out. "You said it could be a person. You said it could be one of us."

"Would it make more sense for it to be an object?" Yvan asked. "If it was a person, then that person would have been in Middleborough all these years, too. Why would the Darklings escalate their attack only recently? They could have taken the person any time."

"Maybe the Voyant didn't need the person before," Wesh suggested. "Or what I really mean is maybe he didn't need whatever it was before. Maybe he only just found out that he did need it—or want it—and now he's trying to get it."

The sandy-haired Watchman looked away, sniffed, and ran his shirt cuff across his nose. "I don't care what you say. I won't give up this ring. You can leave me here while the rest of you go on to safety somewhere else. I'll take my chances. I won't give it up."

"No one is asking you to give it up," Yvan replied. "We have no reason to think your ring is the object the Voyant wants."

"If we're right, the Darklings will come after us here, too," Wesh pointed out. "They'll invade this Island no matter how stable it is—or they'll attack it from out in the Layers until they break it down the way they broke down Middleborough."

"We should find another place to go before that happens," Eliska replied. "We can't stay here forever like what's-his-name says."

She jerked her thumb at the dark-haired Watchman. He spun around to glare at her, but what else was she supposed to call him?

Yvan actually laughed. "I apologize, Eliska. None of us have introduced ourselves to you."

"You have," she pointed out.

"But not the men." He went through the group pointing them out one after the other. "That's Rien Dugas—as I'm sure you've figured out by now. This is Omer Veco, Vidal Rom, Barsali Brun, Niyazi Trahan, Neils Surette, and you know me and Yann."

Eliska tried to connect each name with each face as quickly as possible. She wasn't used to spending this much time getting to know so much about anyone.

The sandy-haired Watchman wearing his mother's wedding band on a chain around his neck was Barsali.

He had a big, thick, muscular frame, but his soft eyes and relaxed features made him seem gentle and cuddly in a soft, comforting way despite his strength.

The sharp, angular, dark-haired, dark-eyed Watchman was Omer. He had a hook nose, a pointed, jutting chin and jaw, quick, watchful eyes, and he spoke with a harsh foreign accent.

Two curved rows of tattooed dots followed the curve of his cheekbones under each eye. They gave him a foreign, exotic look and made his eyes stand out even darker against his dark skin.

Neils had light hair and light blue eyes. He and Yvan were the shortest Watchmen present—even shorter than Yann.

Neils had the kind of boyish good looks that usually go with pale coloring. His finely carved features didn't look right in a Black Watch uniform.

Vidal also had dark hair and dark eyes, but not as dark as Omer. His handsome features gave him a haunted, brooding look. He always seemed to watch everything from outside even when he occupied the center of the group.

Niyazi was as big as Barsali but without the softness or comforting warmth. His uniform did nothing to conceal his hard, chiseled physique.

He walked everywhere with his shoulders braced and his arms flexed to spring into action at any moment.

And then there was Rien. His ordinary, boy-next-door good looks made him the least memorable of the whole party.

If he hadn't imprinted himself on Eliska's mind as the most obnoxious Watchman here, she would have found it easy to convince herself that he didn't exist at all.

Yann brought her back to reality. "Can you search the Coil to find someplace for us to go? You did that before."

Eliska focused on her fingers, snapped, and created the same magical representation of the Coil. "We need another Island," she muttered. "A bigger, more stable Island."

"How do we know if even they will be safe?" Omer asked. "If you're right, then nowhere will be safe."

"The larger, more stable an Island is, the harder it will be to destabilize it. Other, smaller, newer Islands will fall first. It will take more magic and more instability to collapse an Island that's been there for a long time and has built up a great deal of stability."

"If the Voyant is the one causing the Coil to destabilize, then the problem will only get worse," Wesh added. "The Coil has been destabilizing for a long time—and the entire Coil is destabilizing—not just the parts with you in them. Whatever it is the Voyant wants doesn't have anything to do with the Coil becoming unstable."

"Then the whole Coil could fall and we could all die," Niyazi suggested. "If the instability keeps spreading and getting worse, what is there to stop it from destroying everything in the end?"

"It won't," Wesh replied. "Our records in the Temple indicate these cycles happen regularly throughout history. The Coil becomes unstable, chaos ensues, and then the Coil stabilizes again, which leads to centuries of peace and prosperity. We're going into the unstable phase now."

"Going into it?" Yvan asked. "It sounds like we're already in it."

"The records indicate it could get considerably more unstable."

"Wonderful," Rien snarled again. "How long is this likely to take? Are we likely to see the end of it in our lifetimes or will future generations get to enjoy this peace and prosperity while we're rotting in our graves?"

Wesh only smiled at him. "I'm afraid I can't tell you that, either. The cycles don't follow a set pattern. Some follow each other very quickly. Others take centuries."

Yann brought Eliska back to the matter at hand. "Are you finding anything—anything we can use?"

She looked down at the miniature Coil in her hand and frowned when she rotated it in different directions to study it.

Yann noticed her reaction right away. "What's wrong? What do you see?"

"Nothing Wesh didn't just tell you. A lot more Layers are collapsing and reforming more quickly now than I remember from years past.....and we're in an unstable part of the Coil. Look. We can break through to the Ancestral Empire. It will take some doing to get through all those Layers, but if we make it, we should be safe on solid ground for a while....until something else happens."

"The Ancestral Empire is hardly what you would call safe," Wesh countered.

"Why not?" Yvan asked. "What's there?"

"It's a lawless wasteland full of criminals, gypsies, Barbarians, thugs, and organized gangs."

"And they hate the Black Watch," Eliska finished and closed her hand to make the Coil disappear.

"We can't help what we are," Yvan replied. "Anyway, we aren't the Black Watch now because we have no wall to defend. We're just wanderers like everyone else."

"You'll always be Black Watch," she countered. "I don't know much else about you, but I'm certain of that. You'll all be Black Watch until you die. Nothing can change that—not ever."

Chapter 10

Yann sat up and hugged his arms around his shoulders to try to keep warm. The wind whipped across this high rock shelf and cut straight through his clothes.

His father, Wesh, and the other Watchmen lay asleep around him. They huddled close to the center of the shelf so none of them accidentally rolled off it in the middle of the night.

The hard surface made it impossible to sleep. Sitting on it chilled Yann's bones, but he could hardly complain. At least he and the others were still alive—which they might not have been if they hadn't gotten through all those Layers.

Faint shimmers of dark blue shone in the night sky. Were those Dark Layers breaking through to threaten the party?

He tried to shake that thought out of his head. He couldn't start seeing danger everywhere even though it was everywhere.

Fliska's voice whispered to him out of the darkness nearby. "You should be asleep. You'll need it when we leave here tomorrow."

He found himself smiling. Her presence made him happy for some twisted reason. He shouldn't be under the circumstances.

Her being here made it so much better somehow. He could go through all of this because it gave him a chance to spend more time with her.

He didn't even mind the Darklings attacking. Darkling attacks stopped her from leaving.

She could have left whenever she wanted to. She could have abandoned the group in that Island of thorns, but she stayed to make sure they all made it out.

Was she changing her mind about the group—or about him in particular? Could she possibly want to stay?

The thought made him indescribably happy. He couldn't imagine a worse outcome than her leaving. He couldn't explain why because, as she and everyone kept pointing out, she was nothing special.

"You're awake, too," he whispered back. "You should go back to sleep."

"I haven't been able to sleep yet. I keep expecting something to happen."

He didn't have to ask what might happen, so he decided to change the subject. "Thank you for what you said to Barsali. He has a big heart, especially where his family is concerned. I don't know if you meant what you said about them maybe still being alive, but it was kind of you to give him hope either way."

She looked away. "It's always a possibility, I suppose. *We* keep surviving these collapses, so why couldn't they?"

He found himself studying the dark outline of her silhouette. He didn't ask about *her* family.

She already told him she spent years searching. She must have failed and given up—and why shouldn't she? A person couldn't keep living on borrowed hope forever.

Eventually, she must have just reconciled herself to the harsh fact. She was alone and she would stay alone. No amount of searching would change that.

In the end, searching might have caused her more pain than just cutting the cord and moving on. At least then she could stop dwelling on it.

In that moment, Yann thanked High Heaven for his father and the men of the Watch. Yann never had to go looking for any of them.

He never had to wonder who he belonged to or why. He never had to wonder where he came from or where his home was or who would be there waiting for him when he went back.

What a nightmare she must have been living all these years—and to think it had always been like that for her—all the way back to her earliest memories.

She had never known any of those things—not even in the farthest distant reaches of her earliest toddlerhood. She had never known where she came from, who she belonged to, or even who she was.

She never had a home to go back to or anyone who would claim her as their own. She had no one of whom she could even ask those questions.

Thinking of her that way stabbed him in the heart, but the happiness flooded back when he looked at her right now.

She grew up and became strong, powerful, resourceful, self-reliant, and intelligent. She did all of that by herself with no help from anyone.

Now she was out here keeping the Watch alive against impossible odds. She said a thousand times that she would leave them to their deaths, but she never did. Of course not. She was too good for that.

Her voice startled him to high alert. She lowered it to a barely audible hiss, but the words wiped all that happiness out of his mind.

"It's coming!" she whispered. "We have to act now. We can't wait for morning."

She swiveled sideways and grabbed the first man she came to, who happened to be Niyazi.

"Wake up!" she breathed. "All of you—wake up! We have to move!"

She went from man to man shaking everyone awake. She came to Wesh last.

"Wake up, Wesh!" she whispered. "They're coming in fast!"

Yann didn't understand. Wesh floundered out of a sound sleep. "Huh?"

"The Dark!" she hissed. "It's gathering! We can't wait for morning. We have to go now."

"What the hell?!" Rien snarled. "Leave me alone, girl!"

She ignored him. "Hold onto each other. I need to shatter the Layer before they get here. We'll fall through..."

"And then what?" Yann asked. "What do we have to do to get to the Ancestral Empire?"

Eliska opened her mouth to answer, but at that moment, a flying torpedo erupted out of the darkness.

It fired from somewhere deep in the gorges far away from the group's rock shelf.

A torch of light streaked up the gorge and smashed into the pillar's bottommost walls.

The impact shuddered up the walls and through Yann's feet. He and the other Watchmen instinctively moved inward to the center of the shelf.

Wesh stumbled to his feet. "Hurry, Wesh!" Eliska told him. "We have to shatter the Layer before they......"

Another colossal explosion went off deeper inside the gorge. This one fired much faster and struck the pillar much harder.

The blow destroyed the pillar miles below the shelf and the whole granite tower imploded on itself.

Everyone screamed in terror as the floor dropped out from beneath their feet. Yann tried to grab those nearest her, especially Eliska.

Gravity ripped him away. All the Watchmen tumbled apart.

No amount of writhing and twisting in circles would bring Yann closer to the others. Was this the end? Would he ever see them again?

The rock tower evaporated underneath him. He expected to fall and crash again on some hard surface—or maybe just keep falling forever and ever without stopping.

At that moment, an explosion went off somewhere. The whole gorge, the mountains, and the night sky overhead burst apart and vanished to nothing.

At exactly the same instant, a powerful burst of some kind of magnetic force hit him. It sucked him sideways and he slammed into a body—actually, several bodies.

Some invisible effect brought all the Watchmen together and smashed their bodies into a clump so they couldn't separate.

"Hold on!" Eliska yelled. "We'll land in the Layers any second now!"

Yann didn't understand her. Wasn't the group already in the Layers?

The dark blue hues of the night sky above the rock shelf gave way. A strong wind blew red and deep purple vapors across where the sky used to be.

Those vapors surrounded the party until, just as fast, the whole knot of people dropped into another vast landscape.

It looked like some kind of continent full of mountains, rivers, cities, towns, farms, and herds of livestock.

"Is this Ancestral Empire?!" Yvan yelled over the wind.

"It's another Layer!" Wesh called back. "Hold on!"

The cluster of travelers hurtled downward on a collision course for the ground. Nothing checked their fall.

The party would splatter at this speed, but as the group got closer to the moment of impact, the landscape changed.

It heaved in one place and the mountains crumbled. The farmland quaked, fractured, and tilted up. The slabs that buckled out of place grew into new mountains that imploded and vanished a second later.

A brand-new forest erupted out of the farmland. A sweeping carpet of trees stabbed their crowns into the air, darkened that side of the continent, and then a devastating sheet of fire swept across the countryside and erased the forest just as fast.

The landscape shifted, morphed, and transformed in a thousand ways everywhere Yann turned.

"What's happening?" Omer husked.

"This is just another Layer," Eliska replied. "It looks like an Island, but it isn't one. Here we go! Watch out!"

Yann didn't understand what she meant, but he found out when the cluster kept plummeting straight down at terminal velocity.

The landscape looked solid enough until seconds before the moment of impact. Yann winced and braced himself to splat right here. At least he would be able to do it with his father and his friends. He wouldn't have to live without them.

A few feet from the ground, he saw something like shadows moving over the surface. At first, he thought they might be the shadows of clouds cast from the sky.

Then he realized that what he first mistook for solid Earth actually rippled under the ground. Those shadows flowed back and forth through the soil.

The group slammed into the ground full force and punched through. What should have been solid ground turned to some kind of spongy cushion.

The group burst through into another Layer.

This time, the group didn't fall at breakneck speed. The travelers' combined weight slowed more and more as they descended to the surface of a completely different landscape.

Steep hills covered this one with deep river valleys carving between them. Trees, bushes, and clumps of dense woods lined the rivers.

The place looked inhabited, too, with plenty of roads winding in different directions.

"This isn't the Ancestral Empire, either," Wesh announced before anyone could ask. "This is another Layer, so be ready for anything. We need to run to get through this Layer as quickly as possible."

"What happens after that?" Niyazi asked.

The party touched down at that moment and the magic holding them together broke apart. Everyone tumbled onto the ground.

Nothing stopped them from standing up. Yann didn't know what mysterious force held them together. Eliska must have done it again because Wesh thanked her.

She didn't respond. Her wild eyes darted around the countryside.

It couldn't have looked more inviting. It certainly looked like an Island—what Wesh and Eliska called an Island.

Yann couldn't imagine a more stable, peaceful place to settle down. Cows grazed in the fields. Flocks of birds swooped and soared between towns and woods.

Eliska gritted her teeth and tightened her grip on her staff with both hands. She snarled, "Let's go," and started walking down the nearest road toward a town in the distance.

Yann would have given anything for a weapon. He didn't know what he would do when the shrapnel started flying again.

It *would* start flying any second now. He knew now to trust Eliska's instincts—and Wesh's instincts—but he trusted hers more. She had more experience in the Coil even than he did.

The Watchmen gathered around with her in the front leading the way. All the Watchmen kept a sharp eye on the surroundings, but none of them were armed, either.

Yann didn't see anything threatening. None of them did. What if Eliska made a mistake? What if this wasn't a dangerous place after all?

He should have known better than to doubt her. The group traveled over some rolling farmland, topped a rise in the road, and hiked down the other side toward the town.

They made it a dozen yards before the town submerged under the land. The whole group stopped—except for Eliska. She actually picked up her pace as the houses sank out of sight.

"Keep moving!" she ordered. "Don't stop no matter what happens! We have to break through to the Ancestral Empire!"

"How far is it?" Yvan asked.

She turned her head to answer, but at that moment, a wild animal Yann didn't recognize leapt out of the nearby hills.

It sprang straight out of the nearest slope, tossed its head, bared its teeth, and roared at the party.

Everyone spun around to confront the creature, but it turned into a flock of birds and shot into the sky to join the others.

Eliska started walking again right away. "Keep going!" she repeated. "Don't stop!"

The Watchmen took longer to get moving again. Yann felt his nerves nearing the breaking point. He jumped at every sound.

Another monster of some kind erupted out of the road ahead. Eliska stalked the thing down, but it exploded before she got near it.

More ferocious apparitions kept appearing on all sides. They lunged, bellowed, and pawed the group, but none of those creatures attacked—or if they did, they evaporated or changed into something harmless before they got near the party.

All the men of the Watch jumped, spun around, and braced themselves for the worst every time this happened. They stayed so tense and watchful that they found it difficult to keep moving even when Eliska ordered them to.

This went on for over an hour. The sun crossed the sky much too fast here. The day passed in a few minutes and the sky started to darken.

"Pick up the pace!" Eliska called behind her. "We need to move faster!"

She started running. Yann copied her, but he was one of the very few who did. The others only remembered to do it when Yvan and Wesh started running after her.

Darkness fell way too fast. The sky roiled with clouds that weren't there before. The birds changed into whizzing darts shrieking through the air.

They swooped low to the ground, zoomed over the travelers' heads, and screeched off into the sky again.

The road kept rising, swelling, and sinking back in on itself. It twisted and whipped right and left faster than the travelers could run.

It forked up ahead into five different branches. They all snaked back and forth across the ground and changed course in an endless flow of movement.

The landscape transformed at the same rate of ceaseless change. All the stability from earlier disappeared in a sea of chaos.

Eliska darted left toward one of the forks leading that way. The Watchmen veered to keep up with her.

Right then, a different group of Watchmen in black uniforms rushed out of the shadows from the left.

"This way!" a tall man with shoulder-length brown hair called to the group. "That way is a death trap!"

Yann, Neils, and Barsali turned that way to follow him. Before they could go anywhere, Eliska spun around and bombarded the newcomers with a blast from the end of her staff.

The tall Watchman hurtled backward and slammed down hard on his back on the ground. Barsali bellowed at Eliska, "What are you doing?!"

Before she could reply, the strangers transformed into Darklings and pounced on the party.

Yann, Neils, and Barsali staggered backward to get away. Wesh darted in front of them and thrust out his hands to push them away.

"Follow me!" Eliska roared and swerved down the road she'd originally been planning to take.

The others stumbled after her leaving Wesh to fend off the Darklings.

The instant Eliska set foot on that road, the Darklings vanished.

Yvan grabbed Yann by the shirt to pull him into their group, but in a few seconds, Yann saw Eliska running toward a towering mountain blocking their path.

She ran straight up to it, fired a blast of her staff at it, and that eruption of light flared wider and wider.

She yelled one more time, "Follow me!" and plunged straight into the light.

Omer, Vidal, and Rien ran right behind her. None of them hesitated. They jumped through and vanished.

Yann would have hesitated, but his father pushed him forward and shoved Yann through after Neils and Niyazi.

Chapter 11

E liska collapsed on the ground panting hard. She barely kept her eyes open to make sure all the Watchmen made it through the gap followed by Wesh.

She shut her eyes and threw her arm over her face. "Phew! We made it!"

"Are we there?" Yvan asked. "Are we in the Ancestral Empire now? It looks like an ordinary forest."

Something clicked out of sight and a completely different voice Eliska didn't recognize muttered, "The Black Watch. What are you doing here?"

Eliska tore her arm off her face and scrambled to stand up. She didn't notice before where she was or to which part of the Ancestral Empire her portal took her. She'd been too concerned with actually getting here.

Yvan was right. The Watch was in an ordinary forest—a different kind of forest with deciduous trees instead of pines.

Night blanketed this Layer the same way it did in the Layer the group just left. A campfire crackled nearby with a bunch of people sitting around it.

They wore a strange combination of clothes from threadbare versions of glittering finery to patched rags and hand-repaired knitwear.

Seven men wore decorative scarves tied around long hair hanging to their waists. They didn't shave or even trim their beards. Their bright black eyes glittered out of chiseled faces lined by age and long experience in the Coil.

Ten women and a dozen children made up the rest of the group. The women wore dresses down to the ground. These followed the same pattern.

Some of these dresses must once have belonged to royalty, dignitaries, or the extremely wealthy. Glittering gold thread, elaborate embroidery, and lace frills showed at intervals between all the rips, patches, and dirty smudges.

The women wore excessive amounts of jewelry. Each woman wore dozens of necklaces, multiple rings on each hand, extravagant earrings, and countless bangles hanging from both wrists.

Eliska relaxed when she recognized the gypsies. She didn't recognize these people, but she knew and understood their ways.

"We're sorry for stumbling into your camp like this," she told them. "We just escaped from another Layer. We had no idea where we would break through." She waved behind her. "We'll just go on somewhere else and leave you alone. Have a nice evening."

"You don't have to go." One of the men waved at the fire. "Take a seat. Any traveler is welcome."

Eliska took a step forward. Yvan grabbed her arm to stop her. "Do you know these people, Eliska? They could rob us."

"We don't have anything to rob. They can see that perfectly well. Besides, it would be rude to turn down their hospitality. Sit down—all of you."

She set the example by crossing the last few feet to the fire. Its warmth lit up her face and made her sleepy.

The women and children moved out of the way to make room for her and then the whole group rearranged themselves to find space for the Watchmen.

"What are you doing here?" the same man asked. "The Ancestral Empire is no place for the Black Watch."

"Their town collapsed to the Dark," Eliska replied. "These are the only people who survived the destruction. They escaped with the clothes on their backs, so of course they didn't have time to change out of their uniforms."

The man nodded. "You should change your clothes now before anyone sees you." He turned his dark eyes on her. "*You* didn't escape when their town collapsed. Where did you come from—and this one is a member of the Guardian Templars."

"I'm a Coil rat," Eliska replied. "I happened to be passing through their town when the disaster hit. That's why I'm with them."

This explanation seemed to satisfy the gypsies. The man nodded down at the flames. "That makes sense then."

"Have you seen anything unusual in the Coil recently?" Wesh asked.

The man looked up and split into a huge grin. "Do you mean anything unusual like everything?"

"I mean anything even more unusual than everything," Wesh replied. "Have you seen more instability than usual—or anything outright malicious—like Darklings?"

"How can you ask them that after what we've just seen?" Yvan whispered in his ear. "These people could be Darklings."

"They aren't Darklings. They're just gypsies. Look." Eliska passed her hand over the fire in a circle around the group.

A curtain of watery magic passed in front of the gypsies. They didn't change their appearance except to waver for a minute. That wavering stopped the minute she put her hand down.

"See? They aren't Darklings." She turned back to the gypsies. "Please don't take offense. They've never been outside their town before. They don't understand the Coil."

The man only nodded. "Everything here is the same way it always is—a little more unstable, perhaps, but nothing we can't handle. You know what the Ancestral Empire is like. Nothing here ever changes very much."

"So you haven't seen anything that might make you think someone was deliberately manipulating the instability?" Wesh asked. "Something that couldn't be attributed to just instability?"

"What are you saying?!" Yvan gasped again. "Are you saying this landscape....and all these changes.....are you saying this is all the work of....?"

He broke off and didn't finish his sentence.

"It isn't deliberate," Eliska interrupted. "It's always like this. Nothing we've seen has been anything new."

"What about the Darklings always attacking?" Wesh asked. "That's new. They've never acted so coordinated before."

She shrugged. "I disagree."

Wesh's eyes widened. "Are you saying you've seen this behavior before? Have they deliberately attacked *you* before?"

"Darkling attacks aren't deliberate—not the way you're making them sound. They just happen. The Darklings come out of the Layers. Of course they attack. They belong to the Dark."

Wesh looked away.

"How do you survive if things are so bad out here?" Yann asked.

"Just like this—by fighting them off and traveling from one Island to another."

"It's the same for us," the gypsy man added. "We never stay in one place for long."

"Have *you* seen the Darklings organizing their attacks instead of just threatening the Islands randomly?" Wesh asked again.

The gypsy man cocked his head to one side. "I hear you describing two things that are the same. The Darklings come from the Layers. They attack and destroy Islands, people—whatever they can find. This doesn't change no matter how unstable the Coil becomes."

Wesh let the subject drop. One of the women pulled out a bowl piled with some kind of flatbread. She handed it to Eliska. "Eat. You must be hungry."

Eliska took a piece of bread and passed the bowl to Barsali who sat next to her. The Watchmen handed the bowl from man to man until it made the whole circle.

The gypsy man who'd been talking to them took the last piece. No one mentioned everyone else going without. They must already have eaten.

Yvan changed his tune and finally stuck out his hand to the gypsy guy who'd been doing all the talking. "I apologize for implying that you were Darklings. Please forgive my ignorance. My name is Yvan Dilnao. I'm very grateful for your hospitality."

The guy shook his hand. "My name is Ando Dupris. You must stay with us tonight."

Yvan started to say, "I don't think that's....."

"Thank you," Eliska interrupted. "We're grateful for your hospitality. Wesh and I are magic-users. We can help defend you if you meet with any trouble."

Ando sliced his dark eyes at the men of the Watch. "The Black Watch can help defend us if we meet with any trouble, too."

"We're unarmed as you can see," Yvan replied. "We would otherwise."

"We have weapons," Ando breezed around a mouthful of bread. "We can supply you."

A charge of tension went through the Watchmen and their eyes lit up when they exchanged glances. Even Rien brightened up at the thought of getting his hands on a weapon.

Vidal clapped Yann on the shoulder and Yann burst into a huge grin of relief and excitement.

Eliska kicked herself for not thinking of this sooner. She should have armed the Watch.

She let herself think they were helpless because they didn't have magic. She was the one who left them defenseless. That was a mistake.

Now she saw them coming to life when they found out someone was going to arm them.

In a few minutes, the women left the fire and took the children to a bunch of tents set up among the trees. Light glowed through the tents' fabric walls and cast the forest in golden beauty.

The men stayed up talking and passed the time with Wesh and the Watchmen sitting on that side of the fire.

Eliska didn't get involved in their conversation. She didn't want to go to sleep.

Maybe these Watchmen weren't so bad. Being a Coil rat with no family and no one to connect with wasn't all it was cracked up to be. Yvan was right about that.

That didn't mean she planned to stay with them.

She would get them to a town where they would go back to being safe behind the wall. Then she would go her way and they could all forget about each other.

The men started to drift away to their own tents. The gypsies invited the Watchmen to sleep in tents, too, and pitched extra ones for the Watchmen to share.

Eliska stayed by the fire. She didn't expect the gypsies to give her a tent to herself and she didn't want one.

She didn't want to start getting comfortable with anyone if she would only be going back out on her own pretty soon.

She got lost in her own thoughts until someone brought her back to reality. "Eliska?"

She looked up and froze when she saw Barsali still sitting next to her. He stared up at her with wide, searching eyes.

She couldn't hold eye contact with him. She already sensed where this was going. "You should go to bed," she told him. "The Ancestral Empire is a dangerous place even if it remains stable. You'll need your sleep."

"Do you think you could find my family....with that Coil thing of yours?" he blurted out. "You saw which Layers collapsed into which Layers. You could find the Layer they fell into. If they're alive, I would know where to go look for them."

She took a deep breath. She'd never had a conversation like this with anyone. No one had ever asked her anything like this before.

She realized again that she'd stayed with these people just a little too long—or maybe way too long. She knew too much about them. Now she got herself all tangled up with their problems and worries and desires.

She didn't plan to look at Barsali when she answered. She planned to stare into the flames. That would make it easier to completely dash his hopes—which was what she would be doing.

The minute she opened her mouth, she just couldn't do it. She had to face him and look him in the eye. She couldn't give him what he most wanted, but she couldn't stab him in the heart without at least doing that much.

His eyes didn't water the way they did before, but they radiated a depth of misery and longing she'd never witnessed from anyone. What would it be like to care about someone that much—to yearn with all your heart and soul just for one glimpse of their face again?

She couldn't imagine caring about anyone that much—or even more important, that someone might care about her that much. That would never happen. No one out there was hoping to find her lost in the Coil.

Her voice trembled when she finally worked up the nerve to speak. "I could find out which Layer Middleborough collapsed into, but more Layers will have collapsed on top of that one and that one will have collapsed on top of others since then. Even if I looked into my Coil thing, I wouldn't be able to see if your family was alive or where they were. I don't have that power."

He barely heard her. "But you could at least look. Couldn't you? It would be better than nothing."

She sighed and snapped her fingers to create the Coil illusion. It rotated on her palm.

She pointed at it with her other forefinger. "This is where Middleborough used to be. The Layers are still wild there. They haven't started to reform into anything yet. You can see that the Layers above and below are also changing too rapidly."

"Could you expand it....please?"

That one word tore her guts out. God, he needed this!

She couldn't deny him, so she expanded the image of the Layer Middleborough used to occupy. A mass of swirling Dark mingled with the colored vapors.

She adjusted the image to search the Layers above and below that one. She didn't find a single square inch of solid landscape in any of them.

"It doesn't mean they're dead," she told him. "It just means I can't find them—not without actually searching each and every Layer."

He seized on that like the hopeless fool he was. "Then I could look for them! I could find them! I don't care if I have to spend the rest of my life doing it. If they're out there, I'll find them. I have to!"

She closed her hand to shut down the image. As soon as it vanished, that same over-powering drive made her turn around and face him again.

"You couldn't go alone, Barsali. You would have to leave the Watch to go search for your family and you would need a very powerful magic-user to go with you if you hoped to survive in the Coil without protection. You could search forever and never find your family even if they are alive. Believe me. I spent years searching the Coil for my family and never even found the Layer they originally came from—and that was using all my magic."

He definitely heard that. He wilted in defeat, turned away, and slumped while he stared into the flames. "Oh. Of course," he muttered. "I didn't think of that."

She raised her hand to touch his shoulder, but she stopped herself in time.

"If your family is alive out there, they would want to know that you're safe in some Island—not that you're risking your life to go look for them. If they are alive, it means they must have found an Island of their own somewhere—somewhere they can stay and be safe themselves. Don't throw that away."

He didn't answer for a second. He sat there with his shoulders hunched and blinked into the flames as he took all this in.

She didn't expect a response from him. When he finally looked up, he locked his soft brown eyes on her with a very different expression on his face. It wasn't despair or desperation or even pleading.

It was pure heartfelt sympathy—sympathy for her—for the years she spent alone wondering if someone might be out there waiting for her.

It took a long time for her to finally make her peace with the fact that they weren't.

"Thank you, Eliska," he murmured. "Thank you for trying."

"You're welcome," she replied as calmly as she could. "I'm sorry about Middleborough."

"You tried there, too, didn't you?" he breathed. "I'm alive right now because of you. Thank you."

He didn't wait for her to answer. He got up and left to join the other Watchmen in the tents.

She stayed where she was and stared into the flames the way she originally wanted to. She really wished now that she'd never met these people.

Becoming connected to them—understanding them and having them understand her—this was hands down the worst pain she'd ever experienced.

She never felt anything like this when she traveled alone. No one reminded her of how it could have been. She never had to think about how it could have been.

Her life was the way it was for a reason. She was better off alone.

Now all of that fell apart around her ears. She didn't want to feel this. She didn't want to remember what it felt like to ache for someone—anyone who might give a hoot if she lived or died.

She didn't want to remember the brutal agony of searching, coming within a hair's breadth of finding some answer, only to fail and have that hope snatched away at the last possible second.

She would rather do just about anything than feel that. Now she had no choice but to feel it. Just looking at these people brought it all rushing back.

Chapter 12

Yann woke up the next morning and frowned when he looked up at the surface in front of his face. He wasn't in his bed in his room in the Black Watch's house.

Omer coughed right next to him and startled Yann into raising his head and shoulders partway off the floor. He found himself in a tent packed with three other Watchmen.

He remembered everything—everything that happened since the Watch left Middleborough—everything that happened in all the Layers since then—everything that happened between him, Eliska, his father, and all the other Watchmen.

Barsali lay on Omer's other side. Rien lay against Yann's other side. Barsali and Rien were still sound asleep.

Omer twisted in place trying to get comfortable. He frowned to himself and then his hard, dark eyes snapped open.

They sliced to Yann sitting partway up. Yann watched the wheels turning in Omer's head as he remembered everything, too. None of them would ever forget it.

Just then, Yann heard his father talking to two men outside. One of them was Wesh. Then Yann heard Eliska and another woman join in the conversation.

Yann and Omer exchanged one more glance. Then both men got up as carefully as possible so they wouldn't disturb Barsali and Rien.

Yann and Omer went outside. Wesh, Yvan, Eliska, and a bunch of gypsies stood together in the trees at a distance from the gypsy camp.

It looked different in daylight. The sunshine streaming through the treetops gave the camp a stark, rough, brutal atmosphere. It clashed with the air of enchanted mystery from last night.

Niyazi, Niels, and Vidal stood off to one side listening to that conversation. That left only Barsali and Rien out of the loop.

Two gypsy women joined Wesh, Ando, Eliska, and Yvan. The women didn't have a problem interjecting their opinions.

"We're too close to the edge," one of the gypsy women insisted. "We have to move closer to the center—away from the Dark Layers outside."

"Moving closer to the center will bring us closer to the bandits," Ando replied. "We're safer here."

"The edge could crumble and take all of you," Eliska told him. "We'll go with you in case you meet any bandits. We're going that way ourselves. These Watchmen want to find a town that needs the Black Watch."

Ando snorted. "No one in the Ancestral Empire needs the Black Watch."

"Then maybe they need fighting men," Yvan suggested. "We can always change our clothes."

Ando grinned at him, but just then, some movement at the edge of the trees caught all their attention. They turned that way and Yann saw what they were looking at.

The trees shuddered and the leaves parted to show a yawning chasm of wild magic swirling, churning, and seething just beyond the edge of the forest.

The travelers' group hadn't made it more than fifteen feet from the spot where Eliska used that white light to get them to the Ancestral Empire. The boundary between the Island and the Layers beyond must be breaking down.

Yann didn't understand how all this worked. He didn't need to. Wesh and Eliska understood it well enough. If she said they had to move inland, that was good enough for Yann.

He wasn't the one making the decisions on behalf of the Watch, though.

Yvan turned away from the conversation and saw Yann and the others standing there listening. "Wake up Barsali and Rien," Yvan ordered. "We're moving out."

"Are we moving out on our own or with *them?*" Omer asked.

Yvan shot a flinty glance over his shoulder. "It doesn't matter. We're moving out either way. We can't stay here."

Yann hustled back to the tent and shook the other two awake. Barsali sat up right away, rubbed his face to wake himself up, and nodded when he remembered where he was and why.

Rien grumbled, shut his eyes, and rolled onto his other side. "Leave me alone, boy," he snarled.

"You better get up before Father finds you," Yann told him. "He was the one who sent me to wake you up. If he comes looking for you, he'll give you the worst whipping you ever had."

Rien grumbled under his breath again and didn't move. Barsali made significant eye contact with Yann and they both left Rien where he was.

Yann didn't want to be anywhere nearby when Yvan found Rien lounging in his tent.

Barsali must have been thinking the same thing because they both got as far away from the tent as they could before Yvan realized what was going on.

Fortunately for everyone, Rien came to his senses and emerged only a few seconds later. He ran his fingers through his hair and went about his business as if he'd never even considered disobeying his Watch Commander's order.

The three of them left the tent and discovered the gypsies arming the Watchmen. Ando opened a large wooden trunk set against one of the tents.

The trunk was almost as big as the tent itself. Yann didn't see how these people could carry a trunk that size on their travels.

Ando pried back the lid and pulled out a massive battle axe. "This is about your size...." He handed it to Barsali.

He went through the group sizing up each Watchman and handing him a weapon that Ando judged appropriate for each person.

He came to Yann last. Ando's keen eye darted up and down Yann's body. "What will you take, boy? What can you use well?"

Yann's eyes dipped to the contents of the trunk. Swords, axes, maces, clubs, and daggers lay piled inside.

"I'll take that glaive if no one else is using it," Yann replied.

Ando burst into a grin, pulled out the glaive, and tossed it to him. Yann caught it and weighed it in his hands. Damn, it felt good to hold a weapon again!

All the Watchmen adjusted their grips on their weapons.

"Each of you take a second one while you're at it," Ando told them. "We'll need them."

He stepped away and the Watchmen gathered around all talking at once. Yann was too busy examining his new glaive to care what the others left behind for him after they finished.

The tense excitement in their voices infected his blood. They were all going back into battle—armed this time.

Their eyes glistened with fire when they finally turned away from the trunk. They weren't so helpless now.

Yann got himself two short daggers from the trunk, stuck one in his belt and the other in his boot, and walked away to join the rest of the Watch.

He couldn't stop touching and staring at his glaive. It felt perfect—almost like a living thing quivering in his hands.

The others murmured in excited whispers while they all accustomed themselves to their new weapons.

Yann spotted Eliska standing off to one side. She leaned on her staff while she watched the Watchmen. She didn't comment on their change in attitude.

Yvan kept talking away to Wesh and Ando the whole time. He went to the trunk last, got himself an axe and a longsword, and went through the same process of checking their weight, swinging them, and examining every detail of their edges and construction.

His expression changed when he finally faced the other Watchmen. He burst into a glowing grin for a split second before he fought it down and tried to force himself to get serious.

"We're moving out with the gypsies," he announced. "We'll travel with magic-users and Watchmen outside the column and imps, women, and children inside."

Those words set off another explosive reaction in the Watchmen. They didn't show it on the outside, but the charge of energy running through them spiked off the charts. They were back in their element fighting overwhelming forces to protect those less able to defend themselves.

The Watch had to wait a long time for the gypsies to strike their camp. The women had to organize all the children, fold up the tents, and pack everything into more gigantic trunks.

Yann really didn't see how they would carry all this stuff, especially not with the party's strongest men stationed outside the van to defend everyone in case of trouble.

The sun climbed to the top of the trees before the gypsies finally got ready to leave.

Just before Ando gave the order to move out, one of the gypsy women who'd been talking to Wesh and Yvan earlier went around the area and stopped in front of each trunk.

She raised her hand, flexed her fingertips together, and then burst them apart over each trunk.

Yann didn't see anything unusual happen, but she must have magicked them. Each one floated off the ground and hovered there a couple of feet above the spot where it had just been sitting.

Ando called everyone to move out and the company filed through the trees to the nearest road.

The floating trunks followed of their own accord. They bobbed at the same height off the ground. No one had to direct them or even pay attention to them.

Dozens of trunks drifted and hovered behind the column on the way out into the open.

The Watchmen joined Wesh, Eliska, and a group of gypsy magic-users. They formed a loose circle around all the rest of the gypsies at the center.

The trunks stayed behind the party. No matter how fast or slow the column traveled, the trunks always stayed the same distance away.

That would turn out to be important if any bandits attacked the group. Yann didn't want a bunch of wayward magical trunks getting in the way while he tried to fight someone.

The forest edge sat five hundred yards away from the road. The road wound over gentle countryside and vanished into the distance.

The landscape reminded Yann in an unsettling way of the Layer Eliska had guided the party through last night. The two landscapes looked almost identical, but this one didn't keep coming to life and changing into something else every few seconds—or every second.

The walk started out pleasantly enough. The gypsies chatted to each other. Some even laughed. No one made too much effort to keep the children confined to the protective center.

Yann didn't want to let his guard down in this bizarre landscape. The fact that it looked normal seemed to fool him into relaxing.

That was its evil nature. Just when he thought he understood where he was and how it worked, everything changed.

The other Watchmen stayed alert and wary the whole time, too. They stayed much more alert and wary than the gypsies did.

Even the gypsies who armed themselves in the outer protective circle didn't keep an eye on the surroundings as well as they should have.

Yann supposed they didn't need to if nothing was going to happen.

He didn't put his glaive down. Where would the next attack come from?

If he ever felt the slightest temptation to lower his guard, he only had to look at Eliska for confirmation. She stayed alert and wary, too.

She held her staff in front of her with both hands exactly the same way all the Watchmen held their weapons. She didn't talk and laugh with the gypsies.

Some of the gypsies tried to engage her in conversation a few times. She gave them short, blunt answers over her shoulder without taking her eyes off the countryside.

The party traveled for over an hour, climbed low hills and down the other sides, and crossed a few miles of farmland.

"How far are we going?" Niyazi asked Yvan in an undertone.

"However far we have to go to get away from the edge of the Island," Yvan replied under his breath. "The gypsies think it's dangerous—and Wesh and Eliska agree with them."

The party climbed another swell. A large town covered most of the horizon in the distance. Towers rose out of the carpet of house roofs.

"We can stop there," Ando decided. "The townsfolk will be able to tell us how stable this part of the Island is. Then we'll understand better whether it's safe to stay."

No one argued with that. The party climbed down the other side of the rise.

Yann would have liked to pick up the pace. He wanted to get out of the wilderness and back behind walls with other people.

The sight of the town so close turned the gypsies' interactions into something like a celebration. Their mood lightened even more—which only caused an opposite reaction in the Watchmen.

The sense of impending doom became oppressive. Eliska jumped out of her skin every time someone laughed. That sound grated on Yann's nerves.

The group made it halfway across the open countryside before disaster struck. It started with clouds forming in the sky. They darkened the sunshine and the wind picked up.

Eliska's hair tossed in the wind. Her eyes snapped more dangerously in all directions trying to see something.

"It's happening!" Wesh yelled to Ando. "The Dark is overtaking us!"

"That's impossible!" Ando called back. "We're too far away from the edge."

"The edge must be crumbling! It's caving in on us!"

Ando looked around. "I don't see anything."

Yann didn't see anything, either, but right then, Eliska spun backward, stepped out of line, stopped walking, and brandished her staff behind the party.

There was nothing there but the floating trunks. They kept following the gypsies.

Yann stepped out of line and crossed to her side. "What's wrong?" he asked. "What do you see?"

She started to shake her head when a tidal wave of Darkness swept the landscape from behind. It rushed along the ground in shadowy wisps.

Those wisps didn't look like anything at first, but they built to a solid mass of shadow farther away.

The Darkness obliterated the landscape through which the party just passed. The earth fell away and dissolved to join the blackness covering everything.

The shadowy vapors swooped down on the party impossibly fast, overtook the trunks, and would have consumed everyone in the same wave.

Yann tensed for the inevitable. He wouldn't be able to fight this with a glaive or any other kind of weapon.

Eliska reacted lightning quick, stabbed her staff down into the ground, and set off some kind of shockwave through the Darkness.

A blast radiated outward from the point of impact. A ring of energy surrounded the group, but the Darkness kept coming.

It flowed around Eliska's blast and overran the gypsies. For some reason, her attack protected the Watchmen and Wesh but left the gypsies exposed.

The Darkness flooded the party and transformed the gypsies into Darklings before Yann's eyes.

They erupted out of their skins, burst to enormous heights, and changed into fanged monsters covered with whipping tentacles. Even the children changed.

"RUN!!" Eliska roared. "Get to the town! Go, Yann!"

He would have stayed behind to help her, but she took her hand off her staff just long enough to shove him away.

Even then, he had to stagger between dozens of Darklings to continue down the road toward the town.

Darkness enveloped everything. The wind built to a howling, shrieking tempest.

Yann stumbled into Wesh. The other Watchmen raced past him trying to get to the town before the Darklings caught up with them.

Wesh stayed where he was to confront the Darklings, but in the end, he turned tail and ran for it, too.

Eliska planted herself in the road between the Darklings and the fleeing Watchmen.

Yann didn't see what she did. Blast after blast echoed across the crumbling landscape behind him.

Explosions of light, noise, and pounding impacts resounded through the ground and through the air getting farther away the farther he ran.

The Watchmen ran for five minutes before they got to the edge of that Dark wave. It kept advancing toward the town in the distance. Not even that would be safe if something didn't stop the collapse.

Eliska caught up with the men a few seconds later. Sweat drenched her face and hair. She gasped for air so badly that she couldn't talk to explain what she did to the Darklings. Yann didn't want to know.

The town's outer protective walls became more visible as the group got closer. Armed men lined the wall. They all brought up their weapons when they saw the party coming in at a dead run.

Before anyone could act on either side, the Dark wave overtook the Watchmen and kept rushing in an unbroken flow toward the town.

Yann's spirits sank when he saw all that Darkness building to an unstoppable torrent. Nothing could save that town.

His instincts kept him running toward it when he already knew it was hopeless. He kept running out of sheer lack of anything else to do.

The Darkness swallowed him, Eliska, Wesh, and all the other Watchmen. The ground beneath his feet disintegrated and evaporated in a whirlwind of splinters, gravel, and spinning clumps of turf.

He soared off into empty space, but not before the Dark wave washed over the walls, took out all those men, and engulfed the town.

Chapter 13

Eliska crashed down hard on a frozen block of ice dusted with snow. She immediately started shivering.

She struggled to sit up and pull her cloak around her, but it wouldn't be enough to keep her warm in this environment.

She landed in the middle of a completely different landscape. She must have fallen through a dozen different Layers.

Now she lay in the middle of what looked like a frozen lake surrounded by wooded mountains. An iron-grey sky blocked out any sunshine overhead.

Yann, Wesh, and the other Watchmen slammed down on the same lake and they all started shivering, too.

"We....have to.....get to .... those trees.....over there....." Yvan stammered as his lips went numb and blue. "We.....have to....light a fire....."

Eliska stood up and brushed the snow off her clothes. "You go ahead. I'm leaving."

Yann started to open his mouth to protest, but she'd already made up her mind. This disaster had gone on long enough.

Wesh distracted everyone by flicking his empty hand at the ice in front of them. Sparks burst from his fingertips and a fire flared up right there on the ice sheet.

The flames instantly created a pocket of warmth around the party.

"Not here!" Yvan snapped. "The fire will melt the ice! We have to get onto land first."

"The fire won't melt the ice," Wesh muttered. "It's magical fire. Calm down, Watch Commander. We have much bigger problems right now."

"What problem could possibly be bigger than this?" Vidal asked.

"Those Darklings—they went after us to steal whatever it is the Voyant wants."

Rien rolled his eyes and groaned. "Not that again!"

"Don't you see?" Wesh countered. "These aren't random attacks. They can't be. They happen too quickly one on top of the other."

"What are you saying?" Yann asked.

"Did you see the way the Darkness took the gypsies and not you?" Wesh scrambled onto his knees. "The Voyant must have done that. He took possession of them to attack you."

Yvan and the others exchanged glances. "Are you sure about that?" Yvan asked. "Maybe the Darkness took the gypsies because we're imps and they're magic-users."

"Then why did it take the imp gypsies along with the magic-users? Why did it take them and not me or Eliska? Why do you think Eliska's attack protected you and not them?" Wesh fumbled for something under his tunic. "I'm telling you this was no random occurrence. Whatever the Voyant wants is here—in this group right here. One of us must have it."

"This is nuts!" Neils muttered. "None of us is carrying anything."

"We'll see about that," Wesh countered. "I'm going to find it either way. Then we'll know."

The others gathered around the fire. Wesh waved his hands in circles in the air again. He released a sheet of magic in front of his eyes and created another window between himself and the Watchmen.

This one didn't show him any other landscapes. He looked through it at the Watchmen themselves.

The surface morphed and undulated over each person. Wesh widened his hands, took hold of the window from both sides, and moved it up and down in front of each man.

The image wavered with the window's movement, but it didn't show him anything except each Watchmen staring back at him.

The window did start to glow a little when Wesh passed it in front of the ring hanging around Barsali's neck, but the glow faded after only a few seconds.

Wesh must not have thought that glow meant anything. He finally passed the window up and down in front of Yvan.

Wesh wilted, let his hands fall with a shaky sigh, and the window evaporated. "I can't find it," he husked. "The Voyant must be concealing it from detection."

"Unless it doesn't exist," Vidal suggested. "Maybe Ando is right and these are just random Darkling attacks."

"They are not!" Wesh snapped. "I lost my entire party that left the Guardian Temple to protect Middleborough because of this thing! All of you are the only people left from the town. The Darklings wouldn't be coming after you if one of you didn't still have it."

"All the more reason to get as far away from this group as possible," Eliska interrupted. "Being near this group is suicide. I'm going. You'll all be fine now."

"Eliska—wait!" Yvan called after her.

"Don't try to talk me into staying, Watch Commander," she replied over her shoulder. "Be grateful I don't shatter this Island to separate myself from you."

"You can't just leave us here!" Rien bellowed after her. "You can't just leave us to die!"

"I saved your life already, you ungrateful pig," she snarled. "I got you here to a stable Island—and this isn't the first time I've saved your backsides. Wesh will be able to take you back to the Ancestral Empire. You'll be fine without me. Don't worry."

She walked off into the snow without looking back. All the turmoil of the last two days came to a head and drove her away from the Watch.

The connections she made with them only put her at a disadvantage in the Coil. She couldn't afford any disadvantage. Staying alive was hard enough.

Wesh's continued insistence that one of the Watchmen had something or was something that attracted Darkling attacks—that made the decision for her. She couldn't stay around anyone like that.

She had enough problems of her own without going to look for someone else's.

She marched off into the snow and channeled her magic into her feet to walk on top of it so she wouldn't sink into the deep drifts.

She crossed the lake and entered the trees. She walked a long way until she judged she'd gone far enough from the Watch not to make any difference to them.

She stopped under a stand of tall, black pine trees, looked around her in all directions, and planted her staff into the snow at her feet.

She sent a quick burst of magic down the shaft into the ground—just enough to create a hole—not big enough to put the rest of the Island in danger.

The hole opened under her feet and she pitched through it into a different Layer underneath.

She migrated through multiple Layers and landed on her feet in another Island. She came to rest in the middle of a sunbaked grassland with a rustic town not far away.

The land throbbed with heat. A dusty road wound away from her to the town's outermost houses.

This place looked like a different part of the Ancestral Empire, but she couldn't be certain—not after the way the Darkness invaded. The Ancestral Empire might not even exist anymore.

She paused there to check her magical image of the Coil. This was the Ancestral Empire. She and the Watch must not have fallen very far away.

This was the closest Island to the spot where she left the Watch. Wesh would bring the Watch back here as soon as he decided to take them anywhere.

She would just have to avoid meeting up with them. She would leave this Island as soon as possible, but she didn't need to do it immediately.

Wesh would bring the Watch through somewhere else. Then it would take time before their paths crossed. She had some time to regroup before she left for another Layer somewhere else.

She rummaged in her bag while she headed for the town. She searched for something she could trade for supplies, but she didn't find anything.

She would just have to take a job or two to earn some money or some other goods to trade. Then she could buy what she needed and move on.

The houses in this town had all been constructed of logs tied together with leather thongs. Even the roofs consisted of logs laid one against the other and plastered with mud.

Eliska didn't see any forest where the townspeople could have gotten these logs, but what did she know? Maybe they cut down the whole forest to build this town.

Dust covered everything and swirled in the air. She smelled and tasted it the minute she set foot in town.

Everyone in town wore handmade leather clothing in the crudest style.

She passed down the town's one main street until she spotted two men staggering out of a larger building near the center of town.

This building actually had a few glass windows in the front wall—unlike all the other houses in town. Some of their walls were already starting to fall apart. They barely held up their own roofs.

This building appeared sturdy and well taken care of. She knew too much about the Ancestral Empire not to recognize the building.

The door stood open, so she walked in. Sure enough, tables and chairs filled the downstairs room. A man stood behind a long bar along one wall.

Random people who must have belonged to this town sat around the room. A group of ten Barbarians occupied a table to themselves in the corner.

They were all men, all tall, and powerfully built like the rest of Barbarian kind. They stood out from everyone else in town by being tattooed over most of their bodies. Some of the Barbarians even tattooed their faces.

They were also much better dressed than anyone else around here.

Half of them wore their hair shaved except for spikes of greased hair sticking up from their scalps in a line from the forehead to the back of the neck. It was the classic Barbarian headdress.

The other half of the group either kept their heads completely shaved or they had attached other kinds of spikes and horns to their scalps.

Some of these spikes came from wild animal horns. Others had been fashioned out of bone, wood, or anything else the Barbarians could get their hands on.

The Barbarians darkened their eyes with soot to make themselves look even more menacing than usual.

All the men wore black leather pants constructed much more expertly than anything the townspeople could make.

The Barbarian men also wore studded harnesses around their chests and black leather studded or spiked gauntlets around their wrists and biceps.

All of them decorated their clothes and hair with feathers, strings of beads, drilled coins, or any other ornament. Some wore earrings.

Eliska took one look at them and walked past their table. She knew Barbarians. They had magic-users among their tribesmen, but they relied on brute force to get what they wanted when they wanted it.

None of the Barbarians looked sideways at her. A massive collection of cups crowded the table in front of them. They talked and laughed loudly. Eliska didn't see anyone else in the tavern talking.

She went to the bar. A man sat on the nearest stool. His clothes announced him as another local.

The man behind the bar looked and dressed as scruffily as everyone else around here besides the Barbarians. The quality and decoration of their outfits made them look downright regal compared to these people.

The barman came over and asked, "What can I do for you?"

Eliska was just making up her mind what to say when the guy sitting there interjected, "Give her one on me."

"Thank you," she exclaimed. "I was just about to ask if I could get work to pay for supplies."

The customer dipped his eyes to the stool next to him. "Sit down. Where did you come from?"

"I've just been wandering around in the Coil." She settled down on the stool and propped her staff against the bar next to her. "I got caught at the edge of the Ancestral Empire. It's destabilizing from the outside. I'm glad I finally got somewhere solid."

He raised his eyebrows at her. "Is that so? That's no good."

"Do you know anywhere around here I could get some work?" she asked. "I need to make some money."

"That depends. What can you do?"

The barman came back just then and put a rough clay cup in front of her before he left to go do something.

Eliska picked up the cup, sniffed it, and smelled strong, home-fermented grain brew inside it.

She took a gulp. The alcohol fumes rushed to her head.

When she opened her eyes, she discovered the man watching her from the next stool. She took a second to remember that he'd just asked her a question and she hadn't answered it yet.

She opened her hand on the bar, flicked her fingertips, and projected the revolving image of the Coil in front of the man.

Miniature versions of the Layers collapsed on top of each other. The vapors and shadows swirled and reformed into new landscapes buried in countless Layers of wild magic.

The guy raised his eyebrows again when he saw it and again when she made it disappear. "As a matter of fact, I do know someone who might be looking for someone like you. Stay here. I'll go tell him you're here and find out if he's interested. If he is, I'll come back and take you over there to introduce you."

"Thank you," she repeated. "I really appreciate it."

He got up, dropped a handful of coins in front of the barman, and left her sitting there alone. Silence descended over the building—or it would have if the Barbarians didn't talk so loudly.

No one else spoke up. No one wanted to attract the Barbarians' attention to themselves.

Eliska didn't turn around. She took another sip of her drink while she waited. Barbarians were everywhere in the Ancestral Empire. Their presence became just another feature of the landscape like bandits and gypsies.

She could handle Barbarians, even a group as big and powerfully built as these men. She didn't even particularly worry that they might be traveling with a magic user. She'd handled Barbarian magic-users before, too.

They told a bunch of tasteless jokes about how the local women weren't worth their time and they might have better luck in the next, larger town down the road.

Eliska took her third swig of her drink when their conversation changed.

"The travelers should be coming through any minute now," a man with a deep booming voice remarked. "We can catch up with them under the poisonwood stand by the Mossword Bridge."

"Make sure they have some loot this time," another snarled. "We don't have time for these penniless wanderers."

Eliska spread her hand again and let a faint trace of magic flow across her palm. The magical pool widened into a tiny version of Wesh's shimmering window.

It showed her the scene behind her back so she didn't have to turn around. She gazed down at the image and watched the Barbarians plan their next raid.

The first man who spoke had the biggest, blackest hair spikes sticking straight up from his scalp. He also wore more jewelry—probably stolen. He must be their leader.

The second speaker was one of the bald ones with wooden spikes sealed to his scalp with some kind of black sap. They formed two rows down either side of his skull instead of one row down the middle.

He wasn't as big as his leader, but the second was plenty big enough. Eliska probably wouldn't have come up to his chin.

Them talking about ambushing travelers on the road didn't shock her. That was the way life worked in the Ancestral Empire.

The Barbarians lived by the law of power. The biggest and the strongest made the decisions and took what they wanted. All Barbarians made their living by marauding the countryside and preying on anyone not strong enough to stop them.

They weren't the only ones who made their living that way. Plenty of smaller, less organized gangs of bandits did the same thing.

They just didn't do it as effectively as the Barbarians. The bandits didn't have a whole society dedicated to training their young men for it from an early age.

Centuries of Barbarian women marrying the biggest and the strongest made all their fighting men the biggest and the strongest. Eliska couldn't fault them for that.

Their next words made her freeze with her cup halfway to her mouth.

"We're doing this for pay, not for loot," the first Barbarian told the others. "We can get loot anytime."

"We better be careful around them," a third man replied. "The Black Watch is known for the bravery of the Watchmen. We can expect them to fight back. They won't lie down and let us take what we want like that gaggle of hens last week."

"To hell with the Black Watch," the first snapped. "We have a job to do. If any of them are still alive after we return the item to the client, we can go back and finish off the Watch later."

"We'll have to," the third went on. "We can't have the Black Watch running around the Ancestral Empire. They'd ruin everything."

"It doesn't matter," the first countered. "We're getting that item no matter what the Watch does."

Eliska put her cup down without finishing the rest of her drink. So the Barbarians were going after the item now—and not because they knew what it was or because it was so valuable.

Someone paid them to go after it.

She'd never heard of the Barbarians taking a job for pay like this, but why not? Loot was loot regardless of where it came from.

Like they said, they could return whatever it was to the Voyant, get paid, and then go back and loot the Watch for anything of value.

Barsali's ring flashed before her eyes. No way could she stand by and let the Barbarians take that.

They would probably kill Barsali while they were at it. He sure as hell wouldn't give it up without a fight.

What else were the Black Watchmen carrying that the Barbarians would find valuable?

She didn't even have to ask. Yann was with them. Wesh was with them. Barsali and Yvan were with them.

What the holy hell was she thinking walking away and leaving them like that? Each of them was worth a thousand times more than that ring.

Yvan would die fighting before he let anyone lay a finger on Yann. They all would.

Each of them treated him like their own son—because none of them had sons of their own. He was all they had and they were all he had.

She stood up, considered for a split second if she should down the rest of her drink, decided against it, grabbed her staff, and walked out of the building without a word to anyone.

Chapter 14

Yann raised his hand in front of his face and tried to squint through slashing wind. A wall of grey surrounded him on all sides. He couldn't see where he was or where he was going.

He searched the terrain ahead—if there was any terrain ahead. He'd been staggering through this windswept hellscape for hours—or it sure felt like it.

He slowed and eventually stopped walking. He might be moving farther away from the rest of the Watch. He could be walking off into the unknown. He might end up walking around out here forever and never find his way back—to anything.

Without warning, someone rushed him from the side. Wesh appeared out of nowhere and grabbed him. "This way, boy!" Wesh bellowed over the wind. "We thought we'd lost you!"

Yann couldn't find the voice to answer. Wesh tightened his fist in Yann's shirt and dragged him to the right. They eventually stumbled back to the rest of the Watch.

They all held onto each other. Yvan grabbed Yann's shirt by the other shoulder, pulled him into their group, and they all plowed their way deeper into the chaos.

"How much farther do we have to go?!" Yvan had to roar to make himself heard.

"I don't know and I can't stop now to find out!" Wesh called back. "Just stay together—and keep your eyes open for Darklings!"

Yann got a whipping spray of dust and spikes in the face just then. He clamped his eyes shut and tucked his chin into his chest. He couldn't even open his eyes to see where he was going, much less look out for Darklings.

The other Watchmen pulled him where he needed to go. He eventually blinked enough crap out of his eyes, but he didn't see anything but the same wall of debris and flying particles surrounding the Watch on all sides.

The Watchmen even held onto Wesh. He practically towed them through the landscape—if anyone could call it that.

If only Eliska was here....

What would she do differently? What *could* she do differently? Yann didn't understand the Coil well enough to know that.

She could shatter a landscape to fall into another Layer. She'd done it more than once to get herself out of danger.

She knew so much more about the Coil than he did. Then again, he knew nothing about the Coil except what he'd experienced since leaving Middleborough.

She knew more about it even than Wesh. She knew more about it than anyone.

She wasn't here now—which meant the whole Watch would probably die out here.

He heard the men nearest him yelling. Were the Darklings attacking again?

He squinted his eyes open just a little bit. The landscape kept darkening. Did that mean anything? He wouldn't know.

Vidal yanked him sideways. Omer and Niyazi both stumbled. The others tightened their grip on each other to steady each other.

The whole group walked a little faster and Wesh yelled again.

The next instant, the Watch broke through a sheet of thin, stretchy film. It snapped against Yann's face and the wind stopped instantly.

Wesh sagged with a relieved sigh. "We made it!" he panted. "We can rest here for a minute."

"Where are we?" Rien looked around. "This looks like nowhere."

It really did. Darkness surrounded the party on all sides. A faint light shone on everyone's cheekbones and foreheads—just enough for Yann to see who was here and in which positions they were standing.

He couldn't exactly tell where the light was coming from. He didn't see any moon, stars, or any other sign of...well, anything.

From what he could tell, he, Wesh, and the rest of the Watch just walked into a vast container of black. The place had no weather, no features, no nothing.

"We're in one of the Dark Layers." Wesh turned away. "We can't stay here for long..."

"Why are we even here?" Niels asked. "We're trying to get back to safety—back to the Ancestral Empire—although why we would want to go there when it's collapsing, I'll never understand."

"The Ancestral Empire is the most stable Island near here," Wesh replied. "It's the nearest and the safest...."

"Even with all those bandits and Barbarians?" Barsali asked.

"Even with all those bandits and Barbarians." Wesh turned aside and sat down. Yann couldn't even see any surface for him to sit down on. "Sit down and catch your breath. You'll need it when we move on from here—which will be soon."

He folded his legs under him. The Watchmen obeyed him, but they did it reluctantly. Yann didn't want to sit down. He wanted to stand watch or at least fight whatever was out there.

If this was a Dark Layer, then Darklings must live here. Wasn't that the whole point of it being a Dark Layer?

Rien sat down first followed by Vidal and Niyazi. Yvan didn't sit down right away, either. He cast hard glares at the surroundings, but there was nothing to see.

The more Yann looked at it, the more his brain struggled to accept just how little there was here. He didn't know until right now that a place could have so little in it.

Yvan finally gave it up and sat down with Barsali and Omer. Yvan glanced up and saw Yann standing there. "Sit down, son," Yvan ordered. "You might not get another chance."

Yann had no choice but to obey. He crossed to the other Watchmen. Neils and Rien made room for him to sit down.

"Where do we have to go to get to the Ancestral Empire?" Omer asked Wesh. "That girl made it sound like she could break any Layer and get there whenever she wanted to."

"That's her. She has power I don't have," Wesh replied. "It's a pity....."

He didn't say what Yann had been thinking all this time—that the party should have gone to any lengths to keep Eliska with them.

Yann always knew she would leave eventually. He'd even watched her walk away before. He just didn't think it would happen like this.

Her absence violated some unwritten law of nature—kind of like the absence of any distinguishing feature in this Layer. She should be here. She had to be here somewhere.

He didn't want to let go of his glaive, so he rested it across his lap—which made sitting next to the others more complicated.

None of them put down their weapons, either. Everyone kept looking around at everything that wasn't here. Did any of them revolt against Eliska's absence the way he did?

He didn't ask.

"It's too bad we don't have any food," Niyazi muttered.

"I'll get you some once we get to the Ancestral Empire," Wesh told him.

"How will you get that?" Vidal asked. "Will you steal it from someone?"

"Of course I won't steal it!" Wesh snapped. "What do you think I am? The Guardian Templars have a code of honor! We would never....."

"All right, all right, old man," Vidal explained. "I was just asking."

Wesh looked away. "I can use magic to hunt—the way Eliska did."

"Do you have any experience with that?" Omer asked. "She caught that gar thing in less than ten minutes."

Wesh refused to look at anyone. "I'm sure it can't be that hard."

Yann and his fellow Watchmen exchanged glances. They knew how to hunt the old-fashioned imp way—with bows, arrows, spears, knives, and traps.

None of them told Wesh that. No one challenged Wesh to a race to see who would catch something to eat first. Yann didn't want to offend Wesh or make him think he didn't appreciate everything Wesh was doing for the party.

"Where is the Ancestral Empire from here?" Yvan asked. "Can you use a map the way she did?"

Wesh turned his head even farther away. "I'm afraid not. She can do many things I can't. I'm beginning to understand how she moves around the Coil so well. A map like that would be so helpful."

"Why can't you create one?" Yann asked. "Is your magic confined to certain kinds of spells?"

"Hold your tongue, boy," Barsali interjected. "Don't accuse him of parlor tricks. He can do what he can do and not what he can't. We'll just have to accept it."

"Let him ask," Wesh replied. "I don't know how Eliska created that map. I was as amazed as you were."

"What about that window you looked into?" Yann asked. "You saw that forest collapse before it happened."

"My window can only see parts of the Coil and sometimes how different Layers will interact with each other. I can't see the whole Coil. I've never met anyone before who can do that."

"How is it that Eliska is so powerful?" Yann asked. "How can she be more powerful than magic-users who have studied in the Guardian Temple all their lives?"

"I suppose someone has to be the most powerful magic-user," Wesh mumbled. "I guess it just happened to be her. It's such a shame...."

"Can she be more powerful than the Voyant?" Vidal asked. "Could she defeat him?"

"I don't know how powerful the Voyant is," Wesh replied. "I suppose it stands to reason that there must be others as powerful as she is—and as powerful as he is. After all, the Voyant must have come from somewhere...."

"Unless he got his power from somewhere else," Neils suggested. "Maybe this thing he wants will give him more power. Maybe that's what he does. Maybe he goes around taking things that increase his power. Maybe that's how he got as high as he is."

Wesh shrugged again. "I suppose anything is possible."

"I would have expected the Guardian Templars to understand the Voyant better," Yann pointed out. "What do you study if not these forces that affect the whole Coil?"

Wesh didn't look up. He didn't accuse Yann of insulting the Guardian Templars for not understanding the single most powerful wizard in the entire Coil—the wizard who just might hold the key to all of this.

Wesh only mumbled, "You're right, my boy. It's a sign of serious negligence that we didn't at least find out if he *is* controlling the Coil, and if he is, how we could somehow rein him in to stop him from wreaking all this destruction. We failed in our duty....and now I'll probably never live to return to the Temple and tell my brothers what I know."

No one said anything to soften the blow. Those words hung heavy over the whole group.

Would Yann live.....to do anything after this? He could barely see his way to surviving the next few hours.

Building any kind of life after this felt like a million miles away.

The words hardly escaped Wesh's mouth before the floor under the Watchmen's seats collapsed. It buckled in a heartbeat and all the men plummeted into another Layer just below the Dark space where they'd just been sitting.

They fell down one Layer, crashed through some dark tree branches, and landed in a deep snowbank.

All the men took a long time to flounder out of the drifts. By the time they swam out onto the surface, snow clung to their hair and faces. It saturated their clothes.

Black trees towered above a forest packed almost to the branches in snow. "I....I don't know.....if I'll be.....able to find....food here...." Wesh stammered.

"Forget food," Yvan ordered. "Light us a fire. Hurry."

Wesh didn't have a problem doing that. The Watchmen crowded around trying to warm their frozen fingers and dry their clothes.

"Are we in the Ancestral Empire now?" Rien demanded.

Wesh opened his mouth to answer, but before he could make a sound, a blasting hot furnace wind smashed into the forest from the side.

Searing heat melted all the snow, snuffed out his fire, and plastered the Watchmen full force.

The heat scorched the trees away, blew them to scrap, and scoured the landscape of every recognizable feature.

Yann bent his head behind his arm trying to survive the blazing wind. It bombarded every inch of his skin.

The freezing water in his clothes that nearly froze him to death a minute ago—it all evaporated in seconds. He really wished now that his clothes were wet again.

The wind would have ignited his clothes and burned his flesh off his bones, but a second later, the wind changed into a colossal torrent of rushing water.

The wave drowned the Watchmen in the flood, ripped them off their feet, and tumbled Yann head over heel in the chaos.

Chapter 15

Yann felt himself bumping into bodies, objects, and debris. The churning water pounded him against things and then dumped him down on a hard surface.

He didn't want to get up. He didn't want to be alive in this nightmare.

Just lying here and waiting for the Coil to kill him looked like a much more pleasant option, but the sound of his father coughing made him get up.

Wesh and the rest of the Watch lay all around Yann. Tall, dry, yellow grass surrounded them. Yann couldn't see over the top of it from this position.

He crawled over to his father and touched the Watch Commander's shoulder, but Yvan and the others were all unhurt.

They choked and retched the water out of their lungs. It dripped from their hair and formed puddles around their fallen bodies.

All the men lay in a vast field of dry grass three feet tall. A soft, warm wind rustled through it and undulated the grass in waves spreading outward from the Watchmen's position.

The water soaked into the dry soil around the grass roots.

"Now.....now....now we're in the.....Ancestral Empire....." Wesh croaked.

No one answered. The Watchmen panted and gasped for breath. No one moved except to sink down on the ground. Vidal rolled onto his side and curled into a ball. No one told him to get up.

Yvan dragged himself onto his knees and collapsed back on his seat. He grabbed Yann's shoulder and squeezed. They were alive. That was the most anyone could say about them.

"So....." Omer began after a few minutes. "So.....this landscape will stay the same....for a while? It won't change?"

Wesh nodded. "The Ancestral Empire is one of the oldest Islands in the Coil. If anything stays the same, this one will."

"Doesn't any place stay the same for long?" Rien asked. "Middleborough stayed the same for a hundred years. My father and grandfather were born there."

"Some islands stay longer than others," Wesh replied. "Some stay for a long time, but they all fall eventually."

"The Darklings didn't attack us that time," Yvan pointed out. "Why not? You said we were in the Dark Layers. The Darklings should have attacked us there if they were going to attack us anywhere, but the floor collapsed instead."

"Islands and Layers don't usually fall from Darkling attack," Wesh explained. "They become progressively unstable—or it can happen suddenly as we've seen."

Yvan shook his head down at his hands in his lap. "You know so much more about the Coil than we do."

"I don't know so much. What I know comes from studying books in our Temple library. I've only been out in the Coil once before this. If only Eliska was still here, she could tell us....."

He trailed off. No one asked him to finish.

He shook it off and pushed himself upright. "We should move. I'll find us a town—now that we're actually on solid ground again.

He opened his window. Yann tried not to look at all the collapsing Layers. He really, really didn't want to go anywhere near any of them again.

Why couldn't the world just stay nice and solid—the way it always had been his entire life? Why did everything have to start blowing up right now of all times?

It had been like this all along. He knew that. The Coil had always been wild, unstable, and changeable—but only outside the walls of Middleborough.

He always pretended the world was nice and solid and familiar. He could keep pretending that as long as he stayed inside the walls—which was all the time.

He never left the town since the day he was born. He never had to see the Coil except from his post on the wall.

Middleborough always stayed the same the rest of the time—until it didn't.

None of the other Watchmen looked into Wesh's window, either. They must all be thinking the same thing.

Their lives were over—the lives they once knew. Whatever happened to them now, it would never go back to the way it was before.

It *couldn't* go back to the way it was before. They'd all experienced the Coil in ways they never thought they would have to.

No one could wipe out that experience. No one could make them back into the men they used to be when the world was nice and solid and true.

Wesh must have seen something in his window that made him come to some decision. "Yes," he said to no one in particular. "Yes, that's all right, then. We can do that."

He got to his feet. None of the Watchmen asked what they could do.

Yann got up with him and the rest of the Watchmen did the same thing.

As soon as they stood up, they all saw a road nearby. It ran through the grasslands leading away into the distance.

Yann didn't see anything over there the group might head for, but whatever Wesh wanted to do would be better than anything the rest of them could come up with

Wesh set off through the grass. The rest of the Watch fell in with him.

Yann realized he still had his glaive. He'd completely forgotten about it.

His instincts didn't forget to hold onto it when he fell into the snowbank, when he fought his way through the wind, or when the Watch got washed away by that water.

He couldn't loosen his fingers from the weapon if he tried. It remained glued to his hand no matter what.

He didn't try to loosen his fingers. He couldn't lose this weapon, especially not in any country crawling with bandits, gypsies, Barbarians, and God only knew what else.

The other Watchmen still carried their weapons, too, so Yann wasn't the only one. The men scanned the countryside on all sides for anyone coming near them.

Other travelers passed up and down the road. Some pushed handcarts or drove wagons pulled by oxen or draft horses.

Scraggly dogs followed the wagons or tagged at the heels of people on foot. Yann didn't see anyone who fit the category of gypsy, bandit, or Barbarian.

He didn't even know what Barbarians looked like and he'd never dealt with any bandits in Middleborough. That was the Watch's job—to keep people like that out of town.

He hoped he'd recognize them when he did see them. He also hoped someone in this group knew more about them than he did.

He realized on that walk that he really didn't know much about the other Watchmen's backgrounds. He always assumed they came from Middleborough.

He knew Rien and Barsali did. He couldn't be sure about the others.

Omer couldn't have come from Middleborough. His dark skin and hair, his facial features, accent, his sharp way of speaking, and everything else he did—they all gave him away. He came from some other race—so where did he come from?

Yann shivered when he made the connection. He didn't even know if his own father came from Middleborough. Yann always assumed that he did.

Eliska's question came back to haunt Yann now. The men of the Black Watch swore a vow of celibacy when they joined the Watch. They swore off family and women to dedicate themselves to protecting others.

Yvan had belonged to the Watch since Yann's earliest memories—going all the way back to Yann's infancy.

Yvan must have had a girl then. He must have gotten together with her before he joined the Watch—so what happened to her? Where was she now?

She couldn't be alive. Yvan would have told Yann about his mother....wouldn't he?

Either that or.....

Yann refused to think about the other part of that question. He really preferred reality when he thought he understood everything. He didn't want to be aware of all the things he didn't know.

That was the problem. He was aware of them now.......thanks to Eliska.

She asked the questions he never dared to ask himself before. She didn't hide from reality. She had no reason to. She already knew the worst about herself.

Yann distracted himself by turning his attention back to the landscape. It really looked as stable as he could possibly hope.

He didn't see any sign of it transforming into anything else. The wind kept blowing at the same strength and at the same temperature.

The ground beneath his feet didn't change its shape. The road didn't alter its direction. The birds in the air stayed birds. The oxen and dogs and wagons stayed the way they were supposed to stay.

He didn't want to get used to that. He didn't want the safety and calm of this landscape to lull him into a false sense of security.

The simple fact of its safety and calm made him tighten his grip on his weapon. His fellow Watchmen reacted the same way. They became more tense, more watchful, and more ferociously wary with every mile the group covered.

The road went on a lot farther than the others the group had followed before. Then again, the group had never stayed on any road as long as this before. They all collapsed or some other disaster struck before the group had a chance to follow any road very far.

Chapter 16

Wesh kept the lead in front of the gypsy caravan and strode down the road at a steady clip. He definitely seemed to have somewhere he wanted to get.

Yann stared at the spot where the road vanished over the horizon in the distance. He still didn't see any town or destination Wesh might be heading for.

Niyazi snapped everyone back to their senses. "Heads up!" he called. "We got company!"

The Watchmen spun around to check what he meant. Yann's stomach dropped when a line of black figures appeared over a hill to the party's left.

Yann couldn't make the figures out from here. They might have been people, but he didn't recognize their bizarre features. Some seemed taller than others. Some had strangely shaped heads or they might have been some kind of horned creatures.

"Barbarians!" Wesh hissed.

"How can you tell from this distance?" Rien asked.

Wesh pretended not to hear him. He sliced his forefinger at the others. "Stand your ground and get ready to fight. They outnumber us and outsize us. The Barbarians are fierce and bloodthirsty. They won't stop unless you kill or maim them."

"At least they aren't mounted," Omer observed.

"They'll come heavily armed," Wesh went on. "More heavily armed than we are."

"You can take them down with your magic, can't you?" Yvan asked.

"They'll bring magic-users with them—at least one. They always bring at least one—and they'll send multiple fighters after me so the rest can get to you." Wesh narrowed his eyes at all the Watchmen. "I don't know who and what you've fought before, but you'll have to fight your hardest against them."

"We've fought Darklings before, old man," Niels replied. "Remember?"

"I remember well enough," Wesh replied. "I remember you got your asses handed to you—or you would have without our help—and we don't have Eliska with us now. Look out! Here they come!"

The Watchmen closed into a line as the ranks of Barbarians swooped down the hills. They formed a line, too. They crossed the landscape unbelievably fast.

Yann found it difficult to believe these were ordinary human beings and not some otherworldly creatures. How could anyone run that fast?

He still didn't recognize them as human from this distance. Their size and shapes made them look even more monstrous and grotesque as they got closer.

He raised his glaive to strike. He didn't see anything to convince him that they were human until they got twenty yards from the Watch.

By the time he did recognize their bizarre headdresses, costumes, jewelry, and the black face paint around their eyes, it was already too late.

Each of the Barbarians dwarfed every man of the Watch, including Barsali. A few of the Barbarians carried axes. Most carried clubs studded with spikes.

They definitely struck more terror into Yann's heart than the Darklings. He knew how to fight Darklings.

He put it completely out of his mind that these things were human. They weren't. They were some kind of demon from the Dark Realms—even worse than Darklings.

He didn't have to show these people any mercy, but he did have to figure out a way to fight them. He didn't stand a chance of fighting them on strength alone.

He would just have to play his own advantages. He had speed and agility on his side—and then, in a flash of insight, he realized.

These weren't Darklings or demons. They were just people painted up to look fierce.

That thought gave him all the courage he needed to face them.

They must have seen him, Neils, and Rien standing together. By sheer chance, Barsali, Omer, and Niyazi all wound up together on one end of the line with Yvan, Vidal, and Wesh between those three and Yann's end of the line.

The Barbarians turned out to be smarter than they looked. They recognized the three smaller men as the weakest part of the line. The Barbarian assault split into three. The majority turned on Yann, Neils, and Rien.

Three Barbarians with bald heads and less decoration went for Wesh. Those three must be the Barbarian magic-users.

Only three others engaged with Barsali, Niyazi, and Omer. The Barbarians threw everything else at the three smallest Watchmen.

The Barbarians wanted to reduce the Watch's numbers and before diverting their manpower to the bigger, stronger Watchmen.

A huge man with hulking muscles and towering hair spikes charged Yann and swung a massive club. Two other equally enormous Barbarians went after Rien. They flanked him on both sides.

He raised his longsword. One of his attackers hefted his club on high and brought it down with a punishing blow that shattered Rien's longsword. The weapon splintered halfway down and left him with the jagged stump.

Yann couldn't pay attention anymore to what the others were doing. The Barbarian rushing him raised his club with huge arms.

Yann's glaive couldn't take that blow. He had to avoid it and somehow neutralize this attacker as quickly as possible.

Yann went all in with everything he had and sprang forward to meet the Barbarian's charge.

Yann going on the offensive must have been the absolute last thing this Barbarian expected. He didn't hesitate, but he didn't react in time.

He exposed his midsection when he raised his club. Yann sprang sideways under the man's arms, stabbed his glaive between the ribs on the left side, and shoved the weapon in all the way to the heart.

Yann let his own weight drive the glaive shaft forward to slice backward. He kept on going until he wound up behind the incoming line of Barbarians.

The others ran straight past him. He spun around and let his speed take over. He could move so much faster than any of these men.

He leapt for the next nearest assailant. The guy had been trying to flank Yann at the place where Yann had originally been standing.

By the time Yann whipped around to go after the guy, the Barbarian still faced that one spot trying to figure out what happened.

Yann's first victim crumpled and fell right in front of his friends. They looked down at him in surprise and completely missed looking to see where Yann was.

He lunged for the second man, swiped his glaive down the back of the guy's neck in the quickest, shortest stroke possible, and dropped the guy before Yann sprang away to three Barbarians surrounding Neils.

Rien and his broken longsword had no problem handling his two assailants. He pulled out another short sword he got from the gypsies.

The Barbarians came at him from both sides, but these men actually turned out to be easier to fight than the Darklings.

They still had numbers on their side. They sent four more after Yann and surrounded him. He couldn't fight them all—not by himself.

He responded by leaping away and stabbing one of Rien's attackers from behind before Yann's enemies completely cut him off.

Rien yelled, "Thanks!" over the Barbarians' furious yells and the noise of crashing steel.

Yann glanced around trying to figure out who to attack next, but the four Barbarians coming after him understood his tricks now. He got lucky by springing a surprise attack on the first two.

That wouldn't work now. The Barbarians backed him toward the rest of the Watch and closed him in with Neils and Yvan.

The three Barbarian magic-users cornered Wesh exactly the way he said they would. He fired magical pulses at them again and again, but they bombarded him with so many explosions that they brought him to the ground in no time.

One stayed behind to finish him off while the other two turned on Barsali, Omer, and Niyazi. They put up the most resistance, but they couldn't fight magic. None of the Watch could.

Yann bumped into Neils. The two of them turned back to back just as Rien joined them from the other side. Barbarians ringed the three men in a solid pack.

Yann's eyes darted from one Barbarian to another. How much longer did he have before they struck?

How pathetic would it be if the remaining Watchmen fell to these marauders? The Watch survived Darklings, gypsies, hurricanes, heaving landscapes, and freezing cold.

At that moment, another magical explosion went off behind Yann's back. Was that the shot that took out Yvan? Was Yann's father dead now?

Yann didn't believe it when the Barbarian magic-users hurtled away from Wesh and the others.

Yann actually forgot to fight and defend himself when Eliska stormed over the nearest hill and blasted the magic-users flat.

They crashed down in the grass and she rotated around to confront the rest of the Barbarians.

Her arrival surprised the other Watchmen enough that they all forgot to fight, too. Even the Barbarians forgot to fight—but only for a second.

They recovered first and wheeled away from the Watchmen to defend themselves. She bombarded them from a distance, launched magical blasts across the fields, and leveled three more Barbarians who'd been surrounding Yann, Neils, and Rien.

The remaining Barbarians roared in fury and rushed her raising their weapons. The Barbarians completely abandoned the Watchmen, but they never got near her.

She unloaded on them one after the other and cleared the field in a few minutes.

She stalked into the group, went from one Barbarian after another, and jammed her staff into each of them as they tried to get up. She nailed each man with a powerful thump straight into their bodies.

Yann and the others stared down at the unconscious Barbarians. Then everyone stared at her.

Yann still could not bring himself to believe that she came back. She saved them all again.

She pretended not to notice everyone gawking at her with their mouths open. They all still held their weapons ready to fight someone.

"We have to move," she snapped over her shoulder. "We can't stay here."

She went over to Wesh, took hold of his arm, and tried to pick him up.

When he didn't respond right away, she scowled down at him for a minute and then laid her hand on top of his head.

He stayed slumped on the ground with his grey hair hanging over his face. Eliska went very still for a second and then Wesh crumpled the rest of the way to the ground.

He collapsed on his side, rolled in the grass, and groaned with his eyes clamped shut.

"Just lie still for a minute, Wesh," she murmured under her breath. "You'll be all right, but we need to move away from here."

"Eliska! What are you doing here?" Barsali gasped. "You said you would leave us."

"I did," she replied over her shoulder. "I heard these Barbarians talking in a tavern. They were talking about attacking you so I followed them here. Someone hired them to come after you to get whatever it is you're carrying—which means that whoever hired them will either hire someone else or send someone else to get it. We can't stay here—and you can't go to a town. We need to stay off the roads and travel across country."

She cast a hard look around the horizon.

"But if we can't go to a town.....where will we go?" Neils asked.

"We have to stay in the Ancestral Empire," she decided. "The Coil is too unstable elsewhere. We need to stay in an Island. We just need to move to another part of it."

"Is there any part without Barbarians?" Omer asked.

"Barbarians are everywhere, not just in the Ancestral Empire. We would have to deal with them anywhere even if someone didn't hire them to come after you."

"They shouldn't......" Wesh choked. "They shouldn't.....be taking jobs.....for pay....."

"Loot is loot to a Barbarian," she muttered. "They don't care where they get it. We would have to deal with them more in places with people around them. We need to stay away from towns and roads. Follow me. There could be more of the same group around and they could have set up more ambushes for you."

She took hold of Wesh a second time and pulled him upright. The other Watchmen gathered around.

Omer and Vidal both sustained injuries during their fights against the Barbarians. Eliska went through the group one man at a time and healed them where they needed it.

No one said a word, not even to thank her. Did she plan to stick around this time—for how long? Yann didn't dare to ask and no one else did, either. No one asked why she came back in the first place.

She kept shooting sidelong frowns in Wesh's direction. Whatever the Barbarian magic-users did to him left him stunned and wobbly.

He kept tottering on his heels, nearly falling over, and steadying himself. She held onto him to help him keep his balance.

Niyazi grabbed him once on Wesh's other side to stop him from toppling into the grass again. Eliska didn't do anything else to heal him.

She must have decided he was ready to travel. She took a few steps in front of Neils and Rien, passed her hand through the air from her head height down to her knees, and opened another window like Wesh's.

This one didn't tumble around in an array of collapsing landscapes. It opened into another calm scene of sparse trees, bushes, and rocks lining a river somewhere.

Rolling hills rose on either side of the river. Yann didn't see any sign of human habitation or even any footprints in the whole river valley.

"Let's go," Eliska ordered and she stepped through the window into the other landscape.

Chapter 17

E liska stepped through her magical window onto the riverbank. She scanned the countryside up and down the valley.

These hills cut off visibility. She wouldn't be able to see anyone coming closer. That would be a problem.

It would also prevent anyone else from seeing the group here. So that was one advantage.

She waited until Wesh and the Watchmen followed her before she closed the window behind them.

She flicked her fingers and opened a smaller magical vortex on her palm to search the area. No one was around for miles in any direction.

"We can rest here." She walked away to a clump of trees on one of the hillsides. "You might as well all sit down until everyone feels better."

She sank onto the grass and leaned against the nearest tree.

Wesh followed her, buckled onto the sod next to her, and toppled sideways onto his shoulder. He groaned again, shut his eyes, and threw his arm over his face. He didn't move again.

She extended her hand and laid it on his chest to check if she'd healed all his injuries.

She didn't detect any sign of internal damage—or any physical damage at all. The Barbarian magic-users' assault affected him at a deeper level—a magical level.

"Thank you so much, my dear," he husked under his breath. "I'm forever in your debt."

She pulled her hand back and faced front. She didn't want any of these people thanking her. She never should have left them alone.

None of this would have happened if she'd stayed with them. She would have seen the Barbarians coming. They never would have gotten anywhere close to the Watch as long as she defended them.

The Watchmen took a long time before they let their guard down. They stood over there in a loose group. Each man kept a firm grip on his weapons while they all searched the area for any sign of danger.

When they didn't see anything, Rien paced up the riverbank to look around up there. Vidal and Niyazi walked down the valley heading in the other direction before they came back to rejoin the other men.

Eliska stopped herself from looking at them and she didn't want them looking at her, either. She really hoped they didn't ask why she came back.

Wesh stayed where he was with his arm over his face. His breathing lengthened as he fell asleep. Good. He would need plenty of rest after that fight.

Yvan crossed the grass first and sat down a few feet away from Eliska. "Thank you," he told her. "I don't think we'll ever be able to repay you for this—for everything you've done."

"I don't want repayment." She heard herself snapping at him. She shouldn't. She should have been softer to him—and to all of them.

Her conversation with Barsali brought her closer to him. She understood him now, but they all must have stories like his.

Yvan implied that even Rien had a story—a story that explained why he hated her so much for being a Coil rat.

"I wasn't trying to suggest that you were doing it for payment," Yvan murmured. "I was only trying to tell you how grateful we are."

"Well, we can't stay here, either. We have to keep moving. Fortunately, the Ancestral Empire is big enough. We'll be able to travel here for a long time without going near any of the unstable edges."

Omer came over and sat down next to Yvan. "We can't move around forever."

"Why not?" she asked. "I do it."

He shook his head. "We aren't like you. We have to establish ourselves somewhere."

"The only alternative I can see is figuring out which of you has what the Voyant wants—if it is the Voyant sending everyone after you to get it," she replied. "Then you can either give it to him or destroy the thing to make him stop hunting you."

"How can we find out what it is if even Wesh's magic can't locate it?" Yvan asked. "Could *you* find it?"

"I've already tried. I already used my magic to see if one of you was carrying anything—and we all know there's nothing special about any of you."

"But we all know there's something special about *you*," Rien interrupted from a few feet away. "What would a powerful wizard like the Voyant want with a bunch of imps? He wouldn't. He would want the one wizard in the whole Coil who might be able to stop him or kill him or whatever it is he wants from you."

"We already established that Eliska can't be the thing he wants," Yvan countered. "Whatever it is, it's either one of us or something we possess."

"It would have to be something one of us was carrying when we left Middleborough," Yann interjected. He crossed the bank and sat down with Eliska and the others.

Yann sat on her side of the tree. She tried not to read too much meaning into him sitting down near her.

"I had this when I left Middleborough." Omer pulled a dagger out of his boot. "I'm guessing this isn't what he's looking for."

"Maybe he is," Yvan suggested. "Does it have any meaning for you?"

"No, I got it from the Watch armory a week before we left Middleborough. I had never seen or used it before."

Yvan turned away with a sigh. "I wonder if we'll ever find out what it is."

"We'll find out when the Voyant comes to take it—or someone else does," Eliska told him. "If he is the one looking for us, he'll keep coming until he gets it."

Both Yann and Yvan looked up. She realized a second too late that she said the Voyant was looking for "us".

It just slipped out and she stopped herself from making it worse by trying to correct herself after the fact.

Fortunately, the other Watchmen came back just then. Vidal, Neils, and Barsali sat down in a messy circle.

Niyazi squatted. "I'm going hunting. I'm hungry and I saw some animal tracks over there. This place looks like it has more life in it than we've seen before. I'll find something and bring it back."

"You don't have to." Eliska raised her staff and spiked it into the soil near her own foot. She didn't think about it before she did it. Old instinct made her react automatically.

She impaled her staff a foot into the sod and struck a burrowing creature crawling through its tunnel down there.

Her staff ejected a fork of magic into the creature and then magnetized it to the end of her staff.

The Watchmen scrambled out of the way while she pulled the thing out of the ground. It kicked and struggled, but it couldn't break the magic binding it to the end of her staff.

The creature's claws tore up the sod and kicked up a mound of dirt around the hole when she dragged the creature squeaking and screeching into the open.

"What the hell is that?!" Rien roared.

Eliska held the creature up twisting and turning it in all directions. Dirt and clumps of grass fell from its thick black fur while it contorted around in circles trying to free itself.

The noise woke up Wesh. He took his arm down, propped himself up on his elbow, and frowned at the proceedings.

"The local people call them frilled biturongs," Eliska explained. "I don't know what they're really called."

She waited until the creature twisted in her direction. Then passed her forefinger across the creature's throat to kill it the rest of the way.

It drooped from the end of her staff and hung limp with all its limbs pointing down to the ground.

The Watchmen took another long time before they calmed down again. She didn't notice before how jumpy and nervous they all acted.

Yann did it, too.

She never noticed this about herself. She'd become so accustomed to the Coil and its many dangers. Going through all of this just seemed normal.

Some part of her she didn't understand wanted to make it easier for these men, but she nothing would make it easier. She already knew that.

They would probably never find a safe haven. That was the worst part of it. They would have to keep wandering to stay away from the Voyant.

If he was the one who sent Barbarians after them, what would he send next? He already sent Darklings. What could be worse than that?"

She got to work cleaning and gutting the biturong. She released it from the end of her staff, held it up by its foot with one hand, and used her staff to skin it.

She walked away from the group to gut the creature at a distance. She didn't want to leave a pile of steaming entrails lying right there where the men had to sit.

She returned to find Rien standing up compressing all the dirt back into the hole with his foot.

Niyazi scooped up a bunch of twigs from between the trees. He squatted in the center of the group arranging the twigs into a cone shape.

She sat down with her fresh carcass, used her magic to ignite the twigs, and used some other dead sticks to build a spit.

The others sat in silence while Niyazi combed the area for all the dry wood he could find.

The sudden lack of any danger seemed to deflate the Watchmen. They all went slack. Their faces lost all expression. They stared into the flames in a stunned trance.

Only Niyazi stayed active. He fed his sticks into the fire and walked around the area gathering more while Eliska spitted her biturong to cook it.

Then there was nothing to do but sit around and wait. The oppressive silence became unbearable.

Wesh finally gave everyone something to talk about by sitting up.

"How's your head, old man?" Yvan asked.

Wesh snorted. "It's been better. Thank you for asking."

"What did they do to you?" Yann asked.

"They sent a feedback loop through my system to stop me from using my magic against them. It turned my magic back on me to neutralize me so they could finish me off."

Yann looked down at the ground and shook his head. "I'm really starting to be extremely grateful that I don't have magic."

"You should be grateful," Wesh muttered. "Life as a wizard is too complicated. The life of an imp is much better."

Vidal laughed at him. "How do you know that if you've been a wizard all your life?"

"I can see perfectly well how it is," Wesh replied. "I would gladly have lived my life as an imp."

"And get wiped out by Darklings like everyone else in Middleborough?" Neils interjected. "That doesn't sound like much of a life."

"Imps get to raise families and spend their lives working toward building a decent society," Wesh pointed out. "I wouldn't have gotten locked in the Guardian Temple if I'd been an imp."

"No one locked in you the Temple," Eliska interrupted. "The Guardian Templars are a voluntary order just like the Black Watch. They wouldn't take you if you didn't join willingly." She made a face at Niyazi and the others. "Don't listen to a word he says. He's sulking because the other wizards defeated him."

Wesh looked away. "Now I really wish I was an imp. You're too smart for your own good, my dear."

A few of the Watchmen laughed.

"How did you join the Guardian Templars, Wesh?" Yann asked. "Did you grow up with other magic-users?"

"No, I was the only one in my family. My parents saw that I had magic and they sent me to the local wizard to learn. I apprenticed with him using magic in the town to heal, fix things, and solve problems. When I got to the age of maturity, he recommended that I go into the Temple to improve my skill and continue my education."

"Now tell them the rest of it," Eliska interrupted.

He looked up and frowned at her. "What do you mean?"

"A man who joins the Black Watch joins for life. Once they join, they can't leave—not without betraying their oath. That isn't the case with the Guardian Templars, is it? You could leave whenever you want. You stay because you enjoy it and because Temple life suits you. You don't really wish you were an imp householder, do you? Tell the truth."

He winced and looked away. "Of course you're right, my dear. I would have left a long time ago if I didn't take to it."

She found herself smiling at him and feeling something like affection. She'd never spent this much time around another magic-user before, especially not one so much older and more experienced than herself.

Niyazi distracted her by turning the biturong on the spit. It dripped juice into the flames. They sizzled and sent mouth-watering vapors drifting through the air.

Rien groaned at the smell, climbed onto his knees on his side of the fire, and pulled out his knife. "I can't wait any longer. I'm eating it. I don't care if it's raw."

"You better share it with the rest of us," Omer told him. "You talk a lot of crap about Eliska. At least she divided the food evenly."

"I will," Rien replied.

"Only because the rest of us will thump you if you don't," Neils countered. "Just remember you have all eight of us watching you, so don't try to cheat."

A few more people laughed, including Yann. He happened to glance up at Eliska right then.

His eyes twinkled when he looked at her. His cheeks flushed with pleasure and his features lit up, but he wasn't looking at her like that.

The next second, he went back to watching Rien.

Rien carved off a slice of meat, stuffed it into his mouth, and then got to work cutting off equally sized pieces to pass around the circle.

He started by handing the second piece to Niyazi, who happened to be the man on Rien's left. Then Rien worked his way around the circle going in the same direction.

He handed a piece to Eliska after he already served Niyazi, Vidal, Neils, Omer, and Yvan.

She didn't mention that she was the one who caught this biturong so they could all put some food in their stomachs. She waited her turn like the others.

She might have magic, but she didn't want anyone considering her anything exceptional. She was just another person in this group trying to survive until tomorrow.

Chapter 18

Yann sat up and looked around at a different part of the riverbank. Wesh, Yvan, and the other Watchmen lay asleep on the grass under the trees where they'd come through Eliska's portal yesterday.

She was the only person awake besides Yann. She sat against her tree over there feeding sticks into the fire.

Her eyes kept snapping around the group from one man to another. She didn't seem to pay Yann any extra attention except that he was sitting up and looking back at her now.

How long had she been sitting there watching the men sleep? She kept insisting that they didn't have to leave right away and that they could stay here and rest for a change. How long would that last?

She also kept insisting that the group shouldn't stay in one place for very long. She said this was only a reprieve to catch up on some much-needed downtime after their last series of catastrophes.

She didn't say this was the calm before the storm started up again. She didn't have to say it because everybody already knew it.

Wesh never contradicted anything she said or overruled her decisions about anything. If she told everyone they had to move today, the whole Watch would go along with it, including Yvan.

Yann didn't know how to feel about someone taking command in his father's place. Following Wesh didn't seem like too much of a leap considering how much older and more experienced he was.

None of the Watchmen had his magic, either. They would all have been dead without him to protect them.

Yann didn't feel the same way about Eliska doing the same thing. He didn't understand why he had a problem with her doing it. She had more magic and more experience even than Wesh.

Yann did have a problem with it, though.

He wasn't the only one. He caught the other Watchmen all glancing at Yvan and Wesh every time Eliska made any kind of decision or gave anyone an order to do anything. None of the other Watchmen wanted some girl from the middle of nowhere to take their Watch Commander's place.

Yann deliberately looked in the other direction while the other men woke up and eventually dragged themselves off the ground.

The group spent the night sleeping on the bare grass around their fire. Yann fell into a senseless sleep. He didn't stay conscious enough to keep track of who kept the fire going overnight. Maybe Eliska stayed awake all night keeping watch over everyone.

He couldn't fathom why she would take so much care over a bunch of strangers she thought would be too useless not to get her killed. She sure changed fast.

Something must have happened between when she left the group on that frozen lake and when she followed the Barbarians back to the Watch. He didn't like to think about what might have happened, but something must have.

He really hoped nothing happened to hurt her. His temper started rising when he thought about anyone hurting her.

He gritted his teeth and forced himself to inspect his glaive instead of looking around. He didn't want anyone reading his unspoken thoughts, especially not her.

He felt her staring at him even when the other men started talking. She wouldn't be looking only at him, but he didn't want to sit here with these thoughts coursing through his mind.

He pushed himself to his feet. "I'm going hunting for something to eat."

"Don't stray too far away, son," Yvan told him. "Don't make us come looking for you."

Eliska stood up. "I'll go with you. You need someone to keep an eye on you."

His gaze shot up and he discovered her grinning at him. He flushed in spite of himself and looked away. "Or I'll keep an eye on you—one way or the other."

Barsali and Rien both laughed.

Yann headed down the riverbank. She tagged after him until they turned a few corners. Another stand of trees separated them from the group.

He stopped there and used his glaive to hack a long stave from one of the trees. He trimmed it down and sharpened the end into a pointed spear.

He and Eliska kept walking in silence for a while. Yann scrambled in his brain to come up with something to say to her.

Now would have been the perfect time to smooth things over with her—or to smooth things the rest of the way to where he wanted them to go.

He wouldn't have to smooth things over with her because nothing had gone wrong between them—not since Middleborough.

He would have to find some way to advance things in the direction of....something other than them just being traveling companions.

He might never get another chance to talk to her alone. It was now or never.

They rounded a few more corners. She didn't open the conversation nor did she use her magic to find anything to eat.

The silence grated on Yann's nerves. He didn't want her to think he was too timid to talk to her.

They passed through another stand of trees and came out behind an outcropping of rock between themselves and the river.

Yann spotted a long-tailed gar digging in the dirt under one of the rocks.

He eased his glaive down to the ground, crouched low, and crept a few paces closer. He raised his spear, angled his approach the way he judged would give him the best shot, and launched his spear at the creature.

The point grazed the gar's shoulder, scratched a line through the creature's fur, and stabbed into the soil right next to it.

The gar let out a squeal of pain and surprise, leapt away, and took off scurrying into the rocks.

Eliska laughed at him. "Nice shot. You wouldn't survive out here on your own."

He meant to glare at her, but when he saw her eyes shining, he wound up grinning instead. He couldn't stay mad at her, not even when she teased him.

"You might at least pretend that you came out here for my company and not to babysit me," he returned. "Why did you come anyway—to make a joke out of my hunting abilities?"

"Of course," she replied. "My life has been way too serious lately. Who would I laugh at if not you?"

He found himself laughing along with her. Being alone with her gave him new energy. Maybe, just maybe she enjoyed spending time alone with him as much as he enjoyed spending it with her.

He pulled the spear out of the ground and retrieved his glaive. "Don't use your magic to find another one. Let me do it."

She turned bright red and her eyelashes dipped. "All right. The rest of the Watch might starve before you find something. Then you can tell them you said that before you come crawling back to beg me to save you all."

"Cut it out. I will not."

He skirted the rocks looking for another gar. Instead, he found the hole into which the last one ran to hide.

He tried to poke his glaive into it, but it didn't fit. He didn't have any better success with his spear.

She stood off to one side watching. "A gar isn't big enough to feed everyone anyway," she told him. "Why don't you go for something bigger?"

"What else is there? No, don't tell me. I need to prove to you what a skilled hunter I am."

She burst out laughing. "I'm waiting."

He laughed, too, and climbed down from the rocks. They set off walking up the river again, but he didn't really look for anything to hunt.

He didn't want to hunt. He just wanted to talk to her.....and walk next to her like they might actually have come out here to spend time with each other.

"So what did you do with yourself all these years—besides wander around from Layer to Layer and Island to Island?" he asked. "Did you have any particular activity you did to keep yourself occupied?"

"I could ask you the same question. Did you do anything in Middleborough besides train, fight, and avoid looking at the local girls?"

The blood rushed to his cheeks and he laughed again. "Ouch."

"Did you really plan to spend the rest of your life in the Watch? Did you really plan to swear off having a family of your own?"

He shrugged. "I never really thought about it at all. My father did it. I guess I always thought I would do it, too. Middleborough always needed Watchmen. The town needed Watchmen a hell of a lot more than it needed more families. No one would be able to raise families at all without the Watch."

"So did you do anything in particular? Do Watchmen have interests and hobbies like real people?"

He chuckled. "Real people. That's a good one."

"You still haven't answered my question."

"You didn't answer mine, either," he pointed out.

She looked away and her smile slipped, but her cheeks didn't stop glowing. She really looked beautiful when she smiled like that. He never imagined she could come out of her shell this much.

Her eyes captivated him. He stopped walking and turned to face her so he could look at her straight on.

She didn't encourage him to keep going or tell him to go back to his hunting. She looked straight back up at him from inches away.

"Why do you ask about me looking at other girls?" he asked and took a step nearer. "You aren't jealous, are you?"

Her grin cracked a little wider. "What is there to be jealous of if you never look at anyone?"

"Besides, the Watch is finished. We aren't the Black Watch anymore as you keep pointing out so many times. Middleborough has been destroyed. I can marry, build a family, and live an imp life that Wesh says is so wonderful."

He stopped right in front of her—close enough to kiss her—but she turned away this time and kept walking.

"No one will ever build anything with me," she mumbled over her shoulder.

He hurried after her. "Why not? You might have been alone all this time, but you don't have to stay that way. You could....."

He broke off when he heard rustling in the bushes ahead.

Yann stepped around her and eased a little closer. He couldn't see what was in there. It was something alive—something he and the Watch could eat. He didn't need to know anything else.

Whatever it was migrated to his right. He wasn't having any luck with his spear, so he dropped it on the ground and raised his glaive instead.

He tracked sideways keeping pace with the rustling sound. The leaves trembled in the undergrowth.

The bushes ended at another big rock embedded in the riverbank. He stopped there and tensed every muscle. The creature couldn't go anywhere else without showing itself.

He clamped his hand around his glaive shaft and lifted it over his shoulder. Any second now....

The branches parted and another biturong blundered out of the bushes. It didn't see Yann and Eliska standing there. The creature walked right along the lower edge of the rock where it stuck out of the ground.

Yann hurled his glaive and impaled the creature through the torso. The blade severed the top half of the creature's back and bounced off the rock.

"Ha!" he gloated when the creature lay dead. "What did I tell you? Now you can go back to the Watch and crow to the others about how mighty I am."

She dissolved in laughter. "That biturong is definitely not big enough for all of them to share. The men would only end up fighting over it."

"Then you and I can eat it here and tell them that I missed."

She laughed again and beautiful color washed over her cheeks. "You're supposed to be self-sacrificing."

"I told you the Watch is finished. Isn't this enough to prove my devotion to you?"

"Selling out your fellow Watchmen? Not really."

He picked up his glaive, wiped the blade on the grass to clean off the blood, and picked up the biturong. "Anyway, it's better than nothing. We can at least stave off our hunger before we leave for wherever it is we're going to leave for."

He could have taken the biturong back to the Watch, but he didn't want to cut the walk short.

The other Watchmen would already assume he was out here flirting with her. He better make it count.

Chapter 19

Eliska didn't seem in any great hurry to get back to the Watch, either. Neither she nor Yann looked too hard for any other game.

They circled the rocks and returned to the river. Yann would have liked to sit down somewhere and get close to her, but walking turned out to be just as nice.

"Have you been in this part of the Ancestral Empire before?" he asked.

"A few times. It isn't that much different from a lot of other Islands. It's just bigger and has been around longer. That's why it has so many different kinds of people living here. Everyone migrates here for safety."

"Too bad it's so lawless," he remarked. "It would be perfect if there weren't so many Barbarians and thugs running around."

"The Barbarians have to make a living somehow."

"They don't have to do it that way."

"Yes, they do," she replied. "It's the only way they know how to do it. It's their culture. It isn't their fault."

"You only say that because you can defeat them. You might feel differently if they came close to killing you and everyone you care about."

She only smiled at him, but just then, they turned another corner and Yann heard a grunting noise first. A crested sailor hog broke through the nearby undergrowth.

The creature rooted its curved tusks into the soil plowing up a long furrow between the rocks. The hog kept stopping, grunting under its breath, and digging around whenever it found something interesting.

It either didn't see Yann and Eliska or it didn't realize they might pose a threat to it. It kept right on plowing as though they weren't there.

Yann dropped the biturong. He didn't care about it anymore. The hog would definitely be a prize worth taking back to the Watch.

He raised his glaive by the shaft. He would have to hit the hog right in the most vulnerable part of its chest. He would have to kill it with the very first shot before the thing turned on him and Eliska.

If he only injured it, it could charge and try to kill them both. They wouldn't be the first to meet that grisly fate.

The hog accommodated him by turning sideways. It presented its shoulder to him. It was a perfect shot.

He cocked back his arm to throw his glaive, but right then, Eliska stepped in front of him. She shot him a cruel grin over her shoulder, raised her staff, and fired at the hog.

A jet of white light erupted from the end of her staff and hit the hog exactly where Yann had been planning to kill it.

The creature exploded off its feet when the shot hit it. It let out a piercing, high-pitched shriek mixed with a furious roar.

Before Yann or Eliska could move, the creature burst out of its skin, swelled to ten times the size, and transformed into a Darkling looming over both of them.

This Darkling didn't get as big as some of the others Yann had seen in the Coil recently, but it was big enough to kill them both with ease.

Eliska tensed with her hands on her staff. She stayed in front of Yann and aimed her staff at the Darkling to kill it.

The creature roared at her in a voice of thunder. Tentacles slashed from its back and it bared a mouth full of fangs.

Three tentacles came at her from both sides. Yann started to lower his arm and took a step forward to her side. He rotated his glaive to one side to fight the Darkling hand to hand.

The creature's tentacles slashed the air. She fired her staff at them and severed each one where it joined with the monster's body.

They distracted her from seeing another two tentacles winding out of the creature at the same time.

She severed the third tentacle, and the next second, a fourth cracked her across the side of the head. It flattened her instantly.

She sprawled across the grass and her staff fell out of her hands. Her hair scattered across the grass. She must have been either stunned or knocked unconscious.

Before Yann could move, the Darkling's last tentacle spiraled out of nowhere, seized her by the ankle, and hurled her limp body aside.

She smashed into another boulder at the edge of the river and collapsed on the gravel beneath it.

The Darkling turned in her direction even though she wasn't moving anymore. The monster must have sensed that Yann didn't have any magic to fight it. She was the only threat here.

The thing rumbled deep inside its massive, misshapen body. It looked nothing like a hog anymore.

It lumbered toward her hissing and snaking its tentacles all over the place. Every instinct told Yann to charge over there and protect her the way she tried to protect him.

He wouldn't be able to protect her. If he got between her and the Darkling, it would kill him and then nothing would stop it from doing the same thing to her.

He reacted without thinking, raised his glaive over his shoulder again, and launched it at the Darkling with all his strength.

The glaive sang as it wobbled through the air and then dove headfirst into the side of the Darkling's head.

Yann rushed the thing even before he saw the effect of his throw. He sprang off the ground as high as he could leap, grabbed his glaive shaft, and let his own body weight carry him past the creature's yawning mouth.

He wrenched the glaive aside exactly the same way he killed the Barbarians. He let his weight fall against the shaft and the blade cracked the creature's skull in half.

He fell toward the grass on the creature's other side, tucked, and yanked his glaive free as he rolled away.

He somersaulted onto his knees and spun around with his glaive raised to meet the Darkling when it came after him again.

It didn't. It buckled on the spot and crumpled in on itself to become a hog again.

He crouched there panting hard until the creature stopped twitching and lay still. Blood poured from the crack in the side of its head. The hog didn't look right anymore with its head in the wrong shape.

Yann had to shake the tension out of his muscles before he could stand up. He stared down at the thing. It really was a hog. The Dark must have taken it when Eliska's magic hit it.

Thinking that reminded him of her. He shot the hog one last menacing glare over his shoulder and knelt down next to her.

He used one finger to comb the hair out of her face. She was out cold, but at least she was still breathing.

He sat down on one ankle, picked her up, and cradled her while he finished pushing the hair out of her face. "Eliska!" he whispered. "Eliska, can you hear me?"

She didn't respond right away. Yann wouldn't be able to heal whatever was wrong with her. He needed to take her back to Wesh.

He laid her back on the sod and put down his glaive. He made one quick survey of the spot before he made up his mind. He would have to leave his glaive, the hog, the biturong, and her staff behind while he carried her back to the Watch.

He didn't care about any of that as long as Wesh healed her. She was more important.

He bent down to scoop her up in her arms, but when he shoved his hands under her, she stirred.

She groaned and rolled away from him before she opened her eyes. She squirmed and then jolted upright in a flash.

She winced and her hand flew to her head. She swooned and her eyes lost focus for a second before she fell over again.

Yann eased a little closer and squeezed her shoulder. "Take it easy," he murmured. "You fell hard. Just lie down for a second until you feel better. Then I'll take you back to Wesh. He'll take care of you."

She whipped around fast and her eyes popped open when she saw him sitting next to her. "Yann......"

"You're okay," he told her. "The Darkling hit you and you crashed into the rock. Do you remember?"

Her eyes darted around....and she saw the hog.

She pushed herself up on her hand, stared at it, and then looked around everywhere else. Her gaze eventually came to rest on his glaive covered in blood.

"What happened.....to the Darkling?" she stammered.

"I killed it. I saw it coming after you, so I killed it with my glaive. It fell and turned back into the hog. How much do you remember from before you got hit? Maybe your fall affected your memory."

"I remember. I just....." She turned around and winced again. "You....you killed a Darkling?"

He opened his mouth to say something else. Then he realized. He really did kill a Darkling.

He didn't think at the time that he was doing anything special. He just wanted to protect her.

He shrugged it away and looked at the hog instead. "Well, I couldn't let it kill you, could I?" He frowned at her. "We should take you back to Wesh. You could have gotten more hurt than you realize."

She didn't respond right away. She kept looking back and forth between the hog, his glaive, and her staff lying over there where she dropped it when the Darkling first hit her.

Her silence was really starting to worry him. What if Wesh couldn't fix whatever was wrong with her?

Yann got ready to stand up. At least she would be able to walk back to the Watch.

Before he could move, she slipped her hand into his and squeezed.

He spun around in surprise and gaped at her in disbelief, but she didn't let go. She tightened her grip on his hand in one more quick squeeze....and then she burst into the biggest, most beautiful smile he'd ever seen.

"Thank you," she murmured. "I won't forget this."

He blinked at her trying to understand that she was really holding his hand. She was.

Her fingers felt small and vulnerable and soft in his, but they radiated warmth up his arm.

That rush of warmth carried a tremor of excitement with it. She was holding his hand. She took the first step.

He never would have dared to take her hand. He would have expected her to swat him away. Now she was the one doing it.

He couldn't move. He just sat there in shocked silence. The feeling overwhelmed him. He never dreamed taking a walk with her would end like this.

He stared into her shining face. She looked fine. Her eyes shone up at him with all the warmth and understanding with which she'd been smiling at him before the Darkling attacked.

He would have liked to kiss her right now, but he didn't want to spoil the moment. He didn't want to push her farther than she comfortably wanted to go on her own. Holding her hand was enough.

They sat like that for what felt like hours, but it couldn't have been more than a minute.

She finally gave him one last squeeze and pulled her hand away, but that minute changed things for him. It brought them closer than talking and joking around ever could.

"We should go back so I can tell everyone how mighty you are," she teased.

He laughed, and without discussing it further, they both stood up. "At least we'll have something to eat." He went over to the hog. "Would you mind carrying my glaive? I'll carry the spoils of war."

She laughed when she picked up her staff and then his glaive. She also picked up the biturong.

He rolled the hog onto its back and pulled out his knife to cut its head the rest of the way off. He needed to find any way to lighten the load for the trip back. The creature would be heavy enough to carry as it was.

"Wait a minute," Eliska told him.

"What's wrong?" he asked.

She put down the glaive and the biturong and approached the hog from the other side. "Let me help you."

"What are you going to do?" he asked. "Are you going to make it float and follow us the way the gypsies made those trunks follow us?"

"That wouldn't show off how mighty you are. Hold it up by the back legs."

"What are you going to do?"

"Just hold it up."

Yann heaved the hog off the ground by the back legs. It weighed a ton. He didn't look forward to carrying it back alone.

He was just about to suggest much more seriously that she did make it float.

Instead, she used her staff to strip the skin off and then gutted the creature right there on the grass.

The entrails blooped out onto the ground and left the remaining stripped carcass light enough for him to heft it onto his shoulder.

"Is that better?" she asked.

"Yes. Thank you."

She picked up the glaive, the staff, and the biturong again. The two of them started to wind their way back up the riverbank to where they left the Watch.

Yann balanced the hog carcass on his shoulder with one hand. He tried not to think about the fact that he was probably getting blood in his hair and down the side of his neck.

He started to hope she didn't tell the others about him killing the Darkling. He wanted this to stay between them.

He also didn't want the other Watchmen to give him a hard time about protecting her.

Would they think less of her because she needed an imp Watchman to save her life?

That didn't concern him as much as her reaction when she realized what he did. She held his hand. He wanted to keep that secret all to himself and never share it with anyone, not even his own father.

Right then, she slipped her hand into his again. He didn't notice her shift the biturong and the two weapons to her other hand—the one on the side away from Yann.

Her tiny hand slid into his and she squeezed. She didn't let go this time, either.

He looked up at her at the same time she looked up at him. She smiled and blushed.

"Don't think this changes anything between us," she told him.

He found himself grinning back at her. It changed everything. She didn't have to explain that to him.

Whatever direction he'd been hoping to take things with her on this walk, he never imagined they would go this far. He never thought he stood a chance in hell with her.

Now he felt pretty good about it. Now he knew things were going in some particular direction even if he didn't know what direction they were going.

Chapter 20

Yann didn't mention it when Eliska let go of his hand before they returned to the Watch. He let the subject drop and they re-entered the camp as if they'd never held hands at all.

Eliska couldn't decide why she wanted to hold his hand except that she liked him. He saved her life from a Darkling and even managed to kill it. That deserved something.

She didn't hold his hand to reward him, though. She actually wanted to get close to him. She just didn't know how.

She couldn't remember anyone ever saving her life before. She was always the one saving everyone else.

The Watchmen made an enormous fuss over the hog carcass. They all came back to life as if their circumstances never depressed them in the first place.

They laughed and ribbed Yann about killing it. He only blushed and laughed along with them. He didn't tell them how he actually killed it.

He kept looking at her on the side, but he also didn't tell Wesh about her getting hurt.

She saw Yann keeping an eye on her to make sure she was all right. She found it impossible to make eye contact with him, but knowing he cared enough to check felt like nothing she'd ever experienced in her life.

She wished now that she could do something more than just hold his hand. He was worth it—a lot more.

She resumed her former position sitting against the tree. The Watchmen did all the work of quartering the carcass and putting the meat on the spit to cook.

She skinned and gutted the biturong. Then they worked to cook that, too.

"We'll need to take as much food on our journey as we can," Yvan decided.

"This river looks pretty good," Omer pointed out. "We should stay near it. Then we won't have to go looking for game and water when we eventually need to go hunting again."

"No," Wesh interrupted. "We can't stay near the river. Whoever is following us will look for us here first. We should strike out away from this river and cut overland heading west."

The others glanced at Eliska. She didn't get involved in the conversation. She didn't want them to put her in charge.

She didn't see anything wrong with Wesh's suggestion. Staying near the river would be the easiest thing to do, so it would also be the most dangerous thing to do.

The group would more likely meet bandits and Barbarians near the river, but she didn't say that out loud.

She didn't say anything while everyone ate as much as they could possibly hold. Yann talked and joked with the others.

Bringing this meat back gave him a boost of confidence, but he didn't make a big deal about it. He just fell in with their casual banter as if someone else brought it back.

This little victory belonged to him alone. He didn't share it with anyone nor did he imply by any action that anything happened between him and Eliska.

The Watchmen stayed up talking late around the fire while Wesh and Yvan decided that the group would move out in the morning.

Eliska sat up against her tree and watched the firelight play on all their faces. She watched the interplay of relationships between all the men.

They knew each other so well. She'd never known anyone as well as they knew each other.

They eventually stretched out to sleep. Their eyes closed and their features softened.

Eliska would have liked to stay up and watch Yann sleep the way she did last night.

She wouldn't be able to do that a second night in a row. She already felt herself getting exhausted from staying up last night.

Watching him sleep would have been even more important now. She couldn't let anything happen to him—not after she went through all this to find him.

She shuddered at the thought of getting this close to anyone. The danger of getting hurt became unbearable, but she never considered walking away—not again.

Whatever danger getting close to him might pose, she had to risk it just to be near him.

It might come to nothing—whatever "it" was. He might die tomorrow and then she would wind up right back where she started.

She wouldn't wind up back where she started because he changed things for her. She would never go back to being the person who didn't care about anyone.

Whatever else happened to her in her life, she would never be able to forget him. He would haunt her forever.

She would spend the rest of her life knowing this was possible—feeling this way about someone—and knowing that someone might actually care enough to risk his life to save hers.

She eventually couldn't keep her eyes open any longer. The fire dragged her eyelids closed. She stretched out on the ground and fell asleep.

She woke up to sunbeams shining in her eyes. She squinted and then grimaced. Her head ached from yesterday.

She groaned and rubbed her palm across her eyebrow to work the pain out of her head, but it didn't work out too well.

She sat up and discovered Yann sitting up watching her.

Everyone else was already standing up, pacing around, checking their weapons, and studying the surroundings.

"You should have woken me up," she mumbled. "You shouldn't have waited."

"Are you going to talk to Wesh about getting hit by that Darkling?" Yann murmured under his breath. "I'm worried about you."

"You don't have to worry about me," she muttered. "I'll be fine."

"You aren't fine," he snapped in an undertone. "I'm not blind. If you don't talk to him, I will."

"Don't you dare." She picked up her staff. "Are we leaving?"

She got to her feet, but she lost her balance and had to hold onto the tree to stop herself from falling over.

"See what I mean?" Yann pointed out. "Just let him take a look at you."

She shook the stars out of her head, but she couldn't shake off the sick feeling in her stomach.

She didn't want to tell Yann how right he was. That Darkling hit her with something stronger than its tentacle. It weakened her at a magical level. She couldn't remember getting hit like that before—not in a way that affected her this much.

She pushed herself off the tree just as Yvan and Wesh came over with Omer. "We were thinking of moving out when you're ready, Eliska," Yvan began.

"I'm ready." She picked up her staff and turned around. "Let's go."

"Do you agree about heading west like I suggested?" Wesh asked.

"Of course. It's as good a plan as any."

He nodded and led the way to a line of stones crossing the river. The Watchmen fell behind him.

Yann kept narrowing his eyes at Eliska on the way over there. He would have drawn too much attention to her by constantly turning around to check on her, so she went in front.

She followed Vidal and Barsali across the stepping stones. Her head cleared the longer she walked.

The party climbed the nearby hills and came to a broad landscape full of similar hills winding away as far as the eye could see.

Wesh passed into the valleys where the group could travel more easily. The Watchmen walked in silence. They didn't have to stay as alert here.

Eliska checked the surroundings in her hand window, but she didn't see anything.

That on its own should have indicated something wrong. She'd never known any part of the Ancestral Empire to be this deserted.

She closed her hand so she wouldn't look at it anymore. She should just accept the blessing that no one was coming around to bother the party.

The group camped in the open that night and finished off the rest of their available food. No one mentioned where or how they would get any more.

No one spoke above a murmur that night. They definitely didn't talk about their circumstances.

Eliska woke up late again the second morning. The Watchmen's voices woke her up this time, so she didn't sleep as late as she might have.

She stiffened when she saw Yann talking to Wesh at a distance from the others. Yann better not be telling Wesh about her getting hurt.

The day began in silence and stayed that way. The pain in her head faded slightly, but it didn't go away entirely.

She found herself rubbing her eyes and temples every time the group stopped to rest.

Thirst became a serious problem by the second morning. None of the party had drunk more than a few handfuls from random streams since they left the river.

Wesh kept the lead. Vidal, Niyazi, and Barsali stayed behind him with the others following in a loose formation.

Yann always walked behind Eliska. She refused to turn around even to make eye contact with him.

Knowing he was worried about her started to grate on her nerves. She didn't want anyone worrying about her—ever.

By noon, the valley started to climb another set of hills. Wesh wound around a few more slopes and came out on the top.

The party could see everything from up here. The landscape spread away in all directions with a large, wooded river winding through another gentle valley right below this hill where the group stood.

The water flowing through the channel spiked Eliska's thirst off the charts. She needed water before she took another step.

She expected Wesh to lead the others down there. They must have been as thirsty as she was.

Wesh didn't go down there.

She stared down the hill at the water rolling over stones and around eddies....and then she realized. It wasn't normal water.

The angle of sunlight reflecting on its surface made the dark waves look black from this distance. She tried to look away, but she couldn't.

She couldn't tear her gaze away from that river no matter how hard she tried.

The water swirled and tumbled over itself in a sea of black. Waves and eddies of Darkness roiled and crested against each other.

The sight mesmerized her into a trance. She couldn't look away. She heard the others talking nearby and then someone shouted.

That voice came from a long way away. She couldn't understand what the person was saying....and then she felt herself falling....falling deep into that Darkness.....down there.....into that endless Darkness......

Chapter 21

Neils gasped when he saw the river. "Thank God! I'm dying of thirst! Let's go."
He started forward to walk down the hill toward the river not far away.

Wesh shot out a hand to stop him. "Don't go near it. Don't you see the water? It's a river of Dark magic. Don't even look at it if you can help it." He turned away. "We'll have to take another route."

Yann swallowed hard. His dry throat drove him insane. He needed water right now.

The rest of the party must have been suffering from the same thirst, but Wesh's authority won out over everything else.

Yann didn't see anything wrong with the river—except that what looked like water was actually some kind of flowing black Darkness alive with glistening waves and eddies.

Yann tore himself away to follow Wesh back down the hill up which the party just climbed.

Yvan, Rien, Niyazi, and Omer all turned away, too. Yann turned to follow them when Barsali's voice snapped Yann back to his senses real quick.

"Eliska?" Barsali asked. Then his voice spiked with tension and alarm. "Eliska—stop!"

Yann spun around and so did everyone else. Yann's world crumbled when he saw Eliska walking down the hill heading straight for the river.

"ELISKA!!" Yann roared and rushed over to intercept her.

Barsali got there first, planted himself in front of her, and tried to block her from getting to the river. "Eliska—wake up!" he bellowed. "Eliska—answer me!"

She didn't respond. She stared straight through him at nothing and kept walking down the hill.

He grabbed her by the shoulders, shook her, and kept snapping in her face until Yann and the others got there.

Yann yelled in her ear ordering her to stop, but she didn't respond to him, either. She didn't see or hear him.

Wesh tore Barsali out of the way and shoved in front of her. "Eliska!" Wesh roared. "Eliska, look at me!"

Nothing. Yann's blood ran cold. He couldn't even look.

Wesh took a step back to put some distance between him and her. He raised his hand in front of her face.

Before he could do anything, she vanished.

Everyone spun around looking for her everywhere. "There!" Barsali pointed straight at the river.

Eliska stood on a high rock over the widest flow. She wavered there for a second staring down into the Darkness exactly the way Wesh warned everyone not to.

Barsali, Yvan, and Wesh all bellowed, "ELISKA!!" at the same time, but it was too late. She stood too far away for any of them to get there in time. She must have magicked herself there to prevent Wesh from stopping her.

Wesh and the other Watchman sprinted for the river. Yann stood rooted to the spot. He couldn't move to save his own life.

His stomach plummeted into his shoes when she swayed one last time and then toppled off the rock into the river.

She didn't dive or even jump. She just lost her balance for no particular reason and plummeted into the churning flood.

The other Watchmen charged the rest of the way down the hill, up the bank, and tried to scramble onto the rocks, but she was already gone.

Yann's vantage point on the hill gave him a clear view of the river beyond the rock where she fell in. She wasn't there anymore.

She didn't bob to the surface, either. She stayed down.

He gulped down the sting of bile in his throat. He should have known that yesterday was too good to last.

He never would have guessed that she could be in more danger from the Dark than any of them. Why didn't he think of that before?

He had no reason to think the Darkling's blow damaged her. She acted normally—apart from the fact that her injury obviously still caused her pain.

He told himself a hundred times to tell Wesh about what happened and to ask Wesh to at least make sure she was okay.

Yann would never forgive himself for that and now it was too late. She was gone.

His eyes skimmed the river. She didn't come back up.

Barsali, Yvan, Wesh, and Omer clambered up the rock to where she'd just been standing.

They all looked down into the Darkness and saw everything that wasn't there.

Wesh looked away first and clamped his eyes shut. Yann really wished he could look away, too.

Some kind of sick horror made him stand there with his eyes plastered open. She couldn't really be gone—could she?

Rien, Vidal, Neils, and Niyazi spread out down the riverbank searching for any sign of her coming up for air. She didn't.

Barsali, Yvan, and Omer used the rock's height to search the whole landscape....and then everyone saw it at the same time.

Another figure rose out of some shadow on another rock across the river. Yann couldn't tell from here who or what the figure was.

The thing didn't have any arms, legs, or even a head that he could see. Was it another Darkling borne out of this Dark river?

Whatever it was couldn't have been there before. The whole Watch would have seen it. It seemed to grow out of the lichen and dirt clinging to the outcropping over there.

The men on the rock froze when they saw the figure across from them....and then it moved.

As soon as it moved, Yann realized it really was a person. It was a slender female wearing a full-length robe down to her feet.

Her dark brown hair hung straight down to her waist. Her hair and robe blended together in the sunshine and created the illusion that she didn't have arms, legs, head, or even any kind of body under that robe.

The next instant, she dove headfirst into the river. She dove with her arms outstretched. No one could mistake that movement for anything but a deliberate dive.

She dove straight in and plunged out of sight heading for the spot where Eliska disappeared.

The stranger vanished in exactly the same way. The Dark waves closed over her head and she didn't resurface, either.

None of the Watchmen breathed for at least a minute. Yvan, Wesh, Barsali, and Omer stood on the rock staring at the place where both young women went down.

The other Watchmen stood on the bank. They didn't search anymore. Eliska wouldn't come back from this.

The minutes dragged one after another. Now what were the Watchmen supposed to do?

Eliska got them to the Ancestral Empire. If they survived this at all, they would survive because of her. Did she know when she brought them here that she would meet her death here?

Yvan and Omer finally turned away, said something to Wesh and Barsali, and started climbing down the rock.

Yvan and Omer rejoined the others before Wesh and Barsali climbed down.

Barsali waited until last. He kept standing there staring into the Darkness until Yvan called up and ordered him to come down.

The men gathered on the bank shaking their heads. Rien grimaced and turned away first.

Yann suffered another wave of nausea when his father waved the Watchmen to return to the hill where they first spotted the river.

As soon as Yvan got up here, he would order Yann to walk away. He would have to accept that Eliska was never going to come back. Could he really do that?

All the Watchmen turned their backs on the river. It really was over.

They started to walk away, but right at that moment, a splash at the river's edge made everyone spin around.

They rushed forward and then drew back when the stranger dragged Eliska's body out of the river.

Yann shot down the hill running his hardest to get there, but once he did, there was nothing to do but stand with the others while the stranger hauled Eliska onto the grass.

Black sludge covered both of them. It ran off their skin, clothes, and hair in thick, gloopy rivulets. It couldn't be water.

Eliska lay unconscious on the grass, but she was still breathing.

The stranger crouched there like some kind of wild animal. Dark, haunted eyes glared up at the Watchmen from the girl's face smeared with the same black goo.

She hissed and snarled at them through her teeth. Then she burst into feral shrieks, roars, and maniacal laughter.

Wesh completely ignored her and rushed over to Eliska. "Pick her up!" he snapped at the Watchmen. "Pick her up and carry her as far away from the river as possible. Hurry!"

Yann wound up near Eliska's hips. Barsali and Niyazi got on either side of her shoulders and heaved her off the ground by her cloak.

Yann and Neils did the same thing with her pants. Yann hesitated to touch the black stuff. It saturated every inch of her clothes and hair, but he had to help her in whatever small way he could.

Yvan and Rien took hold of Eliska's shirt near her ribs. Wesh and Vidal grabbed her legs.

All the men picked her up and hiked up the hill with her. "Keep going!" Wesh ordered. "The river will cast its spell on her even here. Get her down to one of the other streams. Hurry!"

Yann stumbled under her weight even though she didn't weigh that much. Her head lolled all the way back. No one lifted it.

The effort strained every muscle fiber, but he refused to put her down. He would have carried her by himself if he thought it would help her.

Wesh directed them down a bunch of different valley turnings before he found a stream he liked.

"Put her down here," he ordered. "Bring water. One of you light a fire. Get her cleaned up."

Yann stood looking down at her for a minute. He might have spent the rest of his life looking down at her, but Omer bumped his shoulder and motioned Yann away.

The two of them went into the nearby trees to gather wood for a fire. They both stopped dead when they saw the strange girl hanging around.

The black stuff dripping off her made her look even more feral and inhuman if that was possible. She crouched in the trees eyeing everyone.

She kept shrieking, snarling, and muttering to herself even when the Watchmen didn't look at her. She scuttled in a crouch through the trees to skirt their camp. She never came any closer.

Rien pulled out his broken longsword, rushed her, and stabbed it at her. "Haa!" he yelled. "Get out of here! Leave us alone!"

"Rien!" Yvan snapped from the fire. "Leave her alone. She just saved Eliska—if Eliska can be saved."

"She's an animal!" Rien growled.

Yvan dropped his voice into his chest. "I said leave her alone. Make yourself useful by bringing some water up here."

Rien backed away from the strange girl. She didn't leave.

Yann kept an eye on her while he and Omer scavenged the area for as much firewood as they could find. They formed a large stack next to Wesh.

He spent two hours cleaning all the black stuff out of Eliska's hair and clothes. He stripped her down to her underwear, tore a piece of cloth off his own shirt to scrub as much of the stuff off her as he could, and pulled off his tunic to cover her.

He pointed to her pile of filthy clothes. "You men clean her clothes while I see if I can bring her back. We may have already lost her."

"What is that stuff?" Yann asked.

Wesh shook his head over the fire while he wrung out his dirty rag. "It's pure Darkness made solid. The Coil must be becoming destabilizing even more than we thought if the Darkness is invading the Ancestral Empire this far inland."

"What does that mean?" Yvan asked.

"It means the Darkness will fracture the Ancestral Empire along that river line. It means the Ancestral Empire will fall. We just don't know when."

"Then....it could happen soon?" Omer asked. "It could happen....like...now?"

"Not now. That river is too big. It must have been building for a long time, which means it could keep building for a long time to come before the Island collapses. We don't know. We have to take care of Eliska right now. This is more important."

No one said anything else after that. Yann, Omer, and Neils got to work cleaning Eliska's clothes.

The men didn't have a pot to boil water in, so they found a few flat rocks on the nearby hillsides, heated them in the fire, and then used sticks to lower them into some hollows the men found in the rocks along the streambed.

They boiled water that way and beat out the clothes on the rocks.

The black ooze took a long, long time to wash out. It stuck to every surface with unnatural power.

Yann found himself obsessively washing the stuff off his own hands. He didn't want it to poison him, too.

The men eventually spread Eliska's clothes on sticks over the fire to dry. By that time, Vidal and Niyazi showed up with another long-tailed gar that they cooked for the whole Watch to eat.

Wesh stayed by Eliska's side the whole time. After Yann and the others finished their work, they just had to sit around and wait to see what happened.

Wesh kept laying hands on different parts of Eliska's body and sending currents of magic through her.

Yann didn't see any of Wesh's efforts having any effect—none at all. She remained as unconscious as ever.

Chapter 22

Barsali stood up and dusted off his hands. The party had already demolished what was left of the long-tailed gar. It didn't go very far compared to a hog.

"I'm going to take a look around," he announced. "I'll see if there's another route west that we can take to avoid that river."

"Good idea," Yvan replied. "The rest of you don't need to keep sitting around. Patrol the area and establish a perimeter in case someone comes."

Omer and Niyazi both got to their feet. Rien licked the last of the gar juice off his fingers while he took a few more bites of meat off the bone.

Neils and Vidal were still eating, too. A few scraps still clung to the gar skeleton dangling from the spit.

Wesh didn't turn away from Eliska even once. Yvan took off his jacket, spread it on the grass next to Wesh, and put Wesh's portion of the meat on top of the jacket until Wesh was ready to eat it.

No one disturbed Wesh's work. Yann didn't want to watch anymore. Nothing Wesh did made any difference.

Yann got ready to stand up and go on patrol with the others. Anything was better than sitting here doing nothing.

Just then, Rien shifted around on his seat and flung what was left of his bone in the wild girl's direction.

She kept lurking around the edge of the men's camp. Her occasional muttering and snarling drifted to their ears.

"Here! You can have that!" Rien yelled to her.

The bone landed in a pile of leaf debris under the trees. The girl launched herself at the bone, scrambled in the litter to pick it up, and attacked the leftover meat with her teeth.

"What the hell are you doing?!" Yvan snapped.

Rien looked up. "What? I thought she might be hungry."

"So you feed her like an animal—after she just pulled Eliska out of that river?" Yvan smacked his lips and turned to Wesh's portion of the food. "Now Wesh will have to go short because of you."

"Don't," Neils interrupted. "She can have what's left of mine."

He got up, pulled a bunch of leaves from a nearby tree, and plastered them together into a makeshift plate under what little was left of his food.

"Take mine, too." Vidal handed his food up to Neils. "She looks like she needs it more than we do."

Neils added it to his own portion, crossed the bank, and approached the wild girl.

She scampered away into the trees to get away from him. He stopped and held out the leaves with the meat and bones sitting on top.

"Do you want this?" he called. "You can have it with our thanks. Take it."

He waited, but she bared her teeth and hissed at him. She refused to come any closer.

He finally gave it up, laid the leaf plate on the ground inside the trees, and walked back to the fire.

She crept out as soon as he put a safe distance between them. She advanced slowly and then darted out, snatched the plate, and took off with it. She vanished into the undergrowth.

"Good thinking," Rien remarked. "Now we'll never have to see her again."

"What the hell is wrong with you?!" Yvan snapped again. "Is it absolutely necessary that you be as hateful as you can to everyone?"

"I'm not hateful to everyone. I was trying to be nice to her." Rien wiped his hands on his pants. "I don't see what the problem is. It isn't like we want her hanging around keeping us awake all night with her noise."

"Just keep your mouth shut!" Yvan snapped. "Don't let me hear another word out of you—ever."

"You mean....." Rien faltered. "You mean—like—ever?"

"Not until I tell you to. Don't speak unless I ask you a direct question. Understand?"

Rien made a face and looked away, but he didn't say anything.

He stood up and then Vidal did the same thing. The men divided themselves into pairs and headed off in different directions.

Yann should have gone with them, but he saw this one chance to talk to Wesh while no one else was around.

Yvan still sat there next to Wesh. He would hear everything, but Yann just had to bite the bullet and take the consequences.

He waited for the men to leave and then cleared his throat with difficulty. "Um....Wesh?"

"What is it, my boy?" Wesh muttered without looking up.

Yann summoned all his courage and blurted out, "I think I made a terrible mistake."

Yvan's head shot up exactly the way Yann knew it would, but he couldn't stop now. He had to get this out if it would help Eliska at all.

Wesh looked up for the first time, too. "What did you do?"

Yann poured out the whole story, including everything that happened after he killed the Darkling.

He only left out the part about him flirting with her and then holding hands with her afterward.

He sensed his father sitting there and listening through the whole sorry recital. Yann felt himself explaining all of this to his father more than Wesh—as if anything could explain such a colossal lapse in judgment.

What had Yann been thinking by keeping something so important to himself? He never would have dreamed of keeping an injury like that from his father if it happened to one of the Watchmen.

"I should have told you," he finally stammered. "Her head hurt for two days after that. I wanted her to tell you, but she said not to. I should have.....and now this.....That river did something to her....didn't it?"

Wesh slumped and went back to bending over her. "I don't think it made any difference, my dear boy, if that makes you feel any better," he muttered. "Eliska's power makes her especially susceptible to the Dark. The river would have affected her the same way even if she never got hurt."

"But you said she shuns the Dark," Yann blurted out. "You said she had no affinity for it."

"She does and I never said she had an affinity for it. She has unbelievable power. The Dark twists that power more than it would twist anyone else in the same situation. If you or your father fell into that river, I doubt it would affect you much at all. It might even spit you out unhurt onto the bank. It's different for her."

"So....." Yann gazed down at Eliska's still face. "You don't think the Darkling inflicted any kind of injury on her?"

"If it did, it was purely a physical injury." Wesh laid his hand on her forehead. "I'm not sensing any damage to her skull or her brain. She got a headache from landing so hard. That's all. She would have been fine in a few days—and she would have responded to the river the same way even if she didn't get hurt beforehand."

Yann shook his head. He didn't want to accept that.

If that was true, then he really couldn't do anything to help her.

He wanted so badly to believe that it would help her. He hoped and prayed that telling Wesh the truth would somehow give Wesh the ammunition he needed to drive the Darkness out of her and bring her back.

"Go on patrol, son," Yvan interrupted. "Take your mind off it for a while."

Yann got up and stumbled away in a daze. He almost tripped over the wild girl on his way to join Omer and Barsali.

She sprang in front of him, contorted in strange body positions, and yowled at him. She twisted her face into insane expressions.

He tried to walk around her, but she only leapt in front of him a second time and yelled at him even louder.

She startled him into waking up enough to realize where he was—and where she was.

She no longer scuttled around under the trees where she'd been when Neils gave her that food. She'd moved.

He tried to walk away from her a second time. She rushed in front of him for the third time, got in his face, and went through the same sequence of grimaces, disgusting expressions, and incomprehensible shrieks, snarls, and howls.

Yann froze in place trying to decide what to do, but just then, Vidal, Rien, and Niyazi came back.

Rien pulled his sword on her again and slashed it at her. "Get out of here, you freak!" he bellowed. "Go on! Get out of here!"

Niyazi pulled Yann away. "Did she attack you, boy?"

"No, it sounded like she was trying to talk to me."

"She isn't trying to talk to anyone," Rien snarled and stabbed his weapon at her again. "Go on! Get out of here! Be off!"

She retreated, but not without baring her teeth and snarling at him plenty of times.

The three men must have been on their way back from patrolling. They returned to the fire and took Yann with them.

Barsali, Neils, and Omer returned a few minutes later. Yann had no other option than to sit down with them where he'd been sitting before.

"Everything looks quiet out there," Barsali reported. "We're the only people around."

"Except for *her,*" Rien muttered. "If she doesn't leave, I swear I'll have to...."

He broke off when the girl crept right into their camp.

She circled a few times and inched closer each time. She finally worked her way around to Wesh's side of the group and approached nearer to Eliska.

"Get away from here, you filthy wretch!" Rien barked. He picked up a stone from the ground and winged it at the girl.

Yvan shot out a hand and snatched his wrist, but he sent the rock flying before Yvan could stop him. "What did I tell you about keeping your mouth shut?" Yvan snapped. "I'll be driving *you* out of camp if you make another sound."

The rock missed the girl and landed in the undergrowth behind her. She didn't look at it and she didn't back off. She showed no sign that she even understood that he'd thrown a rock at her.

She crouched there and then gamboled a little closer to Eliska.

"Should we stop her?" Barsali asked. "What if she's a Darkling?"

"She isn't dangerous—not to Eliska," Wesh replied. "She wouldn't have saved Eliska like that if she was."

"But how could she survive that river if she isn't a Darkling?" Neils asked.

"Maybe she doesn't have magic, either," Yann suggested.

Wesh looked up and studied the wild girl. "Yes, she does. She has huge magic. She's almost as strong as Eliska."

"Then how did she survive?" Yann asked. "The river doesn't seem to have affected her at all."

"We don't know what this girl was like before," Wesh replied. "She could have been perfectly normal and the river drove her insane."

"Then why isn't she unconscious the way Eliska is?" Vidal asked.

"The Dark affects everyone differently." Wesh went back to his work. "I don't know who this girl is, but from the way she's acting, I'd say she's as worried about Eliska as we are."

Chapter 23

E liska opened her eyes and stared up at blue sky above her head. Tree leaves swayed at the ends of branches up there.

She glanced around and froze when she saw Yann sitting next to her.

He smiled down at her, but his lips kept twisting all the wrong ways. "Hello," he murmured.

She opened her mouth to say something—and stopped. She picked up her head and looked around.

They were alone. She lay on the ground with her cloak draped over her. Wesh lay asleep in the grass nearby, but it was the middle of the afternoon.

She frowned at the surroundings. They sat at the edge of a small stream. She frowned even more when she recognized it. "Um...where are we?"

"We're somewhere in the Ancestral Empire," Yann replied. "Do you remember the Dark river?"

She furrowed her brow. "I remember it, but...."

A shriek startled her into sitting the rest of the way up. She grabbed her cloak to hold onto it.

The noise came from some kind of creature at the edge of the trees. It took Eliska a minute to register that it was a girl about her own age.

This girl looked nothing like a girl. She wore a filthy dress saturated with some kind of black tar. No one could see what pattern the dress had been originally.

The same thick, black sludge clung to her hair, skin, and hands. She lurked in a crouch under the tree branches across the area.

The Watchmen must have been camping here for a few days now. They'd trampled the whole stream bank. Their tracks led off in multiple directions, but none of the men were here now, not even Yvan.

"You fell into the river," Yann told her. "It cast a spell on you. You went out of your mind and walked straight into it. You even used your magic to stop us from saving you. That girl pulled you out. We don't know who she is or how she did it. She's been hanging around watching us take care of you ever since. She won't go away no matter what anyone does to try to drive her off."

Eliska stared at the wild girl. The wild girl only made fleeting eye contact with Eliska before the girl went back to shrieking, snarling, and pawing her way through the bushes.

Eliska gulped as the puzzle pieces snapped into place. She remembered the Dark river. She didn't remember anything after that.

"How long have I been out?" she husked.

"Three days," Yann replied. "Wesh has been working on you. He told us last night that you were coming out of it and that you were just asleep now. You were out cold the rest of the time."

Her hand flew to her head and she groaned. "Three days! We could have gotten ambushed in that time."

"No one wanted to leave while you were in danger."

She glanced at him and saw him gazing at her with an expression wrenched with misery.

"I'm so sorry, Eliska," he croaked. "I should have told Wesh sooner that you got hurt. He said it didn't matter, but I still should have told him. I never should have taken the chance that something like that would weaken you."

She stretched out her hand to take his and she opened her mouth to say something, but right then, Vidal came back from somewhere.

She yanked her hand away before he saw her about to take hold of Yann's.

"Well, look who's alive and well," Vidal exclaimed and collapsed on the grass. "We didn't think you'd wake up so soon. Are you hungry? Neils caught another hog."

Vidal's voice woke up Wesh. He lifted his head and frowned. "Huh?" Then he saw Eliska sitting up.

"My dear!" he exclaimed. "You woke up early. I didn't expect you to."

"Thank you for taking care of me," she replied. "I don't know what to say except that I'm sorry I slowed everyone down."

"Never mind, never mind." He scooted over and started touching her on the shoulder, on the head, and on the back.

She felt him probing his magic into her and checking her the way he would have checked her for injuries.

She tolerated it. She never would have expected any of these men to go to so much trouble over her. She definitely didn't expect them to delay their travels for three whole days because they were worried about her.

Yann looked away and straightened his expression. Whatever might have passed between them evaporated when the other Watchmen returned.

They gathered around the fire while Neils skinned and gutted his hog.

He grinned at her. "We've been doing things the old-fashioned way. Wesh is useless when it comes to all this outdoor stuff."

"I was a little preoccupied," Wesh fired back. "I'm not completely useless."

"Do you know how to skin and gut an animal with magic the way Eliska does?" Niyazi asked.

Wesh squirmed. "Well...no....but I'm sure I could figure it out."

Neils held up his hands and leaned away from the hog. "Here. Let's see you give it a shot."

Wesh looked away. "Another time, perhaps."

The others laughed at him. Their interaction had become so much more casual and familiar than Eliska remembered it.

No one made a big commotion about her waking up. They went about their business as if she'd only just woken up from a nap.

The wild girl kept interrupting their conversation at random intervals. The Watchmen ignored her, too—right up until the moment when Neils started to divide the cooked meat.

Vidal got to his feet, gathered a bunch of leaves to form a bowl, and Neils deposited a portion of the meat into Vidal's hands.

He carried the meat out into the trees, laid it on a bare patch of ground, and left it there. The wild girl waited for him to leave before she crept out of the undergrowth, snatched the bowl, and took the food deeper into the bushes.

She sat on her haunches and devoured it in wolfish bites.

"What is she?" Eliska asked.

"We don't know," Wesh replied. "She doesn't speak any language that we can understand."

"She doesn't speak any language at all," Rien added. "She's a wild animal. She only hangs around for the food."

"You know that isn't true," Wesh replied and turned back to Eliska. "She keeps coming into camp every now and then to check on you.....and she keeps trying to talk to Yann."

"He's the only person she does try to talk to," Barsali added.

Eliska looked back and forth between the men and the girl. "That's strange. I wonder why she's so interested in me."

"Maybe she's just worried about you falling into the river," Wesh suggested. "She rescued you."

"But why?" Eliska asked. "I sense that she has great magic. She could have gotten herself killed by going into that river."

"I sensed the same thing," Wesh replied. "I was wondering if you could tell us why she did it."

She spun around to stare at him. "Me?! What makes you think I know why she did it?"

"I wondered if you knew her—if you recognized her from somewhere. I wondered if she remembered you from your wanderings and decided to save you for something you might once have done for her—or something like that."

Eliska stared across the clearing. "I don't recognize her. I don't think I've ever seen her before. I think I would remember her if I had."

"You might not remember her if she was sane before," Niyazi pointed out. "She could have been intelligent, graceful, and beautiful the last time you saw her."

"Which explains why she keeps trying to talk to Yann," Vidal finished and the Watchmen laughed.

"That's enough," Yvan snapped.

The Watchmen finished snickering over their joke. Yann looked away. They must have been giving him a hard time for the last three days about the wild girl trying to talk to him.

"If I had to guess, I would say she understands the connection between Yann and Eliska," Wesh suggested. "The two of you were under the river for a long time before she pulled you out. She may have sensed something then, so she may be trying to tell him something about your condition."

Eliska looked down at her hands. She still felt numb all over. "She can't tell us, so I guess we'll never know."

"Maybe she'll leave us alone as soon as we move on and stop feeding her," Rien chimed in.

"We'll keep feeding her as long as she hangs around," Yvan decided. "If she's that out of her mind, she'll probably forget about us long before we forget about her."

"Not if there's food involved," Neils pointed out. "She looks pretty hungry to me."

Eliska found herself studying the wild girl. The girl fascinated Eliska for some reason.

Eliska spent a few years of her early childhood tagging after other travelers and eating whatever scraps they threw her or trash they left behind.

She understood that kind of madness. She saw herself reflected in that girl out there—a girl driven insane by loneliness, confusion, and desperation.

Eliska didn't tell the Watchmen that. She didn't recognize the girl and yet Eliska recognized everything about the girl.

That girl out there was a mirror reflection of Eliska herself. That girl could have been a magical projection of Eliska's memories. Did the Dark river create this shade to haunt Eliska with memories from her past?

She didn't tell Wesh, either. She didn't want the Watchmen to know about that.

The girl's howls, snarls, and insane shrieks confirmed the truth. She wasn't Eliska.

Eliska never made sounds like that. She stayed silent for years and never spoke to anyone. She never sank that far into the realm of lunacy. She came close a few times, but not quite.

Neils served her with her share of the food. She didn't have to join in the conversation. The next time she looked up, she didn't see the wild girl at all.

Eliska suffered a pang of both relief and longing. She didn't want the wild girl to just evaporate into the shadows. At the same time, the wild girl haunted Eliska in terrifying ways.

She didn't want to see that picture of herself right in front of her—the picture of just how far she'd strayed from her own sanity.

"We'll stay here another day while Eliska regains her strength," Yvan was saying. "Save some of the hog meat for our travels or get another one before we leave. We can work our way north to get past the Dark river before we cut west again."

"We don't have to stay," Eliska replied. "I feel strong enough to travel."

"I don't think that's a good idea," Omer told her.

"Don't push it," Barsali added. "You might feel fine sitting here eating your food. Hiking across country all day will be much harder."

"You'll need more strength than just hiking across country," Wesh chimed in. "That river is cutting straight through the Ancestral Empire. If that river made it this far inland, other Dark forces could be at large in this Island. You'll need all your power to fight them."

"We already know they're here," Yann pointed out. "We've seen them elsewhere besides the river."

She couldn't look up at him. So he must have told the others about the Darkling attacking her.

She regretted asking him to keep it a secret. That wasn't fair to him.

She shouldn't have hesitated to tell Wesh herself. She should have confided in him.

Wesh and Yvan both deserved to know about any Darklings this deep inside the Ancestral Empire. They needed that information to plan the group's course and strategy.

She let the whole group down by keeping that to herself.

Chapter 24

Eliska woke up first the next morning, went hunting for the group's breakfast, and had another biturong on the spit by the time the men woke up. She didn't want them to eat all the food before they left on their journey.

"How do you feel this morning, my dear?" Wesh asked. "Do you still feel strong enough to travel?"

"Yes, I feel fine. I don't want us to stay here any longer than we have to just because of....."

She broke off when he put his hand on her head again. She stiffened that someone was touching her this much, but she didn't protest.

She already knew he wouldn't find anything. She didn't ask how he healed her from the river's Darkness. It must have cost him a lot if it took three days.

The wild girl didn't make her appearance while the group ate. "Maybe she found another source of supply," Rien suggested.

"Maybe she found someone else to follow," Vidal suggested.

"Maybe she only stuck around until she saw that Eliska fully recovered," Wesh finished. "Now she sees that Eliska is fine, so the girl left."

Eliska surveyed the surrounding woods. She couldn't decide if she was happy or not about the girl being gone.

It might be kind of nice to have another girl around. Eliska wouldn't have chosen an insane, wild creature with black goo all over her as the most ideal companion, but anything was better than nothing.

She pushed that thought away. That wild girl was no companion. She couldn't even hold a conversation.

The party finished eating and headed up the valleys at a right angle to the direction Wesh had been going four days ago. Eliska cringed when she thought about the men waiting that long just for her to get back on her feet.

The party hiked half the day before Niyazi turned around. "There she is. She's following us."

Everyone stopped and stared at the wild girl hovering in the trees at a distance behind the group.

"What the hell does she want now?" Rien muttered.

"It can't be food," Omer pointed out. "She missed breakfast."

"She isn't bothering anyone." Yvan turned away and started walking again. "Leave her alone."

"Hey!" Rien yelled after him. "How much longer do we have to put up with this?"

"I don't see her attacking you," Yvan replied over his shoulder. "If she poses a threat to your life, then we'll talk about doing something about it."

Rien muttered a string of curses, but he made sure to do it quietly so the Watch Commander didn't hear him—not that Yvan didn't already know Rien's opinion.

The others set off heading north again. Eliska checked over her shoulder every now and then. The wild girl stayed the same distance behind them.

When the group stopped, she stopped. When the group started forward again, she started forward to keep pace with them.

Eliska wasn't the only one who kept looking. She didn't understand Rien's pathological aversion to everything bizarre and out-of-the-ordinary about the Coil, but the wild girl's presence was starting to unnerve Eliska, too.

What if the girl did turn out to be dangerous? She would have done something by now if she had been.

Was she following the group on the Voyant's behalf? Why not attack if that was the case—if all these other attacks really came from the Voyant?

Wouldn't the girl conceal her presence to hide the fact that the Voyant was surveilling the Watch? That would have been better than coming right out in the open where the Watchmen could see her.

The group stopped by a different stream at noon. The wild girl halted a few dozen yards away and didn't come any closer, not even to get water.

"She's a tough old bird. I'll give her that much," Niyazi remarked. "She's holding up better than we are."

Eliska checked her diagram of the Island on her Coil projection. "We've gone far enough north. We can start cutting westward again."

"What's out there?" Yann asked.

"We're leaving the stream system behind and heading back into the open grassland." She revolved a blown-up diagram of the Ancestral Empire in her palm. "There's another river twenty miles due west of here. We can head for that."

"Is it a Dark river or a regular one?" Barsali asked.

She smiled at him. "It's a normal one. No Darkness this time."

He looked away. "Let's keep it that way."

She studied her diagram a little more closely. "Wesh is right. That one is the only Dark river in this Island, but it's growing in strength. It will start to fork and fracture soon. Then it will tear the Island apart."

Yvan stood up. "Let's get past it, then."

Eliska cast one last glance at the wild girl. Would she split off, now that the group was turning in a different direction? Eliska didn't believe that.

The wild girl would keep hanging around to haunt the group. Maybe that's why Rien didn't like her. Maybe she represented something he'd rather forget.

The group climbed out of the hills, crossed a few more streams, and entered the grasslands. The flat countryside made traveling easier.

The party walked single file. Whoever walked in front trampled the grass and made it easier for everyone walking behind him.

The flat, featureless landscape lulled Eliska back into a mindless daze—or maybe her recent experiences made her dull and slow.

She followed whoever happened to be in front of her at the time. She didn't have to look where she was going.

She woke up real quick when Wesh, Yvan, Omer, and Barsali all stopped walking. The others gathered around.

Silence fell over the group when they saw a single person crossing the countryside in front of them.

A ridge of swells divided this part of the grassland from whatever lay beyond it—probably more grasslands.

This figure walked perpendicular to the group's route. The stranger headed east and south—toward the Dark river. The figure would have crossed their path if everyone kept going in the same direction.

Rien shifted his hand to his weapon and hissed through his teeth. "Barbarians!"

"That's impossible," Wesh countered. "Barbarians don't travel alone."

"What is he doing out here, then?" Yvan frowned at the figure. "He doesn't look like the same kind of Barbarian."

"He isn't." Eliska started forward to intercept the guy.

He saw her coming and stopped on top of the swell to wait for her. He turned to face the group and she got a much better look at him as she got closer.

He wore unmistakable Barbarian clothing, but his black leather pants, black leather vest, and the leather gauntlets laced around his forearms didn't have any spikes or studs.

He didn't shave his head or arrange his hair in spikes sticking up. He had dirty blonde hair that hung down his back in tiny braids that had matted into dreadlocks.

His vest lay open to reveal countless tattoos covering his muscular arms, chest, and stomach. The designs even crawled up the side of his neck and disappeared on his back under the armholes of his vest.

He stood taller than Barsali and twice as bulky, but not as tall as the Barbarians who attacked the Watch the first time.

Everything about this man had matured except his face. He still had the boyish freshness of youth despite his size.

He carried a massive battle axe slung across his back. A huge, spiked club hung from a thong on the right side of his belt. A machete-like blade hung on his left side with a leather strap anchoring it above his knee.

He wore a collection of crude decorations such as beads, shells, and colored stones dangling from different parts of his hair and clothing. He wore no other jewelry—not the fancy metal jewelry like the stolen loot most Barbarians wore.

He stood perfectly still with a neutral expression and he didn't react when Eliska hustled up to him panting from the climb.

The grass rustled when the Watchmen stopped behind her back. Were they drawing their weapons on this man?

She opened her mouth more than once trying to decide what to say. "Um....hello....." she began.

The stranger bent over from the waist and bowed once before he straightened up. He shot a flinty glance behind her. She could just imagine what he was seeing back there.

"Um....." she began again. "I'm Eliska....and these men belong to the....."

"If you think you're going to attack us, you can forget about it," Rien blurted out. "Keep moving and don't even think about coming near us again."

Eliska spun around to confront the Watch. "He's not a Barbarian—not that kind."

"Of course he is," Omer countered. "Look at him."

"He's a Servant," Eliska told him. "They wander alone in service to humanity. They're healers and holy men...."

"Like hell," Rien snarled. "A Barbarian is a Barbarian."

"The Servants are different. They don't cut their hair and they take a vow of silence and service." She turned around to face the guy. "Show them."

He went through a slow, lengthy process of taking off his axe, laying it aside, and then removing three leather bags hanging across his body.

He stacked everything on the grass and pulled off his vest. He looked even bigger without it. A carpet of complicated tattoos covered the deep indentations of his muscles.

He left his club and his blade hanging from his belt. He could have squashed every man of the Watch in seconds with either weapon.

"Do you see this?" Eliska pointed to the center of his chest and traced the pattern to both sides. "All the Servants get this design when they take their vow. He's a priest-wanderer with powerful healing magic. He's forsaken the Barbarian way to dedicate himself to service and healing of all humanity. They have strict rules only to use their magic and any violence to defend their own lives and the lives of others. There's no way he could belong to the group that attacked you earlier."

"He sure looks like a Barbarian," Neils remarked. "Who cares what his hair looks like? Look at his weapons."

"His mission is to defend the helpless, heal the sick and injured, and to serve anyone who needs help. He can help us." She turned around to face the guy. "Please excuse them. They've never been out in the Coil before. They don't understand."

He shut his eyes and bowed his head once before he went back to scrutinizing everyone with hard, piercing blue eyes.

"What's wrong with him?" Niyazi asked. "Why doesn't he speak for himself?"

"I told you. He's taken a vow of silence."

"Then what good is he to us?" Omer asked. "He can't help us if he can't tell us when danger is coming."

"Who the hell cares if he talks or not?" Rien interjected. "We don't need any Barbarian anywhere near us."

Rien rushed the stranger before anyone realized what he going to do. Neils and Yann both lunged for him to stop him, but Rien charged too fast.

He had drawn both his blades while Eliska talked to the Barbarian Servant. Now Rien raised both weapons to strike.

He would have hacked the Barbarian to the ground, but Eliska dove in front of him.

She sidestepped between Rien and the Barbarian, turned her back to the stranger, and grabbed her staff in both hands.

She thrust the long edge of the shaft at Rien and nailed him hard with a brutal thump of magic. She hit him square in the chest and sent him flying backward. He landed on his back on the ground and didn't move again.

Vidal and Omer rushed over to him, but they didn't pick him up. Eliska stayed where she was fighting down rising fury.

She heard her voice shaking in spite of her best efforts to control herself. "If any of you raises a finger against this man again, I swear I'll kill you," she snarled. "I told you he can help us. He's one of the few people in the whole Coil who can help us. If you can't accept help from him, you don't deserve to live out here."

She forced herself to stop talking before she said something she really regretted. Her whole body trembled with rage.

The man behind her didn't move or speak. He never once made a move to touch his weapons.

Omer squatted down and touched Rien's shoulder. That movement snapped Eliska back to reality. She might have overreacted and hit Rien too hard.

All the Watchmen got out of her way when she walked forward, planted the end of her staff on Rien's chest, and healed the injuries she just inflicted on him. She didn't stop until she knew he'd be okay—as soon as he regained consciousness.

None of the Watchmen said a word until she finished. She took a deep shuddering breath to steady herself before she returned to the Barbarian.

"Please accept my apologies," she blurted out. "I'm very sorry about that on behalf of everyone here. He doesn't understand. The Barbarians attacked this party a few days ago—and these men have been stranded in the Coil ever since Darklings destroyed their town." She pointed to the south in the direction he'd been going. "You don't want to go there. There's a Dark river there that might enchant you.....and the Barbarians are laying in ambush on a road to the east."

He bowed his head, flattened his hands together in front of his chest, and closed his eyes again.

She took one last steadying breath. "These men belong to the Black Watch. We think someone is hunting for us to kill them."

The Barbarian's head shot up. "The Black Watch?" he repeated in a deep voice. "They are Servants."

"Yes!" She pointed at him. "Yes, they are. We lost a bunch of their brother Watchmen defending their town and now someone is coming after them. We don't know why. Whoever it is keeps sending Darklings after us and we think the same person hired the Barbarians to hunt these men down."

He bowed his head and shut his eyes again. "I will serve."

"You will?!" she gasped. "Oh, thank you so much! You don't know how grateful I am." She thrust out her hand. "I'm Eliska....."

He didn't shake her hand. He only bowed again. "I am Anríq."

She realized a second too late that she was still standing there with her hand outstretched. She shook it and put it down. "Sorry. I forgot."

He bowed again.

"You forgot what?" Yvan asked behind her.

"The Servants take a vow not to touch anyone unless it's in service or healing. It was my mistake." She turned back to the Barbarian and waved to the men behind her. "This is Yvan Dilnao, Commander of the Watch. This is Wesh, a wizard of the Guardian Templars. This is Barsali Brun, Omer Veco, Neils Surette, Niyazi Trahan, Vidal Rom, and this is the Watch Commander's son, Yann. That over there is Rien Dugas."

Anríq bowed to them all, but as usual, he didn't speak.

"I don't know about this, Eliska," Yvan murmured. "What if you're wrong?"

"I'm not wrong. Ask Wesh if you don't believe me."

Everyone turned to Wesh. He frowned and scratched his chin while he scrutinized Anríq. "I've heard of the Servants, but I've never dealt with any of them before."

"I have." Eliska felt herself starting to lose her temper again. She spun around and did her best to straighten her expression when she faced Anríq. "I'm so sorry for their rudeness. They don't know."

"How do we know he is who you claim he is?" Omer asked. "He could turn on us."

"You have my word that he is who I claim he is," she countered. "He's a magic-user and a warrior who is offering to help us. None of us can afford to turn away someone like this—not when he's actually willing to put his life on the line to help us. Use your heads." She turned back to Anríq. "I'm so sorry. Please forgive them."

He compressed his hands, shut his eyes, and bowed to her and to everyone else.

Just then, Rien started to stir. Omer and Niyazi helped him to his feet.

He glared at Anríq. "Get the hell away from my friends," Rien snarled.

"If he walks away, I'm leaving, too," Eliska snapped. "This man is our best chance of survival out here—*your* best chance of survival. You're all suicidal if you turn him away—and you won't deserve my help, either. Either you accept him or we part ways right now."

"You don't have to do that, Eliska," Yvan told her.

"Yes, I do—and if any of you has half a brain, you'll listen to me and realize what a priceless gift I'm giving you—and he's giving you. He doesn't have to help you. He doesn't have to throw himself in front of a murderous wizard who wants to kill all of you. What the hell is wrong with all of you all of a sudden?"

The others shuffled their feet.

Anríq broke the tension by bending over, picking up his vest, and putting it back on. He went through the same slow, methodical process in reverse of hanging his bags across his body and then slinging his axe behind his back.

He straightened up and turned to face the group. Eliska saw exactly what he was trying to tell them.

He could walk away right now. He didn't need any of them. Leaving would cost him nothing.

They needed him. They needed him real bad.

She took a step toward him, and before she thought to stop herself, she took hold of his wrist and tugged him forward. "The sun will be going down soon. Come and make camp with us—please. We have some food. You can share it. Please. We want you to."

He didn't react to her touching him. He didn't pull away.

He allowed her to draw him forward even though there was nowhere nearby for anyone to camp.

Wesh stepped in. "You said there was a river farther west, Eliska. We can go there."

The group set off again in silence. Anríq went with them.

Rien kept glaring at him over his shoulder. Anríq showed no sign of seeing Rein.

The other Watchmen fell in line. Eliska stayed next to Anríq even though she had to forge her own path through the grass.

She had to walk twice as fast to keep up with his long legs. He slowed down to make it easier for her.

She spent the trip telling him the whole story about how she wound up in Middleborough fighting the Darklings, how the Watch Commander arrested her, Mael, and Wesh for breaching the barricade, and how the group got stranded together.

She sensed the others listening when she told all about the Darklings following them through the Layers and then how she overheard the Barbarians talking in the tavern.

Anríq listened to everything in silence and didn't answer.

"And then just a few days ago, we came upon that Dark river," she finished. "It entranced me and I fell in. A wild girl pulled me out and it took three days for me to recover. We don't know who the....."

A shriek cut her off. Everyone stopped and turned around. The wild girl hunkered in the long grass behind the group.

Rien sighed. "And here I thought we finally got rid of her."

"That's her," Eliska told Anríq. "Do you know her? Do you recognize her?"

He squinted across the landscape and shook his head.

Then the group turned away and kept filing west one behind the other.

Chapter 25

Yann squatted down next to Niyazi while he arranged some twigs into a cone. Eliska didn't notice.

She sat down on the ground next to Anríq talking his ear off about everything the group had seen and done, their experience with the gypsies, and Wesh's belief that the Voyant Mendicat wanted something one of these men was carrying.

Wesh ignited the sticks to light a fire. Neils pulled out a length of cured leather.

Eliska had used her magic to tan the hides of the last hog Neils killed and a few gars the other Watchmen had hunted on their travels.

Neils unfolded the hog hide to open the package. It contained the last of the party's food supplies.

He handed out chunks of meat to Wesh and the other Watchmen. Neils gave a piece to Eliska. She didn't stop talking when she handed it to Anríq.

She was too busy talking to notice that Neils didn't give her another piece. She didn't ask nor did she take her attention off Anríq even once.

He listened in silence while he turned the meat over in his hands frowning at it. Then he folded his hands, shut his eyes, and bowed over the food before he started eating it.

Neils glanced at Yvan and Yvan nodded.

"Eliska," Neils interrupted.

She jerked around as though she just noticed the others. Neils held out a second piece of meat to her.

She hesitated like she had to think about why he was giving it to her. Then she remembered and took it before she turned back to Anríq.

He barely acknowledged her. He stared down at the food in his hands while he ate and listened to all the information she kept dumping into his ears.

"And Wesh thinks the girl might have seen something in the river about where we came from and where we were going. If she did, maybe she knows who's coming after us. Wesh thinks that might be why she kept trying to talk to Yann while I was unconscious. She might even know *why* they're coming after us, but we would have to figure out how to communicate with her....."

"How do you know so much about these Servants, Eliska?" Yvan interrupted.

She spun around. "Huh? Everyone knows about the Servants—everyone in the Coil does, at least. The Servants are everywhere."

"If they're everywhere, why haven't we seen them before?" Omer asked.

"I mean they go everywhere. There aren't that many of them, obviously. Not many people go as far as completely turning their backs on the Barbarian way to follow a different path. The Servants get shunned by their people and can never go back to their tribes, but when they do leave, they go everywhere—all through the Coil. They travel around until they find someone who needs help or healing."

"Are you sure it's a good idea to tell him so much about us?" Barsali asked.

"How can he help us if he doesn't understand our situation? Besides, it wouldn't be right to ask him to help us without telling him exactly what he's getting into. He has to understand the danger. If you were going to help someone stay alive against the most powerful wizard in the Coil, wouldn't you want to know going into it that you were going against the most powerful wizard in the Coil? I would. I would think you lied to me beforehand to trick me into something if you didn't tell me everything."

"You have a point," Yvan replied.

"He doesn't look like much," Niyazi remarked. "I mean—he's big and everything, but he's just a kid. How do we know he'll be able to do anything?"

She turned back to Anríq and made eye contact with him. It was the first time he'd ever really acknowledged that the group was talking about him like he wasn't here.

He responded by pulling back the gauntlet on his left arm. He tugged it up to his elbow to reveal a bunch of short parallel lines tattooed onto the inner surface of his wrist and forearm.

Three blocks of five lines each started at the wrist and ended with a block of three lines.

"He's eighteen...." Eliska explained.

Anríq laid the flat edges of his righthand fingers across the top blocks of lines. He covered up six lines.

"He says he's been alone in the Coil for six years," Eliska went on. "He left home when he was twelve."

"Jesus!" Yvan breathed. "That young?"

A hush fell over the group as everyone stared at Anríq. He kept his eyes down while he pulled the gauntlet back into place and tightened the laces to secure it around his wrist where it had been before. It covered up the tattoo that marked how old he was.

No one spoke while he did this. The whole group stared at him as the truth sank in.

Yann didn't think it was possible to meet someone as impressive as Eliska—or maybe even more impressive.

No wonder she made such a big deal about Anríq and went to such lengths to bring him into their company.

He had powerful magic in addition to being one of the most physically intimidating men Yann had ever seen in his life. Anríq was hands down the biggest, strongest man here, but his boyish features and silent ways made him seem almost fragile by comparison.

He was only a year older than Yann and yet Anríq had been alone in the Coil for six years.

He must have strong magic to do all that—strong magic and expert training in the use of his weapons.

He was a Barbarian. He must be devastating when he had to fight anyone—which could turn out to be more often than anyone expected.

He hadn't been wandering around doing whatever he had to do to survive the way Eliska had. He went out into the Coil by choice. He went looking for trouble to help people and serve humanity.

Yann found himself shrinking from Anríq, especially when Yann saw Eliska hovering around him. She pushed herself at Anríq and came up with new topics to keep talking to him. She didn't stop engaging with him once even though he never talked back to her.

She gave him her undivided attention and only engaged the rest of the group when they asked her a specific question.

She gave Anríq no indication at all that anything special ever happened between her and Yann. She barely took the time to introduce Yann to Anríq. She made a bigger effort when it came to Yvan.

Should Yann resent that? Should he be concerned that Eliska suddenly relegated Yann to the background the instant Anríq showed up?

Yann tried not to read too much into it. She was just making Anríq feel welcome. No one else would do it.

She was trying to smooth things over between Anríq and the Watchmen by explaining what he could do for them and why accepting him was the best idea.

Yann couldn't help but simmer over it, though, especially when Neils handed out the second round of food.

He handed Eliska hers first and the same thing happened. She immediately gave her piece to Anríq before she only belatedly remembered to get a second piece for herself.

Anríq reacted the same way. He kept his eyes down and bowed to her when she gave it to him.

"Why doesn't he speak for himself?" Vidal asked. "Why does he let you do all his talking for him?"

"I told you. He's taken a vow of silence," she replied. "You might be some of the only people anywhere in the Coil who don't know about the Servants. Most Servants don't have to explain themselves to anyone. People go searching for them if someone needs help. Then it's up to the person asking for help to explain what they need and ask the Servant to do something about it. Most people don't need an explanation going the way."

"What if he knows something that could put us in danger?" Niyazi asked. "How will he communicate with us to warn us?"

"If it's anything that could threaten us or even benefit us, he'll tell us," she replied.

Yvan turned to Wesh. "You said you knew about these Servants. What can you tell us?"

"Not very much," Wesh replied. "I've only heard of them from my studies in the Temple. I didn't know they were Barbarians who turned away from their people." He looked up at Eliska. "Are they only Barbarians?"

"Of course they're only Barbarians. They're the only ones who have to make such a sacrifice by forsaking everything their people stand for. It wouldn't mean anything if they didn't turn their backs on their tribes, families, and traditions for the sake of all humanity."

Wesh frowned and rubbed his chin again. "I see what you mean. Yes, it makes more sense now when you put it like that."

"Have you heard of these Servants helping people?" Yvan asked.

"No, nothing like that," Wesh replied. "We only heard them mentioned in passing—no actual accounts of their actions. I think the Templars would remember if we heard of Barbarians defending people or using their magic to heal them."

"You can take my word for it," Eliska interjected. "I've done more than heard about it. I've seen it."

Yvan's head shot up to stare at her. "You have? You've met these Servants before?"

She nodded. "I've met three of them. One of them was an old woman. The other was an old man and the other was a middle-aged man. Anríq is the youngest one I've met."

Yvan scrutinized Anríq more closely. "It's a shame he can't explain to us why he left his people so young."

"That's none of our business," Eliska cut in a little too harshly. "Who cares why he left? He's here now."

"So....we just have to go on the same way we were before.....and pretend he really is one of us?" Rien snorted in Anríq's direction. "The rest of you might trust him, but I don't. I'm going to stay up tonight and keep an eye on him to make sure he doesn't do anything to us."

"He won't do anything to us," Eliska sneered. "If he wanted to do anything to us, he would have already done it. None of you would have been able to defend yourselves against him. He could have killed all of you if he wanted to."

"Would you have let him?" Yann blurted out.

She rolled her eyes at him. "I wouldn't have gone near him if I didn't recognize right away what he was. I wouldn't have invited him to join us and he wouldn't be sitting here right now. He isn't dangerous to us. When are you going to admit that? You don't have to resent him just because I knew about him beforehand and you didn't."

That killed the conversation. Anríq didn't interrupt to defend himself.

He kept silently taking bites of the meat Eliska gave him. He kept his eyes down through the whole conversation.

Neils saved the situation again by wiping as much of the grease and fat off his hog hide and folding it up. He put it in his pocket with a sigh.

"That's the last of the food," he remarked. "I wonder if we should hunt along this river before we move on. We could be crossing another grassland for a long way before we find anything else."

"You and Vidal go take a look before the sun goes down." Yvan turned to Wesh. "Can you see what's out there?"

"I'll try." Wesh started to straighten up.

Before he could do anything, Anríq leaned forward and traced his forefinger in the dust at his feet. "The Dark river is here." He scratched a forked, crooked line through the dirt and then drew boxes with crosses inside them. "There are towns here.....and mountains here....."

He drew pointed triangles in a line to indicate mountains.

"Thank you!" Yvan exclaimed. "I don't suppose you can tell us if any of those towns would be safe for us to travel to."

"Nowhere will be safe for us to travel to," Omer pointed out. "The Voyant will follow us no matter where we go. Isn't that what Wesh said? Isn't that the whole reason we're out here—to stay away from people?"

"None of those towns will be safe for you to travel to," Anríq interrupted. "The Dark river will take them soon."

He planted his finger into the forked lines he'd created to indicate the river. He continued it until he bisected the whole landscape.

The forks separated the towns from each other. In some cases, the lines cut straight through the towns themselves.

"You can see all that?!" Wesh gasped. "Can you tell when it will happen?"

Anríq leaned back against the log behind him. "No one can see that."

Yvan scowled at Anríq's drawing. "If you're right about the Dark taking this Island, then we shouldn't go in that direction."

"The only alternative is going back the way we came," Eliska pointed out. "That will take us back to the edges that we already know are unstable."

"Why can't we just travel to another part of the Ancestral Empire?" Barsali asked. "The whole Island can't be unstable."

"It might not be now, but they will be once the Dark starts to spread," Wesh replied.

"Then we should head back toward the south even if we meet more people there," Yvan decided. "At least we'll be in a more stable part of the Island even if we are more likely to bump into someone who is searching for us. At least we won't end up back in the Coil."

Chapter 26

Eliska swung her long-tailed gar by one leg on her way up the riverbank heading for the Watchmen's camp. She felt pretty good about traveling with them, now that they'd found this Barbarian Servant, Anríq.

That was a stroke of good luck and the party needed all the good luck they could get.

She turned a bend in the river on her way back to the camp when she spotted Anríq coming out of the undergrowth farther up the bank.

He wasn't wearing his axe, his club, or any of his shoulder bags. Instead, he carried another gar hanging by its leg from his muscular hand.

He froze when he saw Eliska coming toward him from the other direction with her own catch. The two of them regarded each other from a distance and then he shut his eyes and bowed to her.

She found herself grinning at him and bowed back.

He straightened up, saw her smiling, and froze again. He stared at her with a blank expression....and then his features softened. He didn't exactly smile, but his eyes twinkled a little bit.

She crossed the rest of the way to where he stood. "Good morning," she told him and dipped her eyes to his gar. "Great minds think alike. I didn't think it was a good idea for all these surly Watchmen to go marching across the countryside on empty stomachs."

He actually snorted under his breath and turned aside to return to the camp. She fell in next to him.

She tried to think of something to say to him. His silence made it difficult not to fall into the same silence, but she didn't want to do that. She wanted to keep him engaged. None of the others would do it.

They all kept their distance from Anríq for some reason. Her explanations of who he was and what he was doing out here didn't penetrate their thick heads. They insisted on treating him like a threat.

Rien kept his word by sitting up all night to keep watch on Anríq. Rien had been sitting there awake on his side of the fire when Eliska fell asleep.

Anríq pretended not to see Rien watching him. Anríq had curled up on the ground and slept right alongside the other Watchmen.

Eliska spotted Rien still sitting by the fire now. His stony expression gave him away. He must be in a foul mood from lack of sleep.

He wouldn't be able to keep this up forever. He would eventually pass out from exhaustion. Then he would have to take his eyes off Anríq.

Rien stiffened when Anríq and Eliska reentered the camp. Wesh and the other Watchmen were all waking up, running their fingers through their hair, coughing and spitting into the bushes, washing their faces and necks in the river, and leaving for the undergrowth to relieve themselves.

Neils laughed when he saw Eliska with another gar. "They're your favorite, aren't they?"

"The gars in this Island taste the way I remember them. The others were disgusting."

He got busy erecting a spit over the fire while she held up her gar by its hind legs. She used her staff to skin it.

She was just about to gut it when she noticed Anríq watching her work. She bit back a grin. Something about him made her happy to have him in their group. Maybe it was his boyish appearance. Niyazi was right. Anríq might be big, but he was just a boy like Yann.

She jutted her chin at Anríq's gar and bit back laughter. "Do you need any help with that?"

He responded by holding up his gar with one hand. He swiped his other hand down in front of it in a grasping motion.

The skin stripped off easily and he caught it in his free hand. Then he traced his forefinger down the gar's belly, sliced a thin tendril of magic into the flesh, and cut it open to gut the creature.

"Nice," Eliska remarked. "I'm going to have to practice that one."

Anríq actually smiled at her that time. She used her staff to gut her gar and they both squatted down by the fire while Neils put both carcasses on the spit.

He was the one who divided up the meat this time, too, even though he didn't hunt the animals himself. The group had fallen into a regular routine where everyone trusted him to divide their food between everyone.

He always served everyone the same way starting with whoever happened to be sitting on his immediate left when he cut up the food.

Then he went around the circle in that direction and gave food to everyone one person after another.

Anríq and Eliska sat on his immediate right this time, so he wound up serving them last. Neils handed Anríq his portion first and then Neils handed Eliska hers—so she didn't have to share hers with Anríq.

"I still say we look for a town that needs the Watch," Vidal announced. "If we're in as much danger out here as we are in a town, we should at least take advantage of additional numbers. We might even find a town that already has the Watch. Then we wouldn't have to fight our enemies alone."

"Nowhere in the Ancestral Empire has the Black Watch," Eliska told him.

"We can't go to a town if our presence would put the townsfolk in danger," Yvan pointed out. "Whoever is hunting for us has sent Darklings after us more than anything else. We couldn't lead the Darklings back to any town."

"So what's the solution?" Omer asked. "If you really want to protect everyone by keeping us away from them, then we might as well stay here where we know we can find food. The danger to ourselves will be the same either way."

Yvan turned right and left and nodded at Wesh, Eliska, and Anríq. "What do you three think? Where do you think we should go?"

Wesh shrugged. "I suppose heading back south is as good a place as any. If the Dark river is threatening the west country, then going back toward the more stable parts of the Island only makes sense. It seems a shame to retrace our steps over all that territory we've already covered, but at least we'll be staying on solid ground."

"I agree with Wesh," Eliska replied. "If Anríq is right about the Dark river taking out those towns, then the Island will probably collapse from there first. We should go back toward the center for as long as it lasts. We'll probably wind up back in the Coil anyway, but we can delay it for a little while. We just won't be able to delay the Voyant coming after us—if he is the one who's coming after us."

"What about you?" Yvan asked Anríq. "Do you have anything to suggest—anything other than what these two have already said?"

Anríq kept his eyes down and shook his head.

"Can you find out what it is he wants from us?" Barsali asked.

"He won't be able to," Omer told him. "Wesh already tried."

Anríq looked up and studied each person in the group with those hard, sharp blue eyes. Then Anríq looked away again and shook his head.

Yann broke the silence. Eliska didn't realize until that moment that Yann hadn't spoken since last night. He went quiet and distant since Anríq joined their party.

"We could find out what the thing is if we really wanted to find out," Yann murmured. "It would be easy if we split up. Then whoever is hunting us would go after the person who's carrying the thing. Everyone else would be safe."

The group burst out in protests as everyone started talking at once. The Watchmen rounded on him and yelled at him that they would never split up.

"Are you insane?" Vidal snapped. "We would all die out here if we split up!"

"No one is going anywhere," Omer insisted. "We're staying together. If one of us is in danger, then we're all in danger."

"I'm just saying," Yann replied. "At least those who aren't carrying it would be safer that way."

"We don't know that," Yvan countered. "Maybe it's all of us. Maybe it's some magical combination of all of us together....."

"Then breaking up the group would be better," Yann reasoned.

His father shook his head. "It would only make it easier for whoever it is to hunt us down individually. We'll stick together and head south. Finish eating and let's get out of here."

Finishing eating and packing up their few possessions didn't take long. Anríq carried more baggage than anyone else.

Eliska checked on him while he slung his bags over his shoulder, hung his axe across his back, and hooked the loop thong of his club to his belt.

He kept his hands free while he walked. He didn't do anything to make it easier for him to take his weapons down and get ready to fight if he needed to.

That struck Eliska as a strategic disadvantage, but he didn't exactly go looking for a fight.

Keeping his weapons one step removed from use created a barrier between him and whatever he might actually wind up fighting.

Anyone seeing him for the first time might get the impression he didn't intend to fight at all. No one seeing him for the first time would consider him a threat because he wasn't armed—not yet.

He fell in line with the Watchmen. He didn't try to hurry the journey along. He gave no sign that changing his course or retracing his steps meant anything to him or that he had anywhere else in the world to go.

Eliska found herself three places behind him in line. She would have liked to walk next to him, but that would have made it too obvious that she was trying to keep him engaged.

Yann wound up in the place right behind Anríq with Omer and Niyazi between Eliska and the two boys.

The group walked for an hour before Yann moved forward, stepped out of line, and pulled up alongside Anríq.

"Where did you learn to fight?" Yann asked. "Did you learn with your tribe?"

"Yes," Anríq replied without turning around.

"Did your family know you became a Servant?"

"Yes," Anríq replied in exactly the same tone.

"Eliska says the Barbarians shun anyone who becomes a Servant. Did that happen to you?"

"Yes," Anríq replied.

"Does that mean you can't go home at all? What would happen if you did? Would they try to kill you—or ignore you—or drive you off? What does it mean that they shun you?"

"Leave him be," Niyazi interjected. "You heard what Eliska says. He doesn't want to talk, especially about himself."

"How would you know what he wants?" Yann asked over his shoulder. "Maybe he really does want to talk, especially about himself." He turned back to Anríq. "Well? Are you allowed to go home if you want to—if you want to see your family? Could you if you really wanted to?"

"Yes," Anríq replied.

Yann turned around to look at Niyazi. "You see?" Yann turned back to Anríq. "So they wouldn't try to kill you?"

"No," Anríq replied.

"What about other Barbarians on the road?" Yann asked. "Eliska told you not to go near the roads because the Barbarians were there. Would they attack you, too?"

"Do you plan to talk him to death?" Omer asked. "Eliska said he only talks when it's important to his mission. What the Barbarians do isn't important to his mission."

"It would be important if they tried to kill him. It would be important to all of us, wouldn't it?" Yann turned back to Anríq. "Well? Do other Barbarians attack Servants on the roads?"

"Yes," Anríq asked.

"Do they go out of their way to hunt down Servants?"

"No," Anríq replied.

"Will you leave off already?" Niyazi snapped again. "You can see he doesn't want to talk."

"I'm just trying to be friendly," Yann replied. "Someone has to make up for Rien trying to attack him yesterday."

"Eliska made up for it," Omer pointed out. "She welcomed him."

"She was the only one," Yann replied. "I'm trying to show him that she isn't the only one."

Anríq glanced over at Yann and narrowed his eyes to study Yann more closely. At that moment, a deep rumble broke in on their conversation.

Eliska spun around to stare at the countryside around her. She didn't see anything—not with her eyes.

The Watchmen who'd been in front of her turned backward to search the horizon, too.

A wave of cold dread swept over her even though the sun kept shining as brightly as ever. It baked on the dry grass underfoot. The same gentle breeze blew the smell of fresh hay across the landscape.

"It's coming!" she whispered.

"What is?" Omer asked.

Eliska opened her mouth to say something. She had no idea what she would say. Words failed her.

Before she could make a sound, the rumble coming from the west cracked out of the distant horizon. She swiveled her staff in front of her. Something was coming from there and it wasn't anything good.

Chapter 27

"Get behind me!" Eliska called over her shoulder.

The Watchmen all drew their weapons. Anríq didn't move—not yet.

"What is it?" Yvan asked.

"The river...." Wesh husked. "The river broke."

Yvan snapped around to glare at him. "Is it coming this way?"

"It's coming every way." Pure adrenaline made Eliska spring forward. "Here it comes!"

She leapt in front of the Watchmen and braced herself. She still didn't see anything—not in the landscape.

The cold inside her built to the breaking point. It ate away at her guts and sapped her courage.

Anríq materialized at her side, pulled his axe off his back, gripped it in his left hand, and unhooked his club with his right hand.

He tossed both weapons into the air and switched them—the axe to his right hand and his club to his left hand.

He stepped his left foot back and flexed his knees to fight whatever was coming from that direction.

She didn't know what to expect when it got here, but right at that moment, another image flashed into her mind.

Enormous black Darklings stormed the landscape. Her vision overlaid towns and even massive cities in the Darklings' path.

The Darklings stomped them into the ground, snatched people off their feet, and devoured them in big, greedy mouthfuls.

"Oh, no!" she breathed.

Anríq glanced at her, but her vision evaporated just as fast.

Her mind cleared in time for her to see a dark shadow covering the distant horizon. It only started as a dim outline without shape or substance, but it didn't stay that way.

The Dark rushed the party. As it got nearer, she saw that it was actually a vast network of rapidly forking spikes jerking, stabbing, and fracturing the landscape in front of the forward edge of the wave.

She barely had time to yell, "LOOK OUT!!" before the wave struck the party.

She thrust the long edge of her staff at the wave and ejected all her power into it, but nothing could hold back such a force.

It would overpower her easily and then it would sweep away the whole Watch.

She shifted her power instantly and created a barrier between the Watch and the river. It built to a colossal tide of black sweeping the landscape away under its forward edge.

The wave smashed into her barrier and curved it backward. The Dark river's sheer power bombarding her field curved it backward into a dish surrounding the Watchmen.

She yelled out in fear and rage channeling all her magic into holding that field, but she couldn't hold it forever. She already felt herself slipping.

She caught movement out of the corner of her eye and spotted Anríq standing next to her.

He held his axe in exactly the same position in front of him. The Darkness pounded his axe and a matching curved magical barrier radiated outward from the spot.

Wesh stood on Anríq's other side. Yvan, Omer, Vidal, and Barsali took shelter behind Anríq, but not even all three wizards working together could hold back the flood.

Yann rushed up behind Eliska, slammed into her back from behind, and he, Rien, Neils, and Niyazi braced themselves behind her to hold her in place.

None of the Watchmen could help the three wizards. The Darkness penetrated their protective field and invaded the bubble of safety behind them.

The Darkness kept splitting, forking, and spreading through the air. It worked its way behind the three wizards and laced its many branching fingers toward the Watchmen.

The Watchmen turned outward to slash and hack their weapons at the Dark fibers creeping in on them. Eliska couldn't slacken her posture for an instant—not without the river's full power completely obliterating all of them.

She bellowed again—in frustration this time. She already felt her arms beginning to weaken.

Anríq roared in fury next to her, and without warning, he raised his club and brought it down with a catastrophic blow on the ground at his feet—at the spot between himself and Eliska.

The ground fractured and caved in. All the Watchmen out as the earth crumbled and sent them all pitching through the breach into the Layer below.

Eliska floundered to right herself and see where she was. The instant the group broke through, they landed in another landscape—this one packed to the skies with massive Darklings.

They couldn't have been waiting for the party. The Darklings couldn't have known Anríq would shatter the Ancestral Empire or that the group would fall through to this Layer.

The Darklings must have been here already. All the Watchmen landed on top of the Darklings and then bounced off before hitting the ground.

The landscape itself didn't appear to have any features Eliska could recognize. All the Darklings stood on a wide flat surface stretching away in all directions.

Some kind of red light shone from everywhere at once. It gave both the land and the Darklings a reddish glow.

They bellowed and gnashed their teeth when the Watch landed in their midst. Then all the Darklings turned on the Watch and moved in to attack.

Eliska reacted on pure instinct and fired a lightning bolt from the end of her staff. She had to get rid of as many of these Darklings as possible.

She swiped the lightning sideways and carved a swath of destruction through the Darklings surrounding her. The Watchmen moved into position around her and grasped their weapons to fight for their lives.

Anríq raised his club again and brought it down with another bone-crushing smash on the ground at his feet, but he didn't shatter the Layer this time.

His club set off a magical shockwave through the soil and it started to rumble. It quaked so badly that the Darklings lost their balance—and then the soil erupted out of position.

It jutted upward and started to grow into a hill. Spikes of granite erupted out of the landscape, joined together, and kept rising into a mountain.

The Watchmen got caught on its rapidly growing sides. Vidal almost pitched off into a Darkling's mouth. Neils grabbed him and held him on as the mountain lifted the Watchmen out of the Darkling's reach.

Eliska scrambled to find a stable position on the sharp granite clefts. She couldn't see the other Watchmen as the mountain kept booming out of the landscape until it towered high over the Darklings.

They roared and jumped trying to catch the Watchmen, but Anríq's spire kept growing...and growing..... Would it ever stop?

Eliska tried to see what he was doing or where the mountaintop would take the Watch.

Her throat went dry when she saw Anríq standing on a ledge above her. He had hung his axe over his shoulder again and raised his club with both hands.

"NO!!" she yelled, but he didn't listen.

He pounded it down on the mountain with unbelievable power. His magic discharged with the force of his own strength and the mountain exploded in a cloud of rock shards.

All the Watchmen screamed and so did Eliska. Wesh, the Watchmen, Eliska, and Anríq spun off into space along with massive granite blocks and slabs flying in all directions.

The landscape exploded along with the mountain and the Darklings got thrown, too.

The Darklings tried to snatch anyone who came near them. Eliska revolved in space with no idea of which way was up. She had to keep twisting one way and then the other to fight off Darklings.

They kept falling away and getting replaced by others falling close to her. She couldn't tell which direction was up or if there even was any up in this place.

She had to stay guard at all times for Darklings while she studied her surroundings for some sign of where she could take the Watch to safety.

They appeared to be falling through another vapor Layer—but they didn't fall down. They all just floated in no particular direction.

The Darklings floated in no particular direction, too. They acted as confused about this as the Watchmen. The Darklings only sometimes remembered to attack someone when they got near enough.

"Where are we?!" Yvan yelled from a dozen yards away.

"Hold on!" Eliska called. "I'll try to find us another Island. Just....."

A deafening smash interrupted her. Everyone turned around to see Anríq fighting a Darkling with his axe.

The Darkling floated close enough to wrap its tentacles around Anríq's arms and legs. It tried to yank his limbs aside so it could attack his body.

He swung his axe with almighty force and hacked one of the dual blades into the creature's body right next to its neck.

The Darkling bellowed in a voice of thunder and attracted all the other Darklings' attention.

They spun around to face Anríq. Then they tried to swim in his direction to help subdue him.

He took one hand off his axe and tried to grab the blade from his belt, but right then, the Darkling in front of him lashed another tentacle around his neck.

"Hold on, Anríq!" Eliska yelled and fired her staff across the expanse.

She severed the tentacle from his neck, but the two attacks only infuriated the remaining Darklings.

Some of them were close enough to put her in danger and they came after her instead.

Yann yelled out, "Eliska!" but he was too far away to help her. They all were.

She saw the situation disintegrating before her eyes. Without thinking about it first, she spun her staff in a complete circle and stabbed the end of it into her own palm.

She set off an ear-splitting explosion that shattered the Layer. Gravity caught everyone and yanked them down, including the Darklings.

She plummeted through space and broke into another Layer full of razor shards flying through punishing wind. She couldn't stay here, so she shattered that Layer, too.

The group plummeted down, down, down through three more Layers, each one more dangerous than the last.

She got completely disoriented and forgot all about checking to see if she could find an Island for the group to take refuge.

The party fell through a burning sheet of fire and landed on the steep, grassy slope of some mountain.

Chapter 28

Yann slammed down on the ground and rolled down a slope covered in grass. The fall tore his glaive out of his hand—not that he'd be able to fight anything anyway.

This grass was fresh, green, cool, and clipped short. The air around him chilled him instantly and the fresh smell of lush foliage stung his nose.

He rolled to a slightly flatter place and pitched onto his stomach. He sprawled there trying to make himself as wide as possible so he wouldn't roll anywhere else.

The other Watchmen groaned around him. He heard Eliska whimpering like she might be in pain.

That sound made Yann look up. She lay only a few feet away from him, but she was already pushing herself up onto her hands and knees.

Yann looked around to make sure the other Watchmen were okay. That was the moment when he saw Anríq walking down the mountain toward them.

He wore his axe across his back again and his club on his belt. He looked exactly the same way he looked when the Watch first spotted him. Yann didn't see a single hair out of place on Anríq's head.

He took one look at the Watchmen pulling themselves out of the grass. Anríq halted in his tracks, frowned, and shot a glare to his left.

Yann didn't see anything over there until Omer asked, "Where's Niyazi? He isn't here."

Yann got a horrible feeling in the pit of his stomach when Anríq turned aside and set off across the mountainside.

He had to climb over ridges and rock ledges until he stopped looking down the other side.

"Niyazi!" Yvan yelled. "Niyazi—where are you?"

"I think Anríq knows where he is, Father," Yann murmured.

Every man of the Watch went still and silent staring at the back of Anríq's head. He didn't move for a second—and then he jumped off the edge and vanished behind the mountain.

Everyone hustled over there and looked down into a crevice between two enormous rock cliffs. Niyazi lay broken, bleeding, and unconscious at the bottom.

One of his legs stuck out at the wrong angle. Blood stained the rocks near him and the cliffs up to the crevice's top edge.

"No!" Yvan husked.

Anríq squatted down next to Niyazi and flattened his hand on Niyazi's chest. Nothing happened for a second. Niyazi didn't wake up.

The group watched in silence as Anríq shifted his position down to Niyazi's leg, took hold of it, and compressed it back into a straight line. Niyazi didn't wake up.

Anríq held onto the leg for a few minutes before he went back up to Niyazi's head.

Anríq placed his hand on Niyazi's forehead, shut his eyes, and bowed over the unconscious Watchman.

Yann's throat constricted watching this. If only Anríq could fix what was wrong Niyazi.....

The chaos, danger, and confusion of the last few days somehow shielded Yann from thinking about all the Watchmen—and all the other people—who died when Middleborough went down.

The group had already lost everyone else.

The men in this group were all any of them had left. Wesh lost all the other Guardian Templars who left the Temple with him.

Eliska never had anyone to begin with. None of them could afford to lose anyone else.

How ironically perfect it turned out to be that Anríq met up with this group. He was another lost soul with no family and no home to which he could return. He had no one, either.

After a few minutes of silence, he took his hand off Niyazi's head, scooped up the injured man in his powerful arms, and looked around for a way out of the crevice.

He noticed everyone standing around watching him, but there was no way out. He'd jumped down there to save Niyazi's life. Now Anríq couldn't get out.

Eliska raised her staff to do something, but she didn't get a chance to before Anríq flexed his knees and jumped.

He soared much higher than any normal man should have been able to jump. His magic carried him out of the crevice and he landed on the rocks where the Watchmen stood waiting for him.

"We need to keep him warm," Anríq said to no one in particular.

"I'll take care of it," Wesh offered. "Bring him over here, my boy."

Wesh led the way to a rock overhang against the mountainside. Anríq laid Niyazi on the ground and Wesh squatted down next to him.

Yann surveyed the area. The only trees he could see were more than a mile down the mountain. A few scrubby bushes clung to the rocks nearby, but they wouldn't give the group enough wood for a fire.

Wesh flicked his empty hand at the gravel next to Niyazi. A bunch of sparks flew from Wesh's fingertips and ignited into a blaze.

Vidal and Omer left immediately. They didn't ask for permission. They set off hiking down the mountain on their way toward the trees in the distance.

Yann, Eliska, and the other Watchmen gathered around the blaze.

Anríq took off his axe and all his other weapons, laid his three shoulder bags to one side, and dug around in one of them.

"Can we do anything?" Yvan asked.

Anríq shook his head and started pulling random objects out of one of his bags.

The group sat off to one side while Anríq got to work on Niyazi. Yann found himself sitting between Eliska and Barsali. Everyone watched Anríq in fascinated silence.

He brought some kind of marking pencil made out of chalk. He used it to draw long lines down the two sides of Niyazi's neck and then drew dots down each side of both lines.

Yvan turned white. "What's wrong with him? Did he break his neck?"

"And other things," Anríq muttered.

He sat down cross-legged by Niyazi's head, curved his fingers into a gripping position a few inches above Niyazi's neck, and Anríq closed his eyes.

Yann leaned close to Eliska. "What is he doing?" Yann whispered.

"I don't know," she whispered back. "The Servants have their own way of doing things. Each person develops their own healing skills separate from everyone else."

"You mean they don't train each other?" Barsali hissed. "That's outrageous!"

"They can't train each other. Each one goes alone, so they all develop their own ways of doing everything."

They fell silent when Anríq fired two beams of magical energy—one from his thumb and one from his fingers.

He flexed his hand in what would have been a choking motion around Niyazi's neck, but whatever Anríq did didn't harm Niyazi.

"Are you sure you and Wesh shouldn't try to help him?" Yann asked. "Won't three wizards be better than one?"

"Anríq wouldn't be working on Niyazi if Anríq didn't think he could heal whatever is wrong with him. I think we should stay out of his way and let him do it his own......"

She trailed off when another shriek echoed into the rocks. The whole group spun around to stare at the wild girl crawling up the mountainside to get closer to the party.

The noise distracted Anríq. His eyes snapped open and he stared down the mountain, too, but he didn't release his magic from Niyazi's neck.

"What the hell is she doing here?" Rien snarled.

"She must have followed us through all those Layers," Eliska murmured back. "I wonder what she wants."

"She better not be here for food," Rien muttered.

"You and your food," Barsali returned. "As if you would ever go hungry because of her."

The wild girl didn't come near the overhang. She crept and scrambled over the rock ledges until she got to a flat plateau twenty yards away.

She crouched there with her dingy hair hanging over her face. She didn't come any closer.

The group turned back to Niyazi. Wesh and Yvan sat nearby watching Anríq.

He kept working on Niyazi, drawing on different parts of his body, and rubbing different objects into his injuries.

Omer and Vidal came back before Anríq finished. Both men carried armloads of firewood. Two biturongs hung from Vidal's belt.

He lowered his firewood to the ground next to Wesh. "There are plenty of waterbuck down there," Vidal murmured under his breath. "We could have brought more."

No one said anything else for a long time. Omer and Vidal built up the fire. Eliska cleaned the biturongs for them and Neils took his usual place by the fire to cook them.

Anríq finally sat back on his heels, folded his arms on his knees, buried his face in his elbows, and didn't stir again.

Niyazi still lay on the ground with his eyes closed.

"Should we do anything?" Yann whispered. "Anríq looks exhausted."

"Do anything like what?" Eliska asked.

"I don't know. We should do something, though, shouldn't we?"

"I don't know what we can do besides let him rest."

"Give me your cloak, Eliska," Yann told her.

She hesitated, but she eventually took it off and handed it to him.

He got to his feet, tiptoed around the fire, and draped the cloak around Anríq's shoulders. He didn't respond. He must have fallen asleep.

The others gathered around, but they kept their voices low. "Where are we?" Barsali asked.

Eliska created her Coil projection in her palm. She groaned when she saw it. "Oh, no! The Ancestral Empire is completely gone!" She glanced at Anríq, but he still didn't wake up to get involved in their conversation.

"I wonder if his tribe is there—or was there," she whispered. "Maybe....."

She trailed off staring at him.

"Maybe what?" Yann asked. "Does this have something to do with him?"

"No, nothing like that." She raised her projection and studied it. "We're here—in this Island."

"Are there any other people here?" Omer asked.

"There are some inhabited lands at the base of these mountains. This Island looks quite stable."

"You said that about the Ancestral Empire," Neils pointed out.

"We won't be going anywhere until Niyazi gets better," Yvan decided.

"He will get better," Wesh told him. "He's sleeping now."

Everyone turned around. "Did Anríq heal whatever was wrong with him?" Vidal asked.

"I told you he would," Eliska added. "He's a healer."

"We all see that now," Yvan told her. "You couldn't expect us to believe it when we knew nothing about him."

Just then, Anríq raised his head and rubbed his eyes.

"Here." Neils handed him a piece of the biturong meat—the first piece Neils cut off the roasting carcass. "Do you feel better?"

Anríq took the food, bowed to Neils, and then nodded.

"Thank you for healing our friend," Yvan told him. "I don't know how to tell you how grateful I am."

"The Darkness took him," Anríq replied.

Eliska's head shot up. "It did? He didn't get hurt from the fall?"

"The Darkness made him fall," Anríq replied. "He would have landed with us, but the Darkness sent him over there."

The other Watchmen looked around at each other. "Should we be worried about that?" Barsali asked.

"We're all in equal danger from the Dark," Wesh explained. "It could have happened to any of us."

"It almost did happen to Anríq," Eliska told him. "That Darkling tried to strangle him."

Chapter 29

A growling noise made everyone look up toward the mouth of the overhang. The wild girl sat crouched right next to the overhang, but she still didn't come inside.

She made hideous faces and uttered a steady stream of snarling shrieks. Her eyes rolled in their sockets.

"Get lost!" Rien yelled at her. "We've given you enough food. Go find your own."

Wesh turned to Anríq. "Could you heal her, too—or is she too far gone?"

Anríq barely looked at the girl. "She doesn't need healing. There's nothing wrong with her. She's whole the way she is."

Omer snorted. "There is definitely something wrong with her, little brother. She's out of her mind."

"Her name is Marine," Anríq went on. "She's communing with the Dark. She uses those noises to communicate with the Darklings."

Yvan jolted to high alert. "Are you sure? She's communing with the Dark?"

Anríq nodded. "She passes back and forth between the Coil and the Dark. She can exist in both places at the same time. That's how she appears to be here while she can still talk to them."

"That's it. She has to go." Yvan got to his feet. "This has gone on long enough."

He started to stand up, but Anríq pulled him down. "Leave her alone. She's whole."

"She's wholly Dark, you mean. I only let her hang around because I thought she was harmless. No way will I let any Darkling follow us around the Coil."

Yvan tore his arm out of Anríq's grip and stormed across the overhang to go after Marine.

Anríq stood up after him, but Yvan got there first.

He stalked over to her, grabbed her shoulder, and pushed her away. "Get out!" he snapped. "Go on! Go back where you came from!"

Anríq crossed the overhang right behind him, but not fast enough.

Marine resisted Yvan's efforts and he laid hold of both her shoulders with both hands. He tried to turn her around to push her away.

Before Anríq could intervene, she whipped around fast, opened her mouth, and a blast of some kind of magical energy erupted from her.

It looked like a transparent liquid wave flowing through the air. It had no substance or color that Yann could see.

It smashed the Watch Commander in the face, tore him off his feet, and hurled him across the overhang just as Anríq near them.

All the other men of the Watch shot upright in a flash. Yann grabbed his glaive. The others advanced on the girl and pointed their weapons at her, but they came face to face with Anríq instead.

He held out both hands to the Watch. "She defended herself. Don't touch her. Leave her alone."

He hustled past them to where Yvan lay on his back. Rien, Barsali, and Omer moved to the front. They pointed their weapons at the girl to stop her from coming any closer, but she seemed to forget all about the Watch.

She retreated to the wall nearest to the mouth of the overhang. She huddled close to the wall, peered out at the mountains, and went back to grimacing and baring her teeth at whatever Dark forces she saw out there.

Anríq squatted down next to Yvan and touched the Watch Commander's chest.

Yann wanted to help his fellow Watchmen defend the group against the girl, but concern for his father made him turn away. "Is he....is he dead?" Yann asked.

"He's just injured." Anríq scooped his hand under the back of Yvan's neck and held his head for a second before Anríq put him back down. "He will recover."

Yann glanced over at the girl. She didn't try to enter the overhand again. She completely ignored everyone.

Eliska left the group and went over to her, but the girl only retreated from her, too.

Eliska faced the men. "You heard what he said. She defended herself. Leave her alone. Put your weapons down. Come on, Barsali. Back off."

Barsali responded first followed by Omer. Rien lowered his weapon, but he didn't leave to rejoin the group.

Yann stayed near his father watching Anríq go through the same process of touching and repairing all the internal injuries Yann couldn't see.

"Are you sure he'll be okay?" Yann asked. "What did she do to him?"

"She only protected herself," Anríq muttered. "She didn't damage him."

"Why are you taking so long to heal him then?"

Anríq shot one glance toward the girl. "She's been with the Darklings a long time. I don't think she knows how powerful she is."

Another tense silence fell over the group. Marine's constant growls and snarls kept making everyone jump.

Anríq finally took his hands off Yvan and sat back on his heels again. "He'll sleep now. He'll wake up in the morning." He looked up at made eye contact with Yann. "You should sleep, too. Don't tire yourself."

Yann looked away. He had to resist the urge to ask again if Anríq was sure Yvan would be okay.

Why did Yann doubt anything Anríq did or said? Anríq's presence undid something Yann had come to believe about reality.

How was it possible for one man to be good at absolutely everything? Yann didn't see that Anríq had any flaws at all. He could do anything. Yann didn't even see how anything could defeat Anríq in battle.

Yann knew that wasn't true. Something must be able to defeat him. He was just a kid with all the same problems as everyone else.

Anríq got Eliska's cloak—the one Yann had used to keep Anríq warm. He carried it over to Yvan and laid it over the Watch Commander.

Then everyone returned to the fire and went back to eating their food. Yann sat sideways where he could keep an eye on his father.

Yann should have been more concerned about Niyazi. He got more injured than Yvan. Anríq took a lot longer to heal Niyazi than he did Yvan.

Yann had to force himself to eat. The tension and danger of everything that happened since they left their camp this morning caught up with him.

The girl drew everyone's attention by slinking down the wall working her way deeper into the overhang. She inched closer to the group. She never stopped howling and grimacing the whole time.

"Why did she follow us?" Vidal asked.

"She's a Darkling," Rien replied. "She was probably one of those that attacked us in the red landscape."

"She can't be a Darkling," Eliska pointed out. "She wouldn't have rescued me from the river if she was."

"She serves all humanity," Anríq chimed in. "She communes with the Dark to serve and protect the Coil."

He stood up, flattened his hands together in front of his chest, and bowed to Marine.

She didn't notice. She writhed against the wall, twisted around to glare outside, and then turned the other way to stare off into space.

"If she serves all humanity, maybe she's trying to help us," Eliska suggested. "Maybe she followed us to stop the Voyant from getting whatever it is he wants from us." She glanced at Anríq. "Is that what she's doing?"

He shut his eyes and bowed his head in her direction.

"Just say yes or no like a normal person," Rien snapped. "Don't give us all these stupid coded messages. You're the one who said you would help us. Just tell us what you know without shrouding everything in mystery all the time."

"Not everyone in the Coil thinks and acts the way you do," Eliska fired back. "They aren't dangerous or evil just because you don't understand them."

"Then why didn't he just say that in the first place?" Rien countered. "He could have just told us she was trying to tell us about that."

"He just did," she replied. "What more do you want? It isn't like it made any difference to us that he's telling us now instead of telling us yesterday."

Rien snorted and curled his lip at her to argue back, but the wild girl cut him off with another ear-splitting shriek. Everyone looked up, including Anríq.

He immediately grabbed his head and winced in pain. He squinted his eyes half-closed and gasped.

Eliska spun around the other way to stare at him. "What's wrong?"

"She....she wants....." He yelped as another stab of pain contorted his features in all the wrong ways. "She wants......to......" He actually screamed.

Eliska almost kicked Omer trying to stand up fast enough. "Anríq!" She grabbed Anríq's shoulder and yelled in his face. "What's wrong?! What is she doing to you?"

"She.......she wants.....to talk to you....." He pressed his hand to his eyebrow panting and whining in agony.

Eliska cast a terrified glance over her shoulder toward the wild girl. "She what? Why does she want to talk to *me?*"

Anríq staggered to his feet shivering in pain. He didn't take his hand down from his forehead.

He grabbed Eliska by the wrist with his other hand and towed her across the overhang. "Come here, Eliska," he ordered.

She stumbled after him with her eyes hanging out of her sockets. She stared at Marine in white-faced horror.

Yann couldn't move. His gut told him to intervene and stop what was about to happen.

He didn't want Eliska anywhere near that girl, especially considering the way Anríq was acting.

Yann found it impossible to move. The other Watchmen stood back watching in matching horror. Even Wesh seemed to turn to solid granite.

Anríq stopped in front of Marine and clamped one muscular hand on Eliska's shoulder. "I'm going to.....I'm going to......" He had to stop when another crippling attack hit him in the head.

Eliska stood there in stunned shock while he doubled over with a brutal howl. A trail of blood dripped out of his nose.

"I'm going to.....hold back the Dark......" He broke down in a wretched sob. He couldn't stand upright anymore. "I'm going to.....hold back....the Dark.....so you.....so you.....so you......"

He trailed off with another pathetic whimper. Every ounce of Yann's resolve told him to walk over there and pull Anríq and Eliska away from Marine.

Yann couldn't move. Dread and horror held him in place.

Anríq's knuckles went white on Eliska's shoulder. He stood there convulsing and sobbing in pain. Blood dripped from his ear now.

He finally worked up the energy to fling his other hand at Marine and grabbed her arm near her bicep.

He bellowed in pain as soon as he made contact with her, but he didn't let go of either girl.

Eliska froze with her wide eyes locked on Marine. Marine didn't seem to realize what was happening. She didn't respond to Anríq at all.

His howls of agony escalated to full-throated screams. The sound sent a shiver up Yann's spine, but he couldn't move to intervene. He didn't even know how to.

Eliska didn't see or hear him, either. All her attention riveted on Marine. She didn't look away.

Anríq collapsed onto his knees sobbing and bellowing in torment. His unbreakable grip actually pulled both girls out of position, but he still held on.

Yann couldn't watch this anymore. He shoved between the other Watchmen and attacked Anríq's arms.

"Let go, Anríq!" Yann bellowed in Anríq's face over the noise of Anríq's agonized screams. "LET GO NOW OR YOU'LL DIE!!"

Anríq didn't hear him, either. Yann attacked Anríq's fingers in desperation, but nothing would pry them loose from Eliska's shoulder.

Yann spun the other way and threw all his weight against Anríq's powerful arms to try to knock them away. Blood covered his face and dripped from his nose into his mouth.

Yann almost froze again when he saw blood brimming out of Anríq's eyes where tears should have been. He looked up at Yann in wild, crazed desperation.

Yann swallowed hard. He had to break the connection somehow.

His first thought was to ask Wesh to help. Why wasn't Wesh here now? Why was Yann here all alone trying to save Anríq from this awful fate?

Yann looked up in time to see Wesh and the rest of the Watchmen rushing him to help out, but right then, Anríq collapsed.

His arms and hands went slack. He lost his grip on both girls and buckled into a pile on the floor.

Chapter 30

Eliska slumped on the gravel next to the fire under the overhang. Yvan and Niyazi sat nearby. They were the only Watchmen here.

Yann and the others had left this morning to hike down the mountain to the woods in search of somewhere more comfortable for the group to stay—somewhere everyone didn't have to sleep on bare gravel.

Yvan and Niyazi both recovered exactly the way Anríq said they would. Now he was the one lying insensible on the ground with Eliska's cloak covering his big body.

Wesh bent over him touching different parts of his body and occasionally laying his hand on Anríq's forehead.

"This is my fault," Eliska husked and her voice failed her completely. "He's going to die because of me."

"He did it knowing the risks," Wesh muttered. "He wanted to do it."

"I should have stopped him." Tears choked Eliska's throat and stung her eyes. She tried to see Anríq through her tears, but the sight of him blurred in a sea of misery. "He tried to help us and now this happened."

"He did help us," Wesh murmured. "He helped us against the Darklings in the Layers. He helped Niyazi and the Watch Commander when they both would have died. Anríq did what he set out to do. He gave everything in service to humanity."

Eliska couldn't look up. She couldn't even wipe away the tears streaking down her cheeks.

She didn't have to ask what Wesh really meant. He didn't correct her when she said Anríq was going to die.

"He can't die like this." Overwhelming anguish destroyed the last of her resolve and she broke down sobbing. "He can't die like this—not because of me."

"He isn't dying because of you," Wesh repeated. "He's dying because it's his mission in life to sacrifice himself for others."

She shook her head. "I should have stopped him. I should have realized...."

"When should you have realized? You didn't know until after he already made the connection."

She looked up at him. Wesh's face kept wavering when tears obscured her vision. Then he came back into focus when they ran down her cheeks.

"You have to save him, Wesh!" she blurted out. "You have to!"

He looked away. "I can't save him, my dear. I don't have the magic to cope with this. He took all the Darkness on himself to block it from passing from Marine to you so she could communicate with you. He stopped it. Now it's all in him."

"You can use my magic," she insisted. "You can combine my magic with yours to heal him. You have to, Wesh!"

He shook his head and looked away again. "You would throw your own life away, my dear child."

"Who cares?!" She heard herself shrieking in hysteria right in front of Niyazi and Yvan, but she didn't try to soften her voice. "So he'll be alive and I'll be dead. Who cares? He's so much better than I am. He can do so much good. I'm worthless. No one cares about me....."

"Stop it, my child," Wesh murmured. "You know that isn't true."

"You have to save him!" She grabbed Wesh's arm. "You have to! We can't let him die—not after this. I can't live with it....."

Crushing guilt broke her the rest of the way down. She couldn't look at any of these men.

Thank the stars Yann and the others weren't here to see her completely break down. She could only survive the shame because these three much older men were the ones watching her brought to her lowest point.

She bowed her head and dissolved in silent tears. She couldn't be the cause of Anríq's death—not when he was so much finer and nobler than she was.

She could never be as good and noble and self-sacrificing as he was. She never would have gone willingly into the Coil to help other people—not in a million years.

She would have given anything—or killed anyone she had to kill—for the chance to live behind walls in a normal imp town like Middleborough.

She would have traded just about anything—including all her magic—for the chance at a normal life. She would gladly have died never to set foot in the Coil again as long as she lived.

She couldn't comprehend how someone could be good enough to actually make that choice of his own free will.

Anríq made it in full knowledge of the dangers he would face in the Coil. He knew he would never be welcome in Barbarian society again.

His own people would ambush him on the roads. Every hand would turn against him as an enemy. His family turned him out—and for what? To help a bunch of strangers who could barely offer him a meal in return?

She could never do anything like that—not for anything.

Now he lay here dying right in front of her because he tried to help her. He gave his life so she could communicate with Marine.

Whatever he did left Marine calmer, but she still didn't come back to full sanity.

She sat on a flat rock near the mouth of the overhang. Soft drizzle turned the sky grey outside.

She didn't crouch and shriek and snarl at invisible enemies anymore. She just sat there staring off into space.

She didn't even come around to get food anymore. Neils always left a portion of the Watchmen's food sitting on a plate of leaves near her. She usually ate it hours later when she woke up enough to realize it was there.

Eliska couldn't look at her. Eliska kept staring down at Anríq's still form lying on the ground with his eyes closed.

"You have to save him, Wesh!" she husked. "I can't live with this."

Wesh didn't answer for a long time. When he did, his own voice cracked with buried pain. "You would be taking your life in your hands, my dear. You might not recover at all. His mission in life is to sacrifice himself and that's what he did. He would be utterly destroyed if he woke up and realized you threw away your life to save his."

She shook her head again, but she didn't look up. "At least he would be alive. He could go on and help other people."

"So could you, my dear," Wesh breathed. "You've been helping these men since the beginning. You can honor his sacrifice by continuing....."

She looked up at him through miserable tears. "Please, Wesh..... please......"

He refused to look at her. "And how am I to live with it if anything happens to you? You could be left completely without magic if you survived at all—and then what? Then we would all be finished."

"Please....." She broke down sobbing again. "Please....."

He didn't answer. He went on with his work and left her there, wretched and distraught.

Now what should she do? What *could* she do?

She should walk away right now. She didn't deserve any of these men. Even Rien outclassed her by a mile.

He joined the Black Watch. He swore an oath to give up love and family in service to humanity. Yann did it. Wesh did it. They all did it—all of them except her.

She'd been walking away all her life. She couldn't do it now. If anything she did—even the smallest possible action—if any microscopic decision she made helped them in the tiniest way, she had to stay.

She couldn't let Anríq die, though. He deserved to live if anyone did. Her life meant nothing compared to his.

She shifted closer to him, and the next time Wesh moved off, she extended her hand toward Anríq's head.

Her magic was stronger than Wesh's. She knew that the first minute she met him. She hid the fact from him and told everyone his magic was stronger, but they both knew the truth.

She had to at least try to heal Anríq. If Wesh couldn't do it, maybe she could.

A split second before she touched Anríq's head, Wesh shot out his hand and snatched her arm out of the way. "NO!" he barked. "Don't you dare!"

"I have to! I can't just sit by and watch him die. I have to do something! If he dies anyway, at least I tried."

Wesh tore his eyes away. His whole face spasmed in misery. "Lie down, my dear," he rasped. "I don't know if it will work, but I will do as you ask. I don't know what else to do."

His words flooded her with relief. She swiveled around and stretched out on the gravel next to Anríq.

She stared up at the ceiling while Wesh positioned himself near hers and Anríq's heads. She didn't know what to expect.

She just hoped Wesh would finish before the rest of the Watchmen came back. She didn't want any of them to try to stop her, especially not Yann.

She fixed her gaze on a spot on the ceiling and focused on it. Wesh's weathered old hand came to rest on her forehead. "Concentrate on the Dark, my dear," he murmured. "Concentrate on the Darkness in him......"

She shut her eyes and concentrated. As soon as she closed them, the same image obliterated her mind.

She saw again the massive tide of Darkness forking, streaming, and jagging across the landscape. It chewed up the Ancestral Empire and left nothing in its wake.

All the light went out of the world and Darkness consumed everything. It closed around her and eventually wiped her off the map, too.

Chapter 31

Yann adjusted his armload of firewood on his way down the forest path. He could hear Vidal and Rien talking behind him, but the snow filling the woods muffled their laughter.

Deep drifts piled under the trees and weighed down the branches. Grey snow clouds blocked out any sunshine from shining through the canopy.

He continued down a well-trampled path leading deeper into the woods. The men of the Black Watch traveled this path every day. Their feet packed the snow into ice and made walking easier. None of them had to re-forge the path each time.

He turned a bend in the path and stopped when he saw the wild girl sitting off to one side. A rough cabin built of thatched boughs hovered in the shadows across another clearing. Equally trampled footprints surrounded the area to show where the men had been working.

The men of the Watch built this cabin for their party to stay in while Anríq and Eliska recovered from their ordeal—whatever the hell it had been. Yann still didn't understand what happened—to either of them.

Neither of them had regained consciousness since that disastrous day when Anríq tried to help Marine communicate with Eliska.

No one mentioned leaving the area or going anywhere else. Yann didn't want to leave the area. He didn't want to do this anymore.

He understood these woods. Leaving would only throw the group back into chaos.

Wesh was the party's only functioning wizard now. He didn't mention leaving, either, not even to protect the group from anyone coming after them.

Marine followed the Watch when they moved Anríq and Eliska down here to these woods. Marine hung around in the snow even when Neils and Yvan invited her to come inside and get warm by the fire. She never tried to come near the group again after that day.

At least she didn't howl or snarl or shriek anymore. She just sat off to one side without looking at anyone.

Yann kept walking past her, pushed open the cabin door, and kicked it shut before he crossed to the firepit at the center.

The Watch didn't construct this cabin with any windows. The men had no supplies and warmth took a much higher priority.

The walls cast the interior in permanent shadow. The men chink every crack in the walls whenever anyone spotted hints of light coming through.

That left the little house shadowy even in the middle of the day. A small opening in the ceiling let in the only light.

Yann lowered his pile of wood onto the stack next to the coals. Omer and Barsali sat in one corner cleaning a waterbuck carcass they'd killed for the group's meals. All the other men were still outside.

The Watch took turns gathering firewood, hunting, and heating water for cleaning, drinking, and any other chores the men had to do.

Wesh sat on one side of the fire working over Anríq and Eliska. Wesh spent all his time doing nothing else. He barely ate or slept. He'd aged twenty years since it happened.

Yann sat down on one ankle while he built up the fire. He considered how to break in on Wesh's thoughts to tell him to eat something, drink some water, and maybe get some sleep.

Just then, Anríq stirred for the first time. He hadn't moved since Yann first tried to tear him away from Marine and Eliska. Not even moving him down here got any response from him.

He groaned in his sleep, scowled without opening his eyes, and twisted onto his side before he pried his eyelids open.

He squinted around him trying to figure out where he was. He frowned even more when he saw Yann.

Yann didn't say anything. He watched the wheels turning in Anríq's head as he put the sequence of events back together. Then he propped himself up on his elbows, looked to one side, and saw Eliska lying right next to him.

Anríq froze for a second. Then he shot up into a sitting position. He extended his hand to touch her shoulder the way he did before, but he stopped himself.

He waited a second before he let his hand fall on her shoulder.

"No!" he whispered.

"She got me to use her magic to heal you," Wesh growled. "She insisted that I combine her magic with mine to save your life."

Anríq's voice trembled. "You shouldn't have...."

"She couldn't live with the guilt," Wesh husked. "Seeing you about to die.....It broke her...."

"Guilt!" Anríq croaked. "What guilt?!"

"She blamed herself for what happened to you....and I must admit, my dear boy.....I couldn't live with it myself. None of us could bear to lose you....You'll say I shouldn't have, but I did it and now you're healed exactly the way she wanted."

The misery in Wesh's voice brought a lump into Yann's throat. Anríq stayed there, bowed over Eliska's still form. He left his hand touching her shoulder for a long time before he took it back.

The silence became oppressive.

Wesh came back over to him and laid his own hands on Anríq's head. Anríq barely noticed when Wesh sat back and sighed.

"The Darkness....." Anríq murmured. "It's inside her now."

"I know," Wesh replied. "I've been doing what I can to drain it out of her. It's just taking a long time."

"I have to...." Anríq extended his hand again.

Wesh stopped him. "Don't undo everything we've already done. She risked a lot to bring you back. Don't throw that away."

"I won't, but I have to heal her. I can't leave her like this."

Wesh let him go and moved out of the way. Anríq went through a different procedure of laying on hands and closing his eyes.

Yann had been seeing Wesh working on both Anríq and Eliska for days. Anríq had a completely different way of healing—as if Yann could ever understand any of this.

Anríq didn't touch Eliska for very long. He took his hand away and sat there staring at her for a long time. He was still sitting there when the other men came back.

They tried to make a celebration out of Anríq waking up, but he didn't talk back to them when they spoke to him.

He turned away from Eliska and sat and ate with them around the fire, but he didn't engage. He kept glancing over at her and then staring into the flames.

Eventually, the men noticed and stopped trying to talk to him.

"How much longer do you think it will take before Eliska wakes up?" Yvan asked Wesh.

"It will go quicker now that two of us are working on her," Wesh replied.

Yvan shot a glance at Anríq. "Is that wise after what he's already gone through?"

Wesh shrugged. "He says he won't harm himself by treating her. I believe him."

"It would be nice if she could at least tell us if she found out anything by talking to that wild girl," Niyazi remarked. "It would be nice to know that all of this actually got us somewhere and wasn't just a massive waste of time."

"It got us closer to understanding that Marine trying to help us," Wesh pointed out.

"At what cost?" Barsali asked. "It could have cost us Anríq's life and it might still cost us Eliska's life. I don't call that a fair trade."

"It won't cost us Eliska's life," Wesh replied. "She won't die."

"It still cost too much," Barsali countered. "Whatever Marine knows isn't worth taking a risk like this. It could have been disastrous."

Wesh glanced over at Anríq. "I suppose he thinks it was worth it or he wouldn't have done it. That's his decision to make. He knows more about it than we do."

"Does he know more about it than *you* do?" Yvan asked. "More than the Guardian Templars?"

Wesh nodded down at the food in his hands. "Anríq has more experience in the Coil than all the Guardian Templars put together. He understood Marine better than we did—better than Eliska did."

"How do you think that happened?" Omer asked. "Why couldn't Eliska just communicate with Marine herself if Eliska is so powerful?"

Wesh looked away. "I have my theories, but I wouldn't insult Eliska by voicing them."

"If you think Eliska is communing with the Dark, too, you better tell us," Yvan returned. "You better not keep anything from us that could jeopardize our safety."

Wesh kept his head turned away. He tried to keep the ice out of his voice and failed. "Eliska does not commune with the Dark as I've already explained to you. I only meant that perhaps she held back from trying to make contact with Marine because of Marine's connection to the Dark. Eliska would have wanted to keep away from it. She wouldn't want to go near it even to find out whatever it is Marine wanted to tell her."

"And now Eliska knows what it is and can't tell us." Omer turned to Anríq. "Did you see what Marine was trying to tell Eliska?"

Anríq didn't look up, either. "I didn't see. There was too much Darkness."

"Great," Rien muttered. "So this whole exercise got us a big fat zero."

"Maybe not," Yann chimed in. "Maybe Eliska will be able to tell us when she recovers."

"That's a big maybe, son," Yvan pointed out. "Even if she does recover, she might not have magic anymore." He glanced at Wesh. "Isn't that what you tried to tell her—that she could lose all her magic if she went through with this?"

Wesh opened his mouth to answer, but Anríq answered in his place. "She still has her magic—all of it. She's as strong as ever."

Yvan whipped around to stare at him. "You can tell that?" Anríq nodded down at his hands. All the strength seemed to have drained out of him since he woke up and saw Eliska stricken in his place.

Chapter 32

Eliska groaned and rolled onto her side before her eyes snapped open. She tried to remember everything that happened—and then she shot upright and looked all around her.

She found herself in some kind of primitive house with a fire smoking in the center. Wesh sat nearby sewing the hem of his tunic with a wooden needle.

He looked up and tried to smile at her, but the muscles of his face hardly moved at all. "Ah, you're awake, my dear!" he breathed. "That's wonderful."

She jerked from one side to the other looking all around her. "Anríq—he isn't....."

"He's fine, my child. He's out with the other men doing the chores. He's been awake for three days thanks to you—and he's been helping me to heal you and drain away the Darkness that you took on yourself to heal him."

She slumped in relief. "Thank God he's all right."

"You both are," Wesh murmured. "And you have all your magic. You came through it by the skin of your teeth."

"It was worth it if he survived." She looked up at him. "What about Marine? Where is she?"

"She's out there." Wesh nodded toward the house door. "She followed us down from the mountain when we brought you and Anríq here."

She searched the house a little more closely. The men of the Watch had located some dusty woolen blankets from somewhere.

Ten of them lay stacked in a pile against one wall. Another two lay next to Eliska. They'd fallen off her when she sat up.

She crossed her legs and started folding them.

"How do you feel now, my dear?" Wesh asked. "You should take it easy for a few days before you strain yourself."

"How long have we been here?" She found herself staring at everything. "We shouldn't have stayed here. Someone could have come after us."

"No one came. Anríq and I have been keeping an eye on things to make sure nothing threatens us. I don't know why, but we haven't seen a living soul since Anríq interceded between you and Marine." Wesh frowned at her. "Did you see anything? Did she communicate anything to you?"

"Disconnected images...." She shook her head, but it didn't clear her thoughts. "I don't understand what she did show me."

"What did she show you?" Wesh asked. "Whatever it was, I'm sure it was important."

"She showed me mostly just different Coil landscapes. Some were cities. Some were towns. Others were just chaotic Layers collapsing on top of each other. I wish I could tell you something useful."

Wesh compressed his lips. "Anyway, Anríq thinks it was worth it so it must have been."

"Did he tell you that?" she asked. "Did he see anything when he connected us to each other?"

"No, he says he only saw Darkness. We've all been waiting for you to wake up so you could tell us what it is that Marine knows."

Eliska went back to folding the blankets. Wesh didn't tell her how long the Watch had been hanging around in this shack waiting for her to wake up. It must have been a long time.

She still suffered a pang of guilt when she thought about Anríq getting hurt because of her. At least he made it. She would gladly have not come back at all as long as he was still here.

She stood up to put her blankets on the stack with the others. Her body felt weak, but at least she could move around.

She would regain her strength in time. Wesh was right. She shouldn't push it.

She sat down next to him by the fire. He kept sewing the whole time. God, he looked old! She might have been asleep for years for all the new wrinkles on his face.

She added wood to the fire for lack of anything better to do. This house stayed nice and warm despite the hole in the roof.

She was just wondering if she should do something useful to help with the chores when the door opened.

Yann and Anríq both came in carrying armloads of wood and laughing. Their cheeks shone and their eyes sparkled with more life than she ever remembered before.

Both men wore cloaks made of gar pelts and boots made of the same furry leather. Anríq wore his axe on top of his cloak.

He carried twice as much wood as Yann. Anríq's whole face lit up when he smiled. He looked much younger and much more like an innocent child when he smiled.

He froze on the threshold and stared when he saw Eliska sitting up awake. Her heart flipped at the look on his face. His eyes widened and his lips quivered.

He jolted back to his senses when Yann bumped into him from behind. Yann averted his eyes when he saw the way Anríq was looking at Eliska.

Yann used closing the door to push Anríq into the house and then closed the door behind both of them. Then both young men approached the fire to put their loads of wood down.

Anríq squatted next to Eliska, hesitated, and then laid his hand on her forehead.

His touch sent a charge of energy through her—a charge that didn't have anything to do with him using his magic to check that she was fully healed.

"She's fine," Wesh told him. "She's fully recovered exactly the way you said she would. All the Darkness is gone."

Anríq burst into a massive grin when he took his hand down. She couldn't help but smile back at him.

They shared something. She didn't even know what it was. She healed him and he healed her. That meant something. She just didn't know what it meant.

"Father will be thrilled when he sees you awake," Yann told her. "He was just complaining again outside about how long it was taking for you to recover."

"I'll have a word with him," Wesh interjected. "Eliska won't be ready to travel for a few days—and I don't see any reason why we should travel as long as we're safe here."

"How long can that last?" Eliska asked. "I'm surprised the Voyant hasn't come for us sooner."

"Maybe there's a reason for that," Yann suggested.

She raised her eyebrows at him. "What reason could that be?"

"Maybe Marine is protecting us."

Eliska gasped. "What makes you think that?"

"It's nothing we all haven't been thinking and talking about for days. She's the only thing that's different now. No one has attacked us since she's been traveling with us."

"But…." Eliska's mind went into a tailspin.

The Dark river drove the party out of the Ancestral Empire. Then the group fell through some layers full of Darklings.

No one had attacked or come after the party since Marine pulled Eliska out of the river. Could it be coincidence?

Marine's presence offered a much simpler, more straightforward explanation. She was the missing link in all of this—her and Anríq.

No one had attacked the party since Anríq joined them, either.

Eliska only had to glance at him to know his presence didn't protect them from anything. His magic didn't work that way.

The rest of the men returned a minute later. They made a big noise about Eliska waking up. Everyone talked about nothing but when the group would move on, if they should move on, and what would happen when they did.

"Maybe Marine isn't the one protecting us," Barsali pointed out. "Maybe something in this Island is protecting us. Maybe the Voyant can't find us here."

"That won't stop the instability from eventually taking this Island, too," Wesh replied. "The Temple records indicate we've been in an instability cycle for decades. It will only continue to escalate until the whole Coil becomes chaotic."

"Then we should stay here as long as we can," Omer reasoned. "If the Island is stable and no one is coming after us here, we have no reason to leave. We're comfortable here...."

"You call this comfortable?!" Rien countered. "Give me a feather bed and a pint of beer. Then we'll talk."

The others laughed. Eliska even caught Anríq laughing...and then she spotted Yann watching her.

He looked away and pretended not to be when he saw her looking at Anríq. She couldn't look at either of them, so she paid attention to the other men instead.

"How soon do you think you'll be able to travel, Eliska?" Yvan asked.

She jerked her thumb toward Wesh. "Ask my mother."

The men exploded in laughter again. Their talk flew thick and fast around the circle.

Neils worked non-stop to carve up the waterbuck the men brought in for their dinner. The men ate a lot more, now that they had a steady supply of food.

The whole atmosphere descended into a convivial atmosphere. Eliska could convince herself they were all safe behind walls in Middleborough or somewhere like it.

The men didn't complain at all when they eventually got their blankets, wrapped up on the floor, and fell asleep. They were all used to it by now.

Chapter 33

Yann wrapped a gar-fur cloak around Eliska's shoulders and tied it under her chin. He spent way too much time adjusting it around her and checking the collar to make sure it didn't cut into her neck.

He also looked way too deeply into her eyes while he did it. "How's that?" he asked.

Her cheeks turned bright red. "It's very toasty. Thank you."

He bit his lip to stop himself from grinning and turned away. "Let's go—and you tell me if you start to get tired. I'll bring you back."

"What will you do—carry me over your shoulder?"

He shot her a smirk over his shoulder as he walked out of the cabin. "Don't tempt me." He waited for her to come outside and yelled through the door to Wesh before Yann pulled the door shut. "We're going, Wesh!"

"Take care of Eliska, my boy!" Wesh called back.

Yann pulled the door shut. He would not stop grinning at her. "Oh, I'll take care of you, all right."

She forced herself to look away. So it was going to be like that. "Or I'll take care of you—one or the other."

"You can take care of me anytime you like," he returned. "Just say the word and I'm there."

"Stop it," she muttered.

They set off through the snow. This was the first time Eliska had left the house since she woke up.

She stopped a few yards from the door when she saw Marine sitting in the snow at a distance from the path.

"What is she doing out there?" Eliska whispered.

"She never does anything except sit there," Yann murmured back. "She doesn't come any closer or go any farther away. She's been over there in almost exactly the same spot since we moved down here from the mountain."

"Don't you even invite her inside—or give her anything to eat? I can't believe that."

"It isn't because we haven't tried. She moves off if anyone goes near her. Neils leaves food out for her and he says she eats it. She never comes close enough to come inside. We would be glad to have her if she did."

Eliska could only stand and stare at the girl. Whatever happened between Marine, Anríq, and Eliska affected Eliska.

It connected her to Marine in ways Eliska didn't understand yet. It opened a door that had been closed before.

Marine wasn't a shade of Eliska's past. She understood that now. Marine was a completely different person with a completely different relationship to her magic.

Eliska never would have dared to commune with the Dark the way Marine did—and yet she remained as powerful as ever. Her madness gave her access to a dimension of magic Eliska couldn't even dream of.

Yann got her attention by touching her elbow. "Come on. Let's keep going. She'll be there when we get back and I don't want you to tire yourself."

He set off down the well-beaten path. The light coming through the treetops lit up the snow even though the sun didn't break through the cloud cover.

Eliska followed him. The fur on her new gar-skin boots made her slip on the ice. She had to pay attention to every step.

She only walked a dozen yards before her weakness caught up with her. Walking through the snow took more energy than she realized.

Yann kept stopping to wait for her. She hated slowing him down. He was obviously used to walking much faster out here.

He turned off on a side path leading away from the main walkway. "This is one of the places we usually collect wood," he told her over his shoulder. "I'll cut it for you. Then you can carry one or two sticks back to the house. I'll take the rest."

"Thanks a lot," she grumbled. "Just tell the truth. I'll be carrying one stick if I carry any."

He laughed at her and stopped next to a huge tree that had toppled over in the forest.

The branches had died and the needles had completely fallen off. The branches were completely dry and brittle.

He took out an axe Eliska had never seen before and started chopping the dead branches away from the trunk.

"Where did you get that axe?" she asked. "You didn't have it when we landed on the mountain."

"We found another abandoned cabin deeper in the woods—a much bigger cabin. We got some tools and blankets from there."

"Why didn't you stay there instead of building this cabin here?" she asked.

"The roof had completely collapsed—and we'd already built this cabin. We'd been staying here for almost a month before we found it."

"A month!" she gasped. "Was I out for that long?"

"You weren't the only one. Anríq only woke up three days before you. You were both out the whole time."

She looked away, but just then, he came over to her holding a handful of short, chopped logs. He put them in her arms and started loading her up.

She scanned the woods while she waited. He only gave her a few logs before he started cutting some more for himself.

These woods sure looked bleak in the snow, especially considering how the men of the Black Watch had been living while she'd been out of her senses.

In a way, the very harshness of this Island gave it its unique appeal. No one else would choose to live like this. It was the best protection the group could ask for.

It didn't offer unlimited protection, though. Whoever or whatever was looking for the Watch wouldn't just give up because the party landed in this Island.

Yann came back over to her carrying his own load. "Don't tell me you want to go running back to Anríq so soon," he chided. "We just got here."

"I was just...." She spun around to stare at him. "Why do you mention him? He isn't here."

"That's the point, isn't it? Everyone can see how you look at each other and how you act around him. It's pretty obvious how you feel about each other."

"What are you talking about?!" she countered. Then her jaw dropped. "Are you jealous?!"

"Well, who wouldn't be? He's bigger, stronger, and better looking than I am. You're obviously a lot more attracted to him than you are to me."

She tried to hold eye contact with him, but she wound up looking away.

Any woman would be attracted to Anríq for his looks alone. His pure heart and soul shone through it all. It made him irresistible.

She headed back in the direction from which they'd come. "I don't know what you're talking about," she told Yann over her shoulder.

He followed her. "You can admit it. He's everything I wish I could be but I'm not. He has you practically eating out of his hand....."

She spun around to confront him even as she saw herself reacting overly emotionally to his comments. "He does not! I was worried about him. That's all."

"You said it yourself," he countered. "The men of the Black Watch swear an oath of celibacy and never marry. We're forbidden to take wives or to raise our own children...."

"Have you taken the oath?" Eliska asked. "You never said."

Now it was his turn to look away. "I haven't yet, but I will."

"Why would you if you want to marry and have a family? It isn't too late if you haven't taken the oath."

"I couldn't let the Watch down. I couldn't turn my back on everything my father has done for me. I never asked for this, you know. I never asked to be born into the Watch."

"Then leave it. Your father will understand. I'm sure he will."

He cocked his head to study her. "Would you give me a chance if I did?"

She spun away and started walking again. "You don't understand. It isn't like that."

He dogged her footsteps every step of the way. "Is it not like that because of me—or because of Anríq?"

"Will you stop talking about Anríq?!" she snapped over her shoulder. "This has nothing to do with him."

"What does it have to do with, then? Everything was going fine between us before he showed up."

"Stop it, Yann!" She heard herself screaming at him. Could everyone else hear her—including Anríq?

She summoned every ounce of resolve she possessed and turned around to face him. She fought her voice under control, but it still quavered with buried emotion.

She couldn't even identify what emotion she was feeling right now. Yann was right. Everything had been going so well between them before Anríq turned up.

She couldn't even say she felt something for Anríq—not anything that could draw her away from Yann.

Anríq was in a completely different class of human being. He was so far out of her reach that she never even thought of him like that.

Yann was not out of her reach. He was very real and right here in front of her.

She'd always known she could get together with Yann if she chose to. It never crossed her mind before that she could get together with Anríq.

It didn't cross her mind now, either, because she already knew it was impossible.

She took a deep breath and tried to steady herself.

"Listen," she breathed. "Anríq is a Servant. He's dedicated himself to serving humanity."

"I know that," Yann countered a little too venomously. "He's a better man than I am. He's better at everything than I am—and he's a magic-user. You have that in common with him. You don't have it in common with me."

She held up her hand to steady herself as much as him. "I'm sorry you feel that way about him—and I'm sorry if anything I did gave you the impression that I was interested in him."

"You are interested in him. Do you think I'm blind?"

She had to shut her eyes to stay calm. "I've always been alone....."

"I told you it doesn't have to be that way," he interrupted. "You could change."

"I can't change. You don't understand what I am. You wouldn't suggest that if you did."

"Would you change for Anríq if he asked you to?"

She looked away—mostly to think about how to answer that. What if....?

Yann misunderstood her silence and snorted at her. "So you would change for him but not for me."

"He doesn't think of me that way. He doesn't think of anyone that way. That isn't part of what he thinks about."

"Would you like him to? Of course you would. Any girl would."

She opened her mouth to argue back, but he didn't stick around to listen. He sidestepped around her and took off walking back up the path toward the cabin.

Chapter 34

Yann made it back to the cabin first. He didn't wait for Eliska to catch up with him.

He should have. He should have stayed with her to make sure she didn't fall over and pass out in the snow.

He didn't feel angry or resentful about the obvious chemistry between her and Anríq—not as angry or resentful as he sounded just now.

What girl in her right mind wouldn't be attracted to Anríq? He was everything a girl could possibly find attractive.

He was big, strong, good-looking, and impossibly kind and caring. He obviously cared about Eliska as the special prize that she was.

Why shouldn't he after the way she welcomed him, defended him, gave him her food from her own hand, and went out of her way to make sure everyone else thought the best of him the same way she did?

Yann had to get away from her if only for a few seconds. She would make it back to the cabin and then the whole thing would start all over again when Anríq came back.

He hadn't been able to stop beaming at her ever since she woke up. His awe and esteem for her skyrocketed after the way she convinced Wesh to use her magic to heal him.

Yann didn't want to stand in the way of that. He didn't want to be the reason either of them thought they couldn't be together.

He couldn't know if she was right about Anríq never thinking of her that way. Yann didn't understand the Servant's vow, but Eliska did. Who would know better than she would if Anríq was completely unavailable?

Yann couldn't even be happy about that. If she wanted him, why shouldn't she have him? She deserved the best, and if that wasn't Yann, then he cared about her enough to wish the best for her.

Anríq was the best for her. Yann didn't want to be her second choice. He didn't want to be something mundane and ordinary that she settled for when she couldn't get the man she really wanted.

He didn't even care about any of that. So he held her hand once. That didn't make them anything more than close friends. He saved her life and she saved his. That put him on the same level with Anríq.

Yann could put the whole subject behind him and just be happy to move on, now that both Anríq and Eliska were on the mend. They were both the best thing for this group's survival. Yann could be happy about that.

He just needed to spend a few short minutes away from her while he screwed his head on straight—the way it was before all this started.

He made up his mind years ago to join the Watch and take his vow of celibacy. He couldn't think of any better way to spend his life.

He never once considered throwing over that commitment—not until he met her.

She just distracted him from what he knew he had to do. Now she had passed out of his reach and left him to do what he knew he had to do. Everything worked out better this way.

He walked back into the cabin, put his wood on the pile, and squatted down to warm his hands over the flames until Eliska got back.

Wesh looked up. "Where's Eliska? You said you would take care of her."

"She's fine," Yann replied. "She's coming right behind me."

Wesh opened his mouth—no doubt to give Yann a lecture about how fragile she was.

She came in before Wesh could launch into it. She added her logs to the pile and then Anríq came back with Vidal and Rien.

The three of them had gone hunting, but they didn't bring anything back.

"There's nothing out there," Rien announced. "We have to keep going farther and farther to find game. We must have cleared out the area."

Just then, Yvan returned with Omer, Barsali, Neils, and Niyazi. Yvan took one look at the men's empty hands. "Nothing again?"

"All the waterbuck have migrated," Vidal replied. "Maybe it's time we followed them. At least we'll know where to find food."

Yvan glanced across the cabin. "What do you say, Wesh? How do you feel, Eliska? Are you strong enough to travel?"

"I might not be what I was before, but I'll get stronger as the days go on," she replied. "I say we move out, too."

"I suppose we have nothing to lose and everything to gain," Wesh replied. "We might find somewhere with better weather."

"Have any of you three seen anyone trying to find us?" Yvan asked.

"No, nothing," Eliska replied.

Anríq shook his head. "No."

"I keep checking, but the landscape is empty for a long way around," Wesh replied. "We could travel for days without seeing anyone."

"I find that impossible to believe," Omer muttered.

"So do I," Yvan replied.

"This Island should have turned to spring by now." Eliska created her Coil projection on her hand and rotated it in front of the group. "This Island might already be falling into instability. That might be why the seasons don't change."

"Then we should definitely move," Wesh replied. "It might get colder instead of warmer."

"That settles it," Yvan finished. "We'll move out in the morning. We'll follow the waterbuck. Maybe we'll have better luck."

"We can finish this one tonight." Neils squatted in front of the fire and unfolded the piece of hog hide where he kept the leftover food. "There isn't much left."

"It will be enough," Yvan told him.

Everyone sat down in a circle. Eliska sat next to Wesh with Neils on her other side. Did she do that on purpose so she wouldn't sit next to Anríq?

Anríq sat on Wesh's other side. Anríq and Eliska couldn't see each other or smile at each other or blush at each other or hand each other food the way they usually did.

Yann took the seat on the other side of Neils so he wouldn't be able to see Eliska or Anríq, either.

Yann really needed to put both of them out of his mind. What they did didn't concern him anymore. He was a member of the Black Watch—or as good as.

He succeeded in putting them out of his mind for the evening. He just had to focus on the other Watchmen and pretend that Anríq and Eliska weren't there.

Everyone woke up early the next morning. A current of excitement infected the cabin as everyone folded their blankets into the corner as usual.

"I guess we can just leave everything for the next person," Neils suggested. "Then they won't have to go looking for it."

"If this country is as deserted as Wesh says it is, this cabin will fall apart and decay back into the forest long before anyone finds it," Yann replied.

"Even better," Neils went on. "Then no one ever has to know we were here."

The sense of energized enthusiasm infected everyone when the party stepped outside and filed down the path for the last time.

They all wore their gar-fur cloaks and boots to keep warm in the crisp air.

No one said a word as they all passed Marine. She didn't look up. Was this the last time any of them would see her, too? Yann didn't believe that.

She spent months sitting out here in the snow—just waiting for the group to do something. Wesh was right. Whatever she wanted from them or with them must be something important.

She didn't follow right away. The group came to the end of their trodden path long before they left the woods. Deep snow drifts blocked the way.

Anríq went in front and used his size to plow a channel through the drifts. Barsali and Yvan followed him.

The men of the Watch took turns breaking the path and tramping the snow for those behind. Wesh and Eliska stayed in the back.

Yann stayed near her just because. He should have ignored and avoided her, but he couldn't do that. He didn't start caring for her like this only to turn off those feelings because things didn't work out.

He didn't know how things would work out, but he found as the day wore on that it didn't really matter. He needed to take care of her. Someone had to.

Anríq was too busy breaking the path for everyone. That left Yann in the rear making sure she kept up with the party and didn't tire herself out.

The job of breaking the path slowed everyone down enough. The endless process gave her plenty of time to rest before she had to make another push.

Marine caught up with them an hour later. Her arrival didn't surprise anyone even enough to remark on it. Everyone expected it.

The ordeal of getting through the snow got a thousand times worse when the party left the woods.

The group came to a broad expanse of open country piled in miles and miles of snow.

Anríq collapsed from exhaustion right there at the edge of the woods. "I need....I need to rest....."

Rien marched around him in a circle packing down the snow. "You've taken the front for long enough. You should fall back and let the rest of us take our turns."

Anríq didn't argue. He drank some of the party's water and dropped back to the middle of the line while Barsali, Omer, Niyazi, and Vidal went in front.

Then Yvan, Neils, and Rien rotated to the front to do the heavy work.

No one suggested that Wesh and Eliska do their share. For some reason, no one suggested that Yann go in front, either. They left him in the back with Wesh and Eliska.

They kept on that way until the sky started to get dark. "We'll be camping in the snow tonight," Barsali murmured.

"I see some trees ahead," Omer remarked. "Let's camp there. It will be better than nothing."

Silence fell over the group as they toiled the rest of the way across the field to the tree line. All the men worked together to pack down an area of snow big enough for the whole group.

Wesh started a fire in the center, but no one had any food. Marine lurked around the perimeter. She never came any closer.

"How long do we have to keep doing this?" Rien asked. "How long before we come to the end of this snow country?"

"I have an idea," Eliska blurted out. "I can use my magic to melt a path through it."

Yvan looked up. "You could do that? I mean, you could do it without hurting yourself?"

"My body is weak, but there's nothing wrong with my magic. You'll all die of exhaustion within a few days if we go on like this. I could even shatter this Island and get us to a warmer country."

"Don't do that," Wesh replied. "There must be some warmer part of this Island."

"That's what I was trying to tell you last night. This whole Island should have a warmer climate. Something's wrong with it."

"So is the whole Island snowbound?" Yann asked.

"It looks that way. Breaking through to a different one might be better."

"I don't want to bet our lives on 'might be'," Barsali interjected.

"You didn't tell us what you saw when Marine communicated with you," Wesh told Eliska. "I didn't want to ask before you were ready to tell us, but if we're already traveling into danger, maybe we should have some idea about where we're going and why."

"She didn't show me much and I don't completely understand what she did show me."

"Tell us," Wesh urged. "Anything is better than nothing."

Eliska picked up a stick from the pile the men had been adding to the fire. She scratched the tip onto the packed snow at her feet.

"Most of it was shadowy images or people and Darklings moving around...and then there was this one landscape. I don't remember much of the other landscapes, but this one was the most distinct."

She scrawled a line of square shapes and one large pointed one in the center. She also added a line of hills in the background behind everything else.

"I don't recognize the place," Eliska finished. "I've never been there."

"I recognize it," Wesh replied. "This tall one is the White Spire, the Voyant Mendicat's stronghold."

Eliska looked up. "It is? Are you sure?"

He nodded. "Marine must have been trying to tell you something about him. Either she was trying to find out the connection between you and the Voyant or she was trying to tell you about his plans for us."

"But these visions were too indistinct," Omer pointed out. "We have no idea why Marine showed Eliska this. Marine might not know anything more than we do except that the Voyant is the one coming after us to get whatever it is he thinks we have."

"It does seem a shame that she wasn't able to tell us what it is," Wesh mumbled. "That would have been much more helpful."

Just then, Marine startled everyone by coming into their camp for the first time. She'd never come this close to anyone since she flattened Yvan under the overhang.

Everyone jumped out of their seats to get away from her. Rien and Vidal both yelled out and Barsali accidentally stepped on Yann in his haste to get to his feet.

She ignored them all, pushed her way into their circle, and squatted down next to Eliska's sketch.

Marine picked up a different twig and laid it on the packed snow with its thinner end pointing toward the White Spire—or what Wesh said was the White Spire.

"What does that mean?" Yann asked. "Does that mean we should go toward the White Spire or away from it?"

Eliska stared down at Marine in a trance. Marine looked up at her and made eye contact for what seemed like a long time.

Eliska went still and quiet the way she did when Anríq connected the two girls to each other.

Yann was really starting to hate the hypnotic effect this girl had on Eliska. Nothing good ever came of it.

"Eliska?" he asked again. "What do you think this means?"

Her eyes snapped to his face and her expression cleared. By the time she thought to glance down at Marine, Marine turned away and bent over the drawing again.

She kept picking up more sticks and laying them on top of the sketch with exaggerated care. She took deliberate pains to place each one in exactly the right spot.

She added the second stick with its tip touching the first. She adjusted its angle so its fatter end rested an inch away from the fat end of the first stick. The two sticks converged with their thin ends pointing toward the White Spire.

Then she added a third stick in the same position so the three sticks formed an arrow. She kept adding more and more sticks, all with their ends connected next to the White Spire. She couldn't have made it more obvious that she was pointing at that one feature in this magical landscape.

"This could mean anything," Omer remarked. "She could just be trying to warn us about the Voyant."

"If the Voyant is the one hunting for us, we could go on the offensive and hunt him instead," Niyazi suggested. "We don't have to spend all this time running away from him if we already know where he is."

"We don't know where he is," Eliska countered. "I don't even know which Layer the White Spire is in. We wouldn't be able to find him."

Barsali turned to Wesh. "Do you know where the White Spire is?"

"I'm afraid not. The Temple records list the Voyant Mendicat, the White Spire, and the Voyant's supposed ability to control the Coil as nothing but legends and rumors. We don't even know if they're real."

"Marine seems to think they're real," Yann pointed out. "You said this vision was confirmation that he was the one behind this."

"It does seem coincidental that the Templars' scrying visions indicated he was the one going after Middleborough and now Marine is telling us the same thing," Wesh remarked.

"You mean you think that's what she's telling us," Vidal pointed out. "We don't exactly know what she's trying to tell us. She's showing us a landscape with the White Spire in it. She could be telling us that the Voyant is causing the Coil to become unstable. We don't know that she's telling us he's the one coming after us—or that anyone is coming after us."

"We already know someone is coming after us," Yvan corrected.

"All these incidents could have been caused by something else," Vidal argued. "No one has come after us while we've been in this snow Island. Maybe no one was coming after us in the first place and we misinterpreted what was happening."

"Someone definitely paid the Barbarians to go after the Black Watch," Eliska interjected. "They knew exactly where to ambush you after you crossed multiple Layers—which means that whoever sent them to find you had powerful magic. I don't think the Barbarian magic-users have that kind of power. It would have to be someone else—another wizard."

All eyes turned to Anríq. "What do you say, my boy?" Wesh asked him. "What do you think this vision means?"

"I don't know," Anríq mumbled. "I only serve."

"Do you know anything about the White Spire or where it is?" Omer asked.

"I don't know," Anríq repeated. "I've never heard of it before....or this Voyant you mentioned."

"We can't stay in this snow Island without supplies or at least the ability to hunt for ourselves," Yvan decided. "If you're right about it getting colder and never turning to spring, maybe Eliska is right and we should move to another Island."

"At least wait until morning," Vidal countered. "At least let us get some sleep before we face any more Darklings."

"None of us will be getting any sleep in this cold," Rien grumbled.

"Breaking through to a different Island could take us to a warm country or even a town," Eliska pointed out. "We could wind up there in the middle of the day. Then we wouldn't need all these furs."

Yvan started to answer, but Barsali interrupted by getting to his feet. He pointed across the snowy landscape in the direction the group had come to get here. "Look!"

The long, broken path of their footprints marked a trail through the flat white expanse of snow spreading in every direction.

Everyone else stood up to look—everyone except Marine. She stayed crouched at their feet while everyone stared off into the distance.

A bright light flared at the farthest edge of the horizon. Yann couldn't tell from here what caused that light, but it didn't look right against such dense darkness.

This primitive landscape offered no comforts or conveniences. His brain had become accustomed over the last few months not to expect any kind of sudden change to the environment.

The light contrasted with everything he knew about this rough, bare world—and the light kept getting brighter by the second. It glared in everyone's eyes.

"I don't like this," Rien muttered.

"The Island is collapsing!" Eliska snatched her staff. "Hold on!"

Yann didn't see it quickly enough. The light kept building out of the darkness until, without warning, it flared in the group's direction.

A blast of scorching air slammed into everyone and melted all the snow in an instant. A wall of flame thumped across the barren landscape and almost knocked Yann off his feet.

Everyone had to brace themselves against torrential wind. Flames licked all around the party and then it hit them full force.

Chapter 35

Yann hit the ground somewhere and coughed. He had to double-check every part of his body before he satisfied himself that he didn't break anything.

He couldn't remember if he went through any other Layers before he wound up here or what those Layers had been if he did go through them.

His confusion took a few more minutes to clear. He was definitely on the ground now.

His fingers dug into some more short-clipped, green fresh grass, but he wasn't lying on the side of the rocky mountain.

He dragged his head up and coughed again while he looked around. Anríq lay a few yards away.

Anríq groaned and rolled onto his side before he sat up and looked around, too. He saw Yann and crawled over to him.

Anríq placed his hand an inch above Yann's back and a tingle of energy floated through Yann's skin from Anríq's hand.

"I'm...I'm all right," Yann croaked. "Where is everyone?"

Anríq narrowed his eyes at the surroundings. Yann pushed himself onto all fours and then sat back on his ankles to assess the area.

The two boys had landed in a pasture full of sheep at the edge of a medium-sized town.

It looked bigger and more developed than Middleborough, but he didn't see any Black Watchmen guarding the place. The town didn't have an outer protective perimeter wall for Watchmen to guard.

Marketeers, bakers, and vendors pushed carts or drove wagons through the streets selling goods to the townsfolk. None of them paid any attention to Yann and Anríq.

"The others aren't in this Island," Anríq muttered.

"Can you find them?" Yann asked. "We have to get back to them. *I* have to get back to them. Can you locate them in that Coil thing that Eliska uses?"

"I don't know how," Anríq replied.

He got to his feet and waited for Yann to do the same thing. The two boys started migrating closer to the town without discussing it first. Yann glanced behind him.

He needed to find a way to rejoin his father and the rest of the Watch—but how could he do that if the Watch got lost in the Coil?

Maybe Yann and Anríq were the ones lost in the Coil. His blood ran cold at the thought.

Yann's father would freak when he found Yann gone. Yvan would never stop harassing Wesh and Eliska to find Yann.

Yvan would throw over the rest of the Watchmen's safety to go looking for his son—or maybe Yvan would leave the Watch. That would be a disaster.

No amount of looking around the area would tell Yann how to get back to the Watch. He had no magic he could use to shatter this Island to send himself somewhere else.

Anríq could do it, but that didn't guarantee they would meet back up with the Watch. Yann and Anríq might wander the Coil for years and never find the Watch.

Yann didn't give himself the option to think about that. He followed Anríq toward the town. The road wound over hills and valleys through farmland surrounding the town.

Anríq didn't seem to be going anywhere in particular and he definitely didn't explain himself.

This country posed such a contrast to the rugged, rustic harshness of the snow Island. Everything here had been manicured by centuries of human work.

Hand-constructed wooden fences surrounded all the pastures full of milk cows and freshly shorn sheep. All the houses had been built with hand-shaved boards with glass windows and plenty of ironwork everywhere.

This town was much more refined even than Middleborough.

Anríq paused after a little while, bent his knees, and placed his hand a few inches above the ground on the side of the road.

"What are you doing?" Yann asked.

Anríq muttered under his breath. "I'm trying to find out where we are and how to get back to the others."

"How are you doing that?" Yann asked. "You said you didn't know how to."

Anríq didn't answer for a minute. Then he stood up and started walking, but he stopped to do the same thing again a few minutes later.

"Can you find anything?" Yann asked.

"No," Anríq muttered.

"How are you doing that? Can you feel where we are in the Coil?"

Anríq compressed his lips, straightened up, and cast a hard look over the horizon toward the other towns in the distance.

"Do you know where we are?" Yann asked. "Have you ever come to this Island before?"

"Yes," Anríq replied over his shoulder.

"Is it possible the others landed in another part of the same Island?" Yann asked. "How could that fire bring us here and take the others to a completely different Layer?"

Anríq didn't answer that, either. He started walking.

Yann hustled after him to catch up. Anríq's silence didn't bother Yann so much when they had the rest of the Watch around to talk to instead.

Yann couldn't get stranded out here with someone who wouldn't even talk to him.

"Where are you going?" he asked. "How do you know where to go if you can't find the others?"

Anríq turned around so fast that Yann almost collided with him. Yann had been hurrying to catch up and didn't stop in time.

He had to jump backward to avoid crashing into Anríq's much larger frame.

Anríq narrowed his eyes and scowled at him. Yann shuffled his feet. "What? I'm just trying to understand."

Anríq compressed his lips one more time and then dipped his chin once. "I will serve."

Yann raised his eyebrows. "What does that mean? You'll serve how?"

"I will serve by talking to you the way you want me to. You require healing through talking to me—so I will serve you that way."

Yann's eyes fell the rest of the way out of their sockets. "You will?! Are you sure?"

"Yes, I will." Anríq turned away and started walking again. "What would you like to know?"

Yann stood rooted to the spot watching Anríq walk away. Yann struggled to believe what he'd just heard.

He didn't want to let himself believe that Anríq really invited him to ask as many questions as he wanted to.

Anríq didn't turn around. He kept walking. He made it thirty feet away before Yann woke up enough to run after him.

Yann pulled alongside him and fought his pulse under control, now that he fully realized what Anríq was about to do. Yann didn't want to believe it was real.

He chose his first question with care and cleared his throat before he asked. "Why are you doing so much to help us?"

"You heard what Wesh said. The Voyant is causing all of this instability. Whatever the Watch is carrying gives him the power to wreak havoc in the Coil. If it does, then the highest service will be to stop him."

"Why did you become a servant? Did something happen between you and the Barbarians? Did they throw you out?"

"They didn't throw me out. I left to become a Servant."

"Why?" Yann blurted out. "Did you want to become a Servant?"

"Yes," Anríq replied.

"Why?" Yann repeated. "Why would you turn your back on your tribe and your people? Did you do something to make them shun you?"

"I became a Servant because I didn't want to be a Barbarian. I wanted to be more. I wanted my life and my magic to be good for something other than attacking people, robbing them, and maybe even killing them. I wanted my magic to mean something."

"What about your family? You said they wouldn't welcome you back."

"I don't know if they would welcome me back. I haven't gone home to my tribe since I left."

Yann fell silent for a minute. Anríq hadn't said anything so far that Yann didn't already know or at least guess.

"How did your family react when you became a Servant?" Yann almost stopped walking when he remembered. "You were just a boy then—only twelve."

Anríq didn't turn around or take his eyes off the horizon. He expressed no emotion over whatever happened with his family.

"They didn't like it," he mumbled. "They tried to talk me out of it in more ways than one."

"What do you mean?" Yann asked. "What did they do?"

Anríq shrugged it away. "They beat me up. They even tied me up and kept me confined in a pit for a few weeks."

Yann's jaw dropped and he fell a few more paces behind before he came back to his senses.

He caught up with Anríq, but Yann hesitated to ask any more questions. He regretted asking now.

"What did you do?" Yann finally asked.

"I left," Anríq repeated. "They couldn't keep me locked up forever. My father released me, held a feast for me, and offered to make me his heir over all my brothers if I only stayed. When I refused, he cursed me, turned his back on me, and refused to look at me or talk to me again until I left."

"Wow," Yann breathed. "That sounds terrible."

"He threatened to kill anyone who gave me the Servant's mark," Anríq went on. "I had to go somewhere else to get it. I wandered for a year before I found someone willing to defy my father and give it to me."

"Did you travel to another country where no one knew him? Is that how you did it?"

"No, the person who gave it to me knew him very well. She knew about his threat and she did it anyway."

"She?" Yann repeated. "Who was it?"

"His mother—my grandmother."

Yann swallowed hard. He couldn't ask any more questions—not about that.

He would probably never know the full story of how Anríq became a Servant or all the heinous suffering he had to go through to fully live his destiny.

Yann couldn't ask. He realized now what a colossal mistake he made by bringing it up in the first place.

Eliska was right about Anríq's history being none of Yann's business. Yann should have left it in the past instead of tormenting Anríq by bringing it up and making him remember it all.

Yann followed him in silence for a while.

"What did you mean earlier when you said you wanted you didn't want to be a Barbarian?" Yann asked. "Aren't you still a Barbarian even if you're a Servant?"

"I will always be a Barbarian," Anríq replied. "I can't make myself into anything else."

"Do you still not want to be one? You could change your appearance. You could cut your hair and change your clothes to cover up your tattoos."

"It has nothing to do with being a Barbarian," Anríq replied. "Or maybe it has everything to do with being a Barbarian."

"I don't understand."

Now it was Anríq's turn to fall silent. He took a few minutes before he answered.

"The Barbarians use magic for marauding and stealing and destruction. If other people don't matter enough to protect them or at least to leave them alone, maybe I don't matter, either. If my magic is only good for destroying other people, maybe it's only good for destroying myself, too." Anríq shook his head to clear his thoughts. "I don't understand it. I only know I couldn't stay. I would have turned my magic on myself if I stayed. I wanted to turn it on myself for a long time. It came down to a simple choice—become a Servant or die."

Chapter 36

Yann stood at a distance from Anríq in the center of another town in the same Island. Yann leaned on his glaive while he waited for Anríq to finish haggling with one of the local market vendors.

The two boys had entered this town and Anríq immediately got mobbed by people asking him to heal them or their relatives or to use his magic to do other odd jobs.

He healed everyone they asked him to heal. He spent the morning working his way through town until he finished taking care of everyone anyone asked him to take care of.

Now he stood in the town's central market trading magical favors for food and other supplies.

Yann didn't get involved. He could have traded his fighting skills for food and other supplies, but that would take time. Anríq could accomplish everything so much faster.

Just then, one of the townspeople came over to Yann and pointed at the glaive. "How much for the weapon?"

"It isn't for sale," Yann replied. "I need this to defend myself."

The man rotated around Yann and narrowed his eyes to scrutinize the weapon. "It's very well made—gypsy make, if I'm not mistaken."

"You're right. It is," Yann replied. "That doesn't mean I want to sell it."

"I'll give you three hundred for it. You can buy yourself another glaive for half that and use the money for other things."

"I could buy myself another glaive for half the price and get something half as good," Yann returned. "Thank you, but no thank you."

"Be reasonable," the man insisted. "We don't see weapons like that very often. It's worth a lot of money."

"All the more reason I should keep it for myself." Yann turned away. "Here comes my friend. Thank you anyway. See you later."

Yann pushed himself off his glaive and headed into the market to meet up with Anríq. Yann didn't want anyone tempting him to sell his glaive, not even for food.

The man tagged after him until Yann caught up with Anríq. Then the man turned to Anríq. "Talk some sense into your friend. I can offer top dollar for the weapon. You could invest the money and become a rich man. Think about it. Don't walk away from the deal of a lifetime."

"Leave him alone," Yann fired back. "You can see he's a Servant. He isn't interested in your money or in talking about selling you my glaive. Now go bother someone else. We're leaving."

The two boys turned away and walked out of the market. No one else accosted them the rest of the way through town. Everyone who wanted Anríq's services had already asked him and gotten what they wanted.

He rummaged around in a bag and handed Yann a piece of cheese and a net bag containing five plums.

"Thank you," Yann exclaimed.

Anríq didn't answer. He'd fallen silent again as soon as he entered the town. He only spoke to anyone when he needed information about what was wrong with them or what they wanted him to do.

Yann found himself falling into the same silence. He felt much closer to Anríq after their previous conversation.

Now Yann didn't need to talk to Anríq—about anything. They understood each other well enough that they didn't need to talk.

Anríq ate his own food while they walked the rest of the way out of town and reentered the farmland.

"Will it be like this in all the towns?" Yann finally asked. "Eliska said people go looking for the Servants to ask for help."

Anríq nodded. "All the towns. The Servants just walk around with no destination. People come and find us and take us where we need to go. Then we wander on until the same thing happens."

Yann studied him on the side. "Was it worth it? Are you glad you left your home for this life? Do you ever have doubts that you made the right decision?"

"No, never," Anríq replied. "When I heal someone or help someone, I know I made the right choice."

Yann looked away. "I wish I could feel that way."

"What do you mean?" Anríq asked.

"The Watch. I wish I could be as certain that the Watch is where I really belong."

Anríq frowned at him. "It isn't where you belong?"

"I don't know. I guess everything is up in the air since we lost Middleborough. I don't know if I belong to the Watch anymore. I don't know if any of us do."

"How could you not?" Anríq shot his gaze to Yann's uniform. "You could change your appearance. You could change your clothes. Then no one would think you belonged to the Black Watch."

"I don't belong to the Black Watch," Yann mumbled. "That's the thing. I haven't taken my oath yet. I'm not old enough."

"And yet you fight with them and wear their insignia and do everything they do. Where does the doubt come in?"

Now it was Yann's turn to fall silent. He didn't want to tell Anríq about Eliska.

Yann had already crossed that line. He'd already made up his mind to let Eliska go if she wanted Anríq instead—or if she wanted any other man instead of Yann.

He didn't need her. She only muddied up his thoughts and confused him about his decision.

If he'd never met her, he would have sworn his oath to the Watch and never looked back. He would have spent his life in the Watch and been as happy about that as Anríq was about being a Servant.

Yann had to admire the irony that he met her just months before taking his oath. He couldn't have met her at a more crucial moment.

She stood at the crossroads. He could choose to ignore the temptation and continue to dedicate himself to the Watch. He could treat her as the bait put in his path to lure him away into a trap of pointless carnal satisfaction.

Or he could take her as a warning sign that his heart wasn't as deeply committed to the Watch as he thought it was.

The choice wasn't really about her at all. Did he want to commit himself to the Watch or did he want to find a wife and have a family? He didn't have to do it with her. He could do it with someone else.

Eliska offered him the chance to really decide instead of just doing what his father did.

He shook those thoughts out of his head and noticed Anríq studying him. "What?" Yann asked.

"You tell me," Anríq repeated. "Where does the doubt come in?"

"I don't know. I guess I don't have any."

"Liar," Anríq countered and turned away.

He went back to eating and Yann didn't draw him back into conversation. Yann didn't want to talk about that, either. He wanted to talk about that even less than he wanted to talk about Anríq's past.

"What do you want to do about meeting up with the others?" Yann finally asked.

"We can't meet up with the others if we can't find them," Anríq replied.

"There must be a way to find them," Yann insisted.

"I'm sure your father is trying just as hard to find you."

Yann looked away and didn't say anything about that. He really wished he could somehow pressure Anríq to do more to find the Watch.

Obviously Anríq couldn't find the Watch if he couldn't find the Watch. Constantly nagging him about it didn't change the fact.

The dread and anxiety of not knowing where they were or having any way to get back to them—it sapped Yann's nerves.

He kept searching the surroundings for any sign....but of course he never found any.

Anríq didn't assure him that they would find the Watch eventually. No one could promise that.

Anríq's silence somehow made it so much worse. Anríq must understand Yann's agitation. Anríq just couldn't do anything about it. No one could.

They wandered out of town and through the countryside in silence. Yann should have felt grateful that he even had Anríq.

Anríq knew how to navigate in the Coil. He knew how to deal with people and how to find food, shelter, and resources. He had magic to deal with instability and the ever-changing landscape.

Things could have been worse. Yann could have wound up alone out here. He probably wouldn't have lasted a day.

Of course Anríq didn't remind Yann of that, either. Anríq never told Yann to be grateful for what he had. Yann didn't have to confide his fears to Anríq because Anríq already knew.

Yann marveled for the thousandth time that Anríq actually chose this life of his own free will. No one made him go off into the Coil alone to wander for the rest of his days.

Yann never would have done that, not even if he had Anríq's size, strength, and magic. Nothing would have been worth that. Yann might even have been willing to die to avoid it.

They camped that night by the side of the road in the middle of nowhere. Yann built a fire and the two boys shared the rest of the food Anríq had traded his skills for in town. The two of them had been doing the same thing for three days.

Yann found himself studying Anríq across the fire.

"Ask your questions," Anríq prompted.

Yann tried to look away and failed. "I don't have any questions. You've already answered them all."

"Then why are you looking at me like that?"

"I'm just thinking."

"What are you thinking about?"

"About you—about what it's like for you to go from town to town with no destination."

"The Servant's life is my destination. I don't care where I do it."

"That's what I mean. If you can't meet back up with the Watch, you'll just go back to wandering the way you were before."

"Of course I will," Anríq replied. "What else is there to do? You have nothing else to do, either. Why not do that?"

"That's what I was just thinking about," Yann told him. "You'll keep doing this, and as long as I stay with you, I'll keep doing the same thing."

"You don't have to stay with me," Anríq pointed out. "You could stay in any of these towns. You could get a job or sell your skills or hire yourself out as a guard. I'm sure any number of people would be happy to take you."

Yann stared down into the flames. "I know all that."

"Then why do you stay with me?"

"That's what I was just trying to figure out."

"So what's the answer?" Anríq asked.

Yann looked up. "Why are you talking to me so much? Aren't you supposed to stay silent?"

"I told you. You require healing."

"I do?" Yann asked. "I feel okay?"

"No, you don't feel okay. You feel pain—here." Anríq touched his fingertips to the center of his sternum. "It eats away at you and never goes away. That's why you need to talk to me, even if I'm the one asking the questions."

Yann couldn't look at him again. The gnawing doubt really had been eating away at him.

He should hate Anríq for calling it what it was and blurting out so explicitly how much it bothered Yann.

Yann couldn't hate Anríq for that—or for anything else.

Anríq settled back against the bank by the side of the road and folded one arm under his head. "You'll tell me eventually and then you'll feel better."

"Is that why you're doing this—to make me feel better?"

"Of course," Anríq replied. "I'm a healer. Do you think I can sit by and watch someone suffer without doing something to heal them? Do you think you're any different from all these other people?"

"No, of course not."

"You called me your friend in town," Anríq went on. "Who would need that healing more than a friend?"

Yann didn't answer. He thought at the time that Anríq was too far away to overhear Yann telling that man that Anríq was his friend.

Anríq's power must have allowed him to hear Yann over all the other noise flooding the market.

Yann only said it in passing. Now that word stabbed him in the chest even more brutally than the pain already tormenting him there.

My friend. Yann had never had a friend before—not ever.

Yann couldn't even remember having a conversation with someone he considered a friend. He spent all his time with his father and the other Watchmen.

They had never been his friends and never treated him as one. They were all his superiors and they treated him that way.

They treated him like their son, their little brother, or just some kid they had to train so he could stand his post on the wall without getting killed.

Yann couldn't call Eliska a friend, either. He didn't know what she was, but she was definitely not his friend. He didn't want her as a friend.

He wanted her as more than that even if they never wound up together. She would always be more than that.

Chapter 37

Yann and Anríq woke up the next morning and continued down the same road to the next town. Would this be the town where Yann parted ways with Anríq? Was Yann really ready to go that far?

He couldn't imagine life without Anríq now. Yann's whole destiny seemed to be tied up with Anríq now for some reason Yann couldn't explain it even to himself.

Yann expected everything to play out the same in this town as it did in all the other towns he and Anríq visited.

Yann would have to find some way to occupy himself while Anríq healed all the town's sick and injured people. Then Anríq would have to fix things no one else in town could fix, find things no one else in town could find, and construct things no one else in town could construct.

Anríq went through all of this so methodically. He never asked for payment for healing anyone. He only expected payment for the little conveniences the townspeople could do themselves or would take longer to do.

Yann was just thinking about how to pass the time while he waited for Anríq to finish when the two of them passed a skeleton by the side of the road.

It sat propped against the grassy bank with a placard resting across the skeleton's chest. Someone had painted across the placard in messy black letters, *Danger! Go no further! Death inside!*

"That doesn't look good," Yann remarked.

"They must have a plague or something going on," Anríq replied. "I've seen this before."

He kept going. Yann didn't want to go anywhere with death inside, but being a wandering healer everyone turned to for help must have compelled Anríq to try to help the town.

The two boys passed four more skeletons, each with a placard giving the same warning.

"Can you tell what killed them?" Yann asked.

Anríq approached the last skeleton and placed his hand on its skull. "It was something magical."

"Really? They didn't die of disease?"

"No. I'm certain of it." Anríq turned his sharp gaze toward the town. "They need help. They wouldn't leave these skeletons unless it was serious."

He started forward again. Yann hesitated, but if Anríq was going in, Yann better go, too.

If Anríq could heal whatever was wrong with the town, maybe he could make sure Yann didn't meet the same fate.

A sturdy protective stone wall surrounded the town, but Yann didn't see any men on watch. A heavy wood and iron gate blocked the entrance where the road went into town. The gates were closed and probably locked from the inside.

The boys traveled another few hundred yards before the gates burst open. Ten people rushed out, charged up the road to the two boys, and the townspeople surrounded Anríq all talking at once.

He didn't answer them. He looked from one flushed face to the other trying to hear everything they were saying at the same time.

Yann stood off to one side. Should he avoid touching these people?

None of them noticed him. They seized Anríq by the hands and tried to pull him toward the town even though he was already going there.

They all babbled about the affliction striking their town. From the little Yann could gather, these people gave Anríq a litany of all the various symptoms everyone in town had been suffering from.

Yann didn't know anything about medicine, but he'd seen enough of the world to know these symptoms were too different from each other. They didn't all belong to the same class of disease.

That was the problem. One person suffered from a fever. One person broke out in boils all over his body. Another dropped dead with no symptoms at all.

Each person suffered a completely different form of whatever caused the outbreak—or attack—or whatever the hell it was.

Anríq didn't say a word the whole way back to town. He wouldn't have been able to get a word in edgewise even if he hadn't taken a vow of silence.

One youngish woman and an older man kept hold of his hands all the way back to the gate. They all kept talking right up to the very threshold.

They fell unnaturally silent the minute they got back to the wall. Every eye turned inward to stare at the town.

A few dead bodies lay scattered in the street. Some skeletons sat slumped against the walls of houses. They must have been there for a long time.

Not a living thing moved in town besides these ten people who came out to get Anríq. The streets and shops stood empty. A deadly silence hung over the town.

"It started a year ago," the middle-aged man breathed. "We don't know why. It just started out of nowhere for no apparent reason—and then the Corsairs started their attacks."

Yann spun around fast. "Corsairs—attacking?!"

The man nodded. "They attacked for no reason. They waited until the curse brought us to our weakest point and then they sacked the town. They've sacked us practically every month for two years. We don't know why. They never take anything. They just destroy as much of the town as they can, kill as many people as they can, and then leave so they can do it all over again the following month."

Yann frowned. "That makes no sense."

"Who knows why the Corsairs do anything? They're beasts." The man grabbed Anríq's hand even tighter. "My name is Avol Dyrio. I'm the mayor of this town. Please come to my home. I would be honored to give you hospitality while you carry out your sacred calling."

"He'll do no such thing, Avol!" the woman on Anríq's right cut in. "You only want him to stay with you so he'll heal your family first." The woman seized Anríq's hand. "Please come to my home. I have three young children all on the verge of death. We need you more than he does."

"We all have sick children and relatives at home, Aria," a younger man interrupted. "None of your families are more important than anyone else's."

"You can't talk, Gachu!" Aria snapped over her shoulder. "You haven't lost anyone close to you yet."

"But you will," Avol snarled. "Then you'll know how it feels."

"This Servant can decide who to heal first," Gachu replied. "We brought him here to help us. We'll all abide by his decision—and he and his friend can sleep in the old church house. Then none of us can say we're showing him any favors."

"His name is Anríq," Yann interrupted.

"Oh." Avol frowned at Anríq like it just now occurred to this man that Anríq even had a name. "Well, where would you like to start?"

Anríq shook off both the people holding onto him and headed for the nearest house to the right of the gate.

The ten people who'd gone out to get him stayed where they were and stared after him in horrified shock. They must not have really thought he would choose the nearest house at random.

They didn't follow him over there. That left Yann to go with Anríq.

Yann dreaded finding out whatever was inside that house, but he would be damned if he let Anríq face it alone.

Rickety wooden stairs rose from ground level to a door high on the side of the building. Yann followed Anríq up there and Anríq threw open the door.

Yann peered around Anríq's big shoulders at a filthy room with most of the furniture smashed to matchsticks. A single old woman stood in the center of the room wearing a threadbare cotton slip worn practically transparent with age.

She held a longsword in her skeletal arms and stringy white hair hung over her face. It spilled across her emaciated shoulders where every bone jutted through paper-thin skin.

She whirled from one side to the other swiping her sword at the air. She kept gasping from the effort of holding up the sword.

She turned in Yann's and Anríq's direction. Her glazed eyes and wild features registered not a trace of recognition that the two boys were standing there watching her.

Yann and Anríq exchanged glances. This presented a much different challenge than the other cases of healing Anríq dealt with in previous towns.

"Are you sure this curse is magical?" Yann murmured out the side of his mouth.

"More than ever," Anríq murmured back. "There's nothing wrong with her physically—except that she's been doing this for so long that she's forgotten how to eat."

"How is she even still alive?" Yann asked.

Anríq unhooked his club from his belt. "I'll take care of the sword. As soon as I disarm her, grab her and hold her so I can get near her."

Yann nodded. At least he didn't have to face this insane woman holding any kind of weapon.

The woman didn't see the two boys inch into the room. Yann propped his glaive against the wall. Anríq hefted his club and stepped out right in front of the woman.

He dwarfed the woman by a mile, but she definitely saw him this time. She let out a feral screech, raised her sword, and charged him.

Yann would have jumped in to stop her. He didn't see how she could hurt Anríq when she didn't have a scrap of muscle on her frail bones. He could have crushed her with that club and put her out of her misery in seconds.

She slashed the weapon at him. He hauled back his club, and with one almighty blow, he shattered her sword into a million fragments.

Yann lunged in behind her and hooked his arms around her elbows to pull her arms back.

She kicked and fought a lot harder than he expected. Whatever curse affected the town gave her unnatural strength.

He had to strain every fiber just to hold her still. Even then, she jerked back and forth so hard that she knocked him off balance.

She swung her legs around trying to kick both boys. Anríq rushed in and tried to touch her head, but she kicked him in the chest and then swung her other foot in a high arc to try to kick him in the head.

He dodged back to kept out of range. Yann nearly lost his grip on her. Her skinny body writhed in his grip. She almost broke free before he tightened his arms around her shoulders.

She howled and shrieked to wake the dead. She yanked and tossed from side to side and then hurled what little weight she had back against Yann.

He stumbled and bumped into the bed in the corner. It had survived multiple sword attacks from this woman. Hack marks indented the frame and deep slashes sliced open the mattress and bedspread.

The woman's weight pitched Yann over onto his back. He tried to angle his fall so she fell on top of him. He had to concentrate all his energy just to keep his hold on her so she didn't get away from him.

Anríq rushed them and bent over the woman. "Hold onto her, Yann!" Anríq bellowed over her noises.

"I am holding onto her!" Yann yelled back. "Do whatever you're going to do! Do it now! Hurry!"

Anríq dove on top of the woman and pinned her under his own weight. His bulk crushed her with Yann trapped underneath, but at least the woman couldn't move around now.

Anríq straddled her legs to stop her from kicking—and then he finally grabbed her head in both his massive hands.

He let off a powerful thump of magic into her that knocked her out cold. She wilted on top of Yann and lay still.

Yann took a few agonized seconds before he dared to let go of her. He didn't trust her not to spring back to life any second now.

Anríq sank back onto his knees panting hard.

"Is that it?" Yann asked. "Is she healed now?"

"I haven't even started. I just knocked her out so she wouldn't attack us. You can get up now."

Anríq climbed off the bed and lifted the old woman's body away so Yann could get up. Then Anríq laid her back down.

"What do you have to do to heal her?" Yann asked.

"I don't know yet." Anríq laid the backs of his knuckles on the woman's cheek. "She's ice cold. Get a fire going for me, will you please? I saw a stack of firewood downstairs."

Chapter 38

Yann left the old woman's house, went downstairs, and loaded his arms with firewood. The townspeople who'd brought Anríq in still stood in the same place staring at Yann in slack-jawed horror.

They kept staring at him when he climbed back up the stairs to the woman's house.

"It looks like we aren't the only people who have tried to come in here and do something about her," he told Anríq when Yann returned. "No one will come near the place."

"Could you ask them to bring me some milk, some salt, and some of the white daisies we saw growing on the roadside earlier?" Anríq asked over his shoulder.

Yann got to work. He built a big fire in the woman's fireplace to warm the house. Then he set a kettle of water over the flames.

The women of Middleborough always set a kettle of water on to boil whenever anyone got sick. That was always the first thing they did even if they didn't know what else to do.

Yann didn't know if Anríq would need hot water, but the woman would probably need a hot meal or maybe some soup when she finally got better.

Anríq pulled out all his trinkets from his bag, drew complicated designs on different parts of the woman's body, and then started using his magic on her. Yann went back outside and crossed the road to where the townspeople stood gaping at him.

"You can all go back to your homes now," he told them. "Anríq will get to you in your turn."

"What if our relatives die before he gets to us?" Aria asked.

"I'm sure your sick relatives are no more important than that old woman," Yann replied. "If you really want to make this go quicker, you could always help him. He needs all the help he can get."

"How *can* we help him when we don't have any magic?" Avol asked.

"I don't have any magic, either," Yann replied. "I'm helping him. If you don't want to do that, I suggest you go home."

He walked away from them, unlocked the town gates, and passed down the road until he found the daisies.

By the time he got back, only Gachu remained standing outside the old woman's house. "How can I help him?" Gachu asked. "I don't know anything about magic."

"He asked me to bring him some milk and salt. Do you know where I can find any?"

Gachu nodded. "I'll bring them to you."

"Thank you." Yann went back upstairs.

Anríq stood by the woman's bed and let his hand hover over her face. She lay insensible on the mattress. She didn't regain consciousness.

Anríq's hand trembled for a minute. Then the woman's body started to quake and convulse on the bed in time to the movement in his hand.

The vibration spread through the whole bed until her body bounced off the mattress. Even the bed frame bounced off the floor and thumped each time it banged down.

All at once, the commotion stopped without warning. Anríq doubled over and rested his big arms on the mattress while he gasped for breath. Sweat drenched his face and hair.

Yann went over to him. "Are you okay?"

"It's harder than I thought," Anríq croaked. "It's buried deep inside her—inside all of them."

"Do you want me to do anything? Here. I brought your daisies and one of the men is bringing the milk and salt."

Anríq pushed himself up still breathing heavily. He cupped his hands and Yann scooped the daisies into Anríq's hands.

"Thank you, Yann," Anríq gasped.

"Are you sure you don't want me to do anything else?" Yann asked.

"Hold her down so she doesn't move around so much. I need to concentrate. Her shaking breaks the connection."

Yann didn't understand a word Anríq just said, but whatever.

Anríq scattered the daisies all over the bed. Then he placed two in each of the woman's hands, one of which he laid across her chest. He positioned her so she looked like she was holding the flower because she wanted to.

Just then, Gachu came in with the milk and salt. Anríq dipped his fingertips in the milk, flicked droplets all over the woman, touched a few droplets to her lips, and then sprinkled salt all over her and the surrounding bed.

He glanced up at Yann watching him. "She'll probably fight back again. You'll have to hold her down like you did before. Do you understand? Can you do that?"

Yann nodded even though he didn't understand. He didn't want to get into another fight against this woman, but he would do it to help Anríq heal her—of whatever the hell was wrong with her.

Anríq straightened up, placed his hand above her face where he'd been holding his hand before, and nodded to Yann.

The woman wasn't fighting back now, so he took advantage of the lull, climbed onto the bed, and used his whole body to flatten her into the mattress.

He made sure to hook his leg over her legs to stop her from kicking—just in case she woke up suddenly.

Anríq took a deep breath and his hand started to tremble again. The energy in the room built to a pounding thump.

The bed jumped higher even with Yann's weight on it. Gachu stood back by the door like he wanted to bolt for safety.

The racket escalated louder and louder. The woman's body jolted so badly that she nearly threw Yann off even when he used all his strength to hold her down.

The tremor in Anríq's hand spread to the rest of his body. His whole face shuddered from the effort and sweat poured off him.

All at once, the woman exploded to life with an unearthly roar. She launched herself off the bed.

Yann lunged on top of her to pin her down, and at that moment, a rushing surge of black vapor ejected from her mouth straight into Anríq's hand.

The vapor streaked out of her, into his hand, and vanished beneath the skin.

The woman buckled under Yann's weight and Anríq collapsed onto the floor. He folded like a wet sack and his body slammed down on the hollow boards.

Yann dove off the bed in a flash and tried to grab him. "Anríq!" Yann hauled Anríq up by the shoulders and got in his face. "Anríq!"

Anríq's body weighed a ton. His eyes drifted half-closed. Sweat saturated every inch of his skin and hair.

"You gotta sit up!" Yann panted, but he couldn't lift Anríq off the ground. "Come on! You gotta sit up!"

Yann fought harder than ever to move Anríq's body, but nothing worked. Yann looked around in panic and saw Gachu standing there in the same place.

"Help me!" Yann roared. "Help me pick him up!"

Gachu shook his head fast, took a few stumbling steps backward, and took off staggering down the stairs to get as far away from this cursed house as possible.

Yann cast one last hopeless glance around. Anríq couldn't be cursed himself now. That would be Yann's worst nightmare.

"Come on, Anríq!" Yann husked. "Come on!"

Anríq groaned and tried to lift his head. He didn't straighten up, but at least he responded.

He tried once to sit up and fell back on his seat leaning against the bed. Yann didn't know what to do, so he darted back to the fire, grabbed a cup off the old woman's shelf, dipped it into the bucket of water Yann had brought in, and carried it back to Anríq.

Yann knelt down and held the cup to Anríq's lips. "Drink this. Then I'll find somewhere for you to lie down."

"No...." Anríq rasped. "I have to....keep going....."

"You can't even stand up," Yann pointed out.

"I'll be okay," Anríq whispered. "Just....just let me rest for a minute."

Yann didn't want to let him rest. He wanted to grab Anríq and run for it. He wanted to leave this god-forsaken town behind and run far, far away from whatever curse these people brought upon themselves.

The old woman distracted him. She sighed as if she was just waking up from being asleep and tried to sit up to look around. "Doliva?" she called out in a quavering voice. "Doliva—are you there?"

Yann stood up and looked down at her. The instant he laid eyes on her, he knew she didn't have any memory of using her sword to attack anyone or to destroy her own furniture.

Her face shone with a benign smile. This old woman never fought anyone in her life. Whatever Yann had been fighting since he came into this house wasn't the woman.

He bent over her and stroked her ragged hair out of her face. "Doliva isn't here, but I'll take care of you. Lie quietly and rest. I'll get you something to eat and a hot drink."

She beamed up at him. She definitely recognized the person in front of her now. "Thank you so much, my boy. You're so kind."

He crossed to the fire, took the kettle off, and used a different pan to warm up the leftover milk. Then he ransacked the house until he found some ancient bricks of cheeks.

They must have been sitting on the cupboard shelf for the whole two years of the curse. The rind on the outside had hardened to solid granite. He had to use the hatchet from the fireplace to hack one of the blocks in half.

The inside smelled perfectly good. He carved off the rind and toasted the cheese over the flames.

By the time he got back to the bed, Anríq lay curled up on his side on the floor with his eyes closed.

Yann would have liked to drape a blanket over Anríq, but Yann didn't see one apart from the torn blankets on the woman's bed. Yann used them to cover her.

He sat down next to her and fed her the milk and cheese. She kept mumbling her thanks to him until she finished.

Then came the inevitable moment when Yann bent over Anríq. Yann touched his shoulder thinking Anríq might be asleep.

He opened his eyes immediately and hauled himself off the floor. He couldn't have been asleep.

"I better go to the next house," he mumbled.

"Are you sure you're up for this?" Yann asked. "If everyone is as hard as she was...."

"They will be," Anríq muttered. "The same curse is affecting everyone."

He stood up and frowned down at the woman. Her magnificent smile slipped when she saw him. Then her frightened eyes darted to Yann.

"It's okay," he told her. "This is Anríq. He's a Barbarian Servant. He's the one who healed you. He won't hurt you."

Her smile burst back to life. She brought one of her withered arms out from under the blanket and held it out to Anríq. "Thank you so much, my dear. You're both so kind."

She clasped Anríq's hand. He didn't try to stop her.

"He has to go to the next house and heal the rest of the town," Yann told her. "Stay in bed. Someone will come to check on you soon. If they don't, I'll come back myself. I promise. Stay here."

"All right, my darling," she quavered and smiled up at him like he might be her own grandson.

Yann and Anríq left the house. Anríq paused on the stairs. Yann frowned at him. "Are you sure you're all right?"

"I will be." Anríq started walking again.

Yann had his doubts, but Anríq seemed to rally by the time the pair got to the next house.

Chapter 39

The next house Yann and Anríq came to was on the ground. The case inside appeared much more straightforward than the previous one.

A mother, father, grandmother, and four young children lived there. No one attacked the two men with weapons nor did they fight back.

A different malady afflicted each person. The grandmother sat in a corner rocking on her stool, hugging her arms around her shoulders, and sobbing uncontrollably. She didn't respond at all when Yann told her that Anríq was a healer who was here to help them all.

The father sat at the table with his arms folded on the surface and his face buried in them. He snored nonstop and didn't wake up when Yann and Anríq shook him.

The mother stood in the opposite corner screaming bloody murder and clawing at her face, arms, and body with her fingernails. She'd already bloodied herself enough to soak her dress.

She didn't see Yann or Anríq at all, either.

All four children crowded onto one bed in the corner. The oldest boy convulsed in spasms. His next oldest sister lay on top of him with her back flattening him against the wall to hold him still.

She sprawled her arms and legs wide and stared out into the room with huge eyes. She didn't blink once, not even when Anríq passed his hand in front of her face.

The youngest boy lay near the very edge of the bed with his head hanging off the mattress. His head dangled toward the floor and a line of mucus dripped from his nose and mouth to form a puddle underneath him.

Anríq took hold of the kid's hair to pry his head up. A thick film covered the boy's eyes and crusted around his nose. His head sagged the minute Anríq let go of it.

The middle girl lay flat on her stomach with her face buried in the pillow. Yann didn't see what was wrong with her until he tried to turn her over.

He sprang back in horror and yanked his hands away when he saw that her face wasn't there anymore. Her skull ended at the ears. A solid sheet of bloody flesh covered everything in between her ears where her face should have been.

Anríq came over to take a look when he saw Yann's reaction. "The rest of her looks okay...and she's still breathing," Anríq remarked. "This is just the curse. She should come back to normal when I break it."

Yann's eyes skimmed the room. "Are you telling me....are you telling me you have to go through the same thing with each of them that you went through with the old woman—and then you have to go through the same thing with everyone else in the whole town?"

"Yes, exactly—so we better get to work. I need you to build a fire, bring in more milk, salt, and daisies, and then try to find some food for these people. They're all going to wake up as hungry as the old woman."

Yann gulped and hustled out of the house. This Servant business was turning out to be a thousand times harder than he realized.

He got busy handling everything while Anríq started on the drooling boy. Anríq rolled him over. At least Yann and Anríq didn't have to knock anyone out in this house.

Anríq started drawing his symbols on the boy. Yann tried not to watch when Anríq started pulling the Darkness out of the kid.

Yann bent over the fire to add more wood to it when he heard what sounded like a whimper of agony.

He crossed to the bed to find Anríq grimacing in pain and sweating just as badly. The boy convulsed on the bed and the whole bed started to shudder.

Anríq didn't stop this time, not even to ask Yann to hold the boy down. Anríq kept going until the boy let out a gasp and another flood of black vapor erupted from his mouth.

It all poured into Anríq's hand as before. He crashed down on his knees this time and let his head rest on the mattress. He didn't go as far out into space as he did with the old woman.

He got up much sooner this time, too. Then he started working on the girl with no face.

Yann walked away. Seeing Anríq in pain bothered Yann too much to stand around watching. Anríq already told Yann what to do to help him.

The patients all woke up cheerful—and hungry. Yann had his work cut out for him going through the town and raiding every pantry for all the food he could find.

It wasn't easy. The few healthy people left in this town hoarded their food. The sick had been down for so long that all the food in their houses had either rotted or turned as hard as rock.

It took a lot to convince the healthy people to part with any of their supplies to take care of the newly healed patients, but Anríq's condition worried Yann much more.

He worked his way through the second house. Yann started to fear the worst when they entered the third house.

It was a large, two-story house with four families living under one roof. Each family had at least three children.

Anríq started in the very first bedroom he came to and worked his way from room to room without stopping.

Yann went back and forth to the well for water and back and forth to any firewood pile he laid eyes on. He didn't care if he took wood from one house to supply another.

He lit the fire in the kitchen stove and put on a pot of water to heat. He was on his way back to the house with a second bucket of water when he happened to pass the third bedroom down the hall—the bedroom Anríq had been working in a second ago.

Yann didn't hear any noise in there, so he put the bucket down and went in.

Three children lay on the bed. They all suffered from horrible boils erupting all over their faces, arms, necks, and legs.

Anríq lay unconscious on the floor next to the bed with blood dripping out of his nose. Yann attacked him again, but Anríq didn't respond at all this time. He was out cold.

Yann tried to roll him over. Anríq's body had gone rigid. He didn't uncurl when Yann turned him onto his back.

Yann threw inhibition out the window, left Anríq lying there, and stormed out into the street. Yann had seen enough—and Anríq had done enough.

Yann barged through town until he found the mayor, Avol. "Where's the church house your man said my friend and I could stay in?"

"Um....it's right over there." He pointed to the church in another corner of the town. The mayor frowned at Yann. "Is something wrong?"

"Round up two of your strongest men and tell them to come over to that house there. My friend collapsed and we need a few strong men to carry him to the church house so he can recover."

The mayor turned white as a sheet. "What do you mean—he collapsed?"

"He took the curse on himself to save those people's lives. Do you get it now? He drained the curse out of them and exhausted himself. Now bring your men over there before he dies, too."

Yann walked away fuming. Nothing better happen to Anríq because of this.

Anríq was still out senseless on the floor when Yann got back. Yann could barely lift one of Anríq's arms, let alone any other part of him.

The children in the bed were all waking up. They didn't understand the commotion when the town men came in and hauled Anríq out of the house.

Yann gave orders to the mayor and any other able-bodied people hanging around to take over tending to the newly recovered patients. Yann had more important things to deal with.

He followed the town men to the church house. It turned out to be a little stone building with one main room and one bedroom in the back.

The town men put Anríq on the bed and left Yann blessedly alone.

He turned all his attention to Anríq, but Yann couldn't help him. Yann couldn't fix whatever was wrong with him the way Wesh and Eliska healed Anríq last time.

Yann covered him up with blankets, heated some warming irons on the stove, and slipped them under the blankets to keep Anríq warm. Then Yann tore the town apart a second time to find enough food to make Anríq some soup.

Yann was just taking the soup off the fire when he heard Anríq stirring in the other room. Yann sat down on the mattress next to him. "How do you feel? You look terrible."

"I'm sure I feel much worse," Anríq croaked.

"You should work more slowly so you have time to recover between patients." Yann held out a bowl of soup. "Eat this."

"I don't want anyone else to die. I need to heal as many people as possible as quickly as possible."

"You don't need to do any of that if it costs you your life."

Anríq tried to sit up and failed. Yann took the bowl back, crammed another pillow under Anríq's head, propped him up, and tipped the soup into his mouth while Anríq drank it.

He sank back into place with a shaky sigh. "Thank you, Yann," he breathed.

"Just make sure you get out of this town alive, okay? Don't die on my watch. I didn't sign up for that."

Anríq looked away. "I won't."

"Are you sure? It seems like you're in a hurry to destroy yourself with service the same way you said you wanted to destroy yourself with your magic."

"I have no desire to destroy myself."

"Then slow down. Please. I wouldn't want anything to happen to you before I find a way to take you back to...." Yann stopped himself in time.

Anríq's eyes blazed with an unnatural light considering how weak he was acting. "Before you find a way to take me back to what?"

Yann used that moment to put the bowl down so he wouldn't have to make eye contact with Anríq. "Nothing. I just meant don't die on me."

Anríq didn't answer. He stared at Yann so ferociously that Yann shivered.

He distracted himself by fiddling with a thread that had come loose from the bedspread. "I was about to say....before I take you back to Eliska."

Anríq snorted. "Eliska doesn't want me, my friend. Believe me."

"Of course she does. You're everything I'm not."

"And what am I?" Anríq demanded.

"You're taller, bigger, stronger, better looking...."

"I'm a Barbarian," Anríq countered. "You're smarter, better educated, more socially capable, and better at everything than I am. I'm a brute."

Yann's head shot up. "You.....you mean.....you're actually...jealous of me?"

"If Eliska likes either of us, it's you she likes. Do you think I don't see the way she looks at you and talks to you and smiles at you? I would have to be blind not to see it. Eliska would never have anything to do with a Barbarian like me."

"But what about...." Yann trailed off blinking into space.

Anríq couldn't be jealous—not of Yann. That wasn't possible—and yet Anríq was right about all of that. Yann was smarter, better educated, and more socially capable.

"Is this the secret you've been keeping from me all this time?" Anríq snapped. "You think Eliska likes me instead of you?"

"Well....she does. Look at the way she acted around when she first invited you to join us."

Anríq made a face and looked away. "She was very kind to me, but she only did it because I'm a Servant. She did it to help you—and the rest of the Watch—but mostly because of you. Do you think all this help and effort she's putting into the Watch isn't because of you? Who else would she do it for—Rien?"

"No, but...."

"You can't honestly think Eliska cares about me being taller, stronger, bigger, and better looking. There are countless Barbarians bigger, taller, stronger, and better-looking than I am. She doesn't want them, either. If she likes me the way you say she does, it's not because of any of those things."

"No, she wants you because you're a warrior and a Servant."

"And what are you?" Anríq demanded.

"Me? I'm nothing."

Anríq smacked his lips in annoyance. *"You're* a warrior and a Servant. You've dedicated your life to service in the Black Watch. Look at the way you've been acting in this town ever since we got here. You're an intelligent, educated man in ways I'm not. You're everything that is good about me and more. You know Eliska likes you. I might even go so far as to say she loves you. Why do you doubt that?"

Yann couldn't look at him. The words hurt.

The feelings between him and Eliska had already gone way beyond friendship. He knew that. No one had to tell him.

No one had to tell him they were mutual, either. She did dedicate all this help and effort to the Watch because of him. It started back in Middleborough and it just kept building with every passing day.

Anríq let the silence linger for a long time—too long.

After a few minutes, he pushed himself up on his elbow, picked up the soup bowl, and drank the rest of it without help.

Yann sat defeated on the bed next to him. Just when Yann made up his mind to walk away from Eliska, Anríq threw another piece of bait in front of Yann's nose to tempt him farther down the wrong road.

Anríq lowered his voice to a confidential murmur. "Tell me what's really bothering you. It will only get worse if you don't talk about it."

Yann kept his eyes down. He couldn't keep it to himself any longer.

How painfully obvious it must have been to someone like Anríq. He must have seen from day one that Yann carried a secret burning a hole in the middle of his chest.

"If anything happened....between me and Eliska.....or me and anyone....I would have to leave the Watch," he blurted out. "I would have to betray my oath....and I haven't even taken the oath. How could I walk away from the Watch—and my father—and everything we've all been fighting for all this time—just for a girl?"

"How did it happen with him?" Anríq asked. "How did he have a child before he took the oath?"

"I don't know. I never thought to ask him—and now I might never get another chance. I don't know if I could ask even if I did get a chance. I don't want to pry...."

"But whatever he did affects you," Anríq pointed out. "For all you know, he might regret taking the oath. How do you know he really wants you to join the Watch? Maybe he wants you to have a different life but he doesn't say anything because he thinks this is what you want. You wouldn't know unless you asked him. He might tell you not to make the same mistake and to go off, find a girl, and be happy. If he can do it, you can do it, too."

Yann tore his eyes away again. "I could never ask him that."

"So you would throw your life away because you can't ask him? That's cowardly."

"How do I know I would be throwing my life away? I never thought I would do anything else—and then I met her. What if she's just a temptation to test my resolve? What if joining the Watch is as important to me as being a Servant is to you? What if going off, finding a girl, and raising a family is what would be throwing my life away? Isn't that what you would have done if you stayed with your tribe?"

Now it was Anríq's turn to look away. "You're right. It's exactly the same thing."

"So what's the answer? How am I supposed to know? If I don't take the oath, I'm out of the Watch. I'll never be one of those men again. I might never even see them again. I would stay in whatever town I settled in and they would....do whatever they're going to do."

"You might settle in the same town where they join the Watch," Anríq suggested.

"I would still never be one of them again. I would spend my life thinking I let them down—because I *would* have let them down. I would never be able to look any of them in the eye again without feeling that shame. It would make my married life with my family a living hell."

"And if you join the Watch, you would see all those men raising families and going home to their wives and you would regret your decision. You would come to hate the men of the Watch for robbing you of what you could never have. Then your life in the Watch would become a living hell."

"So what am I supposed to do?" Yann asked. "You must know. You've been through it before."

"I went through it for myself. I didn't go through it for you. Only you can make that decision."

"That doesn't help me. You said talking about it would make me feel better."

"It will make you feel better. I didn't say it would make the decision easier. Nothing can do that." Anríq stretched back out on the bed. "These things are never easy. They're especially not as easy as they appear when someone else does it. Believe me. The decision to leave my family to become a Servant wasn't easy. It was the hardest thing I've ever had to do—much harder than healing these people."

Chapter 40

Yann sat up on the makeshift bed he'd arranged on the floor of the church house bedroom.

Anríq already sat up on the edge of the regular bed—the only bed in the house.

He'd taken off his vest and all his weapons when he went to sleep last night. Now he sat there bare-chested with his arms propped on the mattress.

He looked as big and powerful as ever, but his shoulders slumped and he stared at the floor.

"Are you sure you have to go through with this today?" Yann asked.

"I have to," Anríq mumbled. "Those people brought me here to help them. What kind of Servant would I be if I failed?"

"How long can you keep this up? You only worked for a few hours yesterday and look at you now. You're already weak. You'll be able to do even less today."

"That's a few more people I'll be able to save, at least."

Anríq pushed himself off the bed and started putting his clothes back on.

Yann left him alone and went into the alley behind the church house to wash his face. He had to do something about Anríq's health. Yann couldn't let Anríq work himself into an early grave—which is exactly what he would do if this went on much longer.

Yann didn't even trust Anríq to make it through another day of fighting this curse.

Avol made it a thousand times worse by coming over while Yann and Anríq ate breakfast. Avol bustled around the two of them talking a mile a minute.

"Everyone is up and around!" he exclaimed. "I can't believe it actually worked! You're a miracle! I can't wait for you to come and see my family."

"I wouldn't count on it," Yann muttered.

Avol spun around fast. "What? Why not? This is wonderful! It's the best thing that has ever happened to us."

"You can see Anríq is working his way through town from the gate backward. He healed ten people yesterday before he collapsed. He won't get to your house for a few days at the earliest."

That took the wind out of Avol's sails real quick. He stopped prancing around the room and gaped at the two men.

"But...what's the point of you coming to town if you aren't going to save everyone?" Avol asked.

"That's what he is doing," Yann replied. "You can see he's already saved ten people. Don't tell me you brought Anríq here just to save your family and no one else."

"Of course not, but....." Avol gulped. "Can't you do it any faster than that?"

"Do you mean without Anríq winding up dead, too? Not likely. Anyway, I won't let him. If I see him failing, I'll bring him back here so he can rest. If you have a problem with that, you and I can have a conversation about it another time."

Avol shut his mouth and left the house, thank the stars. Yann went back to eating his food.

"Thank you," Anríq mumbled.

"You better not let it go so far today," Yann countered. "I don't want to find you passed out on someone's bedroom floor. If you feel sick, you better come back here and lie down. I mean it, Anríq."

Anríq bent over his plate. "All right. I will."

Yann let it go at that, but he didn't plan to trust Anríq's word. Anríq was too kind-hearted to leave anyone in danger. He would drive himself to the brink even if it cost him in the end.

Yann made up his mind on the way out of the church house. He would force Anríq to quit before it went that far. Yann would drag Anríq away if he had to—even if it meant one of the townsfolk might die instead.

Yann took his glaive with him on their way up the street to the house where Anríq collapsed yesterday. Yann didn't want to get caught unarmed if one of these cursed townspeople decided to attack him with a weapon again.

Anríq took all his weapons, too. He wore his axe slung across his back and his club and machete hanging from his belt as usual. He never went anywhere unarmed.

More noise of human activity drifted through the town now. The place seemed to come back to life even with that few people back on their feet.

The townsfolk walking around smiled at Yann and Anríq. The townspeople's cheeks shone with more color even if they'd already been healthy yesterday.

Yann and Anríq passed Aria. She smiled at the two boys, but fortunately, she didn't stop to talk.

Anríq turned off toward the house in question. Yann planned to turn off somewhere else and get some firewood from one of the piles he knew about.

Yann glanced up at Anríq to see if Anríq was really okay enough to go off by himself. Anríq started to smile back at him as if to reassure him that Anríq really was okay.

At that moment, the town gates burst open and Gachu stumbled through them from the road outside. "The Corsairs!" he shrieked. "The Corsairs are coming!"

Yann and Anríq both spun around to stare at each other. All thought of healing the sick townsfolk flew out of their heads.

Gachu blundered through the gate and turned back to slam it shut. Yann and Anríq raced over to him, grabbed the heavy wooden beams, and slotted them across the gate to barricade it from the inside.

That wouldn't hold the Corsairs at bay. They'd already sacked the town dozens of times. The wall wouldn't hold them—and two young men wouldn't be able to hold them, either.

Yann scrambled onto the wall and stood on a jutting stone so he could see over the top. The countryside spread out before him.

A cloud of dust rose from the horizon far down the road in the direction Yann and Anríq traveled here. Yann couldn't make out anything from this distance.

Only two other men climbed up on the wall to see. One was Gachu. Yann didn't recognize the other man. Neither of them came armed.

Yann glanced at them down the wall as the penny dropped. The Corsairs would sack this town and might even kill the people Anríq worked so hard to save.

Yann looked up at Anríq at the same moment Anríq looked down at him. They were both thinking the same thing.

Yann flung his leg over the wall and hopped down onto the grass next to the road. Anríq jumped down next to him.

Both men climbed up into the road in front of the gate. Yann hefted his glaive in both hands and braced himself to meet the Corsairs.

Anríq unslung his axe and unhooked his club from his belt. The two men spaced out from each other.

The distant rumble of horses' hooves floated on the breeze. It started as a low hum in the farthest distance. The dust cloud got bigger as the wind caught it and spread it across the countryside.

All Yann's doubts about his place in the Watch evaporated. He was born for this. He trained for it all his life.

He and Anríq wouldn't be able to stop the Corsairs out here any better than the two of them would have been able to stop the Corsairs inside the walls.

Yann made up his mind. He had to do this just to make a point—to himself if not to anyone else. What else was his life worth?

He might never see his father, the Watch, or Eliska again. He would probably die here and that was just fine with him. At least his life would count for something.

He tightened his grip on his glaive. The dust cleared enough for him to see individual horses thundering through the dust cloud.

The dark mob of horsemen charged out of the distance and shrieked in a spine-chilling war cry.

Anríq flexed his knees and raised his weapons. Yann measured the horsemen's distance and decided how he would take out the horses themselves. Bringing the horsemen to the ground would be the best way to reduce the danger to the town.

The Corsairs' long black robes whipped behind them in the wind. Their horses stretched out their necks, flattened their ears, and plunged for the walls at breakneck speed.

The Corsairs saw the two men standing armed in the middle of the road. The Corsairs raised their glittering weapons on high to strike the two men down.

A solid wall of horses closed in on the two friends' position. Yann couldn't see the back of the Corsairs' formation.

No matter how many he fought and killed at the front, those following behind would overwhelm him and Anríq in no time. Then the town would fall.

The horsemen came close enough for Yann to see their facial features now. They tattooed their cheeks in dot patterns under their eyes and across their chins and foreheads. The patterns made the horsemen look exotic and menacing but no less human.

The horses stretched out a little more. Those in the center pulled ahead of those on the sides. The formation narrowed to a point coming straight for the gate.

Yann and Anríq stood alone between the attackers and the defenseless town. This wouldn't end well.

Without warning, the man in the very center of the pack jolted back in his saddle and dragged his horse's reins away. The horse squealed in alarm and skidded in the dirt trying to stop in time.

The man raised his sword and all those around him pulled up short, too. That one guy wore a band of gold around his headdress to hold it on. He must be their captain if they had one.

The horses were running too fast. They came perilously close to trampling Yann and Anríq before the whole Corsair company thundered to a halt.

The horses snorted, stamped, and tossed their heads while their riders tried to control them. The horses kept lunging out of line to keep going, but their riders fought them back each time.

Corsair captain steered his horse to one side. The creature kept pacing back and forth. The man had to turn his head one way and then the other to keep Yann and Anríq in sight.

The Corsair captain glared down at them with brutal dark eyes. He had Omer Veco's dark features, dark skin, hooked nose, and angular jaw as well as Omer's fiery expression.

Yann didn't slacken his stance at all. The horsemen kept their distance from him and Anríq. Yann would have attacked them right here if they came any closer.

Anríq didn't relax at all, either. He raised both his axe and his club to take on the first Corsair to twitch an eyelash.

The whole thing happened in a split second. The Corsair captain vaulted out of his saddle, left his horse standing there, threw down his sword, strode forward unarmed, and fell down on his knees in front of Anríq.

The man raised both hands to Anríq, but the guy didn't touch him. "You're a Servant of the Barbarian tribes!" the guy blurted out. "You defend the helpless and heal the sick. Please....you have to save my daughter! She's in grave danger! Please come! I'll do anything! I'll give you anything you want...."

"How about you leave this town in peace?" Yann interjected.

Anríq stopped him by laying a hand on Yann's arm.

The Corsair captain didn't notice. He kept staring up at Anríq with eyes overflowing with anguish. "Please—my daughter—she was captured by Darklings. She's being held in a Layer we can't find. You're my only hope."

"Why have you been attacking this town?" Yann demanded. "These people are just as helpless as your daughter. That's why we're here. These people can't defend themselves."

The Corsair captain spun around to glare at Yann for the first time. "These people as you call them are the Darklings who kidnapped my daughter! I razed the town a dozen times to find her and now they've used their magic to transport her to another Layer! Do you think I would waste my time with this trash heap if I didn't want to get her back?!"

Yann gaped at the guy in horror. "You think these people are Darklings?! Are you...?"

Yann broke off when the puzzle pieces connected. These people were under a curse. It poisoned the whole town. Was there a connection?

Yann looked up to find Anríq making eye contact with him. Anríq must be thinking the same thing.

Anríq lowered his axe. "I will serve."

"Oh, thank you!" The Corsair captain seized Anríq's wrist, dragged his hand up, and kissed Anríq's knuckles. "I don't know how to thank you."

Anríq shot a sidelong glance at Yann's glaive to remind Yann to put his weapon down.

The Corsair captain scrambled to his feet. Dust covered his robes, especially around the knees where he knelt in front of Anríq.

Yann found it impossible to believe that this whole scene really happened that way. These Corsairs had been about to cut him and Anríq down, not to mention the whole town.

The Corsair captain stalked back to his men and yelled orders at them in another language. A few of them answered him and then the whole company wheeled back the way they came.

The Corsairs took off at a full gallop for the distant horizon. The Corsair captain caught his own horse to stop it from running away with the others.

The dust cloud floated away as the horses retreated into the distance. Gachu and the other man watched the whole scene from behind the wall. They didn't come out to help defend the town.

The Corsair captain held onto his horse's reins, halted in front of Anríq, and bowed from the waist. "You have my eternal gratitude. My name is Costico Nastase."

Anríq bowed back to him. "I am Anríq."

The guy burst into a grin and then his features spasmed in another pang of emotion. He pressed his wrist to his mouth before he got himself under control.

"Please....follow me. I'll take you to my home where I can explain the whole thing to you. Then you will understand how to proceed."

Anríq bowed a second time. "I will serve."

Costico shot a hard glance at Yann. "Who are you, boy?" Costico's eyes darted down to Yann's uniform. "I don't know your insignia."

"My name is Yann Dilnao and I'm a member of the Black Watch," Yann replied. "Anríq is my friend. We're traveling together. I've been helping him try to break the curse on this town."

Costico's features hardened even more. "I see. Then you better come with me. Perhaps when you figure out what these people are doing, you'll be able to solve both problems at once."

He turned away and set off walking up the road in the direction his men just rode off. Costico didn't mount his horse. He walked and led the horse by the reins.

He talked to Yann and Anríq on the way. "You won't believe me when I tell you that these townspeople are Darklings," Costico went on over his shoulder.

"I don't believe it," Yann replied. "I don't think you would believe it, either, if you saw what condition they're in. These people are dying—men, women, and children of all ages. Whatever Darkness took your daughter is affecting the town, too. It's cost dozens of lives."

The muscle of Costico's jaw flexed when he clenched his teeth. "We'll see about that. The Darklings that took my daughter came from that town. People transformed into Darklings, took my daughter, and then spirited her away to another Layer. Then all those people turned back into people as if it never happened. Whoever they are, they're communing with the Dark to carry out some evil purpose—and my daughter isn't the only one. A dozen other people have vanished into that town and never come out."

Yann frowned. "That's strange. The same thing happened to that hog."

Costico jerked around to glare at him. "What hog? I'm talking about my daughter getting captured by Darklings and you're talking about some hog?!"

"I am talking about your daughter getting captured by Darklings. I went hunting with another friend of mine. We tracked down a hog and she hit it with her magic to try to kill it. It changed into a Darkling and knocked her out. I killed it and it turned back into a hog. Maybe the same thing happened to these people. Considering the way they're suffering from this curse, I'd say maybe they don't have any control over whatever Dark powers might be operating through them. Anyway, everyone in that town is too sick to hold anyone as a captive, especially not a dozen people like you say."

Costico scowled even more darkly. "You may be right." He pointed to his left. "Turn here. This is the way to my home."

Chapter 41

Yann didn't see anything on the side road where Costico led Yann and Anríq away from the ordinary towns.

The countryside spread out in a rolling patchwork of farmland with mountains, rivers, and clumps of forest dotted in between.

The sun shone in the sky and fluffy clouds drifted past up there. Flocks of birds winged back and forth on the breeze.

It didn't seem possible that this idyllic landscape could exist in the same dimension as all the chaos, Darklings, danger, and threat that Yann and the Watch had been facing ever since that fateful night in Middleborough.

Costico's presence spoiled the illusion. He brought Yann and Anríq here to save his daughter from the Darklings. Whatever forces threatened the Coil threatened this peaceful Island, too.

Yann couldn't get the cursed townspeople out of his mind, either. If they weren't Darklings themselves, the Dark caused their sickness, too.

He'd seen that with his own eyes when Anríq pulled the Dark out of them.

Yann didn't see any sign of human habitation on this side road—none at all. The Corsair captain must live in a rustic cottage in the woods for it to be so well hidden.

Without warning, the man walked through an invisible barrier across the road. He led his horse through it, too.

The animal followed him without any protest and they both vanished behind a sheet of watery energy.

The sheet wavered once when Costico and his horse passed through. Then the whole thing evaporated as if it was never there. It returned to being invisible and left the view of the landscape as perfect and empty as ever.

Yann stopped in his tracks and stared at the spot. Costico wasn't there.

Anríq kept walking. "Don't worry," he told Yann on the side. "It's his concealment spell. It doesn't mean anything."

Anríq stepped forward, broke the barrier, too, and vanished following Costico.

Yann couldn't stay here, so he stepped forward. He passed through the barrier and wound up on exactly the same road with Costico, the horse, and Anríq all in front of him.

A giant castle rose in front of him. Its high, white marble turrets touched the sky with flags flapping in the breeze and armed men guarding a drawbridge across the moat.

Costico trudged down the road as if he came this way on foot all the time. None of the guards acknowledged him when he crossed the bridge and entered the castle.

"Follow me," he told Yann and Anríq after Costico gave his horse to a boy in the courtyard. "I will show you something that will make everything clear."

Yann couldn't stop staring at the opulent halls, vaulted ceilings, and magnificent furnishings crowding the castle's every room.

Costico led the two boys up a sweeping staircase to the third floor and then up another long flight of stairs into one of the highest turrets.

Costico opened a door carved out of gold and ushered the two boys into a massive drawing room leading to an equally large veranda.

This room must have been on the opposite side of the castle. The view from the veranda didn't match the countryside through which Yann and Anríq had been traveling these last few days.

A bottomless gorge plunged away behind the castle. Towering mountains stood over the castle from behind.

Costico went out onto the veranda and pointed up at the sky. "Take a look. You'll see what I mean."

Yann and Anríq followed him. As soon as they got there, they saw what he was pointing at.

The sky looked different here. The vaulted heavenly blue dome dotted with fluffy clouds and flocks of birds that Yann had just been admiring so much—it wasn't there anymore.

Instead, Layer upon Layer of Darkness swirled and revolved in a never-ending sea of chaos. It covered the whole sky as far up as the human eye could see.

Churning vapors of wild magic rumbled from one side to the other and then revolved in a gigantic whirlpool of Darkness and color.

The funnel plunged toward the earth with Layers collapsing on each other, exploding outward, reforming, and falling in on each other again.

Yann's eye followed the whirlwind downward.....and saw at last what the Corsair captain had been trying to tell him all along.

The point of the funnel—the vortex moving the fastest and wreaking the greatest destruction on both the Coil and everything around it—it came to an apex right on top of the town Anríq had been trying to save.

"All the Darkness channels through that town," Costico murmured. "You can't tell me that just happened by accident. Either those people are communing with the Dark or they *are* the Dark masquerading as people."

"And your daughter?" Yann asked. "You said she vanished into the town."

Costico compressed his lips, clamped his eyes shut, and turned his head aside. "I'll never forget the day it happened. My daughter was riding to another city farther west. She had to pass through that town on her way. She didn't plan to stop there."

"What happened?" Yann asked.

"Some of my warriors and I escorted her to make sure she was safe. We always went with her. It was our usual habit—not anything out of the ordinary. We were approaching the town when Darklings rose out of the streets behind the walls. We saw men transform before our eyes—and they snatched my daughter straight out of her carriage. They took her into the town...."

"How do you know she survived and that they're holding her as a captive?" Yann asked. "How do you know the Darklings didn't kill her right away?"

Costico went back inside and stopped in front of a painting hanging on the wall. An elaborate, carved gold frame surrounded an oil painting of a different landscape.

Costico passed his hand downward in front of the painting and it changed to an image of the town with its entrance gates standing open.

"My father-in-law gave me this painting when my daughter Amala was born," Costico husked. "It is enchanted to show her to me wherever she is—no matter where she is. She appeared in this town for two months after the Darklings took her. They kept her in a house in this town.....here."

He passed his hand downward in front of the painting again and it started to move. It migrated up the road getting closer to the entrance gate.

The painting gave the exact view someone would see walking into town on foot.

The image passed through the gate and down the street between the houses Yann and Anríq just visited.

Yann's hair stood on end when the image turned toward the church and then entered the house where Yann and Anríq spent the night.

"I watched her through this picture every day," Costico rasped. "The Darklings stayed right there inside the house with her. They tormented her and terrorized her with threats and roars around the clock. They reduced her to a nervous wreck....and then she vanished out of the town."

"Are you sure she's still alive?" Yann asked.

"The enchantment on the picture will make it turn black the moment she dies."

Yann glanced over at Anríq. How would anyone test the picture to see if it actually worked? Costico's daughter could have died and the picture didn't show it.

Anríq read Yann's mind, stepped close to the picture, and passed his own hand downward in front of it.

A shimmer of magic radiated from his palm and made the image waver. "No, she is still alive," Anríq announced.

"They took her somewhere under the town," Costico explained. "They're holding her there along with the other captives."

"Did you see that, too?" Yann asked.

"Yes, I saw the vortex strike that house. The Darklings brought in a dozen other captives while they held my daughter. The Darklings kept all those people packed into one small house. Then the vortex hit it and lifted everyone out of the house."

He pointed up at the Layers collapsing over the mountaintops.

"All those people and Darklings tumbled through the air and then the vortex sucked them all down underneath the town—under that very house. They vanished through a breach in the Island and disappeared into the Layer below."

"Have you asked a magic-user to search the Layer below?" Yann asked. "I don't know anything about your magic, but you obviously have it. Someone could have gone to look for her—and the other captives."

Costico turned away again with another pained grimace. "I've spent a fortune hiring magic-users to search the whole Coil. None of them can find her anywhere. You two are my last hope. If you can't find her and bring her back to me, I'll have to give up and accept the fact that I'll never get her back."

Yann and Anríq exchanged another glance. "I will serve," Anríq replied.

"I sure hope so," Costico croaked. "I don't know what I'll do if anything happens to her."

Chapter 42

Yann stepped out of a huge, tiled bathroom and found his uniform freshly laundered and waiting for him. It lay across an ornate, carved armchair in the biggest bedroom he'd ever seen.

Costico insisted that Yann and Anríq spend at least one night in his castle before they set off to find the captives.

Costico didn't come out and say point blank that both boys needed a bath, a decent meal, and a good night's sleep, but he might as well have said it.

Yann knew he needed all those things, especially a bath. He just never expected he would ever take one in a bathroom like that. It was practically a palace all on its own.

He made up his mind while he scrubbed the blood, dirt, and grime out of his hair that he would never tell anyone in the Watch about this. They would never let him live it down.

He didn't ask how Costico's servants snuck into this bedroom while Yann's back was turned or how they laundered his uniform so thoroughly in so short a time. Yann didn't ask questions like that anymore. They must have used magic.

The bedroom Costico assigned to Yann was as big or bigger than the drawing room in which he'd shown the boys the collapsing Layers of the Coil forming that Dark vortex over the town.

Another colossal veranda stuck out from the bedroom. Yann could have housed the entire population of Middleborough in this room and on the veranda.

Yann didn't see the room where Anríq was staying. Yann didn't have to see it. It would be the same.

Yann left his bedroom to go see where Anríq was and find out what they were supposed to do today. Yann didn't even know where to begin to look for the captives—except that they were in a Layer under the church house.

Magical pictures on the wall kept showing different scenes changing in different parts of both this Island and other Layers of the Coil.

Some of them collapsed right there in the picture. They showed people getting caught in the chaos and getting torn apart by Darklings.

Yann stopped in front of one of these pictures to watch. He couldn't understand why it fascinated him so much.

Whoever painted the original picture must have painted a nice, beautiful, calm landscape scene like the one outside this castle right now.

Then, after years or decades or maybe centuries, the picture showed what was happening in that landscape right at this minute.

While Yann stood there marveling at it, Anríq came out of a nearby room with his hair still wet. Someone had cleaned his leather clothing, too, laundered his bags, and even polished his weapons for him.

He cocked his head when he saw Yann studying the picture. Anríq stared into it, too.

Both boys watched in silence until nothing but swirling vapors and Darkness obliterated whatever might have been there before.

The two boys were still standing there when Costico came down the hall from somewhere.

"Ah, you both look much more rested," he remarked. "If you would join me...."

"I think we should get on our way," Yann interrupted. "We've spent enough time in this castle. We won't find your daughter here. We should go."

"Of course, my boy, of course," Costico exclaimed. "If I can provide you with anything...."

"I think we'll be fine," Yann replied. "We know what we have to do."

Costico nodded, but he wouldn't stop frowning. "I could send my men to accompany you...."

"That won't be necessary," Yann replied. "Your men have already done everything to try to get your daughter back. Anríq and I will go out alone. We'll do what we can and hopefully find her and bring her to you. Thank you for your hospitality. I hope we see each other again soon."

"I hope so, too, my boy."

Yann shook hands with him, but Anríq only bowed.

Costico accompanied them as far as the drawbridge. Then the two boys turned the corner, passed through the magical concealment barrier, and the castle vanished.

"You talk very well," Anríq teased on their way back toward town. "You should become a Servant."

"Then I wouldn't be able to talk at all. Be grateful I'm around to get you out of all these sticky spots."

Anríq laughed. "Yes. Thank you. I am most grateful."

"Did you ever think you could have saved a lot more lives if you searched for his daughter on the condition that he stopped attacking that town? You could have protected everyone inside the walls."

"I don't want to protect everyone inside the walls if they're Darklings. I serve all of humanity, including him. The Corsairs are human and his daughter is human. His daughter is as deserving of being saved as those people in the village."

Yann didn't agree, but he didn't argue. Anríq could have saved a lot more people by using the leverage of his position.

That wasn't the Servant's way. Yann understood that, but he didn't agree with it. The Servants walked a fine line between saving people and letting some others get away with murder.

The boys retraced their steps back to the town.

"Are you sure the captives are here?" Yann asked.

"The vortex took them down here," Anríq reminded him.

"It took them into another Layer. Those Layers could have collapsed or changed or shifted anywhere. Amala and the others could be anywhere in the whole Coil by now."

"You didn't see what I saw in that castle of his. He didn't tell us everything."

"What do you mean?"

"One of those paintings worked both ways. It showed a scene on the other side of the painting, but it also gave the subjects of that painting a view of everything in Costico's palace."

Yann frowned. "How can you be sure?"

"Because I spoke to the subjects of the painting. They talked to me and told me a very interesting story about our friend Costico."

"You had a conversation with total strangers? Now I've heard everything."

Anríq laughed again. "It has happened before believe it or not."

"So what did they tell you?"

"Our friend Costico comes from a family of magic-users—very powerful magic-users. They used their power to fight the Darklings, but his family didn't always succeed in killing them. The Voyant Mendicat isn't the only wizard who serves the Dark and uses Darklings to do his bidding. Another one of this family's adversaries named Simion Mihaili sent Darklings after the family and killed some of them. The family counterattacked, tracked Mihaili down, and imprisoned him in a series of tunnels buried between the Layers."

Yann stopped walking. "You're making this up."

"I wish I was. Mihaili escaped many years ago and supposedly vanished. The family lost track of him and Costico and some of his brothers and sisters settled down to live their lives in peace with their families. Mihaili did not forget, however, and set out to get revenge. He created a beautiful painting that would allow him to spy on the family. Mihaili arranged for Costico's wife to see this painting on display and she bought it. Mihaili monitored the family for years and watched Amala and her other more distant relatives grow up. I don't think Costico knows that the other captives are his relatives."

"Are you seriously telling me this wizard used Darklings to kidnap Costico's relatives so he could hold them as captives...."

"In the same tunnels—yes," Anríq finished.

"And he told you all that—through the painting?"

"He was surprised that a Servant would help Costico considering that Mihaili views Costico as an evil sorcerer. Mihaili gloated over his victory and told me everything to prove to me that I won't be able to defeat his system. He plans to keep Amala and the others as prisoners forever to torment Costico and the rest for their mistreatment of him."

"So do you know where the tunnels are?"

"Costico already told us. The tunnels are under the church house."

"But Costico said the vortex took the captives to another Layer...."

"Another Layer under the church house," Anríq finished.

Yann shut his eyes and shook his head. "I don't understand any of this."

"The Layer under the church house will lead us into the tunnels."

"How can you be certain of that? Costico said he sent magic-users to the Layer under the church house to search for the captives."

Anríq made a face. "Don't you think Mihaili is smart enough to stop them from finding him? He must have put measures in place to make sure no one could find the tunnels if they came from Costico or his relatives or planned to tell them where the captives were."

"But you and I fit that description. You and I come from Costico and we plan to tell him where the captives are—if we can't free them ourselves."

"Mihaili wants us to enter the tunnels. He wants us to engage with his Darklings so they'll kill us."

"How do you know that?"

"Because he told me so, my friend. He told me point blank that he wants to kill us. We'll vanish off the face of the earth and Costico will never find out what happened to us."

"Why didn't you at least tell Costico all of this?" Yann asked. "Why did you keep it from him?"

"Apart from my oath keeping me silent? I didn't tell him because it would have made no difference to our mission to rescue Amala and the others. Either Costico would have denied it and claimed Mihaili was making up a story to manipulate me...."

"Which he might have been," Yann pointed out.

"Does it really matter? Either that or Costico would have countered with some claim of his own that Mihaili was evil and Costico's family was somehow justified in holding him as a prisoner to stop his evil plans. None of it makes a difference. We're going after the captives, not Mihaili."

"What if Mihaili comes after us?" Yann asked. "What if we succeed and then he attacks us to stop us?"

"He won't do that. He says that, if we find and free the captives, he'll let us go with his blessing."

Yann snorted. "And you believe him? You're soft in the head."

Anríq only grinned at him. "Yes, I believe him, Yann. Mihaili has no grudge against either of us. I think this must all be some elaborate game to him. He got Amala away from Costico. Mihaili knows now that Costico couldn't find Amala or free her no matter how hard he tried. So Mihaili won his little game against Costico. Now Mihaili is playing a game against us. He has no beef with us, so if we win, he's content to step aside and let us leave with our prize."

"Or we both die. Is that it?"

Anríq burst into another huge grin. "Exactly."

"Wonderful," Yann muttered. "Just wonderful."

"Don't worry. We won't die."

"Says the man who comes close to dying every other day."

"I come close, but I never die."

"Until you do. You are going to die someday. You realize that, don't you?"

"Of course I realize that, Yann."

Yann clamped his mouth shut. He couldn't decide if he should be happy that Anríq was talking this much.

Maybe it would have been better if Yann didn't find out so much about everything that went on inside Anríq's head.

Yann was the one who let that genie out of the bottle. Anríq would probably never put it back in.

He said at first that he started talking because Yann needed healing from all his doubts and uncertainties.

Anríq got Yann to admit what was bothering him, but Anríq didn't stop talking. He didn't go back to being silent.

Yann couldn't ascribe Anríq's behavior to trying to heal Yann. This went way beyond that.

Chapter 43

Gachu and Avol hauled open the town entrance gates to let Yann and Anríq reenter. "We thought you were dead for sure!" Avol whimpered. "We thought they took you off somewhere to torture you!"

Yann frowned at him. Why did Avol mention taking someone off to torture them? Were these townspeople really the ones responsible for Amala's capture—and the capture of all these other people?

Anríq didn't mention it. The two men walked inside and Gachu and Avol barricaded the gate behind them.

Avol rubbed his hands together in excitement. "So? Are you ready to restart healing everyone? You've been gone for so long."

"We're going to break the curse on this town, but not by healing everyone," Yann replied.

Avol's face fell. "You aren't? Why not?"

"First of all, the process is too taxing on Anríq. He'll die if he tries to cure you all, so we're going to cut the process short by going to the source."

Avol frowned. "What does that mean?"

"Never mind. You men can go back to your business. We'll handle it from here."

Neither Gachu nor Avol moved.

Yann shooed them away. "Go on. We don't need you hanging around."

"Are you sure?" Gachu asked. "We can get you anything or help in any way you need us to."

"That's all right. We'll just go back to the church house. We're both tired. We need to rest." Yann eased away. Anríq went with him.

"But you haven't done anything," Avol pointed out.

"Like I said, we're going to the source. We've been doing things you don't know about. Goodbye. See you later. Take care of the town while we're gone."

Yann pulled Anríq the rest of the way down the street. They returned to the church house, but not without Gachu and Avol dogging them every step of the way.

The two men bombarded Yann with questions right up to the threshold.

"Where have you been?" Gachu asked. "We were worried sick about you."

"You saw where we were," Yann replied. "The Corsair captain asked us to go back to his home to save some of his people. Then he invited us to spend the night."

"You abandoned an entire town stricken with a plague so you could save some of *his* people?!" Avol practically shrieked. "Have you lost your minds?"

"Not quite. He told us the secret to breaking this curse at its source—but don't worry. This doesn't concern you anymore." Yann opened the door and Anríq entered first. "Goodbye," Yann repeated. "We'll let you know if and when anything happens."

He shut the door in both men's faces and turned to find Anríq wrinkling his nose in disgust. "Now I know why the Servants take a vow of silence," Anríq remarked.

"Let's get out of here before they break down the door."

Yann took his place on one side of the table in the center of the main room. He grabbed hold of one edge while Anríq took the other side.

They moved the table out of the way along with the chairs and any other household goods lying around.

Anríq unhooked his club and tapped it on the floor.

"I sure hope you know what you're doing," Yann murmured.

"So do I." Anríq hefted his club and made eye contact with Yann once. "Come over here and be ready to fight as soon as we get down into the tunnels."

Yann crossed the room. He didn't like where this was going at all, but he'd come too far to back out.

He took his place next to Anríq and tightened his grip on his glaive. Yann really didn't want to go back into the Layers, but he didn't get a chance to change his mind before Anríq raised his club.

He lifted it above his head and brought it down with a crushing smash on the floor between his spread feet.

The club let off a deafening thump of magic through the floor and the whole structure imploded under Yann's feet.

The floor buckled and both boys pitched through into a Layer of pure Darkness.

It closed over their heads and silent cold cut off every sense. Yann felt himself rushing downward through a bottomless pit of fear and horror.

Then they broke through into another chaos Layer packed from one end of eternity to another with Darklings.

Yann spun around to confront them and slash his glaive at them, but he couldn't find anything solid to push against.

Anríq turned the other way and smashed his club at a Darkling coming from that direction.

Yann swiped his glaive at countless tentacles spinning out of nowhere. He didn't even see the Darklings attached to all those tentacles.

One of the monsters dove for him and cracked its mouth to swallow him. He dove for it, changed his trajectory at the last second, and stabbed for the thing's eyes.

The Darkling bellowed in fury, reared away from him, and its own agonized thrashing blocked the others from getting near him.

He and Anríq fell past them, ricocheted off a dozen other Darklings, and smashed through what felt like a solid stone floor into a long, freezing-cold chute of black stone walls.

The tunnel swept both boys downward and curved sideways to spit them out into a long, horizontal tunnel.

Yann and Anríq tumbled over each other. Anríq's club bounced off Yann's shoulder and made him roar out in pain.

Neither of them could stop themselves until they somersaulted to a standstill somewhere in darkness.

"Yann...." Anríq croaked. "Are you okay?"

"Define, 'okay'," Yann grumbled.

Anríq chuckled. "Now I know you're okay."

"Where are we?" Yann asked even though he already knew.

Anríq's hand brushed Yann's arm. Then Anríq slid his hand down to the glaive shaft in Yann's grasp.

A surge of tingling electricity rushed up the shaft and the glaive blade burst out in a brilliant glow of light. It lit up the tunnel so Yann could see everything that wasn't there.

Neither Yann nor Anríq could stand upright in this tunnel. Anríq had to bend all the way over just to fit his big shoulders under the low ceiling.

"Well, I guess Mihaili got what he wanted," Yann complained. "He got us into the tunnels."

"Now it's up to us to get out of them." Anríq pointed behind him. "This way. You can go first since you have the light."

"You did that on purpose, you coward!"

Anríq only grinned at him and waved his hand to invite Yann to go first.

Yann snorted, held his glaive in front of him as much to defend himself as to light the way, and started down the tunnel.

"Why aren't there any Darklings here?" he asked over his shoulder.

As soon as he said the words, a deep roar echoed up the tunnel from somewhere out of sight. Yann stopped walking.

He tried to see where the roar came from, but this tunnel didn't seem to have any side branches or intersections. It was just one long smooth tube of nothing.

"Keep going!" Anríq murmured from behind.

"*You* keep going!" Yann snapped back. "This was your idea, not mine."

"You want me to go first so you can hide behind me?" Anríq teased.

"NO!" Yann hissed. Another roar cut him off.

This one sounded louder. It could only be coming from directly ahead.

Yann inched forward. He didn't want to meet any Darklings, but what else did he and Anríq come down here to do?

These Darklings stood between him and the captives he and Anríq had to free. Yann had to either fight Darklings or run home in defeat.

Running home in defeat was no longer an option.

That roaring sound called to him. Part of him wanted to meet it as some kind of test of his true destiny. He wanted to fight these Darklings even if he had to do it alone.

This had nothing to do with Anríq's mission anymore. This was between Yann and all the things he'd been avoiding all this time.

He inched down the tunnel heading closer to the sound. It escalated to a steady din. He eventually realized it wasn't just a single voice roaring in the Darkness. It was many.

The tunnel ended in a flared opening. The light from the glaive vanished into nothing.

"Be careful," Anríq whispered. "The tunnel is ending."

Yann could see that perfectly well, but he didn't say that or turn around to make a snide remark.

His attention fixed on that sound in front of him. Where were they? Why didn't they show themselves?

He stopped where the light disappeared and extended his glaive through the opening.

The light spread out beyond where the tunnel walls had confined it before. The light glowed a little brighter and illuminated a vast cavern swarming with Darklings.

They floated in the air, soared around each other, clung to the walls, and seethed on what looked like a floor below.

Anríq tiptoed forward, stopped at Yann's side, and they both looked out at the pandemonium of hundreds of Darklings all jammed into this one cavern.

"The walls must be enchanted to stop them from escaping into the surrounding Layers." Anríq pointed across the cavern. "The captives are over there."

Another pitch-black opening vanished into the cavern's opposite wall. That was the only spot in the whole cavern that didn't reflect the glaive's light back to Yann's eye.

"How do we get across?" he asked.

He didn't really want to know—because he already knew. The only way across was to fight their way across.

"How do you want to do this?" Yann cast one glance downward toward the floor.

He would die in seconds if he went down there, but he didn't say that out loud, either. He didn't think that because he was a coward. He thought it because it was true. It was a pure strategic assessment of fact.

He and his glaive might be able to slice off two or three tentacles before all the Darklings took him.

Anríq read his mind again. "You can't go down there. I'll go down there and fight them while you go for the captives."

"How will I do that?"

"I'll distract them down there. They'll all pile down there to attack me. You'll run around there."

Anríq traced his finger around the cavern's upper rim. Ledges and indentations covered the walls.

Darklings covered the walls, too. They used those ledges and indentations to cling to the surface.

"The fight will draw them away and leave the path clear," Anríq finished.

"Something tells me they won't *all* go down there. Some of them will stay up here."

"Then you'll have to fight them and get to that tunnel over there. Don't wait for me. Free the captives and...." Anríq trailed off.

"And what? How will I get them out? I don't have the magic to take them back through the Layers to the church house—even if I could find it again."

"Just get the captives back into these tunnels—away from the Darklings. The Darklings are too big to fit in here. As soon as you get the captives away, Mihaili will let you go."

"So you want me to leave you behind? Forget it!"

Anríq didn't look up or smile. His eyes remained riveted on the Darklings down in the cavern. "Saving the captives is more important. One of them might have magic. Just get them out of there and back over here. I'll take care of myself."

"You haven't been doing a very stellar job of it so far," Yann countered.

Anríq pretended not to hear, unslung his axe, and took hold of it in one hand and his club in the other. "Get ready, Yann."

Yann gave up trying to convince him. It sure looked like he and Anríq were doing this.

Yann locked his eyes on the opposite tunnel. Nothing mattered but getting over there alive.

He put Anríq as far as possible out of his mind. Yann would just have to trust Anríq to hold up his end of the bargain.

Anríq backed up a dozen feet further from the tunnel opening. He rocked on his heels a few times and then charged.

He yelled out, "GO!!" as he passed Yann and then Anríq launched himself high into open space in the middle of the cavern.

All the Darklings turned on him—and ran straight into his weapons. He arced to the apex of his flight, swung his axe and his club, and both weapons struck the Darklings who came at him first.

A catastrophic explosion went off from the first blow of his axe on a huge, fanged Darkling's head.

The blast detonated three Darklings and cleared a path for the others to hurtle inward to attack him.

The blast also cleared a path for him to start falling through the cavern toward the floor teeming with teeth, tentacles, and spiked bodies.

Yann didn't wait around to see anything else. As soon as Anríq flung himself out of the tunnel, Yann took off running for the perimeter ledge.

Anríq's plan didn't work as quickly as he hoped it would. Too many Darklings crowded the cavern already.

Dozens of them converged on Anríq even as he fell lower through the cavern. The Darklings clinging to the walls couldn't get near enough to attack him. They had to wait their turn—and what better place to wait than on the walls where they belonged?

Yann ran into the first one blocking his path. It stared down into the darkness where continuous explosions kept flashing and blazing from Anríq's club.

Yann took the Darkling by surprise and decided to go for his old strategy. He planted his foot on a higher indentation, launched himself at the creature, stabbed his glaive into one of its eyes, and landed on its head.

The thing reared and thrashed bellowing to the ends of the earth. He had to steady himself before he balanced well enough to stab into the other eye and blind the thing.

It erupted in rage and pain, thrashed even harder, and wound up striking the other Darklings near it.

None of them left the ledge. Yann had to come up with another route across the cavern.

He sprang off that Darkling and vaulted from one to the next getting closer to his destination.

Stepping on them attracted their attention to him, but at that moment, another deafening boom went off far down on the cavern floor.

A brilliant flash of light pounded all the way to the walls and sent dozens of Darklings hurtling away from Anríq standing at the center.

He swung his club in all directions. Magical explosions detonated from his club every time he hit something.

He leveled enough Darklings to make way for more to come in from all sides. The battle lured the Darklings off the walls and they plummeted down to land on top of him.

Yann barely sprang off in time, hit the wall, and scrambled for a foothold before he wheeled off into the void.

He clawed his way back to the ledge and hesitated when he saw the mayhem unfolding below him.

He could barely see Anríq at all under all those Darklings. Only the continuous thumps, booms, and explosions coming from Anríq's club showed that he was still down there and that he was still alive. How could Yann leave Anríq down there alone?

Yann took a deep breath, dragged his eyes away from the battle, and focused on the path in front of him. The opposite tunnel hovered right in front of him. He could make it.

He sidestepped down the ledge, but his own uncertainty seemed to magnetize the Darklings back to him with an irresistible pull.

Four of them rocketed out of the confusion below. One of them hit the wall in front of Yann and stuck there.

The monster turned in his direction hissing and roaring. Its tentacles whipped and slashed the air, cracked toward Yann, and would have knocked him off the ledge.

He swiped with his glaive, but right then, another two Darklings landed on either side of him, one above him and one below him.

They all advanced to close the noose...and then the fourth charged him from out in the middle of the cavern.

Its huge mouth studded with fangs rushed straight for him. It would swallow him entirely. He had to take the only avenue of escape left to him.

He dove off the ledge flying right for the Darkling, hauled back his glaive.....and dropped.

The Darkling sailed toward the wall where Yann had just been standing. It zoomed past his head with all its tentacles snaking through the air.

He fell toward the creature's stomach and drove his glaive into its abdomen with all his strength.

The blade sank past the skin and a foot up the shaft. Yann's body kept going and slammed into the Darkling's underside.

The creature kept going, too, smashed its head into the rock wall, and bellowed as the glaive struck home. All the other Darklings pivoted around on the wall trying to see where he went. He couldn't stay here.

He wrenched his glaive free and dropped onto a different ledge farther below the one leading to the opposite tunnel. He couldn't get there from here.

He didn't care about that. He got away from them, but only for now.

They all leapt off the wall to hunt him down, but he still had one advantage. Too many Darklings crowded this cavern. They couldn't move freely without crashing into each other.

The remaining three dove into the swarm, but they had to fight their way through every other Darkling just to find him.

He took off running around the cavern's perimeter walls. He was probably already dead, so he threw all caution to the wind and sprinted at his top speed.

He sprang from ledge to ledge and foothold to foothold barely keeping ahead of the Darklings pursuing him.

They bounced off the walls, collided with their neighbors, and fought each other to get near him.

By the time they figured out where he was, he was already running off somewhere else.

He made it all the way back around to this original starting place but fifteen feet below the tunnel he and Anríq used to get here.

Yann didn't have time to go back up there and then retrace the route the Darklings already knew he wanted to take.

The deafening booms of Anríq's club kept shuddering the cavern from below. How much longer could Anríq keep this up?

Yann didn't have any more time to screw around, so he took off in the only direction that made sense.

He hurdled out into the cavern's central shaft again, landed on another Darkling, and vaulted from one to another getting closer to the opposite side.

The Darklings he stepped on roared and spun away from Anríq to come after Yann instead, but he leapt so fast from one to the next that they only wound up attacking each other.

His foot slammed down on one last Darkling and he propelled himself up into the opposite tunnel.

Another Darkling dove for him, snapped its teeth together in a devastating chomp, and bit down on empty air as he somersaulted into the tunnel.

Chapter 44

Yann crouched in the tunnel listening to the Darklings thundering in fury out in the cavern. Anríq's club pounded through the walls. He would bring down the whole cavern if this kept up.

The Darklings kept rushing the tunnel entrance right in front of Yann's face. They snapped and snarled trying to get him.

When that failed, they snaked their tentacles down the tunnel to snatch him.

He slashed a dozen tentacles off as he backed away out of range. He was finally safe—for now.

The sound of Anríq's club hammering away down there drove Yann farther away. He had to get the captives out of here and fast. He only prayed he could rescue them in time for Anríq to escape, too.

Yann waited just long enough to make sure none of the Darklings' tentacles could stretch this far. Then he turned away and extended his glaive's glowing blade farther down the tunnel to see where he was going.

He would have given just about anything for a scrap of magic to locate the captives in this Dark maze.

That was never going to happen, so he just had to do it the old-fashioned way.

He picked up his pace, but he got lucky this time. The tunnel turned out to be one long, unbroken tube just like the last one. Simion Mihaili wasn't very creative.

Yann crouched under the low ceiling working his way deeper and deeper into the tunnel. He didn't know how far he'd have to go before he found the captives....and then he saw them.

The light from his glaive picked out some shadowy shapes ahead, but they didn't look like people.

He raced down the tunnel much faster after that...and stopped dead in his tracks when he found the captives.

A dozen people lay embedded in the rock wall. That was the best way Yann could describe it.

Their bodies stuck a few inches out of the surface. They had frozen in attitudes of twisted agony with a thin layer of stone covering every inch of their skin. None of the captives could move.

The stone even covered their mouths so they couldn't make a sound. The rock left their eyes exposed, but their eyes didn't move, either.

Yann studied them one after the other and even touched the rock while he tried to find some vulnerability. How could he free these people with only his glaive?

He didn't want to use the blade to crack the stone. Anríq's enchantment gave the only light for Yann to see what he was doing.

It would also give him the only light to get these people out—if by some miracle he found a way to free them from the rock.

God only knew how he would get them through the cavern. He could just imagine the nightmare of trying.

These people might be just as frozen and immovable outside the wall as they were in it. They might weigh too much for him to carry even one of them. Then he'd be sunk and so would they.

He found Amala. None of these people seemed to be wearing any clothing. The rock outlined their bodies with nothing in between. Would they come out of the rock stark naked into the bargain?

He pushed those thoughts away. Freeing them was much more important.

He rotated his glaive around and drove the wooden shaft end into the rock next to Amala's arm. She didn't react or move in any way. She didn't even move her eyes to show that she knew he was here trying to rescue her.

He slammed his glaive shaft into the rock a dozen times, but the blows didn't even chip the rock.

His frustration escalated to fury. Now what?

He glanced up and down the tunnel. He was just making up his mind to use his glaive blade after all when he heard....the silence.

The booming smashes of Anríq's club no longer thudded through the tunnels. Anríq must be dead down there—which meant Yann had absolutely no hope left of ever getting out of here alive. Forget about rescuing these people.

No wonder Mihaili gloated over Anríq. Mihaili must have seen straight through Anríq. Mihaili must have realized that Anríq would never give up until he found the captives.

Then Anríq would fall into Mihaili's trap and Mihaili would continue to hold Amala and her relatives down here forever. Costico would never find out what happened to Yann, Anríq, or the captives. It was the perfect plan.

Yann's shoulders slumped. He turned back to study Amala. If he had no other option, he might as well use his glaive blade. His situation couldn't possibly get any worse.

He turned his glaive around and cocked back his arms to strike, but at that moment, someone grabbed his arm.

He jumped out of his skin when he found Anríq standing next to him. "Don't do that," Anríq told him. "You'll damage the blade and it won't break the surface."

"You scared the crap out of me!" Yann hissed. "Don't sneak up on me like that! Jesus!"

Anríq furrowed his brow. "I didn't sneak up on you. You looked up the tunnel right at me. I was right there."

Yann turned away gasping for breath. "Just get us the hell out of here. How do we get these people free?"

"They're under a curse," Anríq began.

"I can see that," Yann snapped a lot more harshly than he should have.

Anríq passed down the wall and ran his hands over the rock. "I'll have to break the curse."

"Will these people be able to travel once they get out of the wall?"

"I don't know, but we can't leave them here. Step away, Yann."

Yann backed away from the wall. Anríq laid his flat palms on the surface and shut his eyes. Yann was really starting to hate seeing Anríq do that.

He shuddered and then gritted his teeth. He compressed his lips in deep concentration, bowed his head, and another deep trembling shudder spread through the rock.

The vibration gathered in strength, traveled all the way down the tunnel until it covered all the captives, and in one sudden rush, all the rock covering them sucked inward into Anríq's hands.

It blasted him off and sent him flying into the opposite wall next to Yann. Anríq landed hard on the floor and lay there writhing and groaning in agony.

Yann knelt over him. "How bad is it?"

Anríq bared his teeth through shivering lips. He kept his eyes shut and didn't answer.

Yann glanced up and his heart nearly stopped when all the captives stepped out of their places in the wall. They all looked perfectly healthy, and even better, they were all dressed.

They reappeared wearing the same clothes they must have been wearing when Mihaili captured them.

Amala wore a beautiful, full-length gown studded with pearls. Some of the men wore extremely fancy dinner outfits. Three of the women wore handsewn dresses like the women must have come from country towns.

The captives stepped down to the floor and looked around them in obvious confusion. Amala glanced up and down the tunnel and then frowned at Yann and Anríq. "Um..... where are we?"

Yann straightened up to face all the captives. "It would take too long to explain. We're here to get you out of here and take you home. We just need to figure out...."

Another groan from Anríq interrupted him. Yann squatted down next to his friend and tried to turn him over. "How bad is it?"

Anríq didn't answer for the second time, but at least he tried to sit up.

"You're the only one who can fight your way through the cavern," Yann told him. "If you can't do that....."

"I have....I have.....I have to....."

Anríq choked multiple times, hauled himself to the opposite tunnel wall, and propped himself up on it. Then he retched onto the floor.

Yann kept his hand on Anríq's shoulder. Yann really didn't care anymore about the Servants' rule not to touch people. Anríq did it plenty of times to heal people.

Yann would have traded his own life for the ability to heal Anríq right now. Something told Yann that keeping his hand there would be healing for Anríq even though Yann couldn't explain why he thought this.

Amala and the others gathered around to stare at Anríq. "He's a Barbarian!" Amala murmured. "What is he doing here?"

"He's a Servant," Yann explained again. "Your father asked us to come down here and rescue you. Now we have to go through a cavern full of Darklings and then find our way through the Layers back to your home country."

"How do we do that?" one of the men asked.

"Does any of you have any magic?" Yann asked.

The former captives exchanged glances. Yann's heart sank. So much for that brilliant idea.

He turned back to Anríq. "Can you do this?"

"I have to...." Anríq croaked again.

Yann didn't contradict him. No one among the captives would be big enough, strong enough, or powerful enough to fight those Darklings. Anríq would have to do it or no one would.

Anríq dragged his bleary eyes up to Yann's face. "You need.....you need....to use.....your speed....Yann...."

"You don't worry about me. You're the one we all have to worry about."

Yann opened his mouth to bring up the other elephant in the room.

He and Anríq might, by some distant miracle, find a way to get these captives through the cavern. Yann might be able to stretch his imagination enough to actually entertain that as a viable possibility.

After that, only Anríq could get the party through the Layers. He would need all his strength and magic to do that.

Yann wouldn't be able to help him at all. Yann would be just as defenseless as these other people.

Yann didn't say that. He concentrated on dragging Anríq to his feet.

Anríq's weight sagged against Yann. Anríq's bulk nearly cracked Yann's spine, but he turned away and hobbled down the tunnel getting closer to the tunnel opening.

Yann didn't look behind him to make sure the captives followed. They would have to pull it together real quick when it came to running across that cavern.

He wouldn't be able to rely on them leaping from Darkling to Darkling the way he did. How the hell was he supposed to get them across alive?

Anríq propped his arm against the wall while he unhooked his club. He didn't seem strong enough even to hold it up, much less use both it and his axe to fight the Darklings a second time.

Yann glanced over at him. Anríq didn't look up. He stared down into the pit far below. Would he make it out alive? If he didn't, none of the rest of them would, either.

Yann finally worked up the nerve to turn around and face his group of captives.

"All of you will need to run your fastest to get across. We'll skirt the cavern on that ledge over there. You need to be ready to improvise and use any alternate route available to you to keep out of the Darklings' reach—even if it means stepping on the Darklings themselves."

"But...this is impossible!" the first man exclaimed. "We'll never make it across before they attack!"

"Anríq will distract most of them. Then it will be up to us to get across as fast as we can. I'll do what I can to defend you, but I won't be able to do much with only one weapon. You'll have to fend for yourselves and rely on speed and agility."

Yann tried not to look at Amala's dress. She wouldn't be relying on any speed or agility in that.

She surprised him by nodding. She was one of the first to set her expression in a hard mask of grim determination.

She gathered up her billowing skirts, wadded them into a load in the crook of her elbow, pulled them up to her knees, and dipped her chin at Yann. "I'm ready," she told him. "Let's go."

"NO!" the first man countered. "Are you insane?! We can't go out there! I mean...look at this place!"

"The rest of us are getting the hell out of here," Yann told him. "You have a choice. You can run across there and get into that tunnel over there....or you can stay here. It's up to you."

The guy gaped at him in horror, but Yann was all done babying these people.

He knew one thing for sure now. He would be sending Anríq to certain death down there. Anríq wouldn't be able to fight the Darklings in his condition.

Yann laid his hand on Anríq's shoulder for the last time. "Are you ready?"

Anríq nodded without looking up. Yann couldn't wait any longer. He pushed Anríq forward and yelled, "GO!!"

Anríq didn't run and launch himself into the middle of the cavern. He jumped straight off the edge into the thickest knots of Darklings.

Yann lost sight of him, but that didn't matter anymore. He yelled out one more time, "GO!!" to the people behind him and raced onto the ledge.

Amala followed right behind him, but she had to stop when he ran into his first Darkling.

He rushed in with his glaive flying. He didn't hesitate for a second this time.

He stabbed, slashed, and impaled without really looking at what he was doing or where he was going. He gouged eyes and gutted Darklings at every turn.

He sent the first one flying off into space and ran a dozen more yards before another Darkling landed on the wall in front of him.

He had to stop again, but at that moment, another bone-crushing smash resounded through the cavern from down below.

Yann didn't take the time to see what Anríq was doing. Yann already knew. Anríq was using the last of his strength to buy Yann and the freed captives just a few more precious seconds to get across the cavern.

That one explosion distracted the Darkling into looking down. Yann struck without mercy, slashed his glaive across the Darkling's face, and then contracted every muscle of his core to drive his glaive down into the Darkling's head.

The skull cracked and Yann used the glaive shaft to cartwheel over the Darkling's head.

It started to topple off the ledge. He had to work fast to yank his weapon free. Then he waved to the people behind him. "Come on!" he yelled. "Come now while you have the chance!"

Amala rushed into his arms and he practically hurled her into the other tunnel—the one leading to the surface—or what he hoped led to the surface.

The others followed one after another. Three men had to divert from the ledge to avoid Darkling attacks.

One of the men really did take Yann's advice and jumped from Darkling to Darkling across the middle of the cavern the way Yann did.

The freed captives rushed into the other tunnel. "Keep going!" Yann told them. "Get out of range from their tentacles!"

He pushed the last women through the opening and rushed after them. They took off running up the tunnel.

He stopped again and held his breath to listen when he heard silence coming from the cavern behind him.

It wasn't silence, though. The Darklings kept roaring, but he didn't hear any thumps or booms or explosions.

He turned back and advanced to the edge to look down. The Darklings swarmed all over the place, especially on the floor.

Anríq lay on his back down there with his glazed eyes staring up into space. Darklings pounced all over him, but they couldn't get to him.

He didn't move, but he projected a glistening dome of protection around himself to hold them off.

Something switched in Yann's mind. He got the freed captives across the tunnel. Now they needed Anríq to take them the rest of the way. Yann couldn't do that.

Some hint of recognition in Anríq's dull eyes connected with Yann across the cavern. Anríq saw Yann watching him.

Yann's fear and hesitation vanished and he stepped off the ledge. Gravity stripped him downward at nose-bleed speed.

He didn't even look at the Darklings. He kept his eyes locked on Anríq all the way down.

Yann hit the dome and it caught him enough to break his fall. He floated the rest of the way to the floor and knelt down next to Anríq.

"Make yourself light, Anríq!" Yann yelled in his face over the Darklings' thunderous noise. "Make yourself light enough for me to carry you out of here!"

Anríq didn't respond.

"You're the only one who can get the captives through the Layers!" Yann bellowed. "It has to be you! Come on, Anríq! Make yourself light enough for me to carry you!"

Anríq blinked impossibly slowly. Then he gulped. "I can't.....Yann....." He barely spoke above a whisper. "I....I don't have.....I don't have the....the magic anymore....."

Yann stopped himself from even comprehending those words. No way could Anríq lose his magic.

Yann bent low over Anríq's face, seized two fistfuls of Anríq's vest, and tried in vain to drag Anríq off the floor. "Give me the curse, Anríq!!" Yann roared. "Give me the curse so you can take these people to safety! It's the only way!! Come on, Anríq! Don't give up on me!"

Anríq squeezed his eyes shut. A tear streaked down the side of his face and he gulped again.

"Come on, Anríq!" Yann heard his voice crack. "You know you have to do this! We both do!"

Anríq didn't open his eyes. He hauled one arm off the floor with a massive effort, and still keeping his eyes shut, he clamped his muscular hand around the back of Yann's neck.

A brutal jolt of power hit Yann in the brain when Anríq tightened his grip....and then a sickening flood of poison poured straight into Yann's deepest being.

It spread through his body in seconds infecting every pore with rot and corruption. Yann whimpered in terror. He couldn't handle this, but it just kept invading him more and more and more.

He struggled against Anríq's grip, but Anríq only tightened it. He held Yann in a death clamp as Anríq unloaded the whole horrible curse into Yann's being.

Yann collapsed onto the floor—or he would have if Anríq hadn't caught him.

Yann would have toppled across Anríq's chest, but Anríq shot off the floor at impossible speed.

He grabbed Yann by the back of the shirt and Anríq blasted upward in a headlong streak for the tunnels.

Chapter 45

Yann came to his senses lying on the tunnel floor where he and Anríq started. The stone chilled him through his clothes and he shivered. Once he started, he couldn't stop shaking.

Anríq bent over him. The freed captives stood around staring at Yann in abject horror.

Anríq kept touching him all over. "Don't....." Yann croaked. "Don't....."

Anríq's features pinched. "You'll die if I don't."

"Take them.....take them all......"

"I'll take you, too," Anríq murmured.

Yann tried to shake his head. "Leave me here. I can protect your retreat....."

He didn't know how he would do this. He only knew that Anríq would have his hands full getting everyone through the Layers.

Yann was the last thing Anríq needed to deal with right now.

Just to confirm Yann's deepest suspicions, a tremor vibrated through the rock right then. It came from the cavern, but the group was too far away from the cavern.

Yann couldn't lift his head to see what was causing it. He looked up at Anríq instead and read the truth in those clear blue eyes.

"They're coming," Yann husked. "Give me my glaive and leave me here. Go, Anríq."

Anríq's mouth said, *No,* but no sound came out.

Yann wanted to smile at him, but Yann couldn't summon the energy even to do that.

He couldn't imagine how he would fight the Darklings to protect the fleeing captives. He would just have to dig deep and find a way.

His eyes rolled from one side of the tunnel to the other. "Where's my glaive?" Did he actually say those words out loud or did he just think them?

Amala walked away, came back with his glaive, and squatted down next to him to put it in his hand. "Thank you, Yann," she whimpered. "We'll never forget what you did for us."

Yann could only gaze up at her. She really was beautiful. She had her father's dark hair and eyes, smooth skin, and fine, sculpted features. Her magnificent dress made her look like the princess that she was.

Yann tore his gaze away from her and focused on Anríq. "Help me sit up, Anríq."

Anríq pinched his lips, scooped up Yann by the armpits, and dragged him to the tunnel wall. Anríq propped him there in a sitting position.

The noise coming up the tunnel got louder. Were the Darklings tearing the whole cavern apart to track down the escaped captives?

Did Yann or Anríq really believe Mihaili would just let these captives walk away? Of course he wouldn't. He released his Darklings from their confinement to come after the fleeing captives.

Anríq must have known something like this would happen. He was too smart to fall for a trick like that or delude himself into thinking Mihaili would just drop his vendetta for no reason.

As Anríq said, it didn't make any difference in the end. He and Yann had to come down here to save these people even knowing the danger.

Yann clasped his glaive, but his fingers felt too weak even to hold onto it very tightly. Forget about lifting it.

He couldn't bear the desperate anguish radiating out of Anríq's eyes. "Go, Anríq," Yann repeated. "Get out of here before they get any closer."

"I'll come back for you," Anríq choked. "I'll heal you and take you back. I swear it."

Yann thrust out one hand, grabbed Anríq's wrist once, and then used the last of his strength to push Anríq away. "Go. Go now."

Anríq stood up. Yann shut his eyes so he wouldn't see the others leaving him here to face the Darklings alone.

He still didn't open his eyes when the group's footsteps faded up the tunnel and eventually disappeared.

He would have to open his eyes if he wanted to slow the Darklings down, but for now, he just wanted to rest.

This awful gnawing, grotesque feeling in his gut drained every ounce of courage he possessed. Creeping dread spread through his veins. He really was cursed—far more cursed than those people had been when they were trapped inside the wall.

The Darklings would put him out of his misery. Then he wouldn't have to feel this rot inside him anymore.

The Darklings' roars got louder and louder until they shook the wall behind his back. They were coming—and fast.

After a few minutes, another sound snuck in to mingle with those roars. Deep crashing and exploding sounds echoed up the tunnel. Those sounds got as loud or louder than the Darklings' voices.

Yann shut his eyes again. Now he knew it was really true. The Darklings were caving in the tunnels to make them big enough for the Darklings to pass through. They would get here any second.

He dragged himself away from the wall and sat in the very center of the tunnel. He scooted around to point his legs and his glaive down the tunnel toward where the Darklings would come from.

The enchantment still held to make his glaive glow. It gave enough light for Yann to see the passage in front of him. He would be able to see Darklings coming—whenever they came.

He didn't hold out any hope that he would be able to slow them down—not by fighting them.

With luck, they would pause just long enough to kill him and devour him. Maybe those in the very front would block those behind them. Then his death would delay all the others.

The sound of rock caving in overwhelmed the Darklings' voices. The bedrock under Yann's seat quaked and jolted with individual strikes now, but he still didn't see any Darklings.

He blinked hard trying to see something. How long would it take Anríq to carry the captives back to safety?

Then he saw it. The tunnel at the farthest distance of the light ring crumbled. It imploded on itself and an avalanche of rock rained into the tunnel.

The cave-in blocked the tunnel. Nothing would be able to get through that, but the advantage only lasted a second before a giant mouth chomped the fallen rock out of the way.

The two sets of fangs smashed together and closed in a huge Darkling face where the tunnel had been.

The next instant, two more Darklings moved in from the side slashing and gobbling their way through solid granite on a dead course for Yann.

He raised his glaive. He should have met these creatures on his feet, but he couldn't stand. He would just have to do as much damage as possible from here.

The Darklings didn't see him right away. They chomped another fifteen feet up the tunnel before the Darkling in the center spotted the light from his glaive.

The three Darklings leading the way paused there to study him. They took a minute before they reacted to his presence.

He roared back at them and jabbed his glaive to antagonize them. "COME ON!!" he bellowed. "COME ON!!"

They lunged for him, but they had to chew through more rock to get to him.

His awareness dropped into the deepest, darkest, most silent part of himself as he watched them come closer. Time crawled to a standstill.

Every bite of their teeth tore the cavern walls apart with ease. They would make short work of him, too, once they got here.

None of that mattered anymore. He wouldn't be able to rely on speed or agility. He would just have to stop them with pure tenacious brutality. He could do that.

He clamped his hands much tighter on his glaive. Some kind of crazy explosion went off inside him. It didn't get rid of the curse nor did it bring his strength back. It just gave him the boost of determination he needed to face this moment as his last.

The Darklings roared in fury that someone had the nerve to stand in their way. They plunged into the rock, smashed their heads against it, and wound up slowing themselves down.

Nothing could slow them down completely. They eventually worked their way close enough. The center Darkling chomped into the floor just beyond Yann's legs.

He yanked his feet back before the Darkling could pull him into its mouth.

Adrenaline took over. He dove onto his knees and stabbed his glaive into the creature's forehead. The Darklings couldn't use their tentacles in this confined space. They were all mouth.

Yann hurled his weight against the glaive shaft the way he did before, twisted the weapon in place, and cracked the Darkling's skull. That seemed to be the best way to kill them.

The creature froze there with its mouth open. Its size blocked the other two Darklings from getting near Yann.

They had to chew their way through the tunnel's side walls to crawl around their dead friend. Yann scrambled backward to put more distance between himself and them.

Those two came at him from either side this time. He wouldn't be able to fight them both.

They plunged through the walls at the same time. They would have squashed him between their two heads.

He tried one last desperate time to scuttle backward out of range. His legs gave out and he sprawled on his backside across the floor.

What might have been a disaster turned out to work in his favor. He fell below both Darklings and they crashed into each other instead.

He got trapped beneath them with both Darklings right on top of him.

He stabbed out with his glaive. He didn't care what he hit as long as he hit something.

He stabbed into one of their necks and severed a blood vessel. Thick, black, sticky blood gushed all over him, got in his eyes, nose, and mouth, and stopped him from seeing anything for a minute.

The Darkling he hit roared out in deafening rage and then collapsed right on top of him. It pinned him under its colossal weight. He couldn't move even to raise his glaive.

More Darkling voices thundered from inches away. They couldn't get to him with this monster on top of him and another dead Darkling blocking the tunnel. Now what was he supposed to do?

He didn't have to wait long to find out. The Darklings went to work tearing down the tunnel and then more tremors vibrated through the big body on top of Yann. The Darklings must be tearing their dead comrade apart to get to him.

He scraped his face against the shoulder of his uniform to clear the crap out of his eyes. He still couldn't see much with this hulk on top of him.

He *could* see the two walls on either side...and he definitely saw the cracks skidding down the walls. They spread outward as the Darklings destroyed the structure around him.

His glaive got trapped under the Darkling's body. If the Darklings had a brain between them, they would leave him trapped there and bite his head off to stop him from using his weapon against them.

The Darklings didn't have a brain between them. They didn't think. They attacked in berserk fury unless something directed them to do things in a particular way.

The vibrations coming through the Darkling's dead body escalated faster than the vibrations coming through the walls. Yann really wished he could see what the hell was going on out there.

Without warning, some almighty force ripped the Darkling off him and left him lying there completely exposed.

He had half a second to see an endless void of Coil Layers spreading into nothing beyond his feet. The Darklings had completely obliterated the tunnel system and whatever structure housed it.

Dozens of them floated in the Layers out there. This one small stretch of floor ended there. This was the only part of the tunnels left standing—and the tunnels behind him leading to the surface.

At the same moment, four more Darklings smashed through the walls on either side of him. They tossed their heads from side to side and shook all the broken rock out of the way.

Now nothing stood between them and him lying helpless and weak on the floor.

He ripped up his glaive just as they all lunged for him, but as usual, they couldn't all attack him at once. They were too big and he was too small. They would up crashing into each other and slowing each other down again.

He played that to his advantage. He didn't even try to stand up or even sit up.

He dove sideways and rolled under another Darkling that came through the side wall. He tried to pull the same trick by slashing its throat, but he missed.

Being underneath the Darklings definitely protected him in ways he never thought possible. All the other Darklings dove in to attack him and attacked their friend instead.

He might have been able to protect himself and even delay them indefinitely if he just stayed down there.

The temptation to kill them proved overpowering. He took a few more seconds to check his aim, slashed again, and drained that Darkling, too.

He didn't stick around long enough for it to fall on top of him. He launched himself across the floor, rolled under another Darkling, and swiped his glaive through its ribcage this time.

Their size cramped them in the tunnel. They couldn't move as fast as he could. He kept darting and rolling from one Darkling to another trying to stay underneath them where they couldn't get him.

He worked his way farther up the tunnel to get away from the edge. The tunnels gave him his only other advantage. He couldn't lose that.

He planned to roll over and pick out his next target when a tentacle snaked out of nowhere. It lashed around his ankle and brought him crashing down on his stomach on the hard stone.

He tried to kick the tentacle off, but before he could move, it yanked him backward and dragged him skidding across the floor.

He flipped over and brought up his glaive thinking to sever the tentacle and free himself. He almost forgot to fight back when he saw the Darklings pulling him toward the void.

They gathered out there with their mouths open. One jerk and he would sail off into one of those mouths.

He rotated his glaive and contracted his stomach to sit up. He had to cut that tentacle at all costs, but at the same instant, another tentacle shot out of nowhere and caught his wrist—the wrist of the hand holding his glaive.

The tentacle tugged his hand aside. He couldn't aim well enough to make his strike... .and now he couldn't use his glaive to free his hand, either. He couldn't use his glaive for anything.

Another tentacle slithered around his neck and tightened. The Darklings snarled at him from all sides. They had him. He was finished.

He stared up at them, completely helpless. The world stopped for the second time and he didn't move or make a sound to break the spell.

As long as he lay here with all their attention on him, Anríq and the freed captives could keep getting farther away. That was the whole point of Yann's life right now—to give someone else a chance.

He relaxed into the inevitable. Anríq was right about him. Yann was a Servant—as much a Servant as Anríq himself.

He couldn't even remember when it started. He admired his father and the men of the Watch. Yann wanted to join them so he could be as good and selfless as they were by protecting those who couldn't protect themselves.

He felt the same way about Eliska even though she was so much more powerful than he was.

Her magic didn't protect her from......something else. She needed someone or something to take care of her. He sensed that about her from the beginning. She was scared—probably more scared than anyone in the Watch.

Yann helped Anríq heal those people—as much as Yann could help Anríq. Yann would have done more....and now this.

That one thought gave him the inner peace he needed to face his own death. He was a Servant. He would die as a Servant. He didn't have to take an oath of celibacy to the Black Watch. He already was one.

He sank back on the stone floor waiting for the Darklings to attack and finish him off. At least it would end quickly. He wouldn't suffer.

He only hoped Mihaili's curse died with him. No one else had to suffer like this.

The Darklings roared in unison and they all plunged in together. More tentacles hissed and whipcracked from every side to tear him apart.

The Darklings dove on top of him, and at that moment, a catastrophic boom went off somewhere above Yann's head.

He had a split second to see Anríq leap over his face, land in a crouch straddling Yann's knees, and then Anríq's club hit the Darklings.

The club made contact with a Darkling's head and the whole Layer detonated in a deafening explosion that wiped out everything else.

Chapter 46

Yann woke up in a completely different bedroom in Costico's palace. Yann pried his head off the pillow and looked around. He'd never seen this room before.

It was just as big and palatial as the room in which he'd stayed last time, but its giant veranda and garden faced a different part of the mountains.

The bed and furniture also sat in different positions than Yann remembered.

Anríq lay curled up asleep on top of the bed next to Yann. The blankets covered Yann with Anríq on the outside.

Anríq looked peaceful when he slept. He must have brought Yann back from the Layers.

Yann felt good, but still a little weak. He wasn't wearing his uniform. A pair of thin linen pajamas surrounded him in softness.

He collapsed back on the pillow and that movement roused Anríq. He cracked his eyes open and squinted at Yann before Anríq let his head fall down with a sigh.

"I thought you might die," Anríq husked. "Thank the stars you're all right."

"Thank you for coming back for me," Yann replied. "I really thought I was going to die down there."

"I wouldn't let that happen." Anríq pushed himself upright. "You should eat. You've been unconscious for almost a week."

"I don't want to lie in bed anymore." Yann threw back the covers.

He tried to sit up on the edge of the bed, but sitting up made him realize he was weaker than he thought. He couldn't stand up—or at least he didn't trust himself to stand up.

Anríq crossed the room, picked up a bowl of fruit, brought it back, sat down on the edge of the bed next to Yann, and put the bowl between them.

"Thank you," Yann repeated.

Anríq took an apple out of the bowl and started eating it. Yann took a plum. It tasted incredible.

"What's happening out there?" Yann asked. "Did all the captives get back all right?"

Anríq nodded. "They're all home thanks to you. Amala won't stop talking about you."

Yann looked up. "Is she here?"

"Of course. Costico wouldn't let her go anywhere else. They've already had several arguments because he doesn't want to let her leave the house again—ever."

Yann had to laugh. "I think I can guess how that will end."

Anríq kept eating his apple while he crossed the room going in a different direction. "Here's your uniform in case you're feeling strong enough to walk around."

"How long are we staying here?"

Anríq shrugged and sat down again. "I suppose we'll stay until you feel strong enough to travel. We have no more reason to stay." He pointed outside. "The vortex is gone and so is the curse on the town. I went to check. Everyone is recovering, now that the Darklings aren't living directly under the town anymore."

"Where are they?" Yann asked. "What happened after you found me?"

"I collapsed the Layer to send them somewhere else. The caverns caved in completely. There's nothing under the town anymore except more Layers—the same chaos Layers that have always been there. The curse is lifted."

"Wow," Yann breathed. "Well done."

"We both did it—you especially. You healed more people this time than I did."

Yann looked away and concentrated on eating his plum. He didn't tell Anríq about his revelation when the Darklings were about to kill him.

Anríq didn't need anyone to tell him. He knew before Yann did—not that it made any difference.

It didn't make any difference between the two of them, but it made all the difference in the world to Yann.

He knew what he was now. He just didn't know how it would affect his life. Waking up to the fact that he was a Servant—or the Black Watch equivalent of one—didn't clarify which direction he should go.

He didn't find the answers to any of those questions, but they didn't bother him anymore. He would just keep following the road in front of him.

Maybe something would happen between now and when he actually had to take the oath. Something might show him what he had to do. He could only keep going and find out.

Yann finished his plum. He would have put the pit back in the bowl, but Anríq held out his hand for it and then tossed the pit off the side of the veranda.

"Where are you staying?" Yann asked when Anríq came back inside.

"I'm staying here with you. I didn't want to leave you alone until I knew you were going to make it."

Yann forced a laugh. "You mean we've been sleeping in the same bed all this time? Why am I only hearing about this now?"

Anríq laughed along with him, but just then, Costico came in with a bunch of other men wearing Corsair robes.

Costico's eyebrows shot up when he saw Yann sitting up. "Ah! This is a pleasant surprise. We thought the curse would be harder to break."

Yann glanced at all the other men standing around. "Am I missing something here?"

"These are my doctors and healers. They've been working to break your curse since you came back from the Layers."

Yann shot a look at Anríq. Yann thought Anríq was the one who had been working to break Yann's curse.

Yann didn't want some strangers working on him, but what difference did it make as long as the curse broke in the end?

"I suppose you have to take some time to recover and build up your strength," Costico went on. "I'm going out for a few days raiding with my men. Make my home your home. I'll see you when I return."

Yann stiffened when Costico mentioned going raiding with his men. Were they going back to the same town after everyone there just recovered?

If Costico and his men didn't go for that town, they would go for another. They would sack it and probably kill a bunch of other innocent, defenseless people.

Yann didn't speak up to try to talk him out of it, though. Yann would have tried to talk him out of it before, but something changed in those tunnels.

He no longer considered it his place to talk anyone out of anything. Who was he to decide who was right and who was wrong?

What if Costico had been right about the townspeople communing with the Dark? What if they weren't innocent pawns of Mihaili or whatever Dark force captured those people?

Yann would never know.

He did know one thing. He didn't want to stick around this palace accepting Costico's hospitality as long as Costico was out there raiding anybody.

"We probably won't be here when you get back," Yann told him. "We'll leave as soon as I can travel. If you aren't back before then, we'll be gone when you come back."

Costico only smiled at him. "I expected that. You have your own mission to fulfill. I'm supremely grateful for everything you've done."

He came forward and hugged Yann. Costico remembered to bow to Anríq and Anríq bowed back.

"Thank you both—for everything," Costico repeated. "My servants have orders to give you anything you need—anything at all. I hope our paths cross again."

"Thank you for taking such good care of us," Yann replied. "I'm glad we could bring your daughter back."

Costico left the room and took his doctors with him. That left Yann and Anríq alone in the silence.

Anríq broke it. "I'm glad I'm not the only one who wants to move on."

"Did you really think I would want to stay here?" Yann made a face at the room around him. "This place gives me the creeps. Give me a thatch cabin in the woods any day."

Anríq grinned at him. "Are you sure you don't want to stay, marry Amala, and inherit Costico's fortune? I'm sure he would be delighted to welcome you as his son-in-law."

"You better shut up," Yann snarled. "Make that the last time you ever mention me getting married."

Anríq laughed at him, but Anríq didn't mention it again.

The boys spent the rest of the day lounging and eating way too much. The servants figured out pretty quick that Yann was awake—or maybe Costico told them.

The servants brought in massive platters of every kind of delicacy known to man—most of which Yann had never seen or heard of before.

The boys helped themselves, went to bed early, and slept like rocks until the next morning.

Yann woke up restless on the second day. "Let's get the hell out of here before Costico comes back," he told Anríq.

Anríq only nodded. "All right, but I want to do something before we leave."

"What is it?"

"Get your glaive and follow me. We'll leave as soon as I take care of it."

Yann felt better after he put on his uniform. Anríq seemed to feel better with his bags slung over his shoulder and his axe hanging on his back. Both of them felt more normal like this.

Anríq led the way to a different bedroom—an unused one. Yann seemed to remember Anríq coming out of this room the first time the boys stayed in this castle.

Anríq checked both ways to make sure none of the servants saw them, opened the door to let Yann inside, and shut the door behind them.

"What are we doing here?" Yann asked.

Anríq crossed the room to the opposite wall. "This is the painting Mihaili used to talk to me."

Both boys faced an elaborate oil painting surrounded by an expensive wooden frame painted gold.

The image inside depicted the interior of a grand house and a wide living area full of expensive furniture. The room led onto another marble veranda with a mountain scene behind it. The picture looked eerily similar to something from this very castle.

"The picture is different now than when I saw it last time," Anríq murmured. "Mihaili must have changed it."

"What did it show you before?"

"It was a poor house with one room, one table, one bed, and a fireplace. An old woman and an old man lived there."

"So is Mihaili the old man?"

"No, he looked like a young man. I don't think the old man and the old woman realized he was using their house as a staging area to spy on someone else. They didn't even notice him. I think he must have used magic to conceal his presence."

"How is that even possible?" Yann countered. "Surely they must have noticed something."

"I doubt it. I saw them in the picture multiple times. They didn't notice anyone watching them from the picture—and when I saw Mihaili there, the old people were gone."

"So what are we doing here?" Yann asked. "What do you want to do about it?"

"I want to break the spell on the picture so he can't spy on Costico's family anymore."

"So what's stopping you?"

Anríq gazed into the picture. "Nothing, I guess."

Yann studied Anríq more closely than the picture. Yann didn't understand Anríq's hesitation, but something obviously did make him hesitate.

Yann didn't see anything that made Anríq act, either. When he did, he did it decisively.

He stepped forward and passed his hand down the picture the way Costico activated the picture of the town—the one he said showed him where his daughter was.

The scene in the magnificent living room vanished. The picture didn't turn back into a poor, one-room house with an old man and an old woman living in it, either.

The image changed to a sunny field with a split-rail fence and horses grazing in the sunshine. The long grass waved in the breeze and birds soared against the clouds.

Anríq stood back.

"Is it finished?" Yann asked.

Anríq nodded. "It will stay like this forever now."

Yann waited, but Anríq didn't turn away from the picture. "Are you ready to go?" Yann asked.

Anríq nodded again without turning away from the picture. He might have stayed like that forever.

Yann bumped his elbow to get his attention. "Let's go."

Anríq tore himself away and the two boys left the castle. No one tried to stop them.

Chapter 47

Yann and Anríq crossed the drawbridge, passed through the invisible barrier, and headed back out to the road heading in the direction they'd been traveling when Avol and the others brought Anríq to their cursed town.

The boys had to travel through the same town to continue down the road, but no one stopped them there this time.

The gates stood open at both ends of town to let anyone in and out. No one had remembered yet to remove the skeletons and warning signs, but the townspeople would get to that eventually.

People smiled at the two boys when they walked into town, but everyone was too busy putting their lives back together to stop and talk.

Bustling energy filled the town. People worked in the streets and in their yards. Different people went into and out of each other's houses.

Voices drifted from every window. A few children played outside and Yann even heard laughter in the distance. It didn't feel like the same town.

He and Anríq passed all the way through town without talking to anyone. No one stopped them. No one even acknowledged that these two young men were the ones who lifted the curse.

Yann and Anríq left town by the other gate, passed down the road, and returned to the open countryside on their way to the horizon. Yann reconciled himself to go through the whole process again when they got to the next town.

Word would spread that a Servant was traveling this way. Anyone who needed help would come out to find Anríq.

Yann settled into that cycle as the basic formula of his life now—and not just because he was traveling with Anríq.

It made sense for Yann to do that, too. This process completed what he started in Middleborough. He only just came to accept it in the tunnels under the church house.

This was his life now—at least until he caught up with the rest of the Watch. This was his life now even after he caught up with the rest of the Watch.

He was still a member of the Watch. He was actually more a member of the Watch now than he had been before. He was as much a member of the Watch now as if he'd already taken his oath.

He'd already let go of the idea of getting together with Eliska—or anyone else. Did it really matter in the end?

His desire to get together with her—it had really just been a desire to protect her—to give her the care and connection she never got from anyone else.

So that was all part of service, too. It really just came down to that.

He wanted to serve her by helping her, protecting her, and caring for her the way she needed him to. He didn't need anything for himself. He didn't even really want anything for himself.

The boys camped by the side of the road that night. They didn't talk around the fire. Yann settled into the comfortable intimacy between him and Anríq. Their connection had grown beyond words.

Yann would keep traveling with Anríq—probably forever. Yann no longer doubted that.

Eliska said the Servants traveled alone, but Anríq didn't say anything about Yann going off to do his own thing.

Yann made up his mind to stay with Anríq until Anríq did say something. If Yann's presence somehow violated Anríq's oath, then Yann would have to go.

He wouldn't stop being a Servant when he did. Nothing would ever change that.

They both woke up and left camp in silence the next morning. Yann didn't even ask how far away they were from the next town. It would happen one way or the other whenever it happened.

He zoned out thinking about what the next town would be. Would it be another peaceful market scene or a magical catastrophe that would cost both boys their lives to fix?

He wasn't thinking about anything in particular when Anríq stopped in the middle of the road, scowled, and looked around.

Yann stiffened instantly. He knew that expression too well. "What's wrong?"

Anríq shook his head, and before he could answer, the same vortex of collapsing Layers blasted down from the sky.

It never happened like that before. Yann had never seen the vortex anywhere else besides Costico's castle.

The vortex erupted out of thin air, spiraled toward the ground in a whirlwind of swirling color and shadow, and forked into the hills a dozen miles west of the road.

Punishing wind struck both boys in the face. Yann raised his glaive, but he didn't see anything over there—nothing but chaos.

Booming thunder echoed out of the Layers high above as they crashed down one on top of the other. They buckled with flashes of magical discharge going off all the way up to the heavens.

Yann squinted at the surrounding countryside. Would this Island collapse now, too?

He turned to Anríq to ask, but right then, the vortex ejected a solid wall of wild magic. It hurtled across the countryside. Yann couldn't identify what this was except that it rushed him unbelievably fast.

The wall shimmered with colorful hues playing on its surface and then it smashed into him with bone-crushing force.

It didn't sweep him away like so many other collapses. This one flooded over him and surrounded him on all sides like a vast sea of water—except that this was crystal clear with brilliant light shining through it from somewhere.

The water—or magic or whatever it was—blocked off his nose and mouth. He couldn't breathe—and he could swim through it like water.

He floundered to figure out which direction was up or down. Anríq paddled a few feet away trying to hold his breath and orient himself at the same time.

Cows, wagons, household utensils, fence posts, and even a few windows got caught in the same magical flood. They floated in the substance, bumped into each other, and bobbed weightless in the sunlight.

The cows thrashed their legs trying to swim out of the stuff. They tried to swim up, but there didn't seem to be any up to swim toward. The light came from everywhere and nowhere at once.

Yann's chest strained holding in the last mouthful of air before he suffocated. Would this Layer collapse and spit him and Anríq out somewhere else? It better happen soon before everyone ran out of air.

Yann kicked out to get closer to Anríq, but right then, another cow shot downward from somewhere above him.

The animal streaked through the magical substance as if the cow just fell into a giant lake or something. It crashed down on top of him and pushed him twenty feet below Anríq.

Yann scrambled to get out from under the cow. He had to swim sideways to get clear of the animal's hooves striking out in panic.

Yann kicked sideways...and bumped into something else. He didn't think anything of it at first until he glanced behind him. Whatever it was felt sold enough that he might be able to push off it to propel himself closer to Anríq.

Yann froze when he saw what it was—and what it wasn't. He didn't see anything at first—not anything he might have bumped into. Whatever it was, it was invisible.

A mysterious invisible barrier separated him from a completely different landscape on the other side. That landscape was not inundated with water or any magical substance.

He stared through the transparent surface at his father, Wesh, and the men of the Watch engaged in a deadly battle against a completely different breed of Darklings.

They fought at the edge of a wood where the trees met open farmland. That landscape looked stable. The men must have found their way to another Island.

These Darklings weren't massive fanged monsters covered in spikes and whipping tentacles. These were smaller but somehow even more deadly.

These Darklings looked more like misshapen humans with multiple limbs where their arms and legs should be.

They didn't have any heads, either. Their bodies moved around on five or six regular human legs with six or seven regular human arms sprouting from the headless shoulders.

These Darklings could move much faster and they used conventional weapons. Each arm held a sword, battle axe, club, or mace.

Dozens of these Darklings surrounded the Watch with countless weapons. The Watchmen couldn't get away.

Yann looked everywhere for Eliska, but he didn't see her anywhere in the other landscape. Where was she? Did she finally abandon the Watch to its fate?

Yann put out his hand and touched the invisible surface. It felt like a sheet of glass blocking him from getting out there.

He looked around everywhere, but he only came face to face with the hopeless reality on the other side of the barrier. He was about to watch his father and his friends go down against these Darklings. Yann couldn't do anything to stop it.

Desperate fury drove him insane. He pushed off from the surface, grabbed his glaive, and nailed the blade into the surface with all his might.

He delivered one blow after another, but he couldn't break the surface. His efforts didn't even attract the Watch's attention.

He floated close enough that they should have been able to see him right next to them. He would have been able to call out to them if the barrier didn't separate him from them.

He nearly broke his shoulders hammering his glaive into the surface as hard as he possibly could. Nothing.

Someone grabbed him and he spun around in wild panic. He almost turned his glaive on Anríq before Yann realized who it was.

Anríq scowled at him and pushed him away. Anríq puffed out his cheeks holding his breath, straightened his arm to hold Yann at a distance, and unhooked his club from his belt.

Yann's heart threatened to explode out of his chest. He couldn't hold his breath much longer and seeing the Watch in danger drove him ballistic.

Anríq swam in front of the surface and turned sideways to wind back his club. The battle outside escalated as the Darklings moved in for the kill.

Anríq swung his club and it smashed into the surface with a ground-shaking explosion. The blast shattered the surface and all that magical water crashed into the other landscape.

The flood slammed into the Watch carrying Yann and Anríq with it. All the cows, fenceposts, windows, and furniture swept away into the trees and took the Darklings with them.

Chapter 48

Eliska pushed herself off the ground and blinked the stars out of her eyes. She frowned while she tried to remember where she was and why.

She remembered the snow Island....and the conversation about the White Spire....and Marine adding those sticks to Eliska's drawing....

And the fire. Eliska definitely remembered the fire that wiped out the snow Island.

There was no fire here. She woke up in a different Layer. It couldn't be an Island because the landscape kept morphing and changing.

She woke up on a rock ledge in the middle of a sea of some glassy silver liquid. It blooped and shimmered all around this ledge.

The ledge didn't float in the middle of the liquid nor was it attached to anything.

Marine sat at the other end of the ledge. She bent over the side, dipped her finger into whatever this substance was, and it clung to her skin when she pulled her hand back.

"Um....Marine?" Eliska ventured.

Marine looked up at her, and right then, the liquid sea erupted out of whatever bed it might be floating in.

It crested in waves that grew into mountains. The mountains turned into monsters and then caved in on themselves. They shattered into rock that turned into birds that flew away past Eliska's head.

She grabbed her staff and scrambled to her feet. The furs she'd been wearing in the snow Island just slowed her down now.

She yanked off the cloak and discarded it on the ledge at her feet—but it wasn't a ledge anymore.

The ledge grew outward into a river of ever-changing shapes. The surrounding landscape that had once been mountains changed to a solid carpet of gears, wires, machinery, and cogs all grinding against each other in constant motion.

The machinery chewed away at the rock ledge until it crumbled under her feet. She couldn't stay here.

She flexed her legs to spring off. She spotted a large piece of machinery fifteen feet away. Its metal housing looked big enough for her to balance on....and then she saw Marine.

Marine balanced on a different slab of metal bobbing and tilting in the confusion. The slab wobbled and Marine almost fell off into the grinding cogs.

"Hold on, Marine!" Eliska yelled. "I'm coming for you!"

Eliska reacted without thinking, leapt off what was left of the ledge, and threw herself into the mayhem.

She started to descend between her starting point and Marine's slab, planted her staff into the boiling, devouring mass of parts underneath her, and propelled herself the rest of the way to Marine's slab.

Eliska landed on its edge. Her weight made it tip even more dangerously, but she didn't plan to stay here.

She grabbed Marine around the waist and launched away carrying Marine with her.

Eliska pole-vaulted on her staff one more time and landed on the large machine she noticed earlier. She held onto Marine to stop the other girl from falling off.

The minute they landed, the landscape changed again. All the machinery locked together in a deafening sequence of clicks, snaps, and bangs.

The pieces formed modular components rising into some monstrous machine city. They carried the two girls high off the ground—if this Layer even had any ground.

Without warning, burning fireballs pelted out of the sky and smashed into all the machinery. The components caught fire and one of the fireballs bounced off Marine's head.

She screamed and threw up her arms to protect herself. Eliska couldn't wait any longer.

She scooped her arm around Marine's waist to make sure the girl didn't get lost, stabbed her staff down hard into the machine at her feet, and discharged a deep thump of magic through the mass of parts underneath her.

The Layer collapsed. Eliska held onto Marine at all costs and they dropped into a Layer full of gnashing mouths not attached to any kind of bodies.

All those mouths rushed the two girls. Eliska fought them off with her staff clutched in one hand. She didn't dare to let go of Marine with her other hand.

They plummeted through the headless mouths, fell through a solid sheet of fire, and came out in the clouds.

Gravity caught them both and yanked them toward the ground falling faster and faster and faster.

The clouds parted and Eliska's heart stopped when she saw a huge Island landscape spread out below her.

Towns and even cities rose out of a massive plane as wide as Eliska could see. The earth rushed her way too fast. Nothing would break the girls' fall.

Eliska twisted around the other way, pointed her staff downward, and fired a jet of magic. It formed a bowl-shaped container that broke the wind. Both girls slowed until they floated toward the ground at a safe, gentle speed.

Eliska couldn't stop staring at everything in amazed shock. This Island resembled nothing she'd ever seen in the Coil before.

Towering buildings of glass and steel raised their spires to the sky. Flying vehicles soared around the buildings and buzzed over streets teeming with different kinds of vehicles running along the ground.

Blazing lighted signs covered the walls of buildings, flashed different images and written messages, and then changed to completely different pictures of people, objects, and landscapes.

The bowl she used to slow her fall passed some of these buildings so she could see through the windows.

People in fancy clothes sat inside talking to each other, working on more screens, and talking into them to converse with people at a distance.

Others stood in front of larger screens and pointed at diagrams, scenery, and pictures on them while they lectured others about what they were seeing.

Wild whoops of crazy laughter startled Eliska back to her senses. She went through another torrent of confusion when she realized the laughter came from Marine.

She shot to her feet, teetered on the edge of Eliska's magical bowl, and yelled out in crazy glee. "Whoo! Come on, Eliska!"

Before Eliska could move or fully comprehend what was happening, Marine grabbed her hand and yanked her out of the bowl.

Both girls sailed through the air and started to fall again. Eliska was too stunned and horrified to do anything, but Marine must have known exactly what she was doing.

She landed on top of one of the flying vehicles and crouched there to keep her balance as the vehicle shot away across the landscape.

Now Eliska was the one who wobbled and almost fell off to her death in the streets below. Marine caught her.

Eliska gaped in slack-jawed disbelief at the mischievous grin spreading across Marine's smudged face.

"Oops!" Marine giggled. "Be careful there!"

She held onto Eliska's hand and then pulled her lower onto the vehicle's roof. It zoomed between buildings, skirted signs, and fired out of the city heading for the distant countryside.

"This is where we get off!" Marine yelled over the wind, and without giving Eliska any further warning, Marine launched herself over the side.

Eliska screamed in terror, fired her staff again, and created another bowl to slow them down.

This time, they drifted the rest of the way to the ground. They landed on a grassy knoll next to a glistening stream.

Eliska collapsed back on the ground fighting to breathe, but she couldn't stop staring at the city just a few miles away. Its buildings touched the sky. The sun reflected off all those windows.

The tide of engine noise and thousands of voices, laughter, music, banging sounds, and crashes floated on the breeze.

Marine brought Eliska back to reality real quick. Marine laughed again. "Come on! Don't act so surprised! You must have seen cities like this in the Coil before."

Eliska turned around extra slowly. She wasn't sure she really wanted to see this, but she had to.

She faced Marine and discovered Marine grinning back at her. Marine's deep, dark eyes glowed with fun and mischief.

Her cheeks glowed with pleasure at her trick—or they would have glowed if so much dirt and muck didn't obscure her features.

"Um.....Marine?" Eliska stammered. "Um....what the hell is wrong with you?"

Marine burst out laughing again. She had a full, musical, uninhibited laugh like she really enjoyed laughter and joking around.

"I'm not what you expected, am I?" She smirked outright and passed her hand across her face to push her hair out of her eyes.

Touching it drew her attention to it. She looked down at the stringy, matted, greasy locks hanging on each side of her face.

She wrinkled her nose at her hair. "Ugh! That's disgusting! We can't have that, can we?"

She passed her hand down her hair a second time from her forehead all the way to the tips. A wave of magical sparks erupted from her palm, flowed down her hair with the motion of her hand, and left her hair clean and shiny in a waterfall of glistening darkness.

She stroked her hair all over until it shone in the sun. Then she rubbed her hands over her face.

All the grime came off in more sparks. They left her face as fresh, clean, and glowing as any princess.

"How's that?" she asked and grinned again.

Eliska gaped at her in stupid disbelief. This was definitely not the same person Eliska had been used to. This was no wild, crazy girl sitting in the snow and snarling at unseen Darklings.

Marine laughed at Eliska's reaction. "Oh, come on! You didn't think I was like that all the time, did you?"

"What did you...I mean...what are you....who the....?" Eliska stammered and faltered to a stop.

Marine squinted at the city in the distance and raised her arm to shield her eyes from the sun. "We should go inside and see what they can tell us about the Voyant."

"The Voyant?!" Eliska blurted out. "What about him?"

"About why he's hunting the Black Watch, of course." Marine turned around to study her. "Isn't that what you're all trying to find out—why the Voyant is hunting the Watch? You want to find out what he wants from them, don't you? Isn't that your whole quest or whatever you call it?"

Eliska's jaw dropped again. "You know all that?"

Marine made a face. "Come on. What do you take me for? I saw it all in the Dark river—and even if I didn't, it isn't like I didn't hear you all talking about it. What did you think—that I was so out of my mind that I didn't understand what you were talking about?"

Eliska opened her mouth to answer, but she stopped herself. She really did think Marine was so out of her mind that she didn't understand what the Watch had been talking about.

Eliska started to say, "Um....." again, but just then, Marine noticed her dress.

"Ooo! Look at this!" she squealed. "Have I really been walking around like this?"

She passed her hands down the length of her dress from her neck to her ankles. She used her magic to change her torn, muddy rags into a completely different dress.

This one glistened with silver thread and tiny gemstones embedded in the fabric. The skirts puffed out in a cone from her tiny, corseted waist to her ankles.

She somehow made white stockings appear on her legs and tiny white leather slippers on her feet where she'd been barefoot until just a second ago.

Eliska gawked at her with her jaw on the ground. Marine really did look like a princess.

The self-satisfied grin of pure wicked mischief sealed the deal. No way could this be the same girl.

"Come on! Stop staring!" Marine grabbed Eliska's hand and towed her forward. They started walking down the riverbank heading for the city.

"Do you know what city this is?" Marine asked over her shoulder. "You know so much more about the Coil than I do."

"Um.....are you sure about that?" Eliska didn't ask what other secrets Marine might be hiding behind a mask of insanity.

"Of course I'm sure about that!" Marine fired back. "I've only been in the Coil a year or so. You've been in it your whole life." She cocked her head to study Eliska more closely. "Don't tell me you've never seen this city before!"

"I haven't. I've never seen anything like it."

Marine stopped dead in her tracks. Now she was the one whose jaw hit the ground. "You haven't?! Are you serious?"

Eliska shook her head. "I didn't think places like this existed in the Coil."

"Aha!" Marine practically yelled and pointed into Eliska's face. "So you *have* seen it before! I knew it!"

"I've seen it before, but not in real life. I only saw it in the Layers."

Marine punched her fist into her palm. "I knew it! What did you see? Tell me everything."

"I just told you. I saw visions of it in the Layers. I didn't think it was real. I've definitely never been here before. I thought it was some construct or an illusion created by the instability."

"Well, we're here now. These people must know something about the Voyant."

"What makes you say that?" Eliska asked. "They look like normal people to me even though they have all these amazing machines."

Marine spun around and gasped. "Are you telling me you don't know?!"

"Know what?"

Marine gaped at her. Then Marine shut her mouth and turned away shaking her head. "I don't believe it! All this time! I would have told you a long time ago if I thought you didn't know."

"What are you talking about?" Eliska asked. "What do you know that I don't?"

"The Voyant lives in a city like this. He lives in a city full of machines and flying vehicles and computers and...."

"Whats?" Eliska interrupted.

"Computers. They're the machines you saw people using in their offices. They process information and allow everyone to communicate as fast as thought."

"Wow!" Eliska breathed. "That sounds amazing."

Marine waved at the city in front of them. "He lives in a city exactly like this. The White Spire is in a city like this."

"Really?" Eliska gasped. "How do you know all this?"

Marine smirked and turned away. "We have our little ways."

"So.....you think these people have been keeping track of the Voyant on their...."

"Computers," Marine finished. "I didn't say that. I think the Voyant keeps his activities a secret from everyone, including whoever lives in the same city with him."

"So....the city he lives in....it isn't this one?"

"You don't see the White Spire here, do you?" Marine laughed again. She laughed a lot. "No, it isn't the same city, but it's similar. All the cities with this level of technology communicate with each other. Whoever these people are, they'll be in constant communication with the people in the Voyant's city....."

"Do you know what city he lives in?" Eliska asked. "Wesh didn't know where the White Spire was."

Marine rolled her eyes again. "I don't think Wesh's branch of the Guardian Templars has been keeping up with their studies. They're seriously behind on current events. He isn't even certain the Voyant is real or that he holds the power to control the Coil."

Eliska stopped dead in her tracks. "Are you saying the Voyant *is* real—and that he really does have the power to control the Coil?"

Marine nodded. "He's the one causing all this instability. If we can stop him, we can bring peace to the Coil. Then the whole Coil will become as stable as the Islands and people can start to build new civilizations. Wouldn't that be worth it?"

"Yes," Eliska breathed. "Of course."

"So we have to find him, figure out what he wants from the Black Watch, and stop him somehow."

Chapter 49

Marine set off walking toward the city in the distance. Eliska fell in next to her.

Eliska's head spun on their way there. She floundered trying to take in everything Marine told her.

Marine herself presented the biggest surprise yet. Eliska still found it nearly impossible to believe that the wild girl from the forest was actually walking, talking, reasoning, laughing, and joking around.

The wild girl from the forest really was this exquisite princess. She was funny, vivacious, friendly, mischievous, and warm.

Eliska cast sidelong glances at Marine on the way. Eliska had trouble taking her eyes off Marine. Eliska had to stop herself from staring too hard.

Marine noticed and smirked at Eliska every time Marine caught her looking. Eliska averted her gaze, but pretty soon, she found her eyes migrating back to study Marine again.

The pair walked for over an hour.

"Why do you think the Voyant wants the Black Watch?" Eliska finally asked.

"It must be something related to building up his power," Marine replied. "That's all the Voyant cares about. That's how he got so powerful in the first place."

"How do you know that? How is it that you know so much more about the Voyant than the Guardian Templars?"

"I don't. Like I said, some orders of the Templars are better informed than others."

"So you found out from the Guardian Templars? Wesh's order was the one that found out the Voyant sent the Darklings to attack Middleborough in the first place."

Marine spun around and pointed in Eliska's face again. Marine's eyes sparkled with wicked mischief. "Aha! I got you again! Wesh's order *didn't* find out that the Voyant sent the Darklings to attack Middleborough. Wesh's order found out that *someone* sent the Darklings to attack Middleborough. Wesh's order *suspected* that the Voyant was behind it, but since the order couldn't confirm that the Voyant was even real, they couldn't say exactly who sent the Darklings to attack Middleborough—which is also why the order couldn't figure out *why* he sent the Darklings to attack Middleborough."

"But the order knew the Darklings were after something in the town," Eliska pointed out. "That's why the order sent out Wesh and the others to try to protect the town—to stop the Darklings from getting it. Besides, why don't *you* tell me what it is he wants if you're so smart and so well-informed?"

Marine burst out laughing again and threw her arm over Eliska's shoulders. "That's what I like about you. You aren't afraid to tell it like it is."

Eliska turned bright red. No one had ever acted this friendly toward her before, not even Yann.

"You don't know, do you?" Eliska asked. "You don't know what it is the Voyant wants. Just admit it."

Marine sighed and took her arm down. "No, I don't. I wish I did. I thought I would be able to figure it out once I met up with the Watch, but it's just as much a mystery now as it was before."

Eliska skidded to a halt again. "You....you met up with the Watch....on purpose? You...you actually set out to intercept the Watch.....to find out what they're carrying?"

Marine turned around to eye Eliska again, but Marine didn't smirk this time. "Why is that so shocking to you?"

"But...you were communing with Darklings! Anríq said so."

"Ah, Anríq," Marine murmured. "Now we get to the heart of the matter."

"What about him? Don't tell me you had something to do with bringing him to us. I'll never believe that. He was just walking across country minding his own business. He couldn't be a part of this."

"No, *you* had something to do with bringing him into your group, didn't you? You were the one who went out and asked him to help the Watch."

"Well, why shouldn't I? He's a Servant and I was the only magic-user the Watch had besides Wesh. The two of us sure as hell weren't getting the job done on our own. Who better to ask than one of the Servants?"

Marine shrugged and kept walking. "You might be right."

"You can't tell me there's anything Dark about him. He's one of the best men I've ever met. He practically died so you could communicate with me."

Marine nodded. "I know."

"Then what are you saying about Anríq?" Eliska heard herself losing her cool over Anríq. Where was he now? She really hoped he was safe—and that Yann and the rest of the Watch were safe.

"I don't know that Anríq has anything to do with any of this," Marine replied. "Like you say, he was just minding his own business when you asked him to help the Watch, but he's up to his neck in it now. He won't be able to get out of it any more than you can."

"What does that mean? What does this have to do with me? We already know that whatever the Voyant wants was already in Middleborough before I ever set foot in the town. Whatever he wants, it isn't anything to do with me or Anríq or even Wesh."

"Maybe not, but all three of you are tied up in this now—by your own choice if not by some other means. Would you really just walk away from this, now that you know what's going on? Of course you wouldn't. Whatever happens to the Watch is as much your business and Anríq's business and Wesh's business as it is Yann's, Yvan's, and the rest of the Watch's business."

Eliska looked away. She'd been coming to this realization for a long time—long before she heard those Barbarians talking in the tavern.

For some reason unknown even to herself, she just kept involving herself in this mess. Now it was her mess as much as the Watchmen's.

She was the one who roped Anríq into it. Now he wouldn't be able to walk away, either. Did she make a catastrophic error by asking for his help?

She forced herself to keep walking. "I guess it doesn't matter. The Watch isn't here and we have no way of getting back to them."

"We can still try to find out what the Voyant is doing......but I don't think we'll be able to do it here."

Eliska spun around. "What do you mean? Why not?"

"Look." Marine shaded her eyes again and pointed at the city in the distance. "We've been walking for almost two hours, but we never get any closer to the city."

"What does that mean?"

"Maybe something is stopping us," Marine suggested.

"Or maybe this is an illusion Layer like I said," Eliska pointed out. "Maybe the city isn't real."

Marine laughed again. "Of course it's real, silly! Don't joke around about that!"

"I'm not joking. How do you know it's real? You said you don't even know what city this is, which means you've never been here before, either."

Marine smirked even more wickedly. "Are you telling me that vehicle we jumped on to ride here wasn't real? Please."

Eliska tried to shrug it off. "Okay. That part was real."

Marine finished chuckling to herself and threw herself down on the grass with a sigh. "Oh, well. I guess we might as well take it easy—since we can't go to the city the way we planned. Maybe we fell into some kind of loop. I suppose we can shatter the Layer and go somewhere else to get out of this, but we might as well relax and enjoy it while it lasts."

"The way *you* planned," Eliska corrected. "This was your idea, remember?"

Marine grinned and then covered her eyes to search the city. She was right. The two girls never got any closer to it no matter how far they walked.

Eliska found herself studying Marine instead. Marine turned around too soon before Eliska remembered to avert her gaze.

Marine burst into another huge smirk, lunged forward, grabbed Eliska's hand, and hauled her down onto the grass next to her. "Sit down and stay a while. Talk to me. Don't tell me you want to run off back to those guys when we've just made friends."

Eliska's cheeks flamed. "Are we friends?"

"Of course we're friends! What do you think we've been doing all this time—plotting each other's assassinations?! Of course we're friends! What else would we be?"

Eliska looked away.

"What's the matter now?" Marine demanded. "Are you offended because I said Anríq is involved in this because of you?"

"No," Eliska muttered into her collar. "I'm not offended because of that. I mean, he *is* involved in this because of me."

"Why are you offended, then?"

"I'm not offended—not at all."

"Then what's the problem? Why don't you want to talk to me?"

"I do want to talk to you." Eliska looked away again. "I like talking to you."

Marine exploded in another massive cheesy grin. "I like talking to you, too. It gets so boring communing with Darklings all the time."

"Why do you do it, then? Why do you go so far out into the Dark when you could be like....like *this?*" Eliska waved her hand up and down in front of Marine's beautiful face and dress.

"I do it for the mission, of course," Marine replied. "I do it to get information about what the Voyant is doing, how we can stop him, and how we can stabilize the Coil so it doesn't keep collapsing on people and wiping out whole towns and even cities. Can you imagine the loss of life if an Island like this collapsed? It would be disastrous—and yet it happens all the time. It happens because of the Voyant. Someone has to stop him and I can't do that alone."

Eliska looked away again. She didn't have to wonder about the loss of life from collapsing Layers, towns submerging into chaos, and whole civilizations getting wiped off the map.

She'd witnessed it countless times. Her magic saved her each time. She could just travel to another Island or migrate through the Layers from one place of stability to the next.

Other people didn't have that luxury. They just had to die.

Marine read her mind. "Looking like this and acting like this aren't the most important things—not even close. Some things are more important."

Eliska couldn't stop herself from turning around to stare at Marine's glowing face. It glowed with something more than just physical beauty.

Her radiant personality shone through. Eliska's mind staggered that she'd spent so much time around Marine and never even seen this person before.

"You're beautiful," Eliska whispered.

"You're beautiful, too," Marine replied. "Why do you think Yann and Anríq both like you so much?"

Eliska turned her head away so Marine wouldn't see her cheeks flush. "They don't like me—not like that—or Anríq doesn't."

"Of course he does," Marine insisted. "Everyone can see the way he looks at you and the way he acts around you. You really won his heart. That's obvious—and then there's Yann."

Eliska didn't want to talk about Yann, so she changed the subject. "I've never had a friend before. You're the first person who has ever called me that."

Marine split in another broad grin. "Aw! Pals!" She dove for Eliska and gave her a crude hug before Marine leaned back and sat up straight. "I've never had a friend before, either, if you really want to know the truth."

Eliska gasped out loud. "You're lying! You're so outgoing....and beautiful....and fun ny.....and vivacious...."

Marine laughed again. "Ha ha."

"How can you not have friends?! You're...like....perfect. You're everything I wish I could be." Eliska opened her mouth to say something else, faltered, and then gulped before she blurted out, "I don't want it to end. I don't want you to lose your mind when we leave here."

Marine smiled at her, but this was a sad smile. "I don't want it to end, either, but some things are more important. I have to commune with the Dark to find out what the Darklings know and to track Dark forces through the Layers. I can't do that in places like this—in places where there are no Darklings and no Darkness."

Eliska didn't answer. She was really starting to dread the prospect of losing this version of Marine and getting back the old one.

"What makes you say Yann and Anríq don't like you?" Marine asked. "You know they do."

"They only like me because I'm there." Eliska's eyes darted to Marine. "They would both like you better if they knew what you were really like."

Marine didn't turn that into a joke. "I wouldn't be so sure about that. You're everything either of them could want—much more than I am."

Eliska stared down at her hands. "It doesn't matter because Anríq is a Servant and Yann will join the Watch as soon as he gets old enough to take the oath."

"What do you really know about Anríq?" Marine asked. "What do you know about him, really?"

"Well....nothing. How could I when he's never told me anything about himself?"

Marine nodded at nothing. "Maybe you just don't understand him the way you didn't understand me. Maybe something would happen that would pull aside the veil and you would see the way he really is underneath."

Eliska looked away again. Marine's dark eyes made Eliska uncomfortable. "That will never happen. He doesn't want to get close to anyone, especially not me. If you understand him that way, then you're lucky. I never will."

"You saved his life," Marine pointed out. "He cares about you very much. How could he not?"

"Anyone would be grateful for that. It doesn't mean anything."

Marine broke the tension by slapping both hands on her thighs. "Welp, rest time is over. Let's get out of here. Maybe we'll have better luck somewhere else."

She got to her feet. Eliska hesitated to do the same. "Are you sure there isn't some way to contact these people?"

"The Voyant is probably blocking us from going in there."

Now it was Eliska's turn to make a face. "Don't start assigning everything that happens to the Voyant. It's more likely that this is an illusion Layer that shows us something unreal."

Marine laughed. "You and your illusion Layers! I swear I never met anyone more committed to believing the world isn't real." She jutted her chin at Eliska's staff. "Do you want to do the honors or shall I?"

"Do you know how to?" Eliska asked.

"Of course I know how to! How do you think I found you?"

Eliska didn't know or want to know how or why Marine found her. Eliska turned away, raised her staff, and stabbed it down into the grass.

She didn't do it as hard as she might have. She didn't want the whole Island to collapse—if it was a real Island and not just some hallucination in the Layers.

She opened a hole just big enough for her and Marine to fall through into the next Layer.

Chapter 50

M arine and Eliska fell through the crust of soil, plunged through a few Layers, and landed in another Island.

This one looked like another countryside of gently rolling farmland, but instead of people and houses, enormous monsters of every variety covered the terrain from one horizon to another.

The monsters roared at each other, charged, and attacked each other, but for some reason, they completely ignored the two girls.

Marine and Eliska moved closer together. Marine bumped into Eliska and they wound up holding onto each other.

"They aren't Darklings!" Marine called over the noise. "I don't know what they are, but they don't belong to the Dark."

"I know!" Eliska yelled back and she opened her palm to check her diagram of the Coil. "This shows a few more cities to the west. Let's head that way and see if we can find some people. These monsters don't look dangerous."

Marine rolled her eyes to heaven. "Yes, they do."

"I mean they don't look dangerous to us. Come on."

The two girls inched across the landscape. This place didn't have any roads, so the girls just had to cut straight overland and hope for the best.

They held onto each other and had to keep springing out of the way to avoid getting trampled by ongoing conflicts between the monsters.

Their roars made conversation nearly impossible.

"How do you think they got here?" Eliska yelled over the noise.

"Some of them look like people—or like they used to be people!" Marine hollered back. "Maybe the Dark took them and transformed them."

"They aren't Dark!" Eliska pointed out. "Something else must have caused it."

"Maybe the landscape changed them," Marine suggested.

Eliska nodded. "That makes more sense."

Another bone-shaking roar startled her into turning around, but the monsters still didn't attack the girls.

Some of the monsters attacked others if they even came close to the girls.

"They're trying to protect us!" Eliska pointed out.

Marine looked over her shoulder. "I don't like this. Something isn't right about this landscape."

"Everything isn't right about this landscape." Eliska created her Coil projection again. "I'm not picking up any instability. The Island is holding steady—which explains why the environment is so pleasant."

Saying that out loud only reminded her that everything wasn't all right with this Island. Everything about it was pleasant except the monsters.

The girls' presence triggered some kind of reaction in them. Monsters blundered into each other or outright attacked each other for no reason.

Others lunged in to tear these monsters apart if even one of them accidentally stumbled close to the girls.

Brutal fights broke out right near the girls. Dozens of monsters nearly trampled both girls even when the monsters tried to protect them.

"We gotta get out of here!" Eliska yelled.

Marine nodded fast. "Should we shatter the Island? I don't want to wreck such a nice place—and these monsters are some of the very few we've seen who don't belong to the Dark. They don't deserve us destroying their home for no reason."

Eliska opened her mouth to suggest that the girls transport themselves to another Layer without shattering this Island.

Before she could say a word, another group of dozens of monsters barreled toward her and Marine from the side.

Multiple fights broke out over there and another three monsters came perilously to squashing the girls between the monsters' giant bodies.

This new group might have decided they needed to protect the girls from the same monsters who had already been trying to protect the girls.

The new group thundered across the plane, collided with those they wanted to attack, and the whole pack toppled right onto Marine and Eliska.

Instinct took over. Eliska grabbed Marine, hugged her close to her body, magicked both girls out of the way.

She acted in time to save them from getting crushed, but it didn't take them completely out of danger.

More monsters barreled in from all directions. That one collision set off a chain reaction in all the other monsters. It seemed to give them the license they needed to all pile in at the same time.

Eliska transported her and Marine from one place to another and sent them whizzing across the landscape. Eliska had to keep zooming, dodging, and blinking off somewhere else to skid around more monsters charging in.

Marine craned her neck to look over Eliska's shoulder. Eliska really hoped Marine saw something over there—like a way out of this death trap.

Too many monsters crowded the landscape even before the girls showed up. Once the fight started, what looked like every monster in the whole country charged in to converge on that one spot.

The two girls bounced off monsters roaring and pounding across the terrain. Eliska had to work her hardest to direct herself and Marine out of the monsters' path.

The fight spread. More monsters tried to protect the girls from each other. The fight followed the girls even as they tried to flee.

So many of these massive creatures gathered from all over, ran everywhere, and hammered their weight on the ground that it trembled under all those pounding feet.

A deadly crack jutted under Eliska's feet the next time she landed somewhere. She transported somewhere else and landed on the ground fifty feet away only for the same crack to fork in her direction.

The earthquakes set off another ballistic response from the monsters. Eliska didn't see how they could get any heavier. Their jumping up and down must have fractured the Island's structure.

It imploded and the girls, the monsters, and tons of bedrock plummeted into the next Layer down.

Marine screamed as the two girls hit a Dark Layer just beneath the monsters' country. The Dark Layer might have been responsible for transforming the monsters, but Eliska didn't have time to think about that right now.

She crushed Marine in a death grip and Eliska shut her eyes against hurricane winds.

She could always defend herself in any Layer she happened to fall through or any Island she happened to fall into.

She couldn't find another friend—not one like Marine.

The girls struck something brutally solid, crashed through that, and then plunged into a frigid snowbank that didn't seem to have any bottom.

Eliska had to let go of Marine to flounder out of the snow, but neither girl could tell anymore which way was up.

"Marine...." Eliska choked on a mouthful of snow. "Hold onto me! Stay with me, Marine!"

"Eliska!" Marine yelled back and tried to say something else before the snow muffled her.

Eliska tried to paddle through the snow toward the sound of Marine's voice, but they couldn't find each other.

The monsters must have fallen into the same Layer. One enormous furry behemoth slammed down right on top of the same snowbank.

The creature's weight drove the girls all the way down, down, down, into the Dark before whatever lay at the bottom of this Layer broke, too.

The girls tumbled out onto another riverbank somewhere, but this one didn't pass by a beautiful city of glass and flying vehicles.

Eliska rolled onto her stomach on a bed of cinders that scorched her through her clothes. She jumped herself up immediately to get away from the heat searing her skin. Then she saw where she was.

She and Marine landed on a sloping mat of hot ash and smoking rock chips leading down to a black river oozing through a Dark landscape.

Four gargantuan wolves stood on the other side of the river. Their coal-grey fur stood up in ridges along their backs, flared outward in thick ruffs around their necks, and stuck out in spikes up their tails.

The wolves paced back and forth on the opposite bank, bared their fangs, and narrowed dark, glowing red eyes at the two girls.

Marine scrambled onto her hands and knees and scooted closer to Eliska. The fall turned Marine's beautiful dress back into a shredded mass of soot-stained rags.

Grime and filth covered her face, arms, and hands and clung to her hair in stringy, greasy ropes, but at least Marine's eyes still registered all her old vivacious personality. She didn't lose her sanity when she landed in this place.

Eliska grabbed her and pulled her away from the river. Eliska didn't have to wonder what the wolves were doing over there.

The wolves paced back and forth between the river and another city spreading from the opposite riverbank—or it used to be a city.

The charred remains of buildings, smoking piles of rubble, and blackened streets littered with bodies and destroyed vehicles bore silent witness to exactly what this city used to be.

And there, on the horizon, towering over the whole horrid scene, stood the White Spire.

Chapter 51

Eliska took hold of Marine's arm to pull her away from the Dark river. "We have to get away from the river. It could enchant us and pull us into the Dark Layers."

Marine didn't hear her. She stood frozen to the spot and stared across the river at the White Spire in the distance.

Eliska shivered at the sight. She would have recognized it anywhere after seeing it in the vision Marine sent her. The characteristic cornice around the spire's topmost peak stood out against the swirling vapor Layers above it.

The spire itself wasn't white—not now. It might once have been white before whatever disaster struck this country hit the spire, too.

Now it towered over the landscape as black and foreboding as everything else in this wasteland.

"No!" Marine stammered. "No, it can't be! This is all wrong! The White Spire ruled over a beautiful land—a paradise Island full of prosperous trade and productive people! They had the greatest technology in the whole Coil! They can't all be....gone! This is all wrong!"

Eliska pulled Marine's arm one more time. "Don't you get it? The Voyant turned this place to the Dark. Come on. We gotta get out of here."

"NO!!" Marine's voice spiked. "We can't leave! This is our chance to stop him! We finally found him! We can't just walk away. He's right there! We can...."

She broke off when a ball of light rocketed out of the heavens from deep in the Layers above the spire.

The light plunged out of the vapors and shadow up there, burned a fiery path through the atmosphere, and dove straight into the spire's highest peak. The light vanished inside.

"There!" Marine yelled and pointed to the light just as it disappeared. "That's him! He's inside the spire right now! We have to go over there and find out what he's doing! We'll never get another chance like this, Eliska. Come on!"

Marine grabbed Eliska's hand and pulled her toward the river instead of away from it.

Eliska reared away in alarm. "Hell no! We are NOT going over there! Are you out of your mind?! Look around you! We would have to cross that river—a Dark river—and then we'd have to deal with those wolves. We aren't going over there, Marine. Forget it!"

"Come on!" Marine countered. "We have to stop the Voyant! He's the one doing all of this. Look at this city! It used to look like that other one we just left! Don't you see? All those people—all that technology—he wiped them all out! He killed all those people...."

"You don't know that. The Dark could have taken them or the landscape could have changed exactly the way you said it changed those monsters. A firestorm could have hit this city. It could have injured or changed the Voyant, too. He could be an innocent victim in all this....."

"Innocent!" Marine bellowed. "That's outrageous! He controls the Coil! Don't you understand? If the Dark took this city or the landscape changed or a firestorm hit it, any of those things happening would have been his doing! He's the only one who would cause that to happen!"

Eliska glanced toward the spire. "I don't know....."

Marine spun away again and tried to tow Eliska with her. "We're going over there...."

"What about the wolves?" Eliska asked.

"We'll just have to fight them."

"How do you plan to cross the river? We would get sucked into the Dark Layers if we tried to swim it."

Marine waved that away. "The Dark Layers aren't dangerous. I go into them all the time. They're no big deal."

"No big deal?!" Eliska yanked her hand out of Marine's grip for the second time. "You saw what happened after I fell into the Dark river last time. No way am I going in there—not for all the tea in China."

"No! It will be fine!" Marine countered. "You'll see."

"It definitely will not be fine." Eliska planted herself there and refused to move. "None of us will be able to fight the Voyant if we're dead. You go if you really want to kill yourself. I'll find another way out of this Island on my own."

"Then you'll be turning your back on even more deaths. Would I let anything happen to you? Would I ask you to go into the Dark Layers if I thought it would kill you or leave you in danger? I'll be with you. I'll get you out in one piece. I promise."

Eliska didn't believe that for a second, but right at that moment, Marine grinned at her again.

Marine really had been going into the Dark Layers all this time. She went into and out of them all the time.

She dove into that river and came out untouched—or mostly untouched.

Eliska, Wesh, and the Watchmen would never know just how untouched she came out of it because none of them knew what condition she was in before she went into it.

Eliska didn't want to end up insane or permanently trapped in the Dark, but something drove her forward.

No one knew what the Voyant was doing, what he planned to do, what he wanted, or why he went after the Black Watch.

What if Marine and Eliska really could find that out—just by crossing this river? Wouldn't that be worth it?

Eliska couldn't explain why she trusted Marine, but she did trust Marine. Marine could go into the Dark Layers and survive if anyone could.

Eliska didn't argue when Marine took hold of her hand again and marched straight down to the river's edge.

The river's Darkness didn't cast the same spell on Eliska's mind. Did Marine do that?

Marine halted at the edge and shot Eliska one last wild grin. That grin was really starting to give Eliska a terrible feeling.

She should have resisted harder, but for some reason unknown to human rationality, she allowed Marine to pull her to the river's edge.

Marine shot her one more crazy smirk. "Ready?"

"No," Eliska replied.

Marine only laughed. "On three—one....two....THREE!!"

On three, Marine dove into the river. She didn't give Eliska a chance to back out. Marine kept a hold on Eliska's hand the whole time.

Eliska told herself not to do it right up until the moment when her face broke the surface....and then the black ooze closed over her head and she sank into the Dark.

The two girls plunged into a solid black Layer full of objects that pummeled the girls from all sides. Darklings roared in the shadows.

Eliska turned in all directions, but she couldn't see a thing. Only Marine's grip on her hand oriented her that the two girls were still together.

In half a second, they broke through to a vapor Layer, but this was nothing like the chaos Layers Eliska had traveled through before.

She always avoided the Dark Layers at all costs and for good reason.

The instant the girls entered, the vapors of shadow and deep hues at the outermost edges came together to form Darklings. They reared and roared at the girls.

Marine spun to her left, raised her hands, and fired magical bursts from her palms the way Wesh and Mael did.

Eliska wheeled to the right and blasted her staff at four Darklings. The vapors exploded and faded into the wind, but more Darklings gathered from every side.

The Darklings didn't concern Eliska as much as the shadows themselves. They hit her every time she fell through one of them.

They infected her soul with fear, rage, menacing jealousy, and every other Dark emotion. She couldn't get rid of them.

Bitter resentment flared in her mind against everyone she'd ever met—everyone who failed to help her when she needed it most.

The Darkness twisted every memory into a torment and every face into a nightmare.

She lashed out even harder against the Darklings and slashed her magic at them to tear them to shreds.

She saw herself losing control, but at that moment, one of the Darklings behind her let off a pulse of its own.

The shot hit the two girls and sent them cartwheeling backward.

They broke through some barrier that felt like a hedge full of thorns......and the girls somersaulted onto the cinder bank right next to the same Dark river.

The spire raked the horizon in the distance. The smoking rubble marked the spots where buildings once stood.

The wolves kept pacing back and forth and raising their hackles every time the girls looked in their direction.

The Layers stripped all the Dark goo off Eliska's clothes and hair, thank goodness. She landed dry and relatively clean if she could call it that. At least the stuff didn't drip off her.

Marine clambered to her feet, pushed her hair out of her eyes, and ran her hands down her dress. All these falls and battles left her as ragged and filthy as when Eliska first met her.

"Right," Marine snapped. "We'll just have to try again."

"No," Eliska countered. "It's a waste of time—and don't argue about it, Marine. Do you honestly think the Voyant didn't surround his spire with magical protections to stop people like you from getting inside?"

"Well, we have to try something!"

"If you really absolutely have to cross the river, I'll transport you across. I'll transport both of us across. Then we have to deal with the wolves."

Marine blinked at her, stunned. "Transport! I never thought of that."

Eliska snorted. "You know a lot about the Dark Layers but not much about the Coil."

Marine glanced behind her. The wolves didn't suddenly decide to go away while the girls had been gone.

"We'll have to use magic to get into the spire," Marine remarked.

"Obviously," Eliska countered. "The Voyant won't just let us walk in."

Marine frowned. "How would we do it?"

"You tell me. You're the Voyant expert around here."

"We should try breaking into the spire from here," Marine decided. "That way, if it doesn't work, we won't be on the other side when it happens. We won't have to fight our way past those wolves only to find out that we don't have the magic to break in."

"Now you're thinking. Let's try it."

The two girls swiveled shoulder to shoulder. Eliska concentrated all her mental attention on the spire's highest tower. The light went inside there.

She pointed her staff at it and Marine ejected a stream of magic from her hands. Eliska fired her staff at the spire.

The wolves burst into a torrent of baying, howling, snarling, and roaring when the girls' combined magic jetted over the wolves' heads.

The wolves couldn't stop the girls' assault. Both beams hit the spire's highest point.

Nothing happened. The girls' magic didn't even seem to touch the spire. It didn't bounce off. It didn't shake the spire. It just....vanished.

The spire remained untouched and as formidable as ever.

Eliska cut her fire and lowered her staff. She didn't want to admit defeat.

Marine let her arms fall to her sides. "I don't understand!" she quavered.

"The Voyant is stronger than any of us understands. That spire is probably the best-protected building in the whole Coil."

Marine's shoulders drooped, but at that moment, the same light rocketed out of the high vaporous clouds, shot across the landscape, and plunged into the spire's highest pinnacle again.

The light vanished exactly the way it did before.

Marine jolted to high alert. She spun around to look back and forth between the spire and the place where the light came from.

"That's impossible!" she cried. "I didn't see him leave! Did you see him leave?! How did he get out of the spire without us seeing?"

"Isn't it obvious?" Eliska asked. "He must have left it after we went into the river."

"You have to transport us across, Eliska," Marine insisted. "It's our only option."

"All right. Just be ready to fight those wolves the minute we set our feet on the other side. The Voyant must have channeled all his power into them to protect the spire. They're likely to overpower us—which means we'll have to run for it if the fight turns against us."

Marine dipped her chin once. "Got it. You can count on me."

Eliska didn't hold out much hope for this plan, either. She was beginning to see a pattern here.

Why on earth would a wizard as powerful as the Voyant Mendicat leave his spire unprotected?

If he really did control the whole Coil, then he must already know that people were trying to stop him.

He probably knew exactly what the girls were doing right at this moment. He could probably hear every word they said to each other.

He might be sitting up there in his spire sending all these countermeasures against them depending on what method they tried. Eliska wouldn't have been surprised.

That's what she would have done in his position. She wouldn't let some pesky teenage girls mess up his carefully constructed plans.

She didn't want to completely dash Marine's hopes. The Voyant would do that just fine on his own. She would realize she couldn't defeat him. Then she would have no choice but to give up.

Eliska took Marine's hand, planted her staff into the cinders at her feet, and magicked both girls off the ground heading straight for the wolves.

They all turned on the girls and bared their teeth. The girls would have soared straight into the wolves' jaws, but at the river's exact midpoint, another almighty slam hit both girls.

The blow sent them flying backward and they both landed hard on the riverbank where they started. Neither of them got anywhere near the wolves.

Eliska picked herself up and dusted herself off. "Well, that went about as well as I expected. Come on, Marine. We're leaving."

"Leaving!" Marine gasped. "We can't leave!"

Eliska turned her back and started climbing the cinder bank. "If you want to try again, go ahead. I'll see you when you get back."

"Hey!" Marine yelled. "You can't just walk away!"

"I've been traveling in the Coil my whole life and this is the first time I have ever gone through the Layers and wound up in the same place. The same thing will happen. Trust me. I'm going to those trees over there to make camp for the night. Come and join me when you get tired of playing his little game."

Chapter 52

Eliska walked off toward the trees on the distant edges of the cinder landscape. She didn't wait around to see if Marine followed.

Marine hesitated a lot longer than Eliska expected, but Marine didn't go back into the river.

She hustled up behind Eliska a few minutes later. Neither girl spoke on their way to the trees.

Eliska couldn't see them very well from the riverbank. The trees were too far away, but anything was better than staying here under the wolves' watchful eyes.

The girls had to hike a few miles before they came to the tree line. This stand of woods stood far enough away from the Dark river and the White Spire. Whatever inferno torched the city didn't damage the woods—or not as much.

The fields between the river and the woods lay charred and bare. The heat left the leaves on the trees shriveled.

The fire burned the bark on the side facing the river, but at least the trees were still alive. These woods would recover eventually. Eliska couldn't say the same thing about the city itself.

She passed into the woods and continued through them for a long way until she couldn't see the burned countryside anymore.

She found a clearing, gathered some sticks, and lit a fire. Neither she nor Marine had any food, but Eliska didn't offer to go hunting. She wasn't hungry and she didn't feel like eating.

Marine sat down near her. Marine recovered her former cheery nature on the walk there. She grinned at Eliska like they were on vacation or something.

Eliska stared into the flames while she decided what she should say to restart the conversation or *if* she should say anything to restart the conversation. Nothing came to mind.

Marine didn't restart the conversation, either. That left Eliska to her own thoughts. Eliska wouldn't have known how to handle Marine's mischievous joking at a time like this.

Marine finally broke that silence after what seemed like hours. She heaved a contented sigh and gazed into the flames when she murmured, "I admire you, Eliska."

"Me!" Eliska countered. "What do you admire about *me?* There is nothing admirable about me. Believe me."

Marine's eyes darted up to meet Eliska's and Marine smiled. A deeper level of understanding and sympathy in those dark pools caught Eliska in an undertow. "You don't see what other people see."

Eliska had to look away. "You have more power than I do. You're the one everyone admires—or they would if they knew what you've been doing."

"Why do you think Yann and Anríq like you so much?"

Eliska snorted. "Don't start up about Yann and Anríq liking me so much."

"They do. They both admire you."

Eliska groaned. "Can we please talk about something else? Tell me anything else you know about the Voyant and his plans."

"I don't know his plans. That's what I'm trying to figure out."

"Then tell me what you do know about him. How did you find out that he controls the Coil's movements?"

"I read about it in the Guardian Templars' library."

Eliska's head snapped around so fast she gave herself whiplash. "You....what?"

"I belong to the Guardian Templars. That's how I learned so much about him and how to travel in the Dark Layers. That's how I know that Wesh's order isn't as informed as they should be. Some orders fall behind the others."

Eliska gaped at Marine in dumbfounded shock—almost as much dumbfounded shock as she stared at Marine when Eliska found out that Marine wasn't really insane.

Marine gave her another sad little smile of pure, warm understanding. Of course Marine understood why Eliska would react like that.

"My father sent me to the Templars when I was fifteen," Marine explained. "I didn't want to go, but he didn't give me a choice."

"But...." Eliska stammered. "The Guardian Templars is a voluntary order. You should have been able to leave whenever you wanted and you....." Eliska's eyes darted down to Marine's ruined dress. "I thought you were a princess."

"I am a princess," Marine chirped. "My father is a king in the Hallowed Vales."

Eliska's jaw hit the ground. She couldn't speak. She couldn't even think. She wasn't hearing this.

Marine grinned more broadly at Eliska sitting there slack-jawed in shock. How long had Marine been sitting on this bomb just waiting to blow Eliska away with it?

"Now maybe you'll understand why I admire you so much," Marine went on. "I grew up surrounded by luxury. I never wanted for anything....and I had an older brother who loved me more than the whole world. Anríq reminds me of him......"

Marine turned back to the flames and stared into them in brooding silence. Words failed Eliska.

Marine said she *had* an older brother. Did he die? Eliska couldn't ask. She and Marine had been friends for less than a day.

She didn't see how losing a brother could ruin Marine's usual bubbly mood. She grew up in luxury with every advantage and a family that loved her. What could possibly be wrong about that?

Marine pulled herself out of her thoughts, straightened up, and shook her hair out of her eyes before she smiled at Eliska again.

"I was the only magic-user in my family—the only magic-user in twelve generations," Marine explained. "I didn't know how to use my magic, so my father sent me to the Guardian Templars for training and education."

"That doesn't sound too bad," Eliska remarked. "I guess he had to send you somewhere if he couldn't teach you himself."

"The day I left my father's palace for the Temple was the worst day of my life," Marine went on. "I begged my brother not to let me go, but my father said I had to. I begged the Templars every day to let me go home. They said my magic could do my people some good if I learned how to use it and they promised I could go as soon as I finished my training....." Marine heaved another sigh—a broken one this time. "And then all of this happened and I never saw my father or my brother or my family ever again. Now I probably never will see."

"Um....." Eliska hardly dared to ask. "And then what happened?"

"All of this." Marine waved her hand at the countryside around them, but she still did it casually like she was talking about the weather or a normal day's activities.

"The Voyant started twisting the Coil to raze cities and kill millions of people. The chaos and instability escalated and it will only keep getting worse. My order took it as our mission to find out what he's doing and try to stop him. I learned in my training how to go into the Dark to commune with the Darklings, so I volunteered to do that to find out about his plans." Marine turned away from the fire to gaze down into Eliska's eyes. "Don't you see? I'm not strong like you, Eliska. I could never do what you do. You can handle anything. You know how to survive in the Coil. I go into the Dark....and I like it. It's terrible...and dangerous....and I like it.....and I can't stop." She turned away with the first grimace of disgust and misery Eliska had ever seen. "I just want to go home, but I know now that I can never go home—not after all the Darkness that has passed through me. I couldn't take that back to my family. I hate what I am—and yet this is the only way I know how to make any difference to what's happening. My family wouldn't even know me—and I wouldn't go home anyway—not with the threat hanging over everyone....."

She trailed off and went all silent and serious staring into the flames. Eliska told herself again and again to say something—anything.

Marine's joking, casual nature unsettled Eliska. Eliska liked this version of Marine much better.

At least now Eliska knew there was a real person under all that sunshine—a person who understood the gravity of the situation and was doing everything possible to save people from it.

Eliska forced herself to say the words she'd always kept buried before now. "I'm not strong, Marine. I'm not strong at all. I'm weak and scared to death of everything in the Coil. I would never go into the Dark Layers the way you do. I've only survived as long as I have by staying away from them. You're so much stronger and more powerful than I am. You're everything I wish I could be. You're beautiful and alive and warm and happy. You know how to talk to people. You know how to have fun. That's something I could never do."

Eliska had to stop when her throat constricted the rest of the way. Whatever happened to her today crushed her under an unbearable weight.

She never admitted to anyone just how terrifying her life had become. She stayed away from people and towns—not because they posed any threat to her—not like that.

She stayed away because they scared her. People scared her.

She never learned how to talk to them and make them like her. Part of her was too afraid to go looking for Yann and the others in case she started liking them too much.

She already did like them too much. She should have run from them to stop herself from liking anyone this much. Liking them and having them like her scared the crap out of her.

Marine snapped back to life in a flash, sat up straight, and went back to grinning at everything. "Anyway, that's enough of all that doom and gloom."

"Don't worry about it," Eliska murmured. "You can tell me anything anytime."

"I just haven't talked to anyone about all of this before. I never told anyone....." Her features started to darken again, but she waved her hand in front of her face and shook that off, too. "Anyway, I don't want to blabber about it anymore. That's where I found out about the Voyant....so yes, he controls the Coil and he's the one causing all this instability. We would be in a stability cycle now if not for him."

"Wesh says the Coil goes through patterns of stability and instability all the time. He says it's a natural cycle that repeats forever. He says he got that information from the Guardian Templars."

"Either his order has incorrect information or they're interpreting it incorrectly. The cycles can be shorter or longer, but they always happen at the Voyant's direction."

"Are you saying the Voyant Mendicat is a recurring position....or something? Are you saying there have been others like him....and that they're the ones who are causing these cycles—all of them together?"

"I don't know about that, but if he's the one causing this one, then it follows that other people caused the other cycles."

"I don't see it that way, but okay. You know more about it than I do."

"What other explanation is there?" Marine countered.

"That the Voyant is causing this cycle and the others occurred naturally. Maybe he has some reason to cause the instability—like maybe he thinks the instability will give him a better chance of finding whatever it is that he wants to use to boost his power."

Marine shrugged that away. "Maybe."

"The question is how we can find out what he wants from the Black Watch. Did you see anything when you were with them to indicate which of them has it—or which of them *is* it?"

"No, I didn't see anything." Marine turned back to stare into the flames. "Whatever it is must be masked somehow."

"How can we find out what he wants—apart from waiting for him to attack the Watch again?"

"We could get Wesh and Anríq to help us break into the spire," Marine suggested. "The four of us could combine our magic."

"That means we have to find our way back to the Watch—and we can't find the Watch."

"We might be able to," Marine suggested.

"I doubt it."

Marine's eyes suddenly burst open and she pointed at Eliska with an excited gasp. "I got it! We could combine our magic! Yes! That will work!"

"It *might* work, you mean," Eliska corrected. "We hope it will work."

"Yes, it will!" Marine shot to her feet. "Come on! Let's go."

Eliska didn't move. "Sit down. We aren't going anywhere tonight."

"But we have to!" Marine insisted. "We have to stop the Voyant as soon as possible. We can't let this instability cost any more lives."

"If we can stop him at all, we won't do it tonight. It will take us a long time to find our way back to the Watch even if you're right that combining our magic *will* lead us back to them. Even then, all four of us working together might not be able to overcome the Voyant's defenses. Sit down. Losing sleep over this won't help anything."

Marine said, "But......" and stopped.

Eliska stayed where she was and stared into the flames. She'd seen enough of the Voyant's defenses today. It would take a lot more than Marine's youthful enthusiasm to convince Eliska that Wesh's, Anríq's, Marine's, and Eliska's combined magic would defeat him.

Marine finally sat down and sighed again. "This is why you know so much more about this stuff than I do. I don't know how to plan a campaign like this."

"I don't know anything about stuff like this—as you call it," Eliska countered. "I have no idea what I'm doing out here."

Marine brightened up and looked all around her with interest. "So.....where should we sleep tonight?"

"Um.....right here," Eliska replied. "Where else would we sleep?"

"You mean right here on the ground?!" Marine practically shrieked.

"Where have you been sleeping all this time while you've been out of your mind and communing with Darklings? You must have slept on the ground. You slept in the snow when the Watch stayed in that cabin."

"I don't remember that," Marine replied.

Eliska's eyes fell out of their sockets. "You don't remember.....any of it?"

"I don't remember where I was. I remember the Dark Layers I passed through and the Darklings I tried to communicate with. I don't remember sleeping in the snow." She made a face and snorted. "I would have remembered that."

"Well, we don't have any castles or servants or feather beds for you to sleep in here. I've been sleeping on the ground practically every night my entire life. We're lucky to have this fire."

Marine heaved another tortured sigh. "I suppose this is the price of sanity—dealing with the real world."

Eliska laughed at her. "Maybe you should go back into the Dark Layers so you don't feel it."

Marine cracked a grin. "I wouldn't be able to talk to you if I did that."

"How is it that you're so sane here and not in other Layers?"

"I can't explain it. I can commune with Darklings in some Layers and not in others, so I'm sane in some and not in others. I don't know if I'll be able to until I get somewhere. My whole mission is communing with them, so I try to stay in the Layers where I can do it." She looked around at the night closing in on their fire. "This is the first Island I've come to in a long time where I can't connect to the Dark."

Eliska looked down into the flames and shook her head. "It's amazing. I would never dare to go into the Dark. I've been doing everything the opposite way and staying away from Dark Layers."

Marine burst into another brilliant grin. "Then I guess it's a good thing that we met here so we could get to know each other."

"Yeah," Eliska breathed and gazed at her friend. "I'm glad about that even if we can't do anything about the rest of it."

Chapter 53

Eliska woke up first the next morning. She sat up, built up the fire, and watched Marine sleep.

Marine slept soundly considering she'd never slept on the ground before—or never been aware that she was sleeping on the ground.

She lay curled up on her side with one arm folded under her head. Her smudged face relaxed in sleep. She looked angelic like this—almost as angelic as she looked when she cleaned herself up into a stunningly beautiful princess.

Eliska took that moment of silence to truly marvel at what and who Marine was. No one in the Black Watch would ever have believed it if they didn't see Marine change with their own eyes.

Eliska didn't want to take Marine back to them.

Eliska didn't have to wonder how Yann and Anríq would both react to seeing Marine like that—all happy and bubbling with fun and excitement and glowing with magnificent beauty.

Eliska didn't even really feel jealous at the thought of Yann and Anríq liking Marine better. Any guy would jump at the chance at her attention.

No guy in his right mind would look sideways at Eliska as long as Marine was around. No one had to explain that to Eliska. She understood the world well enough to expect that.

She wouldn't have resented either of the boys for liking Marine better. That wasn't the reason Eliska wanted to delay going back to them.

She didn't want to share Marine with anyone. Eliska might be the only person alive who knew what Marine was really like when she wasn't out of her mind in the Dark Layers.

Eliska wanted to keep Marine to herself for as long as possible. Eliska didn't want to take Marine out of this Island. Eliska didn't want Marine to go back to being a raving mad woman snarling and hissing at unseen forces.

The thought of losing Marine hurt worse than anything. Eliska finally made friends with someone. Marine liked and admired Eliska as much as Eliska liked and admired Marine. Eliska couldn't lose that—not after everything she'd already gone through.

Eliska didn't even really want Marine to wake up this morning. Eliska didn't want to face the moment when the two girls had to leave this Island.

She would rather preserve Marine like this—happy and contented despite her circumstances.

Marine did wake up eventually. She sat up, frowned at her surroundings until she remembered where she was, and then grinned when she saw Eliska sitting there.

"What's for breakfast?" Marine joked.

Eliska had to laugh. "Chocolate truffles with a side of quadruple-layer chocolate cake."

"Now you're speaking my language." Marine looked around again. "I guess we don't have anything else to do but leave."

"I guess not," Eliska murmured.

"How do we find our way back to the Watch?"

"How should I know? I already told you I can't find them on my own. What's your master plan?"

"Combine our magic."

"How?" Eliska asked.

"How would you look for them if you were by yourself?"

Eliska opened her palm and projected her miniature version of the Coil. It revolved there while Layers collapsed and others expanded.

She scrolled through a few different Layers trying to find...well...anything.

"What are you looking for?" Marine asked. "You said you wouldn't be able to find the Watchmen."

"I was trying to find some of the Islands we visited before. Some of them might still be intact. If I can find them, I might be able to trace the Watch back to the last place we saw them."

Marine extended her hand and placed it an inch below Eliska's. A rush of heat flooded through Eliska's hand as Marine radiated her magic into the Coil projection.

It blew up to three times the size. Eliska could see tiny landscapes in some of the Layers along with Islands of towns, cities, and settlements, but she couldn't see any people.

She gasped out loud. "How are you doing this?!"

"I've never done it before," Marine replied. "I've never met anyone who can create something like this."

The image of the Coil revolved to its other side, and in a second, golden lines started to trace their way between Layers.

They threaded back and forth, up and down, from one Layer to another. Some of the lines broke off in certain places and reformed in others.

"Ooo, look!" Marine pointed her other hand at a Layer billowing with fire. "The lines all separate there. That must be the snow Island where we lost track of the Watch."

"This shows three different lines going off in different directions," Eliska pointed out. "So the Watch might not be together."

"You don't know that. Wesh or Anríq or both of them could have gone off somewhere else to do something. The Watch could still all be together in one place."

Eliska frowned at the projection. The more magic Marine added to the image, the bigger and more distinct its Layers became.

"All of the lines seem to be traveling through stable Islands," Eliska pointed out. "That's good."

"Not this one." Marine pointed to one particular line. "This one is going into the Dark Layers. I wonder why."

Eliska got ready to shut her hand. She didn't want to find out about the Watchmen going into the Dark Layers. "This is getting us nowhere...."

"Wait!" Marine grabbed her wrist and forced Eliska's fingers open. "Look! They're coming together again! These two are rejoining!"

Eliska stared as the lines converged. "They're in a different Island. We have to go there and find them....."

"Wait a minute!" Marine pointed to another Layer. "That's us."

"Yeah?" Eliska asked. "We already know where we are."

"Look at it. It looks different from here."

Eliska opened her mouth to say that it didn't look any different from here. The miniature version of the landscape looked the same.

The scorched planes, the Dark river, the enormous wolves, and the not-white White Spire in the distance—they all looked the same.

The rest of the Layer surrounding this Island didn't look the same, though. The vapors moved the same way with shadows morphing, taking shape, dissolving, and reforming between clouds of dark color.

Different random images of people, landscapes, buildings, and animals formed in the Layer, but they didn't come together to form Islands. She also didn't see any Darklings. The shadows didn't form Darklings.

"Oh, my God!" Eliska breathed. "It's an illusion Layer!"

"Then all of this...." Marine's gaze skated over the woods and the horizon beyond. The White Spire framed the skyline in the distance. "This is all an illusion, too."

"That explains why we couldn't get near that city," Eliska pointed out.

"It doesn't explain why the Voyant is using so many defenses to stop us from getting near the spire."

"It could explain...." Eliska broke off, gasped, and her eyes popped. "Marine! Do you realize what this means?!"

Marine frowned at her. "What do you mean? What *does* it mean?"

"It means we don't have to go near the tower! It means we can find out what he's doing without triggering any of his defenses! It means we can use the illusion Layer to spy on him right inside his spire!" Eliska clapped her hands. "This is perfect!"

Marine furrowed her brow. "Are you sure? Wouldn't the Voyant have defenses against that, too?"

"He might not that this illusion Layer is showing us the Island with the White Spire in it. The Layer could be showing us something from a completely different Island. We might not be in an Island at all. We could be completely trapped in an illusion."

"Then why are the other defenses still working?"

"Because the illusion shows us exactly what's happening in the other Island!" Eliska grabbed Marine's arm. "Come on! This is great! We're going to find out what he's doing and how to stop him."

She pulled Marine back into the woods out of sight of the spire—not that it made any difference.

Marine dragged her heels. "I don't know about this," she murmured when Eliska finally returned to the spot where they camped the night before.

"Just help me," Eliska told her. "We'll combine our magic and manipulate the illusion. Understand?"

"No," Marine replied.

Eliska laughed. She was too happy about this discovery to care about much else.

"What do you want me to do?" Marine asked.

"Give me your hands."

Marine placed both her hands in Eliska's. "Do you know what you're doing?"

"Nope," Eliska replied. "I'm making this up as I go along."

Marine rolled her eyes and smirked. "You're as bad as I am."

"Here we go. Send your magic into me and we'll use it to morph the Layer."

"Morph it to what?"

"To get ourselves close enough to the spire to see inside it. The Voyant should be...."

A flash of brilliant light cut her off. It blinded her for a second.

She forgot to hold onto Marine. Eliska raised one hand in front of her face to shield her eyes from the glare.

The flash burst a dozen yards to her left. It appeared in the trees—and then her blood ran cold when she saw an old man with long white hair and a long white robe standing there.

Light radiated all around him. It lit him up as bright as the sun, but his cold black eyes glittered with menace.

He didn't wear a handlebar mustache like Wesh's. His clean-shaven face showed a hard, compressed mouth tightened with fury. The muscle of his jaw clenched and his eyebrows came together in a deadly scowl.

Eliska didn't recognize him, but the power coming from him blasted across the clearing and drained her of all hope.

She would definitely remember if she ever met a wizard as powerful as this. This had to be the Voyant.

He didn't do anything but appear to them. Marine and Eliska both whirled around to confront him. Eliska raised her staff and Marine raised her hands to attack him.

At that moment, the whole landscape around them vanished along with the Voyant himself. The woods, the river, the wolves, the spire—the landscape didn't crumble or implode or collapse like a normal Layer. It just....wasn't there anymore.

It changed to a massive vortex of multiple Layers all colliding and churning together.

Eliska and Marine still stood on some solid surface, but everything else solid around them evaporated in a blink.

Entire landscapes revolved through multiple Layers and came close to crushing the two girls before the Layers wheeled off somewhere into the chaos.

Eliska and Marine moved closer together and grabbed onto each other.

"We need to get onto one of these Islands!" Eliska yelled over the noise.

"What about that one?" Marine pointed at a bunch of mountains shrouded in clouds.

"That looks good. Let's go!"

Eliska pulled her forward and both girls burst into a run to get to the Island before it rotated off somewhere else.

Eliska launched herself off whatever surface the two girls had been standing on. She and Marine soared through the vortex, but at that moment, another Layer whipped across them and smacked them down into a completely different Layer.

The two girls burst through and landed on an ice sheet with no visible landscape features at all.

Freezing wind slammed into Eliska from the side. "Hold onto me!" she bellowed. "I'm going to shatter the Layer to get us out of here!"

Marine yelled something back, but Eliska couldn't make out the words. The wind shrieked in her ears and numbed her lips and nose. The girls couldn't survive here.

Chapter 54

Eliska spiked her staff down into the ice sheet under her feet. The Island exploded in a rain of boulders and ice shards.

The rupture didn't collapse this time. The ice sheet shot straight up and fired Marine and Eliska into the air.

Both girls screamed and then snapped through what felt like a curtain of water into a pitch-black Layer with no light anywhere.

The wind died. All trace of movement and upheaval disappeared in a split second.

Eliska and Marine held onto each other even tighter.

"Are you okay?" Eliska whispered.

"Yeah!" Marine whispered back. "Are you?"

"Yeah! Any idea where we are?"

"Somewhere in the Dark, I'd say," Marine whispered. "Do you want to check?"

Eliska created her Coil projection and Marine placed her hand under Eliska's hand to make the image bigger.

The golden lines still traced through the Coil showing where the Watch separated and came back together.

The lines followed the girls' route and ended in a pocket of Darkness between a bunch of chaos Layers.

"Well, that doesn't tell us anything we don't already know," Eliska remarked.

"How do we get out of here?" Marine asked.

"We can shatter this Layer, too." Eliska held up the projection and used its light to try to see anything around her. "It doesn't look like there's anything here."

She raised her staff and stabbed it into whatever solid surface she and Marine happened to be standing on this time.

Nothing happened. Eliska repeated the process three times, but it didn't work. The Layer didn't shatter.

"There must be some way out of here," Marine muttered.

"You're the one who's so big on joining our power together. Take hold of my staff."

Marine smirked at her and grabbed Eliska's staff. They both held on when Eliska jabbed it down again.

Both girls channeled their magic through the staff but it still produced no effect.

"Nice try, though," Marine remarked.

Eliska looked around again, but the more she looked, the more there just kept not being anything there to see.

She started to say, "I guess we can just...."

At that moment, a deep, menacing growl broke the silence from her right. She spun around.

She wouldn't have been able to see the Darkling without the light from her projection. Even that bright glow didn't make the Darkling any easier to see.

This Darkling grew out of the shadows—except that there were no shadows. The Darkness itself took shape into a giant black outline craved out of Darkness.

Eliska raised her staff to protect herself, but she didn't dare to close her other hand. This light was her only advantage.

Right then, another Darkling growled from her other side. Marine spun that way and created a blazing orb of light in her left hand to shine on more black Darklings closing on both girls.

"Why are they so Dark?" Eliska asked over her shoulder.

"I guess they come from this Layer," Marine replied. "I can't think of any other reason."

Movement caught Eliska's eye from both sides. More Darklings drifted out of the Dark all around the girls. The Dark gave birth to these monstrous shapes creeping closer by the second.

Eliska braced herself to fight. If this had been any ordinary Layer, she would have shattered it to send herself somewhere else to get out of it.

She couldn't do that now. She had to stand and fight.

At least she had Marine with her. Marine backed up a few steps and the two girls sealed their backs together.

"What's the plan?" Marine called over her shoulder.

"I say we go on the offensive and strike first," Eliska countered.

"Sounds good! You say when."

"When!" Eliska yelled and hurled her Coil projection down at the floor.

It smashed in front of the Darklings, exploded, and flashed outward in a blinding sheet of light.

It lit up dozens of these black Darklings all around the girls, but Eliska didn't hold back. She grabbed her staff in both hands and ejected a torrent of magic from the tip.

The energy burst to life and lit up the Dark Layer better than the Coil projection. She swiped the beam sideways cutting down as many Darklings as possible.

Marine attacked at the same time. Eliska kept her back sealed against Marine's, so Eliska couldn't see what Marine did.

Eliska heard Darklings roaring and explosions going off behind her. She didn't dare to turn around.

She didn't stop pouring her magic through her staff to bombard the Darklings with every ounce of her power.

She slashed her staff back and forth. Darklings exploded in front of her, but more came out of the Dark behind those in front.

They waited until she turned one way and charged from the other side. She barely turned in that direction in time to hit them and drive them back.

One of them got within a few feet of her and detonated in her face. A curtain of Dark goo splattered her from head to foot. It got into her eyes and mouth.

Her head swam and Marine screamed. Eliska lost control of her staff, but her own desperation kept shooting endlessly even if she didn't know what she was shooting at.

Four more Darklings hit her from behind. She tried to turn around when another punishing concussion hit her from somewhere else. She didn't know where it came from.

The Layer ruptured without warning and she, Marine, and the Darklings plummeted through a void.

Eliska's mind cleared enough to see forks of Darkness shooting at her from all sides. They converged on her at the center. She didn't see Marine anywhere.

Eliska rotated from one side to the other trying to see Marine, but all the black Darklings fell through the Layers with her. They surrounded her trying to attack her and orient themselves at the same time.

The Dark came perilously close to enveloping her. She struck out with her staff at one of the forks and it burst in her face the same way.

The Layer exploded in an outward starburst shockwave and she landed hard on the ground somewhere. A flood of cold water washed over her, but it soaked into the ground in a few seconds.

She really was on the ground. Grass poked her in the face. She lifted her head out of the puddle and found herself in some kind of woods.

She froze when she saw Yann, Anríq, Wesh, and the Watchmen battling a different kind of Darklings in the trees. These Darklings looked like people with multiple limbs and no heads.

Every hand held a weapon and the Darklings surrounded the Watchmen in droves.

Wesh kept blasting magical eruptions from both hands. Anríq stood off to one side swinging his axe in one hand and his club in the other.

Magic detonated from his club every time he hit one of the Darklings. His strikes exploded a dozen Darklings with each blow, but more Darklings flooded out of the woods behind those he killed.

Neither he nor Wesh could stem the tide. Darklings passed both wizards by and went after the Watchmen.

They fought their hardest, but they couldn't do much with so few weapons in so few hands.

Eliska launched to her feet still holding onto her staff. Her feet splashed in what was left of the water on her way deeper into the trees.

She opened fire and slashed down dozens of Darklings surrounding Vidal and Niyazi.

She carved a path through the horde, pivoted sideways, and cleared a little bit of space around Rien, Omer, and Barsali who stood in a clump to one side.

A massive swarm of Darklings surrounded Yann and Yvan. Eliska couldn't see Neils anywhere. He better not be dead.

She stormed into the clearing dropping Darklings on all sides, but she couldn't stop more of them coming out of the forest.

She threw caution to the wind, swung her staff over her head, and nailed the tip down into the ground.

She didn't shatter the Island. She didn't want to send the Watchmen back into the Layers after she just found them.

She sent out a powerful shockwave of magic radiating outward from her position. The pulse leveled dozens of Darklings and kept spreading deeper into the trees.

The blast knocked the Watchmen off their feet, too. Only Anríq kept his balance.

He never stopped fighting, not even when her blast took out most of the Darklings surrounding him.

Eliska swiveled toward the trees facing a few scattered Darklings coming from there.

With so many dead Darklings lying on the ground, she could finally see a breach in the Island farther away in the trees. The Darklings poured from another Layer beyond the opening.

She grabbed her staff in both hands, thrust it longways at the oncoming Darklings, and sent out another blast to finish off the last of them.

Then she aimed the point of her staff at the rift to close it.

The Watchmen, Wesh, and Anríq started to relax when they saw the Darklings defeated. It was over.

She fired her staff at the top of the rift to pass the beam down the two edges. It would close and then the Watch would be safe in another Island.

The instant she fired, another blazing light shot through the rift from the other side. The Voyant rushed her from the Dark Layer beyond. She tried to run her magic down the breach faster to close it, but he came too fast.

He didn't seem to fly through the air the way she and Marine saw that light dive into the White Spire.

She saw the light in the Dark Layers, and the next instant, he stood in front of her glowing the way he did last time.

He flew straight into the blast from her staff, but the jet of magic just vanished inside his halo.

Wesh sprang forward before Eliska had a chance to cut off the beam or even to think about trying something else.

"Stay behind me!" Wesh yelled to the others and he raised his hands to attack the Voyant.

Without warning, a plume of fire ejected out of the ground right underneath Wesh. The Voyant didn't move even to look at him before a geyser of flame vaporized Wesh to nothing. Not even a wisp of smoke remained where he just stood.

Eliska dove for him, but it was all over in a split second. "NO!!" she bellowed, but Wesh was already gone.

She landed five feet in front of where she started, and almost as if her own movement made it happen, the Island collapsed.

The ground beneath her feet buckled and the group plunged through the surface into another Layer just below it.

Chapter 55

Yann slammed down hard on the ground. A bunch of thumps shook the ground around him as the rest of the Watch landed in the same area.

He rolled onto his side....and his heart soared when saw Eliska just a few yards away. She made it back!

Marine also landed on the ground ten feet beyond Eliska. Eliska wasn't wearing her furs anymore. None of the Watch wore them anymore, either. No one needed them.

Other than that, the two girls looked exactly the same as he remembered from the moment when they got separated in the snow Island.

Eliska rolled onto her knees and her eyes skidded around the landscape. Yann burst into a smile that she was back with the group—and him.

She barely looked at him. Her eyes widened when she saw their surroundings. She didn't look at anyone else in the group, either, not even Anríq.

The group landed in a wide valley of cracked mudflats surrounded by rocky mountains a few miles away. Blazing sunshine beat on those flats and heat radiated off them.

"Gone!" Eliska choked. Her features spasmed. "All gone.....!"

She buckled onto her knees and slumped staring down at the staff in her hands.

Yann pulled himself to his feet and went over to her, but before he got there, Marine yowled again.

She crouched at a distance from the rest of the group. Black grime caked her stringy hair. It hung over her crazed eyes and smudged face.

She turned from one side to another glaring at everything, baring her teeth, hissing and snarling, but she didn't hiss and snarl at Eliska, Anríq, or the Watchmen. Marine didn't even see them.

Eliska squatted in front of her, grabbed Marine's shoulders, and tried to turn Marine to face her.

"Marine!" Eliska called. "Marine—come on! Snap out of it!"

Marine rounded on her with an animal snarl and gnashed her teeth at Eliska. Eliska dropped her hands and reared back to get out of the way in time.

Eliska blinked at her for a second and then crumpled again. "Damn! She's crazy again."

"Of course she's crazy," Rien cut in. "She always is."

"You don't understand." Eliska's voice broke. She stood up and looked down at Marine from above. "She was beautiful—and funny—and excited—and helpful.....We made friends....."

"You....made friends....with *that*......?" Niyazi blurted out.

"She wasn't like this! Don't you get it?" Eliska cast a desperate look at the landscape on all sides. "This Island....there must be Dark forces here. She said she communes with the Dark in some Layers and not in others. She was perfectly sane....and bubbly.....and kind....." She shut her eyes and her chin fell onto her chest. "She's a princess.....and she looked and acted like one. I wouldn't have believed it if I didn't see it for myself."

"I don't believe it," Rien countered.

Eliska's features convulsed again and she shuddered when she opened her eyes to assess the situation. "We have to get out of here. We can't stay in this Layer."

"What's wrong with it?" Yvan asked. "It looks stable enough. That's better than nearly getting killed when the Layers collapse."

Eliska spun around and shrieked out in a sudden explosion of hysterical panic. "My magic is gone! This Layer....it has no magic! I can't get us out! I can't do anything!"

Her voice spiked to the stratosphere and cracked with terror and frantic despair.

"You.....you don't have magic?" Yann stammered. "But....that's impossible."

Eliska didn't hear him. She looked down at her staff and suddenly yanked her hand away from it in horror.

The staff hit the ground and she backed away. She stared at her hands in front of her and then her crazed eyes skimmed the horizon. "We gotta get out of here...." she croaked.

Yvan and the other Watchmen exchanged glances. Then they all looked around at the horizon as the truth sank in.

Wesh and Eliska had been the only things keeping the Watchmen alive. The Watchmen would have been dead a dozen times without Wesh's and Eliska's magic to protect them and save them from every disaster.

Now Wesh was gone.

Without Eliska's magic.....

Yvan turned to Anríq. "What about you, young one? Do you still have magic? Is your magic gone, too?"

Anríq stood silently off to one side looking at the ground. He didn't raise his eyes.

He barely murmured above a whisper. "No, it's all gone."

Now Yvan was the one to cast a wild look of desperate realization at the broad, baking mudflats all around the party. Every last one of these people was utterly defenseless against the Coil's dangers, including Eliska and Marine.

"We gotta get out of here," Yvan muttered.

"Where will we go?" Omer asked.

"I don't know, but we can't stay here." The Watch Commander squared his shoulders, tightened his lips, and dipped his chin once at nothing. "Let's go. Follow me."

He set off across the landscape heading.....somewhere. Yann and the other Watchmen exchanged glances. Anríq didn't raise his eyes to look at anyone.

Omer and Niyazi fell in line behind Yvan. Yann made sure Eliska got in line with the others.

He probably should have taken the time to make sure Marine went with them, but as soon as the group got moving, she trailed them at a distance.

The minute they all started walking, the land trembled under their feet. Everyone stopped to check themselves, but the rumbles vibrating through the mudflats only got stronger.

They built to an earthquake. The surrounding mountains boomed and thundered.

"Run!" Yvan yelled. "Come on!"

He took off for the distant mountains and everyone else burst into a run to follow him.

End of Book 1.

Keep Reading

Corrupted Coil Series; Book 2; Staff Of Life

When the last survivors of the Middleborough disaster escape into the Coil with nothing but the clothes on their backs, the only thing keeping them alive was Wesh's and Eliska's magic.

Now Wesh is dead and the ever-shifting Coil has stripped Eliska of the magic that has kept her going all her life. With her world in turmoil and no way to save herself or anyone around her, she must fall back on the most unlikely allies—the Black Watchmen who escaped from Middleborough with her.

With everything at stake, the group is going to find out that it takes more than just magic to survive the Corrupted Coil. Human relationships, friendship, and even the love of family are much more important when the chips are really down, but what will the friends do when they lose that, too?

Read it here for free.

You can find it at your favorite book retailer.

Sign Up Once--Get all Theo Mann's free books including brand new releases

S ign Up Once--Get all Theo Mann's free books including brand new releases

With the Corrupted Coil becoming increasingly unstable and the human world torn apart by war, the Barbarians expects their Chieftain's sons to become his greatest warriors and take over his power after him.

When twelve-year-old Anríq's dormant magic comes to the surface, it will destroy everything he knows about his life, his family, and his future.

When those he most cares about turn against him, he'll have to find a new source of strength within himself and the allies to help him do what must be done before it's too late.

Sign up at www.theomann.com to read it for free

About Theo Mann

I write 70 books per year—and yes, before you ask, all these books are my original creative work. Nothing written under my name is AI-generated or ghostwritten because I write better than AI and any ghostwriter out there.

People don't read fiction for entertainment or to escape from reality. People read fiction to see their humanity reflected in another person's character and story.

This is my promise to you. When you read my books, you'll see your own humanity reflected in the characters and stories. I take this commitment to my readers very seriously. My books are an intimate form of communication between us. I would never disrespect my readers by turning that over to a machine or another writer. This is my bond between me and you as my reader.

I write 20,000 words per day as my daily work output. If anyone with a public platform would like to challenge me to prove this in a controlled environment, feel free to contact me on this website's contact page.

I worked as a professional ghostwriter for fifteen years. Now I'm on a mission to set a Guinness World Record by writing 700 books over the next ten years and 1400 books over the next twenty years, all originally written by me. See my website for the full book list.

I'm also the author of *Proof for the Existence of God* and the *Crimes Against Fiction* blog. You can find all my nonfiction work at www.crimes-against-fiction.com.

If you have a story idea, or if you would like me to explore a series in more depth, or if you'd like me to explore a character by writing a spinoff series about that character or world, leave me a message on my website's contact page. I answer all reader emails, so ask me anything, tell me what you liked and didn't like, and let me know where you'd like your favorite series to go. I would love to hear your ideas and find out what you'd like to read next.

Find out more at www.theomann.com.

Also by Theo Mann (so far)

Standalone Novels
Kingdom of Heaven
The Verge

Series
Onyx Series (Books 1-6)
Prideland Series (Books 1-4)
Ultra Meridian Series (Books 1-7)
Hellhounds Series (Books 1-7)
Battlefleet Series (Books 1-4)
Highland Heroes Series (Books 1-6)
Battalion 1 Series (Books 1-5)
The Network Series (Books 1-6)
Corrupted Coil (Books 1-5)
Rise of the Giants Series (Books 1-10)
The Edge of Chaos Series (Books 1-5)
The White Series (Books 1-7)

www.ingramcontent.com/pod-product-compliance
Lightning Source LLC
Chambersburg PA
CBHW070358260626
47161CB00001B/178